Fall with Me

Also by Becka Mack

Consider Me
Play with Me
Unravel Me

Fall with Me

BECKA MACK

SLOWBURN

A zando IMPRINT

SLOWBURN

Slowburn is an imprint of Zando.
zandoprojects.com

First Edition: September 2024

Text design by Midland Typesetters, Australia
Cover design by Jessica L. Boudreau
Cover image: watercolor landscape © Adobe Stock/Elena M.

The publisher does not have control over and is not responsible for author or other third-party websites (or their content).

Library of Congress Cataloging-in-Publication Data Available Upon Request

978-1-63893-244-4 (Paperback)

10 9 8 7 6 5 4 3 2 1
Manufactured in the United States of America

For those who think they're better off alone,
that they're not worthy of the love they crave,
because they've dealt with the pain of people leaving.

The power to let them win or rise above it with your head
held high is yours and yours alone.

The only person who needs to think you're worth it is you.

1

AND THE NAME FOR THE DRINK?

Jaxon

"Fucking on the beach, in our private pool, and on our deck. Bent over the bed, up against the wall, and on the bathroom counter." I brush a long gold ponytail off a flushed neck. "I'll spend the week fucking you any way you want, anywhere you want."

Her blue eyes twinkle as she twists back and forth. "Your treat?"

"Of course, my treat. I'm rich, aren't I?"

She bites back her grin. "That's what Google says."

I resist the urge to roll my eyes, only because I rarely get time off during the hockey season. Despite her having clearly looked up my net worth, I still want to spend my limited vacation time buried in something hot and wet. I'm certain she'll do the trick.

"You haven't even asked my name."

Oops. "Haven't I?" I trail the tip of my finger along the strap of her sports bra, down to the dip in her cleavage. How is this flimsy thing holding those girls up? "Guess I just feel like I really know you, you know? It's like you've always been a part of my life." *Fuck no*, but I hear my friends say shit like this to their girls all the time. "You just fit."

She bats thick, coated lashes. Mascara feels like a bad idea at the gym. Doesn't that shit get in your eyes and burn? "You are so sweet, Jaxon Riley. I can't believe they call you the NHL's bad boy."

I wink, sliding my hand down to palm her hip. "I'm not always sweet . . ."

She presses her chest against mine. "Brielle."

"Huh?"

"Brielle. That's my name."

Oh. Right.

I hook a finger under her chin. "When you're on my arm, I only plan on calling you *mine*."

I swear to God, her pupils dilate at that four-letter word. "Okay. I'm in. I'll go to Cabo with you."

As if there was any chance of her saying no. I first saw her at the gym three weeks ago. She'd just finished trying out a Pilates class, and I commented on her flexibility. She told me she was a cheerleader in college, and five days later when I was back after an away series, she'd told me she'd missed seeing me through the studio window. That's when she found out who I was, and now she just happens to be at the gym every time I'm here.

Is it uncomfy? Sure, a little, but it's January on the west coast, my hockey team has a bye week starting in two days, and I can't bear hanging around my friends for it. They're fucking fantastic, but I'm tired of being the ninth wheel in their overbearing lovefest.

Brielle slips her hand in mine, towing me toward the locker rooms. I follow, even though I'm not done with my workout.

"I'll have to pack, which normally takes me two to three weeks, but I can figure it out. And, *oh*! I'll have to go shopping. I have time to go shopping, right? I wanna get a new bikini for you." She spins into me, tossing her arms around my neck. "Maybe I'll get a spray tan. That way I'll have no tan lines."

I'm about to ask her if it'll rub off on me while I'm fucking her, because no way I wanna be orange, but she keeps going. Of fucking course she does. She talks a lot. It's annoying, but not unbearable. If I keep her mouth busy most of the week, we'll make it out just fine.

"Will you have room in your suitcase for my heels? I'll want a different pair for all my outfits. Or can you pay for my extra baggage? I have to bring my hair dryer, and my straightener, and my curling iron, and my makeup bag; that alone will take up one suitcase. Then I need casual outfits for the beach, and fancy outfits for each meal."

I wonder what Mittens is doing right now. He was sleeping in the window when I left, but I bet he's looking for me now. He always misses me when I'm gone.

"We'll go out, right? I want to show off, not be cooped up and eating room service all week. Do you think people will recognize you? I bet they will. People might even take pictures of us."

He's probably waiting on his back by the front door. He likes to do that, pudgy belly out, paws up. He pretends he's dead when I've left him alone too long. Dramatic as fuck, just the way I like him.

"Do you mind if I document our trip on my Instagram? I'll be subtle, like, tag you, but say nothing, you know? You can post pictures of me without any context too. People will speculate who I am and if we're serious, which will create a buzz. Imagine? Me, being the one to tame Jaxon Riley? Trixie Forsyth will be *so* bitter when she sees. She was always a jealous bitch in high school, thought she was better than *everyone*."

I'm gonna get him some catnip on my way home. He goes batshit over it; it's my favorite thing to watch. Especially when I pull out the laser pointer after. It's the only time he willingly exercises.

"Jaxon? Are you listening?"

"Mmm?" My eyes flick to hers. "Yeah, baby. Of course I'm listening."

She melts, clasping my hand. "I was asking if we're taking a limo to the airport."

A limo? What the fuck for?

"Uh, I'll just pick you up, leave my car at the airport."

"Oh." She frowns, rebounding quickly with a broad grin. "That's okay."

"Well, hey, you should probably get going. Get your tan on and all that." I open the contacts on my phone, then drop it in her hand. "Gimme your number. I'll text you the details tomorrow."

Her fingers fly across my screen, then she presses my phone to my chest and pops up on her toes . . . rubbing the tip of her nose against mine. *Huh. Don't fucking like that.*

"Bye, Jaxon," she whispers against my lips. "See you in two days."

It's not until she disappears into the locker room and I amble back to the squat rack that I realize she's typed *Mine* and a heart into her contact details.

"Shit." I drop my ass to a bench, scratching a hand along my stubbled jaw. "What was her name again?"

I can't believe I left my fucking cat for this.

"*Stop* looking at me that way!" the blonde shrieks at me from across our private deck.

"What way?" I scream back.

"With your eyes!"

"Sorry I have eyes on my face!"

She narrows her blue ones, aggressively drying off her body before chucking the towel to my feet. "I *hate* you! You're so dry about everything!"

"Oh, *sor-ry* I'm not more enthusiastic about taking seventeen fucking thousand pictures of your goddamn ass from every angle just for your fucking Instagram!"

She rolls her eyes. "You're exaggerating!"

I roll mine right back. "No fucking shit, I'm exaggerating!"

"And don't think I don't know the only reason you took me to Starbucks on the way to the airport is because you couldn't remember my name!"

"Oh, *here we go!*"

"The barista asked the name for my drink and you looked at me and *raised your eyebrows*, Jaxon!"

"I'm a feminist! I don't believe in answering questions for women!" When she only stares at me, arms crossed over her chest, I hurl mine in the air. "Am I supposed to be expected to remember the name of every person I meet?"

"The ones you bring on vacation, at least!"

"Well, I'm fucking regretting that right now, aren't I? I haven't had a goddamn minute of silence since you slid your ass into my car three days ago! *Jaxon, can we listen to my drunk girl playlist? Jaxon, can you take a picture of me laughing but make it look not staged? Jaxon, does my ass look too big in this dress? Jaxon, how many carbs do you think are in this croissant?*" I drag my hands down my face in slow motion. "Christ, Breanne, does it ever. Fucking. *End?*"

She gasps, and this is quite literally the first time I've been able to render her silent. Sweet *fuck*, do I ever savor the moment while it lasts.

Her hands ball into angry fists. "How. Many. Times. Do. I. Have. To. Tell. You. It's. Bri-*elle*. Not. Bre-*anne*."

I swallow my laughter, but our neighbor fails to, letting that snort out. My eyes flick to the villa next door where she sits on the edge of her deck, copper legs shining beneath the bright Mexican sun, toes dipped in her private dunk pool while she eavesdrops on our conversation.

"Right," I mumble. "Brielle. I said that."

"You said *Breanne*. Again. You've called me it at least five times in the last three days, *despite* the Starbucks!"

It's hard to see from here, but I'm nearly positive our neighbor's shoulders shake. She gathers her chestnut coils off her back, twists them around her hand, and secures them in some sort of clawlike contraption. The sun touches her shoulders and dances down her spine, guiding my gaze to the dip in her lower back, where her bikini bottom clings to an ass I know for a fact is round as *fuck*.

"*Jaxon!* You are *not* seriously checking out the girl next door right now!"

My eyes snap back to Bre—aahhh . . . elle. Brielle. "What? No? Obviously not."

Brielle stomps her foot. "You're not paying attention to me!"

"Oh my *God*, how much more attention do you need?" If I give her any more of it, I will simply pass away. "You're worse than my fucking cat."

Her face crumples with devastation. "You have a cat? But I'm allergic! How are we gonna make this work?"

"Make this work? Make *what* work?"

"Oh. My. *God!*" Our neighbor leaps to her feet, snatching her towel off her deck, glaring at us. "Would you two shut *up*? I can't take it anymore! All you do is fight! I'm so fucking *sick* of hearing your voices!"

Brielle gasps, slapping a hand to her throat. "Jaxon, she told me to shut up!"

"Newsflash, Brielle! He's been telling you to shut up for the last three days!" Our neighbor shakes her head, and that claw thing buried in her hair somehow detaches, clattering to her feet, where she stoops to pick it up, curls springing free and bouncing around her face. "I'm done. This is supposed to be my honeymoon, and you two are ruining it for me."

"Honeymoon?" I lift a brow. "Honey, I hate to break it to you, but typically you bring your significant other on your honeymoon."

My gaze coasts down, then back up. She doesn't look thoroughly fucked enough for my liking. If she were my bride, she'd be in bed all week on account of her legs no longer working. Instead, she's been sunning on that deck for the past three days, tablet in her hands, curls piled on top of her head, buds in her ears, probably listening to some podcast about the art of homemaking or some boring shit.

Her mouth scrunches, gaze narrowing. "I'm requesting a new villa."

"Good luck with that." This place was sold out seven months ago, but maybe she can find a . . . *standard* room. *Shudder.* "Don't let the door hit your ass on the way out, honey."

"You're a jerk." She stomps to her sliding door, flings it open, and shoots me one last menacing glare. "And *don't* call me honey."

"Whatever you say, honey." Huffing out a breath, I turn back to Breanne, cross my arms over my chest, and rock back on my heels. "Wild, huh?"

She rolls her eyes and stalks into our villa, opening her pink suitcase, throwing her clothes inside. I follow her, opening the bar fridge and cracking a beer.

"What're you doing?"

"Leaving."

I sip my beer, savoring the refreshing way it slides down my throat. "Leaving? Oh, no. Please stay."

"You didn't even tell her off for telling me to shut up. And you were *totally* checking her out." She slams her suitcase closed, pouting. "And I asked you this morning if I looked sexy and you didn't even look at me when you said yes. So yes, Jaxon, I'm leaving."

I pick at the label on the beer bottle. "Well, if you think that's best."

"You know, I thought you were finally ready to settle down. All your friends are doing it."

"You don't know shit about my friends."

"You're the only single one left. It's not a secret."

My jaw tics, only because I'm tired of being compared to them. I'm nothing like them, and I don't need the reminder that I'm the outlier.

I stand, sipping my beer before walking toward Breanne. Her breath hitches when I crowd her space, hopeful blue eyes holding mine. I could do it. I could say the word, only four letters. I could tell her to stay, and she'd toss that suitcase right to the floor, throw her arms around my neck, press her tits to my chest and her mouth to mine. I could spend the rest of the week fucking the hours away.

Or I could spend the rest of the week lying naked on my deck, all alone, getting drunk under the sun, every meal delivered to my doorstep.

"Breanne," I whisper.

"Brielle," she whispers back, licking her lips.

"Brielle." I reach past her, scoop her thong off the table, and drop it on her suitcase. "Don't forget this."

She blinks at me, and I don't need to savor the moment of silence. I'm about to have days of it.

"*Urgh!*" She stuffs her feet into those fluffy leopard-print sandals I hate, snatches her big purse out of the closet, drags her suitcase to the door, and scowls at me one last time. "You're a jerk, Jaxon Riley. I'm switching gyms."

"Safe flight, baby."

The door slams behind her, and I stuff a handful of honey-roasted nuts into my mouth as I pick up the corded phone next to the king-size bed. I didn't even know corded phones existed anymore.

"Good afternoon, Grand Siesta Paradise Suites. This is Maria at the front desk. How may I help you?"

"Hey, can I get a fridge restock and order some lunch?" I toss another handful of nuts into my mouth and follow it with a swig of beer. "I'm fucking starving."

2

RATHER BE FUCKING
MY DRAGON DILDO

Lennon

IT'S QUIET. *TOO* QUIET.

The first half of my week was like this. Blissful. Peaceful. *Quiet.* Ever since Thing One and Thing Two showed up three days ago, it's been anything but. I swear, the only time those two stop fighting is to fuck.

And *oh boy*, have I heard it all.

Jaxon has magical fingers. A magical tongue, and, apparently, an *incredibly* magical cock, based on the way Brielle hasn't been able to stop screaming his name.

Is that how I also know *her* name? Oh no. I know her name because *she's* been shrieking it at *him* every time he fucks it up and calls her some version of Breanne, Breanna, or Brenda. He seemed to learn well enough after the first forty-eight hours, settling on *baby*.

I tiptoe across the cold ceramic floor, kicking aside the purple-and-gold dildo I tossed there, along with my clit sucker, after failed orgasm number . . . honestly, I've lost count. Honeymoons are supposed to be spent fucking. Since that's out of the question, I picked up a few toys on the way to the airport to get the job done.

And they haven't. Not a single time.

No, instead I've been listening to my neighbors fuck for the past three days they've been here, and I'm 99 percent sure *Jaxon* is only continuing to participate because it's the only time Brielle actually stops talking.

I shove aside the sheer curtains and peek through the patio door. Jaxon is alone on the deck, which is a first. The only time he's out here alone is in the middle of the night, long after Brielle is quiet.

Now he's lying on the wooden planks, one leg bent, the other dangling in his dunk pool. A pair of shades guard his eyes, and the sunshine glitters against his golden skin. He's covered in tattoos, arms painted with colorful designs, bathing suit shorts showing off one thick thigh covered with what looks from here like mountains and trees.

I swallow against the desire lumping in my throat, the one that reminds me *I'm* supposed to be the one getting fucked into the floorboards, and *he* looks like he could do it well, no matter if his voice is enough to drive me to drink.

Okay, I don't need a reason to drink; I've been doing it all week. So has Jaxon, I guess, because right now he's surrounded by beer bottles and platters of food.

Where's Brielle? She seems to enjoy spending her time posing on the deck, in the pool, in the ocean, halfway out of the ocean, halfway into the pool, looking over her shoulder, laughing at nothing, and fixing her bikini bottom when it doesn't need to be fixed, all while Jaxon mumbles half-assed encouragement while he's forced to take pictures. Yesterday he drawled out the most unenthused *yas, queen*, before chugging his beer and muttering out a *fuck my life*.

I'm still trying to figure out how they wound up here together. Surely no one goes on vacation with a total stranger, but then how come he can't remember her name?

Jaxon's hand reaches out, slapping at the planks around him

until he finds a platter of fruit. He hooks a finger over the edge and drags it closer, plucking a chocolate-covered strawberry off the plate, biting into it. My lower belly pulls taut when red juice dribbles down his chin, and when he flicks his tongue over his lips, I squeeze my thighs together.

Truly, it's unfair how gorgeous he is. Shouldn't he be as ugly as his rude, annoying, arrogant personality?

"Hey, honey?" he calls suddenly, and my heart pounds as I look around. I don't see Brielle. He's not . . . he's not talking to me. Right? "You gonna keep eye fuckin' me through your patio door, at least don't stand where I can see you." Another chocolate-covered strawberry, and my eyes hook on his thumb as he drags it up his chest, along his chin, catching that line of red and sucking it into his mouth. "And if you're gonna stay where I can see you, feel free to make it interesting and strip down to as few layers as I have on."

The curtain balls in my fist, and before I tear it across, I toss a *screw you* out the door and storm away. I'm standing over my toys, contemplating what to do with my life and my last day in Cabo, when my phone rings, my brother's name on the screen.

"Hey, Dev."

"What's up, Len? Ready to go home?"

Home? "I don't have a home anymore."

"Ah, don't say that. If you want me to fly to Seattle and boot Ryne out on his punk ass, just say the word."

I sniff. "No, I don't want you to do that." *But, like, maybe.*

"You wanna crash at my place for a bit? I'm heading to Florida for spring training, so you'll have the place to yourself."

It's a tempting offer, and would be even if he was going to be there. Devin is the second baseman for the Toronto Jays, and along with my cousin Serena, my best friend. Hiding out in his pristine condo sounds comfortable. Safe.

Instead, I tell him quietly, "I'm thinking of relocating."

"Yeah? You take that interview for the job I sent you?"

I nod, though he can't see. "They offered me the job on the spot. The start date is one week today if I want it."

"Shit. That fast, huh?"

Apparently their current photographer quit unexpectedly, and they're super eager to start building their fan base up on social media. They said I was just the type of talent they were looking for, but I'm sure having my superstar brother hand my name over didn't hurt. I don't often use his name, but desperate times and all that.

I nibble the tip of my thumbnail. "What should I do? I can't leave Mom and Dad. And Mimi—"

"Mom and Dad will miss you, but they'll understand. And fuck Mimi. Respectfully," he tacks on, because we're still not convinced the woman doesn't have eyes and ears everywhere. "You wouldn't be here if she'd never set you up with that douche to begin with. What kinda name is Ryne anyway? And plus, two days ago she texted and asked what a respectable seventy-four-year-old woman might wear at midnight if she wanted to egg someone's car and not get caught."

I snicker, and his answering chuckle thaws my cold, dead heart just a touch.

"You gotta do what's best for you, Len. If that means starting over somewhere new, then do it. Put yourself first for once."

I can't remember the last time I did that. Every decision has been led by someone else, altered in one way or another to suit the type of life they wanted for me. But what about the life *I* want?

"What time's your flight at?" Devin asks.

I flip through the itinerary I made for me and Ryne, trailing my finger over my return flight details. "Eleven. Have to be at the airport by eight. I should get—"

"Fucking wasted."

"—to bed early."

Devin sighs, loud and long-suffering. "How many times you been to a bar this week?"

I pick at imaginary lint on my cropped tank. "They restock my mini fridge every day."

"Lennon, how many times have you been to a bar this week?"

"Zero." I do, however, venture to the breakfast buffet every morning at six a.m. before most other guests are up.

"Have you made any friends?"

"Yes," I scoff. "Just this morning, I had breakfast with Joyce and her husband, Harold."

"*Joyce and her husband, Harold*? How the fuck old are they?"

I cough the answer into my fist.

"What?"

I throw one arm up. "They're in their seventies, okay? There, are you happy now? My only friends are the old lady who keeps trying to set me up with her eighteen-year-old great-grandson, and her husband who keeps missing his mouth and dropping food on his Hawaiian shirt and shouting 'Eh?' at his wife every time she says something to him."

Devin is quiet for a solid five Mississippis before he barks a laugh. "For shit's sake, Len. Drag your ass out to a bar tonight, have some drinks, and try to make a friend. C'mon, there's gotta be someone around your age you can hang out with."

My mind goes to the surly, arrogant prick lounging on the deck next door. The only type of hanging out he knows how to do is fighting and fucking, and I'm certainly not doing either of those things with him.

Even if he was the last man on earth, there's no way I'd spend my last night in Cabo with *Jaxon*.

"I SWEAR ON MY TITS, if you sit down next to me, I'll break every one of your fingers, and I'll do it so fucking slowly."

The man that stops beside me stares down at me, a wicked grin spreading across his handsome face. He should have devil horns protruding from his temples, but instead there's just a messy mop of light brown waves covering them, capped by a baseball hat.

"I hope for your sake you're prepared to follow through on that threat." Jaxon can't-remember-his-date's-name Fuckboy sinks down to the stool next to me, signaling the bartender. "I hate to see perfectly good tits go to waste."

I grab my frozen Bahama Mama and twist away, propping my chin on my fist, letting my hair block him from sight. "I was having a good time before you showed up."

"Really? Was that while you were sitting here by yourself for the last hour looking like a kicked puppy, or was it when that old guy with no shirt suggested taking the night back to his room?"

I frown at my drink. That was Gregory. He sat with me at breakfast two mornings ago, telling me all about his late wife and how they used to come here every year on their anniversary. Imagine my surprise when he showed up at my side fifteen minutes ago, drunk as a skunk, and asked if I wanted to give him an anniversary present, clothing optional. Imagine *his* surprise when I sweetly told him to go fuck himself. Offered up my dildo and everything.

"Don't you have someone else to annoy?" I grumble.

"Nope."

"Tall, blonde, big tits, loves screaming your name?"

"Nope."

"Did you knock her out with an Ambien or something?"

"Shit," he breathes out. "Why didn't I think of that sooner? Nah, she's gone."

"What?" I lift my head out of my hand, start to spin back to him, and the second I catch his self-assured smirk, I turn away again.

He grips my stool, spinning me back to him. "Breanne left."

I spin away. "Brielle."

"Yeah, her." He spins me back. "She's gone."

I kick at his stool, spinning again. "Wow, you chased her out of the country. Good for you."

When he spins me back this time, he holds my seat in place, tattooed forearm flexing. "Just one of my many talents."

I judo chop his arm, and he lets go with a silent scream, clutching the spot. "Annoying women? Yeah, you deserve a trophy."

The bartender joins us, grinning from ear to ear. His name tag says Luis, and I liked him well enough, until now. "Honeymoon?"

"No," I snap, as Jaxon says, "Yeah."

I glare at him, and he grins back.

"I live to annoy her. Get her all riled up, then fuck the angry outta her later."

Heat floods my cheeks, and Jaxon takes my hand, lifting it to his mouth, brushing a feather-soft kiss across the engagement ring I'm still wearing, for some inconceivable reason.

"Tell him, honey. Tell him how you love to scream at me."

"Jaxon," I whisper, watching as his thumb slowly brushes across my palm, over my allergy alert bracelet, coasts up the inside of my forearm.

He chuckles lowly, winking. "Something like that, but a lot louder."

Luis laughs, hearty and loud, and when he turns back to his bottles, I use the opportunity to mouth a *fuck you* to Jaxon and rip my hand back. "Allow me to make you something special to celebrate your wedding."

"Oh, that's not necessa—"

"That's great, Luis. Thank you. Don't mind my bride. She loves to argue." Jaxon winks at me. "It's her love language."

Luis returns with two glass goblets filled with blue slush. The empty bottle of tequila on the counter is alarming, but before I can question it, Jaxon is closing my fingers around the stem, clinking his glass to mine.

"To my beautiful wife."

"I—I'm not—" I frown at Jaxon, then Luis. The poor bartender wears the most hopeful expression while he waits for me to try his concoction. I roll my eyes, lifting the glass to my lips. Sweet, tangy notes erupt in my mouth, sliding way too easily down my throat, where a low moan rumbles. "Shit, that's good."

Luis pumps a fist through the air, then points at us as he jogs to a group waiting at the other end of the bar. "I got you! All night, I'm refilling your cups! Tonight, when you make love, you'll think of me!"

Okay, well, that's oddly disturbing. I don't want to be thinking of anyone when we're—

"I'm not sleeping with you," I bite out, shoving my finger in Jaxon's chest.

"Please." He pushes my hand away. "As if I wanna subject myself to your loud mouth all night long. I've just had the week from hell—"

"You've been here three days."

"—and the last thing I'm doing is getting into bed with another stage-five clinger."

I gasp. "How *dare* you. I'm not a stage-five clinger. I'm not even a stage-*one* clinger! I don't cling, period. And if I did cling, you'd be the last person I'd cling to."

"You tryin' to convince me, or yourself?" Hazel eyes move over me in a slow sweep as he sips his drink. "Where's your lucky other half anyway? It's your honeymoon."

My spine stiffens, breath rattling in my rib cage as I spin away from Jaxon. "Do you see a wedding band on my finger?"

"No, but I see a mediocre engagement ring."

Mediocre? This ring is worth half my salary. "The center stone is two carats. The paved band adds another."

"Mmm. Is that all?"

"Is that—" I stop, swallowing my frustration. "It's a very expensive ring."

"Is that why you're still wearing it?"

My gaze swings to his. "Are you calling me a gold digger?"

He takes another drink, shaking his head. "Don't put words in my mouth."

"Don't insinuate you know anything about me or my life."

"I know you're on your honeymoon, but you're here alone."

"And I know you arrived three days ago with a girlfriend, and now you've got no one."

"She wasn't my girlfriend."

"You brought someone who wasn't your girlfriend on vacation? Here?" I look around, palms up. "We're at an exclusive resort. You rented a honeymoon villa, for fuck's sake, Jaxon."

He grins.

"What are you smiling at?"

"You, saying my name. Bet you hate that you know it."

I roll my eyes. "You're so full of yourself."

"Someone's gotta be." Amusement dances in his eyes as he watches me drain my drink in four consecutive guzzles before he signals Luis for another round. "What's your name?"

"Bite me."

"You'd like that."

"I'd hate it."

His gaze dips to my mouth. "Trust me, you wouldn't."

"You're infuriating." I flash Luis a smile when he drops two new drinks in front of us. "No wonder Brielle left you. How'd you even convince her to come in the first place? Kidnapping? Bribery? What did you have on her?"

FALL WITH ME 19

He simply shrugs, like he knows the answer but doesn't want to share it with me. "What's your name?"

I pin him with my sweetest smile. "Now, honey, shouldn't you already know that, given that we're married?"

He smiles again, or maybe it's never dimmed. It's an incredibly handsome and devilish sight, and I'm definitely going to be thinking of him when I head back to my room later, drunk, lonely, and horny, trying one last time to give myself an orgasm at least once on my fucking honeymoon.

Fuck him, and fuck Ryne.

"That's okay." He tips his head toward my drink, and I realize I'm halfway through my second. "Another one of those and you'll be spilling a lot more than your name."

"Are you saying I'm an easy drunk?"

He lifts a shoulder, playful gaze heating as it glides down the length of my body. "Can't be more than five-three, and I'm a betting man."

Damn it. Bang on. "And what are you betting on?"

"I'm betting on you—being a lightweight and spilling your deepest, darkest secrets."

"Well, bet again." *He's totally fucking right.* I've never been able to keep my mouth shut when I've been drinking. But I'm tired of entertaining him, and I don't plan to do it for more than another five minutes, give or take. There's an electric buzz warming my body, and all I wanna do is go back to my room, slip my ear buds in, pop on the bodyguard threesome romance I'm listening to, and fuck the eight-inch dragon dildo currently resting on my bathroom sink after its afternoon bath. "I was a sorority girl. I know how to handle my alcohol."

His brows quirk. "Yeah? Care to play a game, then?"

"I'm not entertaining you and your childish desire to win." I toss my curls over my shoulder. "What game?" Blame my competitive childhood. I spent it vying for the attention my superstar brother was given freely by anyone and everyone.

"Let's keep it easy. It's our honeymoon, after all."

I roll my eyes.

"Never Have I Ever."

I sputter on my drink, clapping my hand to my mouth to catch the liquid. "Are we in high school?"

"How else am I getting all your secrets?"

"I'm not giving you anything, least of all my name."

"All right, honey." Jaxon reaches for his wallet when Luis drops more drinks in front of us, even though we aren't finished. This one is bright pink. Jaxon slips him a fifty-dollar bill. "Thanks so much for taking care of my wife and I tonight, Luis. I'm Jaxon." He takes Luis's hand, shaking it firmly, and I follow his lead, giving our bartender a bright smile.

"You're amazing, Luis. I'm Lennon."

I realize my mistake the moment the grown man beside me snickers into his pink drink.

"You motherfucker," I seethe as Luis leaves us.

"Aw, c'mon, Lennon. Don't be like that. I—" He stops abruptly, gaze dropping to my feet when I sling one leg over the other. "What the fuck are those?"

"They're shoes, Jaxon. Has your pink drink gone straight to your oversized head?"

"Those aren't shoes."

I glance at my tie-dye Crocs. Perhaps *shoes* isn't right, but what they are is fucking *comfortable*. Ryne hated when I wore these in public, so they were the only shoes I packed for this trip.

"They're fucking hideous."

"Yeah, well, I'm not taking them off." I grab my bag, spin away, and hop down. "See ya."

"Hang on." Jaxon catches my waist, hauling me back onto the

stool. "I said they were hideous; I didn't tell you to take them off. Wear whatever the fuck you want." He pushes my glass back into my hands. "Never have I ever had a pair of Crocs."

The tension stacked in my jaw dissipates, and I hide my smile behind my drink before Jaxon can see it. "Um . . . Oh, I know. Never have I ever had a threesome."

Jaxon drinks, which is unsurprising, but my eyes bug anyway. "Foursome?"

"It's my turn, not yours," he argues, which sounds a lot like a yes. Hazel eyes move over me, and I know he's about to go in for the kill. "Never have I ever left someone at the altar."

My hands shake as I lift my glass to my lips. Technically, we didn't make it to the altar; not for real, at least. That doesn't stop the alcohol from turning bitter in my mouth, sliding down my throat, and settling like lead in my belly. "Never have I ever slept with someone whose name I didn't know."

"Aw, c'mon. Cheap shot, Len. I remembered the first two letters."

"You and I both know she wasn't the first nameless girl."

"Excuse me for having a short attention span and a bad memory." He gulps his drink and squints at me. "Never have I ever spied on my neighbor on vacation."

My heartbeat trips. "What? I didn't—that wasn't—you were—" Face flushed, I finish my drink. "Never have I ever had sex in a public place."

My eyes widen as he drinks.

"Never have I ever listened to my neighbors have sex."

"I—" Close my eyes, sipping my drink. The nerve of this man. "It's not as if I had a choice. Brielle was incredibly loud." I narrow my eyes. "Never have I ever thought myself God's gift to women."

An easy tilt of his mouth. Another drink. "Never have I ever been in a relationship."

"Like, *ever*? That's—" I sigh when he aims a pointed look at my drink, the one I then finish. There's a new one in front of me before I can blink, this one lime green, and I've lost count of how many I've had. My body feels alive with the kind of energy that makes you want to get up and dance, throw your arms out wide, and soak up life.

That must be the only reason I continue to entertain Jaxon and this ridiculous game. Why twenty minutes turns to sixty, and one hour turns to two, until we're both drunk, inches away from each other as we pepper more truths between half-assed insults, meaningless conversation, and easy laughter.

"Never have I ever gone streaking." I lick the sugar from the rim of my margarita glass, then swipe his, cleaning it too. "Can you believe that? Twenty-six years old, former sorority girl, never, not once, have I ran my bare ass down the street."

Jaxon groans, dropping his face toward the bar before giving me an exasperated look. "Lennon, have you even *lived* your life? You were engaged, not dead."

"Maybe I'm still engaged."

"No, you're not."

"How do you know? Just because I didn't go through with the wedding doesn't mean—"

"Never have I ever called off my engagement."

Wow, okay, so, that was rude. "Well, I have no drink left, and would you look at that? The bar is closing. Guess we'll never know."

I hop down from my stool, swaying a little. Jaxon catches me, but he's no better off.

"Don't follow me," I shoot over my shoulder, pushing away and sauntering down the dark sandy path leading back to our villas. I twirl back to him, shoving my bag and Crocs into his chest. "Can you carry these for me? Thanks." Another twirl, this one in the open air, gaze set on the sky, all those stars I always wanted to build my life around. "Isn't it beautiful here? Look at all the stars. Makes me want to never go home."

"Where's home?"

A frisson of longing tugs at me, but I shove it away. "Wherever I want it to be."

"You're not going back to him."

I think it's a question, but he doesn't really word it that way. Instead of answering him, I dance ahead, onto the boardwalk and all the way down to the last two oceanfront villas.

"Lennon."

I swing around, pressing my back against my front door beneath the dim glow of the moon and the stars above. Jaxon pauses at the edge of my walkway, watching me for a beat before slowly closing the distance between us. The barstools really fucked with my perception of him. As he towers over me, I become acutely aware that this man could destroy me without effort.

My heartbeat trips, and I couldn't look away if I tried. There's something so magnetic about his gaze, the way it tracks every inch of my face, sparks when I laugh, darkens when I sweep my spirals off my neck and over my shoulder.

"You're not going back to him."

"Are you asking or telling?"

"Both."

"Well, I hate to break it to you, Jaxon, but you are, in fact, *not* God's gift to women. So you don't get to—" My words are cut short by the gasp that works its way out of my throat when Jaxon pins me against my door, his hips against mine, fingers closing gently around my throat.

Dark eyes stare down at me, his chest heaving in time with mine, and the heat radiating between us muddles every thought in my brain. I can't remember the last time I felt anything like this with Ryne, this intense hunger.

Jaxon twines his fingers through mine, lifting my left hand to rest by my head, his words softer this time. "You're not going back to him."

"No," I whisper, biting my bottom lip to stave off the whimper that nearly slips out when I feel the press of his weight between my legs.

He twirls my engagement ring around my finger with his thumb. "Why are you wearing this ring, Lennon?"

"I . . . because I . . . I don't know." I really, really don't. Maybe I'm still in denial. Maybe the disappointed faces are too scary a notion to face when I return home, ringless. Or maybe . . . "Maybe it makes me feel like someone still wants me."

Something like a growl rumbles in his chest, tearing up his throat. He throws the door open and forces me through it. I stumble backward, staring up at him as he matches each of my steps with his own.

A rough palm grips my neck, hauling me forward, fingers fisting the curls at the back of my head as his mouth drops to mine.

"Ditch the fucking ring," he whispers against my lips, and the second that platinum band princess cut diamond is skipping over the ceramic tiles, his mouth is on mine.

Hot, wet, and *starved*, his tongue sweeps into my mouth, laying claim to everything I have to give, fingertips scraping down my sides, tearing at my dress. I yank at his shirt, pulling it over his head, and we break away, breathless and feral.

Jaxon shoves me down to the mess of blankets on my bed.

"I'm gonna fuck you the way a bride deserves to be fucked on her honeymoon, and when I'm done, you're going to thank me and ask for more." He whips his belt free from his shorts. "Got it?"

I swallow. "Got it."

"Good girl. Now take off those panties and show me how badly your pussy wants my cock, honey."

3

HUMAN COCK: 1, DRAGON COCK: 0

Jaxon

LENNON DOES EXACTLY WHAT I expect her to.

Slowly drags her teeth across that plump lower lip. Bats those dark lashes. And ignores my demand. Fucking infuriating, and I eat it up.

"You suddenly lose your hearing? Or just too distracted by my beauty to pay attention to the words leaving my mouth?"

She grins, stands, and in *slow fucking motion*, shimmies her panties over her hips, letting them drop at her feet. Then she sits that round ass on the edge of the bed, props her feet up, spreads her legs, and I die inside.

The moonlight slides through the windows, glistening against her soaked pussy, and I nearly fall to my knees. Christ, I wanna fucking taste her. Bury my face between her thighs and never come up for air. I've never been a jealous man, but a scorching fire blazes through me at the thought of another man being in my position, having her spread out before me like a feast.

I step toward her, and she presses pretty pink-painted toes against my abdomen.

"Ah-ah, Jaxon. You want this pussy, you need to ask nicely." Dark eyes hook on the bulge in my boxer briefs. "In fact, I'm not opposed to begging."

"I don't beg, Lennon."

"Mmm. Shame." She slips off the bed, moving by me and into the bathroom, emerging a moment later with a giant . . . *something.* "Feel free to see yourself out," she murmurs.

I grip her wrist, stopping her when she tries to stroll by me.

There she goes, batting those lashes again like she's some kind of angel. "Something you need, Jaxon?"

Uh, yeah. "What in the fuck is this?"

Eyes as smooth and smoky as whiskey flick to the . . . fuck, I don't even know what to call this . . . *thing* in her hand. "It's a dildo, Jaxon. They're modeled off cocks. You know, that thing tenting your pants right now?"

"I dunno what kinda cocks you been fuckin', but mine doesn't have all these bumps and . . ." I flick one of the protruding . . . "Ridges?"

"I should hope not. It'd be alarming if you had a dragon cock."

"Drag—the fuck? What're you doing with a dragon cock?"

"You can put it anywhere if you're creative, but this one's made itself a nice home in my vagina for the last week."

Any blood left in my body rushes to my cock, throbbing with the need to show her how much better I can fuck her.

"You're not using that," I manage, super croaky as she presses every inch of herself against me, slinging one arm around my neck, dildo flopping against my shoulder, her hand sliding down my torso, cupping me.

Warm lips touch my jaw, working their way up to my ear. "You're worried you won't stack up; I get it. You probably won't. But hey, there's no shame in trying, right?"

I'm not sure how it happens, but next thing I know, that dildo is soaring through the air and I've got her pinned against the wall.

"You talk a lot of shit for someone who's here alone on her honeymoon. You wanna rile me up so you can fuck out all that anger you're holding on to?" I shove her thighs apart and dip my hand, running two fingers up her soaked slit, right up to her clit. When she gasps and grinds against me, I smile, plunging my fingers inside her. "Or you wanna sit back and let me fuck you the way a bride deserves to be fucked?"

Her fingernails bite into my shoulders as she rides my hand like a good, needy girl. "How do I deserve to be fucked?"

Wrapping an arm around her waist, I toss her to the bed and crawl on top of her, gripping her hips. "If you were my bride, my fingertips would be imprinted in your waist, because I'd never be able to let you go." My mouth finds hers, forcing it open while I circle her clit, pulling moans from her lips. "If you were my bride, your lips would be swollen because I'd never stop kissing you."

Climbing to my feet, I drop my pants, smiling when her eyes widen as my cock springs free. I fist it, working my hand over the throbbing, rock-hard length while I push my fingers inside her, press my thumb to her clit. Her back bows, my name tumbling off her tongue when she cries out. When she tries to pull my hand away, I give that beautiful brown pussy a swift slap.

"*Holy fuck.*" She weeps from behind the hand she clamps over her mouth, hips arching like she wants more.

So I give her another, then yank her hand off her mouth. Those noises are *mine.* I want them all.

"If you were my bride," I rasp, pulling her to the edge of the bed, sinking to my knees between her legs, "your pussy would be so sore you'd wonder if you'd ever walk again."

Hooded eyes lock on me as my mouth presses against the inside of her knee, slowly working itself up her thigh. I stop when I get where I want to be more than anything, breathing in the damp scent of her.

"If you were my bride, you'd be addicted to the taste of me and you, because after I finished fucking you, I'd clean up the mess between your legs before burying my tongue in your mouth."

Her fingers plow through my hair. *"Jaxon."*

I kiss the spot where her thigh meets her pussy, dragging my tongue around her, everywhere but the place she wants me most. Hooking my arms around her thighs, I jerk her as close to my face as I can get her. Her eyes don't leave mine, and the only thing I can hear in this room is her staggered, desperate breathing as I flick the tip of my tongue over her clit, the smallest tease.

"If you were my bride, I'd fuck you like you were my lifeline. I'd eat your pussy like it was my last meal, and I'd drive myself inside you over and over again, like you were the only place I'd find my salvation."

Pressing my tongue flat against her, I lick her slowly from bottom to top, and every inch of her trembles as she curls over me. Gripping her jaw, I force her gaze back to mine.

"If you were my bride, Lennon, I'd have spent the week worshiping you. We've missed a few days, but that's okay. I'm gonna worship you now, and I'll do it until you can't remember your own name. Do you want that, honey? You wanna be worshiped?"

She nods frantically, a light in her eyes that's been missing since I first spotted her bathing in the sun three days ago, ass up and topless.

"Ask nicely. Say, 'Please, Jaxon.' Tell me you want me."

Fire sparks in her gaze, and Jesus, all I wanna do is stoke it.

"You wanna tell me to go fuck myself?" I whisper against her thigh. "That you'll escort my ass out of here before you beg?"

She moans, fisting my hair as I slowly sink a finger inside her, curling it, thumb on her clit. "Y-e-e-esss."

"But you won't. Will you, honey? You want this. *Need it.* So ask nicely, honey, and I'll give it to you."

"Please, Jaxon," she breathes out, eyes tracking my hand as I pull it back, my finger as it disappears inside my mouth. "I want you."

With a grin, I spread her wider and bury my face between her thighs like I haven't eaten in days. I swear her soul leaves her body as she yanks at my hair and collapses against the mattress, heels digging into my back.

"Oh, *fuck*," she whimpers. "Oh God, oh God, *oh God*."

Her hips lift, and she grinds herself against my face as I eat her, lap at every inch of her, tug her swollen clit between my teeth. She's so goddamn wet, my trimmed beard is drenched, sliding effortlessly against her. I don't pull my face from her pussy until I need to breathe, gasping for air as I plunge three fingers inside her.

She's tight, squeezing my fingers so snug, it's no wonder she's so desperate for this. I'd bet that fiancé of hers never fucked her properly. Probably didn't know how.

Lennon sits up, chest heaving. Wide eyes go to my beard, and she reaches forward, touching the soaked hair. She pulls her hand back, looking at her glistening fingers like she's embarrassed. Silly. I've never had a better beard conditioner than her, so I force those fingertips into her own mouth, making her taste herself.

"Fuckin' delicious," I rumble, flicking my tongue back over her clit.

A pair of perfect bronzed tits beg for attention, so I lean forward, pulling a taut nipple into my mouth.

"Jaxon," she moans, arching against me. "Oh my . . . I-I-I . . . I can't."

"You can, honey."

Sucking her clit into my mouth, I keep my eyes on her as I drive my fingers deeper. Her head rolls over her shoulders and her thighs squeeze my neck. She's so damn close, hips lifting, chasing my touch, and when her walls clamp down around my fingers, I pull them out, taking her into my mouth.

She cries out my name, cries out for God, cries out for more and *please please please* as she comes on my tongue, legs shaking as I lick her clean.

Standing over her, I grip her jaw, tilt her face to mine, and show her what she tastes like on my tongue. She moans, fingernails raking down my arms, desperate for more.

"You like slow, Len?" I ask, my hand on her chest as I force her backward. Finding my pants, I keep my eyes on her as I pull a condom from my wallet, sheath my cock. "That what you want?"

She licks her lips, takes that plump bottom one between her teeth, worries it.

"Answer me, Lennon. You want slow?"

I push her down to the pillows, crawling toward her, her eyes bouncing between mine.

"No," she whispers. "I've had slow. Fuck me like I'm the reason your date left you here."

A smile tugs at the corner of my mouth as I settle myself between her legs. "Anything for my beautiful bride." Pushing her thighs up, I bare her to me. She's a fucking vision, brown pussy so beautiful and wet, like honey dripped over the forest in late October.

"You gonna fuck it or just keep staring at it, Jaxon?"

My gaze flicks to hers, and I grin as I drop a kiss to her lips, running the head of my cock through her slick pussy. "Don't get mouthy, honey. I'd hate to have to shut you up on our honeymoon."

She drags her thumb across my lower lip. "It's cute you think your cock holds that much power."

My head drops, a dark chuckle shaking my shoulders. Pressing my palm against the base of her throat, I tell her lowly, "I'd give you the chance to take that back, one last opportunity for soft and slow, maybe even a little sweet." I nip her lower lip. "But I'm afraid I'm all out of those."

I drive myself inside her without warning, and fucking *fuck*, I'm in goddamn *heaven*, right there with her as her lips part. The only sound that leaves her throat is something so hungry, so desperate, I swallow it, not wanting to share it with anyone else.

"Fuck, Lennon. Fucking . . . *fuck*." I toss her legs over my shoulders, one hand on her throat, the other clutching the mattress beside her head as I bury my cock so damn *deep* inside her, over and over.

She's breathless, speechless, shaking her head, fingernails tearing at my arms as I pound into her. She squeezes around me, and the filthiest smile I've ever smiled splits my cheeks.

"Already, honey? It's not even been a minute."

Her eyes roll to the ceiling. "I . . . fucking . . . *hate* . . . you."

"Take it back, baby. You love this cock. You wanna come all over it."

Her body quivers, and she chokes out her weak comeback. "It'll do."

I angle my hips, driving myself deeper, my pelvis slapping against her clit as I run my tongue up her neck, pressing my whispered words to her ear. "Ask me. Beg me to let you come on my cock. Make it pretty, honey. Say please."

"Fuuuck. *Jaxon*. P-p . . . please."

"Keep going." My fingertips dig into her trembling thighs. "You're running out of time."

"Please, Jaxon," she begs. "P-p-please. I want to come on your cock."

I roll my hips hard, grinding against her clit, and she shatters around me, eyes closed, back bowed, hands fisted in the sheets as she drenches my cock. Christ, what a spectacular fucking sight.

Pulling out of her, I slap her pussy, sending another round of tremors through her before I yank her onto her hands and knees, ass in the air. I run my tongue up her delicious cunt before turning her head, plunging my tongue into her mouth and my cock back inside her.

I hold her hips as I bury myself balls deep and just stay there for a moment, basking in the euphoria of the magnificent way her pussy molds to me, like she's been waiting for my cock to fill her up.

"Jaxon," she whimpers, wriggling her ass. "Fuck me, please." She sinks down to the mattress, gripping two fistfuls of sheets. "I can't take it."

I clap a hand to one plush ass cheek, something inside me pulling taut as I watch the tips of my fingers disappear. "You'll take what I give you," I growl, fingertips digging into her hips as I drag my cock out of her before slamming back inside, harder, fast, deeper.

My gaze roams her, desperate to see all of her at once. To watch the way she stretches around my cock every time I sink inside her, the curl of her fingers as they tangle in the bedding, the way her curls bounce with each thrust and fall around her shoulders, frame the deep flush of her cheeks when her head flops to one side like she can't take it anymore.

Moonlight dances through the windows, glinting off the delicate metal wrapped around her left wrist. I run the pad of my thumb over the etched words that tell me Lennon has a tree nut and peanut allergy, and then I slide my palm over the back of her hand, linking my fingers with hers.

She looks up at me, her gaze slowly tracking mine like it's been drenched in molasses. There's something there, something so open and raw, and when she tells me, "Nothing's ever felt so good," something inside me snaps.

I pull out of her, tug her onto my lap, and yank her down on my cock, her curls tight in my fist as I hold her head taut and fuck her. Her breath kisses my lips, her tits bouncing against my chest, and my brow furrows as we watch each other. I don't want to stop looking at her, and the feeling throws me. I want her eyes on me at all times. I want to drink her in while she bounces on my cock, while I sink inside her, make her come undone while she chants my name. I want to erase the memories of a week spent alone and replace them with memories of being so full she can't remember what it was like before she had my cock.

I want her to think about me every time she fucks anyone else. I want her to remember how good it was, how perfectly we moved together, and I want her to wish it was me inside her instead of whatever dipshit is having the luckiest night of his life.

Her brows tug together, so slightly I barely notice the crease in her forehead, but then she closes her eyes and presses her lips to mine, devouring my mouth. She breaks away with a gasp, clinging to me as she rides me, her face in my neck.

"Look at me," I demand, but she shakes her head. "Lennon."

"You're gonna fall in love with me."

I snort a laugh, my grip on her hips tightening. "Okay."

"It's true. I saw it in your eyes. You're an open book."

"Gimme your fuckin' eyes," I growl, and when she does, the light is back in them. They dance with amusement, and she grins, a fucking brilliant sight, pink tongue dragging across lips I want to spend my night feasting on. "I don't fall in love."

"Of course not," she barely manages as I pull her harder down on my cock. "You fuck. Love is for losers."

I don't know about that, but it's definitely not for me.

"I love lots of things. Like pussy. I *love* pussy."

She smiles wider. "You've made it quite obvious it's your favorite meal."

"I was talking about my cat."

The amusement slides off her face, and she glares at me. I chuckle, and she shivers, squeezing around my cock, the sensation tingling in my balls. My palms scrape up her sides, but hers land on my chest, shoving me down to my back.

Lennon leans over me, hands braced on my chest, curls curtaining her face as she pulls herself off my cock and then slams herself back down.

"Fuuuck. That's it, honey. Take what you want."

"I want you to come," she breathes out. "I want to watch you fall apart, just for me." She sinks all the way down, hands in her hair, eyes closed as she rolls her hips slowly, making herself feel good, making me feel like a fucking god.

"Jesus, Lennon." My balls tighten, cock throbbing at the sight of her as she moves, like no one knows her body better than she does. Like she's perfectly happy with loving herself. She doesn't need anyone else to do it for her. "This is how I wanna go. Most beautiful girl I've ever seen riding my cock. Take care of my cat for me, honey."

She giggles, lifting herself off me, sinking slowly. "You wanna come?"

"Fuck, I wanna *explode*."

"Ask nicely, Jaxon. 'Can I come, Lennon? Can I come in your beautiful, perfect pussy?' But oh, wait." She frowns, cocking her head as her hips roll to a stop. "You don't beg. Right. I forgot." Her lower lip slides between her teeth, one brow quirking. "That's okay. You can finish yourself off when I'm done."

Her hand drops to the cleft of her thighs, right where we're connected, and she starts stroking her clit, moaning as she brings herself closer to her own release, squeezing around me. I grin, because fuck me, I like her; I'll play whatever game she wants to play.

I cup her tits in my hands, brushing my thumbs over her dark nipples, tweaking them as her mouth falls open. Her fingers slow as I rock into her, one hand dropping back to my chest to steady herself. "I wanna come, Lennon. Can I come in your beautiful, perfect pussy? It's so wet for me, so soaked, hugging my cock so good." I knock her hands out of the way, grip her hips, hold her in place, and drill up into her. "You feel that, honey? Feel how hard I am for you?"

She nods, over and over, whimpers spilling from her throat, pussy squeezing me so tightly I know I can make her give it all up. But if she only gets one thing this week, I want it to be this.

So I bring her lips to mine and whisper the plea she wants against them. "I can't take it, Lennon. Let me come. Please."

"Yes," she cries out. "Yes, you can come!"

My head drops back, and I drive myself inside her once, twice, three more times before I hold her against me. My balls tighten, and I rub her clit with my thumb, waiting for her to fall apart around me before I explode inside her, sealing her mouth to mine as we ride out our release together.

Lennon collapses, breathless and boneless, on top of me. "A-plus for effort," she wheezes, and I bark a laugh.

I shove her off me, turn onto my side, and gather her back against my chest, my face nestling into her curls. They smell like coconut. "Your hair's in my way."

"Then get out of its way."

"You're more annoying than Breanne."

"Brielle."

I chuckle against her shoulder, and when my hand slides over her stomach, her body softens to fit against mine.

"Jaxon?"

"Mmm."

"What will you call me tomorrow when you forget my name?"

I crack my lids, sifting through the dark room. It smells like sex in here, which is exactly the way every honeymoon suite should smell. "Wife."

"You wish, fuckboy."

I close a hand around her throat. "Shhh. Go to sleep. I'm waking you up in fifteen minutes with your dragon cock."

And I do. I watch her come apart around it before she comes apart around me. I fuck her on every inch of her honeymoon suite all night long, fifteen minutes of rest in between each round. I don't pass out until sometime after five, and when I wake up at eight and reach for her, she's not there.

I sit up, squinting against the sun, and search for Lennon.

There's no sign of her. Her hideous Crocs are gone. Her luggage is gone. *She's* gone.

I flop back down to the pillows, and something crunches under my head. Finding the piece of paper, I read the scrawled note she left for me.

I hate you, but I love your cock. Thanks for letting me ride it. Bye, Jason.

4

HUH. WASN'T EXPECTING THAT.

Jaxon

ONE THING ABOUT ME? I'M gonna serenade my cat every chance I get so he knows how much I love him.

"Silly kitty, chunky kitty, I kiss your tiny nose. Fluffy kitty, handsome kitty, I love your extra toes."

Mittens meows, rolling onto his back when I reach the end of my song—his version of a standing ovation. I nuzzle my face into the soft white fur on his belly. He plops one orange paw on my nose, which roughly translates to *I love you, Daddy*. I guess he's forgiven me for leaving him. It's my first real day back to reality, so when I rolled out of bed earlier, still dreaming of the best sex I've ever had, I forgot to slap a hand over my junk.

I know what you're thinking: Jaxon, why would you have to slap a hand over your junk?

Uh, because my cat likes to attack my balls like they're his favorite dangly toys.

"I'm really worried about you, bud."

The words startle me right off Mittens's chaise lounge, where I've been sprawled beneath the sunrise seeping through the windows of my condo. I scramble to my feet as Garrett strolls through my door and into my kitchen. "Do you ever *knock* anymore?"

"Never," he mumbles, pulling a granola bar from my pantry. He stuffs the entire thing in his mouth, watching me while he chews.

His beanie—or toque, as he and Carter call it, 'cause Canadians are weird—is covered in a dusting of snowflakes, same as the shoulders of his blue Vancouver Vipers hoodie. "You singing to your cat again?"

"No." I press a kiss to Mittens's nose. "Love you, marshmallow." I tug on a hoodie and beanie that match Garrett's. "Why are you worried about me? And why are you eating my food?" I slap the bag of Sour Keys out of his hand before he can open them. First of all, they're mine. Second, they're gonna make him sick on the ice in an hour if he eats them now.

"'Cause you're singing to your *cat*."

"You sing to Jennie." Caught him singing Justin Bieber in her ear just yesterday. When he saw me, he slowly backed away.

"Jennie's my fiancée. I'll do anything she wants me to do." He steals a banana off my counter, peeling it as he follows me to the door, where I step into a pair of sneakers. "She hired an assistant manager for her dance studio. Want me to see if she'll set you up?"

Heaving a sigh, I lock my door behind us before jamming the elevator button seventeen hundred times. "Why would I wanna be set up?"

He lifts a shoulder. "You seem—"

"I'm not lonely."

Garrett grins, extra fucking irritating. "Like you might be ready to meet someone, is what I was gonna say."

"I don't need to meet someone. I already have eight friends. I'm at capacity. In fact, I could probably do with ditching a few of you." I step out of the elevator and follow Garrett to his car out front. "Plus, I know where to meet people if I wanna. But I don't. I'm perfectly happy, just me and Mitts."

"Uh-huh." He's still grinning, and if it were a year ago when we didn't like each other, I probably wouldn't hesitate to wipe it off his face. But I guess now Garrett Andersen's, like . . . one of my best friends, or whatever. "Well, forget I asked. Wouldn't wanna mess with whatever you and Mitts got going on."

What Mitts and I have going on is possibly the best arrangement ever. Adopting him from the shelter in September was my brightest idea yet, not just because he keeps me company while I drink my morning coffee, but because he hates everyone except my friends. When I bring a woman home, he's sitting outside the bedroom door glaring at her after we're done. When she inevitably reaches for him, because *awww he's so sweet*, he hisses and swats at her. I apologize profusely for my poorly behaved cat as I walk my date to the elevator, and then Mittens drapes himself over my shoulders on the couch and bops the shit out of my jaw with his cute little head while we eat snacks and watch *One Tree Hill* reruns. I couldn't have asked for a better partner in crime.

I get it, though. Or at least I think I do. I've got eight friends, and they're all married/dating/engaged to one another. I'm the only single one left, which means I'm always the odd man out. Truthfully, I'm used to being on my own. Before being traded to Vancouver just over a year ago, I played for Nashville. Before Nashville, it was Carolina, and before Carolina, it was Los Angeles. At twenty-seven years old, I've already played for four NHL teams. I've never been anywhere long enough to plant roots, or make the kind of friends I have in my teammates Garrett, Carter, Adam, and Emmett.

But those four have been playing together for years, built a bond you dream of when you think about a career as a professional hockey player, and I'm just the defenseman who stepped off the plane fourteen months ago after one too many fights that led to too much time off the ice. They took me in because they had to, and they do a damn good job of treating me like, for the time being, I'm really one of them.

When I inevitably get booted from Vancouver, though, they'll forget about me, just like all my former teammates.

I settle into the passenger seat with a sigh. I've had a slow return to life after Cabo, and I can't wait to get back on the ice this morning, back to the one thing I was born to do. Maybe the only thing I'm good at.

Garrett fiddles with one of the Starbucks cups in his console, reading the label before he passes it to me. "Here."

I blink at the drink warming my hand. "You got me a coffee?"

"Caramel brulée latte."

Something thick settles in my throat.

"Isn't that what you like?"

I clear my throat, nod, and let the drink warm my belly. Instead of asking him why he thought to get me my favorite winter drink on the way to pick me up, I just say, "Thanks."

By the time we're in our gear at the arena, I've managed to bury my useless thoughts and simply enjoy the way the cool air nips at my cheeks as I whip around the ice for the first time in ten days. I've missed this. Missed the way my legs move without thought, gliding quickly down the ice, hands moving effortlessly as I cradle a puck back and forth on the blade of my stick. Out here, on a pair of skates and with a stick in my hands, is maybe the only place I really feel at home.

I pull my stick back, shift my weight to my left foot, and send the puck flying toward Adam.

And like he does 99 percent of the time, he stops the puck from soaring past him and into his net. His legs split as he dives to his right, and his catcher comes up, scooping the puck out of the air. He grins at me as I skid to a stop in front of him.

"When you gonna let me score?"

"The only person I let score is Rosie." He shifts his mask on top of his head to squirt water into his mouth. "I always know exactly where you're aiming. You look there right before you let the puck fly."

"Fuck. I have a tell?"

"You got a fucking tell, bud."

A body connects with mine from behind, shoving me into Adam. Carter Beckett, our captain, spins with flourish, and for the hundredth time I wonder if he was really meant to be a figure skater, not the leading goal-scorer in the NHL. "You guys hear about Tim?"

"Tim?" I scan the arena seats for our team photographer. "Where is he?"

"Gone. He quit, right after our last game."

"What? Why?"

Emmett Brodie, our left winger, stops beside us. "Cara says he was having an affair with one of the stewardesses. His wife chased him out of town."

"What? No way." Garrett joins us, grabbing Adam's water bottle, coating his sweat-soaked face. "His wife's mom was sick. Jennie said they probably moved back home to help take care of her."

Carter inches closer, voice dropping. "What if, this entire time, he's been here undercover to run an exposé on us?"

We go quiet, staring at Carter. Slowly, his eyebrows hike higher and higher, his grin growing like he thinks he's really nailed it, and he's so impressed with himself.

Adam shakes his head, puts his gloves back on, and turns away. "Yeah, no."

"Absolutely not," Emmett agrees.

"What is with you and all your conspiracy theories?" I ask.

"And why do they all revolve around someone being obsessed with us?" Garrett adds.

Carter's face falls, reminiscent of a six-year-old who's just found out Santa isn't real. He aimlessly handles a puck on the tip of his stick. "Well, *excuse me* for having a creative imagination."

I snort a laugh, skating off with a shake of my head when my defense coach calls for the defensemen to join him at the other end of the ice. A flash of light catches my attention, and I look up, finding the backside of a woman with a beanie shoved over her head as she crouches on the stairs and aims an oversized camera up them. I can't imagine what makes dirty concrete stairs and shitty red vinyl seats photographable, but I don't really have an eye for art. If this is the team's new photographer, I'm not sure she does either.

By the time practice is done, I'm ready for a nap. I keep my head down as we stomp through the tunnel, heading back to our dressing room while a camera clicks and flashes. I hate having my picture taken. Everyone always comments on how I'm never smiling. Our team's Instagram comment section is always at least 30 percent filled with remarks about how I don't look as friendly or as happy as my friends, another reminder that I don't fit with them.

"Dude." Charlie McCarthy, my D partner, elbows my side. "You see her?"

"Her who?"

He tips his head behind us. "The new photographer. She's hot as balls."

"Not interested," I mumble, pulling off my helmet and sinking to the bench at my cubby. I like to fuck around, sure, but with someone involved with the team? Doesn't seem like the brightest idea, no matter how hot she is.

"Suit yourself." Charlie shrugs. "Maybe I'll shoot my shot."

"Go for it, bud."

By the time I'm showered and back in my sweats, I'm fucking starving. We've got a team meeting, and the breakfast buffet is the only reason we race there. A full belly always makes for a banging midday nap cuddled up on the couch with Mitts.

"Fuck yeah," Carter mutters, shouldering me out of the way

to hit the spread at the back of the conference room. "Come to Daddy."

"Hey." I tug the paper plate from his hand, shoving him down the table. "No butting. And stop calling yourself Daddy in every scenario that presents itself."

"I cannot simply *stop* calling myself Daddy. Not when the opportunity arises. Plus"—he grabs two giant blueberry muffins, shoving half of one in his mouth—"I'm wike da team daddy, wight?"

It's best not to entertain him in these types of scenarios, so I don't.

"Technically . . ." Axel Larsen, the Vipers' general manager, pokes his head over our shoulders. "*I'm* the team daddy." He winks at Carter. "Maybe I'll be *your* daddy, Beckett."

Carter gasps, shoving a finger in Axel's shoulder. "Holly Beckett is so far out of your league, she's in outer space."

I roll my eyes, filling my plate and finding a seat near the back of the room. The boys collapse beside me a minute later, plates full, talking about how they spent their week off.

Carter and his wife, Olivia, took their daughter, Ireland, to Disneyland. Adam and Rosie took their kid, Connor, to Colorado to visit Adam's parents, and then spent the rest of the week making up one of their spare bedrooms for Lily, a little girl they're hoping to foster as soon as they've finished their training. Emmett and his wife, Cara, spent the week—

"—fucking like animals. Literally everywhere. Kitchen counter, bathroom counter, dining room table, living room couch, basement couch, the chaise lounge in the bedroom, you name it. If it supports my weight, I fucked her on it."

"That's how I should've spent my week," I grumble, shoving a gooey pastry topped with cinnamon sugar into my mouth. That was my plan when I originally invited Brenda, but by the time we stepped off the plane in Cabo I already couldn't stand her. It was still my plan three days later when I found God inside Lennon's pussy, but then she took off on me. Easiest one-night stand of my life, but I would've preferred to spend the rest of my week fucking the attitude out of her before never seeing her again.

"I see you're still bitter about being ditched by *two* girls on your vacation," Garrett says.

"I don't care about Brenda."

"Brielle," Adam corrects. "Or was it Breanne?" He frowns. "Breann*a*? I feel like you've called her a million different names that all start with B."

I wave him off. "Dunno, can't remember. But the girl next door—"

"The one who was supposed to be on her honeymoon," Carter confirms, nodding.

"Yeah, her. She was—"

"The reason Breanna left?" Emmett asks.

"No. Well, yeah, kinda. 'Cause I was checking her out, and Breanna got pissed 'cause I wasn't giving her enough attention."

"What was her name again?" Adam asks.

Garrett snickers. "He probably doesn't remember."

"Actually, I do. Her name was—"

"Is there something you'd like to share with the class, gentlemen?" Coach's voice cuts through the room, and the sharp look in his eyes silences us immediately. "Christ, the number of times I wonder if I'm coaching men's professional hockey or teaching kindergarten is astounding."

"Sorry, Coach," the five of us mumble, picking quietly at our food.

"All right, let's get on with this. I know you're all probably ready for a nap, and I want everyone fresh for our game tomorrow, so I won't keep you long." Coach sighs, sifting through the papers spread out on the table in front of him, his other hand buried in his hair. "Oh, right. If you haven't heard by now, Tim's no longer with us."

The five of us perk up, leaning toward Coach. Carter's particularly eager, and Garrett's hand is already outstretched over Carter's lap, waiting.

"His mother-in-law isn't doing well, so he and his wife moved back home to help out."

"Aw, *fuck*," Carter groans beneath his breath.

"Fuck yeah," Garrett mutters, curling his fingers into his palm. "Pay up."

Carter slaps a handful of bills into Garrett's hand before crossing his arms over his chest, glaring at the front of the room.

"We're really excited about the new addition to our Vipers crew, though. She's got a great eye, and promises to get our social media buzzing." Chatter trickles in from the hallway, and Coach peeks out the door. "Ah, here she is now."

I swear I've heard this voice before, the one growing closer. It itches my brain in a funny way, and I slip my fingers beneath my beanie, scratching my head as I try to place it.

She laughs, a carefree giggle that has my mind flashing back to a humid night with too many drinks, trading truths for insults, sweat-soaked bodies, tequila kisses, and trying to outfuck a dragon dildo.

"Boys, please give a warm welcome to our new photographer and social media content manager: Miss Hayes."

She steps into the room, and my world spins to a stop. My pastry might make a reappearance, along with my caramel brulée latte.

"Hey, guys," she says with a wave and a wide smile. "Super stoked to be jumping on board. Thanks for having . . . having . . ."

Dark amber eyes lock on mine, widening, and a deep flush works its way into those sharp copper cheekbones. She's ditched the beanie she was wearing in the rink while she was hiding behind her camera, and now all I can see is her hair, the chestnut curls I had fisted in my hands while I pounded into her, fucked her the way a bride deserves to be fucked on her honeymoon. She swallows then, finally tacking on that last word she's been searching for. "Me."

"Lennon," I whisper, the contents of my plate falling to my feet.

Adam snaps his fingers. "Lennon! Yeah! That was the name of the girl you . . ." His smile falls. "You . . ." From the corner of my eye, I catch the way his head whips back and forth, between me and the woman at the front of the room as we watch each other. He swallows. "Oh. Oh no."

Oh no is right.

Somewhere, I'm conscious of Carter short-circuiting over my food scattered on the ground, the fact that I haven't swooped down to save it yet.

But I can't take my eyes off the woman who rode my cock like a queen a week ago, made me beg before *she* snuck out on *me*. And right now, she looks like she's come face-to-face with the ghost of her worst mistake.

"Excuse me," she murmurs, covering her mouth. "I think I'm going to be sick."

Adam's eyes stay straight ahead, head bobbing as Lennon flees the room. "So that was the girl you met in Cabo."

"Correction," Garrett mumbles around a doughnut. "That was the girl he *fucked* in Cabo."

Emmett's typing out a message on his phone. "Cara's gonna eat this the *fuck* up."

"Unbelievable," Carter mutters, stooping down to swipe my

food off the ground. He aggressively shoves it back on the plate, shooting his disappointment at me through narrowed eyes. "We do *not* waste baked goods, Riley."

He sinks down to his seat, slipping mini doughnuts on each of his fingers like rings. "Anyway. What did I miss?"

5

IT WAS ALL A FEVER DREAM

Lennon

THIS ISN'T MY WEEK.

Really, the whole year's been rough.

"It's only January," my mom murmurs, blue eyes twinkling with amusement from my phone screen.

"Exactly." I flop onto the couch in my new living room. "It's *only* January. I'll never survive the rest of the year when it's already burning in the fiery depths of *hell*."

"Right along with Ryne," my dad mutters from somewhere off-screen.

Mom rolls her eyes. "You two are the biggest drama queens I know. You have plenty of time to turn the year around, Len. You'll make new friends in Vancouver—"

"Unlikely."

"—and maybe you'll meet a—"

"No."

"For all you know, you might even spark a romance with one of the boys on the t—"

"Nope."

"But Lennon—"

"Absolutely not, Mom. I'm not dating a hockey player." Fucking one, maybe.

No. *Fucked*, past tense.

And holy tits, *that* was a mistake. A glorious, incredible, magnificent, *orgasmic* mistake that I've been regretting for the last . . . twenty-seven hours, give or take. Basically, since I walked into the Vancouver Vipers' conference room and came face-to-face with my one-night stand from Cabo, who, as it turns out, is not just *ohhh God, yes, Jaxon, please,* but Jaxon Riley, star defenseman for the team I'm now—*oh fuck, I'm gonna be sick*—working for.

Yeah, that sounds bad, doesn't it? Otherwise, I could've happily lived the rest of my life walking around in a dazed bliss, the memory of that one night, Jaxon, his filthy mouth, and a cock that blew my dragon dildo out of the water, nothing more than exactly that: a memory.

Instead, I'm going to need to come to work every day and pretend I've never had that man's face buried between my legs.

Mom frowns, pushing her ashy hair back. She quit dying her roots last year at my dad's encouragement, and now her sleek blonde bob is streaked with silver. "Why not? I looked up the roster. There's some cuties over there."

I press a hand to the headache forming behind my eyes. "I'm here to get away from one horrible relationship, not chase another." And certainly never, ever tell anyone about the player whose cock I accidentally impaled myself on after one too many colorful drinks.

"Yeah, Len," my cousin Serena murmurs, brown eyes alight as she smirks at me from the split screen on my phone. "Surely there's at least one cute player over there that's caught your eye. Why not let him dick you down good?"

Okay, so I accidentally told Serena about Jaxon. That was mistake number two (Jaxon was number one) because Serena keeps secrets about as well as my ex-fiancé kept himself off Tinder, which is to say not at fucking all.

Shit, Ryne was mistake number one, wasn't he?

"For fuck's sake, Rena." Mom sighs. "I said date, not dick down."

Dad appears next to Mom. "I'm not a fan of this conversation. Nobody needs to get dicked down." His mouth dips to my mom's ear. "Except for you."

"*Ew*," Serena screams while I gag. "TMI, Uncle Trev!"

"And athletes are bad news," he adds.

"Your son is a professional baseball player," I remind him. "*You're* a retired coach."

"Coach, not player. And Devin is terrible news."

Mom arches her brow. "Devin is exactly like you when you were that age."

He grins, hand over his heart. "Fiercely charming and devilishly handsome. Thank you, I know."

Mom, Serena, and I roll our eyes in unison.

When Mom's gaze comes to mine, she's still frowning. It's about all I've seen from her since she watched me get on the plane to Vancouver a few days ago, like it's so deeply ingrained. She's never been a frowner. But her hope for my bleak future has been slowly dying, right along with her smile.

"I want you to find happiness, Lennon. Whatever that looks like. And I would hate to see you avoid relationships forever because one—"

"—piece of motherfucking shit," Serena and my dad supply, which, coincidentally, is Ryne's name in my phone.

"—isn't a real man."

I tug at the hem of my pajama shorts. "Is Mimi still mad at me?"

"She's not mad at you, per se . . ."

Serena snorts a laugh. "Mimi said if you're not back for good in time for the family cookout in the spring, she's dragging you back herself."

"She's just upset you've run away," Mom clarifies.

"I didn't run away! I just needed to get away!"

Serena checks her nails. "Most people call that running."

"I flew." I stick my nose in the air. "The two are distinctly different." I twirl a coil around my finger, watching it slip off and spring back up. "I still don't want her to be mad at me, though."

Dad smiles, and like it always does, it transforms his face. All the hard lines melt, softening into the warmth I've always felt safe in. Beneath his nearly black facial hair, the dimples in his cheeks pull in, and I swear his brown skin glows, the same as his deep brown eyes. My dad, just like this, has always been one of my favorite safe places.

"She's not mad at you, sweetheart. She understands. She misses you, that's all. We all do. But we want you to be happy, here with us or in Vancouver, but definitely not getting dicked down by any athlete." His expression brightens. "Oh, hey, what about that girlfriend you had in sophomore year? She was nice! Yeah, I liked her." He points at me with two finger guns, pumping his brows once, and yes, he's always been embarrassing. "You should look her up."

I hide my groan behind the palm I drag down my face. "Hillary is happily married with two kids and a third on the way, Dad, but I'm glad she left a lasting impression on you nearly ten years ago." Dragging myself off the couch and to my feet, I head to the kitchen to make myself a coffee with the machine Amazon delivered last night. "I'm just going to lay low for a while. Be on my own."

The three of them exchange a look, one I pretend not to notice. I haven't been on my own since . . . well, ever. I had my first kiss at thirteen in Serena's closet during her fourteenth birthday party and I never looked back. I floated from one relationship to another until Mimi introduced me to Ryne when I was in my junior year in high school, and he was a freshman in college. After high school, I joined him at the University of Georgia, moved into a student house with seven other girls, and when I graduated, Ryne proposed. I said yes because I didn't think there was any other future for me without him in it, and I moved into the house he stayed in while he was in town for work. Now here I am, twenty-six and without a clue about how to be on my own.

And I hate it.

Both being alone, and that I don't know how to be.

"Anyway, I'm totally fine." I shove a coffee pod in the little hole thingie, slam the lid, and panic when I see three sets of flashing lights blinking up at me. I don't know which one to press, so I jab the middle one, because that seems like the safest bet. The little machine whirs to life, and I smile, proud of myself when it starts making a grinding sound.

"What's that sound?" Dad asks cautiously.

"I'm making coffee. It's grinding the beans right now."

Serena snorts a laugh. "I know you didn't just say it was grinding the beans. Len, that's a damn Keurig box on your counter. The beans are already ground!"

"Huh?" The machine squeals like a car in desperate need of new brakes, and when it starts sputtering, shooting spurts of faintly tinted water out at me, I grit my teeth. "Fuck."

"Oh my God," Mom murmurs. "Honey, she doesn't know how to make coffee."

"No!" I shove my phone against my chest as I jab another button, then the other, and eventually all three. Water keeps shooting out at me, and the machine is making a furious fizzing sound, like I've personally offended it. "Everything's fine! I gotta—" The water turns brown suddenly, and as it starts spraying in all directions, I shriek. Somehow managing to get a handle on myself, I pull my phone screen back to my face, plastering on a ginormous smile that looks 100 percent genuine, if I were a betting woman. "So, hey, everything's totally fine over here, but I gotta go. Furniture shopping. Because I'm so excited to be on my own, and I happen to be incredibly excellent at it so far."

My family blinks at me, and before they can call me on my bullshit, I half-scream, *"Okayloveyabye!"*

I slam my phone down and yank the cord for the coffee machine from the wall, sagging with relief when the fountain of coffee stops.

My phone pings, and I look down at the email notification from Starbucks.

Your next Starbucks visit is on Dad! Dad sent you an eGift card for $200 and said, "Don't burn your apartment down."

Oh, thank *fuck.*

I shoot off a *thank you* to my dad before changing out of my pajamas and getting on with my day. I don't have to be at the arena for the game until later this afternoon, which leaves me plenty of time to head to Starbucks, spend the day getting lost in IKEA, and maybe even head back to Starbucks for round two.

Because if I'm going to successfully ~~ignore Jaxon Riley~~ put together IKEA furniture, I need all the caffeine my body can reasonably handle.

And possibly a *strong* cocktail.

"SURELY IT'S NOT CONSIDERED DRINKING on the job if they *serve* alcohol here."

"I vote no, and I'm always right."

My wishful thought is muttered aloud, but the blonde five feet to my left still answers. I peek over my shoulder, heat pooling in my cheeks when she winks at me and speaks again.

"Go for it, girlie. Get your drink on."

"I can't." I reluctantly pick my camera back up, aiming it at the ice as the players whip around it, take shots on the goalie, stretch, or goof around. Then I pull my camera back again, just an inch, and look at the blonde. "But it's almost like they're inviting me to drink, right?"

"Oh, for sure. Taunting, at the very least."

"It's almost rude."

"So fucking rude." She discreetly offers me a wine cooler, brows raised.

"Thanks, but I need this job. I'll have to find another way to make it through."

She holds her hand up, nodding. "If you change your mind, though." With a wink, she turns her attention back to the group of girls to her left.

I spend the next several minutes listening to them interact, whispering, laughing together, bickering in that way that tells me they're not just friends, but family. I've never had that type of friendship with anyone who wasn't *actually* family, and I didn't realize how much I craved it until right now. Sororities give you that fake sense of security, of importance, in college. You feel invincible, like you're surrounded by a force field of friends who would do anything for you. But then you're torn apart by the silliest, most inconsequential things, like having a crush on the same person, or trying out for the same spot on the cheer team. If you're lucky enough to make it through college with them still by your side, chances are you'll never see them again after graduation, instead watching their life unfold over social media and exchanging half-assed promises to get together next time you're both in town.

Maybe Vancouver is my shot at finding that. Maybe now it's my turn to find my people, to find friends that turn into family, people that want to stick around forever.

I swallow the eager thoughts and focus on my job: taking pictures of hot hockey players. It isn't exactly the career I'd envisioned for myself, photographing a semi-violent sport I know nothing about. Once upon a time, I dreamed of photographing the skies. Brilliant sunrises and spectacular meteor showers.

Constellations, blood moons, and the Northern Lights. Everything beautiful in this life.

But sometimes, dreams are meant to be dreams, not realities. That's why I stopped chasing my dream a long time ago.

It's also why, up until two weeks ago, I was responsible for home staging, photography, and social media for a home design company owned by the wife of one of Ryne's business partners. A horribly lonely and boring job that left me wanting to put down my camera for good. At least now I actually have a chance to interact with people and make friends.

I follow the view from my camera lens across the ice, heart tripping when I accidentally zero in on Jaxon's face. He's chewing a piece of pink bubble gum, laughing with a blond man. It's a weird scene, Jaxon laughing and smiling. I seem to remember him being a rude, arrogant, broody asshole who only laughed at my expense. But he looks . . . happy here. He reminds me of my brother, the way he changes on the baseball diamond, like he's finally come home.

And then those hazel eyes peel across the ice, landing on me.

"Oh, shit. Fuck." The camera slips from my hands, and I swallow a shriek as I dive for it. "Fuck, fuck, fuck." Cradling my baby in my hands, I slip the strap around my neck for safekeeping, and look back at the ice. My stomach flip-flops when I find the man still watching me, and I twist left to right, looking for something to do, anything to keep me from looking at him while he looks at me. Isn't he supposed to be busy? Not very committed to his craft, now, is he?

I sink down to the seat reserved for me and pull out my phone, clicking to the team's Instagram page. This team has a wild fan base, but a lackluster social media presence, and one of my jobs is to turn that around, a task I'm incredibly excited for. Social media can be a fun place to engage fans, and the photo I posted only forty-five minutes ago of the Vipers' team captain, Carter Beckett, walking into the arena in a three-piece suit with a pin attached to his lapel that reads "World's Greatest DILF" is proof of that. The simple picture already has more than three hundred comments and fifty thousand likes. Apparently, the Vipers' fans love their ostentatious captain.

"You're Lennon, right?" the grinning blonde to my left asks. She's stunning, one of those women you see all the time on the arm of a famous athlete, lean, leggy, with spectacularly vivacious blond hair. I can only assume she's one of the players' wives, or WAGs, as all wives and girlfriends have been affectionately labeled. Maybe she's even married to the captain. "The new photographer?"

I hold up my camera and smile. "That's me."

Her grin grows impossibly wider, and the longer she stares, the more I wonder if I have something in my teeth. I turn away, discreetly running my tongue over my them, swatting at my boobs, which happen to catch 99 percent of messes on my shirt, even though they're not that big.

I come up empty, and a quick side glance at the woman tells me she's still watching me, and *still* grinning. In fact, it's so big, it's borderline terrifying. I'm not even sure it's her grin, but rather her entire vibe, like she's always ready to go to war for her people.

"Can I, uh . . . help you?" I finally ask, much squeakier than I'd like.

She relaxes into her seat, pops her feet up on the plexiglass, tosses a handful of—oh *gross*, are those M&Ms *and* Skittles?—into her mouth, shares a quick look at her friends, and winks. "We know."

My brows rise. "You know?"

"We know."

"You know . . . what?"

Her eyes flick to the ice, and I follow their path to the man currently sinking into a deep lunge. He looks suspiciously like the man who fucked me nearly into a coma a week ago, but I can't be sure. It may have been a fever dream.

"We know," she repeats, except this time it's punctuated by the flick of her brows and the thrust of her tongue against the inside of her cheek.

"I . . . I don't know what you're . . . are you . . ."

"Oh, for fuck's sake, Care. Put her out of her misery." The petite brunette at her side leans around her, smiling sympathetically. "We know you rode Jaxon straight into the Mexican sunrise. I'm sorry about Cara. She's always like this." She waves. "I'm Olivia. I'm nothing like her, and I'm married to—"

"*Ollie!* Hey, Ollie, look at me! Princess, look!"

She shuts her eyes, pulling in a deep breath that takes her several seconds to exhale as the team captain waves his arms over his head from the ice, trying to garner her attention. "Carter."

"Oh, wow. I don't know why, but I assumed Carter and you"—I point to Cara—"were married."

Cara and Olivia look at each other, a long moment of silence that drags out so long I desperately want to shove the words back down my throat.

But then they both explode with laughter.

"Oh my *God*," Cara cries, swiping beneath a pair of brilliant blue eyes. "You thought—"

"Cara and *Carter*?" Olivia barely manages.

Another brunette peeks around Olivia, deep dimples pulling in as she cackles. "Lennon, *please.*"

The woman on the end with a cute blonde-and-pink bob gives me a sympathetic smile, but when she tries to speak, her snickers slip free. "Leave her alone." She giggles. "She couldn't have known."

"Oh, babe." Cara pulls in a steadying breath, reaching over to pat my hand. "That's cute. If Carter and I ever dated, the Vipers would need a new captain, because the man would cease to exist on this planet." A body collides with the plexiglass, and Cara's eyes warm as she grins at the man pumping his brows at her. "That's my man. Emmett."

"And that's mine," the woman with the pink hair says, wistful smile directed at the humongous goalie currently watching her from across the ice. Adam Lockwood pulls off his catcher, taps his heart, points at her, and her cheeks turn the same color as her hair. "I'm Rosie," she tells me.

"Jennie," the other brunette says to me with a dazzling, dimpled smile. "The better Beckett sibling, and—oh, fuck." Her eyes snap to the ice as a new song starts, pumped extra loud across the arena, and she leaps from her seat. "Garrett, for shit's sake, you have to shake your ass! Your ass!" She points to hers, giving it a wiggle for good measure. Then she sighs, collapses back in her seat, and gestures haphazardly toward the ice. "I belong to the one who can't dance. God, he's hopeless, but I'm so in love with him."

I turn toward the ice, finding the four men lined up in front of the net. Carter is tugging on number 69's arm, trying to get him to join in, and I'm trying to place the nostalgic tune as the boys dance along to the words.

"Is this the 'Cha Cha Slide'?"

"Yup." Cara shoves another handful of candy into her mouth. "Jaxon always does this, puts on this big show like he doesn't want to join. He's being really difficult about it right now, though, isn't he? Maybe he's embarrassed because you're watching."

I look for the man, but I can't find him. Carter's still pulling on number 69's—

Sighing, I drag a hand down my face. "Of course Jaxon's number sixty-nine."

"I knew it!" Cara screeches. "Jaxon's the sixty-nine king, isn't he? That man looks like his only dream in this life is to go out suffocated by a pussy sitting on his face."

"*Care!*" Olivia glares at her friend, but the shock that should be there seems to be missing from her expression. "This is a family-friendly event! There are children here!" She settles back into her seat. "Besides, Carter's the sixty-nine king."

"Uh, I hate to break it to you guys." Rosie holds a finger up. "But Adam's *definitely* the sixty-nine king."

The girls erupt with hoots and hollers, and I stifle my laughter. It's not until they're completely silent that I realize they're watching me.

"So?" Jennie asks expectantly.

"So . . . what?"

"Does Jaxon live up to his number or what?"

"Oh. Um . . . I don't know, we didn't really, um . . ." I bury my burning face behind my camera, documenting this horrifying choreographic rendition of the Cha Cha Slide. Jaxon's still not dancing, just standing there with his grumpy arms across his grumpy chest. "Yes."

And I swear, their squeals rival the rest of the fans'.

As it turns out, pussy isn't the only thing Jaxon Riley has an immense appetite for.

By the time we're down to the final five minutes of the game, it's clear Jaxon also has a penchant for extreme shit-talking, and getting a little physical with the other team. His teammates drag him away from most altercations before they can turn into something more, but judging by the roar of the crowd every time he gets in someone's face, followed by the resounding sighs when a fight is avoided, I'd say these fans enjoy his aggressive attitude problem.

I . . . don't blame them. That aggressive attitude problem led to the most mind-blowing sex I've ever had. Sometimes I swear I can still feel his fingers wrapped around my hips. As it is, I'm still trying to pretend the hollow feeling left in my vagina after Jaxon went and carved out a home for his cock for one night has always been there. It's irritating, and what's more irritating is how hot his attitude on the ice is making me.

Through my camera, I follow his warpath as he tears down the ice, matching the forward from the other team stride for stride. He spins around, so effortless, like a beautiful Olympic figure skater, not a 250-pound brick house of a man, and I'm mesmerized, watching his hips sway as he skates backward, blocking the path of his opponent. The forward on the red team makes to slip by him, and Jaxon throws his shoulder into his side, knocking him off his path. He grabs the puck, fires it off the boards, and Emmett Brodie receives it, barreling toward the opposing net.

"*Yes, Emmy!*" Cara shrieks, leaping to her feet, slamming her palms on the glass. "Go, baby! Do it for the blow job!" She winks at me. "I'm gonna blow him even if he misses."

I chuckle, and Emmett sends the puck soaring. The arena erupts as the puck finds a home in the back of the net, and my finger goes trigger-happy as the boys dogpile on top of Emmett. Cara's still shrieking, the fiercest WAG I've ever seen, so I snap her picture, too, because she deserves her own post on the Vipers' Instagram page tonight.

On the way back to center ice, Jaxon and the forward he stole the puck from get tangled up in a dance of some sort, exchanging words that have both of them grinning from ear to ear. Despite the smiles, something tells me there's nothing pleasant about what they're saying. Jaxon dips his face, whispering something to the other man, wiping the smile from his face, the one on Jaxon's growing as he skates away.

"Just wait," the man calls after him. It's nearly impossible to hear over the crowd and music, but I manage to make out the words. "It's only a matter of time till you're gone from here too. Nobody ever keeps you."

Jaxon's body goes rigid as he comes to a stop, and my heart patters in my chest at the dark look that storms through his expression, like a mask sliding into place. He spins back to the man, and the two of them toss their gloves to the ice at the same time, the roar of the crowd blocking out the pounding in my ears. My blood runs hot as Jaxon grips the neck of his opponent's jersey, and when he flings his fist forward, nailing him square in the jaw, I'm horrified by how turned on I am. I accidentally take one picture, then two. Three, and suddenly I have ten pictures of Jaxon, sweat-soaked hair slapping against his forehead after his helmet goes tumbling to the ice, hazel eyes sparked and determined as he wrestles with a man who looks every bit as angry.

The officials pry them apart, shoving them both toward the penalty boxes. I snap a photo of Jaxon as he scoops his helmet and gloves off the ice, tucks his stick under his arm while the tip of his tongue flicks over the bloodstained split in the center of his lower lip. Dark eyes flip to mine, and I drop the camera and my gaze to my lap, swallowing the heady feeling brewing low in my belly.

"Does he always do that?" I ask, watching on the jumbotron as he climbs into the penalty box, dousing his face with water while someone tends to his bloodied lip.

"Fight? Isn't he amazing at it?" Cara watches me for a moment, a curious look in her eyes that turns to mischief when she smiles. "Hey, what are you doing after the game?"

"Me? Getting wine-drunk and attempting IKEA furniture assembly."

Olivia laughs. "The only way to assemble it."

"You should come out with us," Cara says. "Ollie and Rosie are kid-free tonight. Come get wine-drunk with us. If you can hold off a couple of days, we can come over and help."

I blink, watching as the other three nod. My insides spark like fireworks, lighting at the chance for connection, for friends in an otherwise lonely world. "Really?"

"We could enlist the guys to do it while we go get brunch," Olivia says, "but this could be a nice bonding experience."

"And guys suck at assembling IKEA furniture," Jennie adds. "They skip the instructions because, 'I *think* I know how to put together a simple coffee table,'" she says in a deep voice, punctuating it with an eye roll. "Spoiler alert: Garrett and Carter put five holes in the coffee table. *Five.*"

"Adam follows the instructions," Rosie says proudly. "Actually, he built Connor's learning stool, and he's been designing a tree house for the backyard—"

"She nailed the only one of the boys with humility and life skills, is what Rosie is trying to say," Cara finishes for her. "C'mon, Lennon. Come have some drinks."

My gaze flicks to Jaxon, his eyes moving between me and the girls with what looks suspiciously like fear. "I kinda planned on never seeing Jaxon again."

Cara snorts. "Do you have a Plan B?"

"Pretend I don't recognize him."

"Perfect." She tosses her feet up on the plexiglass, shoveling candy into her mouth. "Sometimes, when we really piss him off, he gets this little tic in his jaw. It makes this vein in his neck pop, and I always have the urge to poke it."

Another handful of candy, a devious smile, and a coy wave at the man watching us from across the ice. "Let's see if we can make that vein explode tonight."

6

HOW DARE SHE?

Jaxon

I'VE GOT A HEADACHE, AND I'm 99 percent sure it has nothing to do with the punch I took to the mouth in the third period.

"Cara says she has a new friend."

I roll my eyes, burying my face in my hands. I don't need Emmett to point out the obvious, which is that the girls befriended my one-night stand and the team's new photographer during the game. But when I look up, Emmett's still grinning at me, his phone in his hand. It pings again, and he chuckles.

"What? What's it say?"

His eyes snap to mine, and he folds his lips into his mouth. "Nothing." He shrugs, turns his back on me, strips his boxers off, and heads for the showers. "Not a thing."

"You're a fucking *liar!*" I shout after him. "What'd they say about me?"

"Nothing!"

I groan, yanking my shin pads off. Carter's humming a song, staring at his phone while he shakes his hips, which only serves to piss me off more.

"Hey." He smiles at us. "Does anyone wanna do a T—"

"Nobody wants to do a fucking TikTok!"

His eyes widen, and he exchanges a look with Garrett and Adam, mouthing *wow*.

"Someone's testy," Garrett mutters, but we both know he doesn't want to be forced into one of Carter's dance routines right now either.

Sighing, I yank off the rest of my equipment, stuffing it out of sight. The only thing keeping me from heading straight home to curl up on the couch with my emotional support cat is the promise of an ice-cold beer or two at the bar. Maybe that'll take this edge off, the jagged one that's been a thorn in my side ever since Lennon Hayes strolled into *my* arena with her perfect fucking curls and her perfect fucking tits, just to open her perfect fucking mouth and act like she was going to vomit at the sight of me.

Also, my gran's sent me a photo of herself sprawled out on her living room floor, one hand over her forehead, eyes closed, with a text that says, *Me, post–heart attack after your fight.* Her dark sense of humor never ceases to amaze me.

A shadow slides over me, and a throat clears as Adam drops down to the bench beside me, already showered and dressed.

"Hey, big guy," he starts cautiously. "Great game tonight."

It physically pains me to keep my eyes from rolling, but it's almost impossible to be snippy with Adam. He might be a beast in the net, but everywhere else, he's our gentle giant. He's also the friendliest guy you'll ever meet, kind to a fault, and always looking on the bright side.

But there's no bright side to your one-night stand suddenly being at your work every damn day.

"I spent seven minutes in the penalty box," I remind him.

His head bobs, and he cracks a teeth-gritting grin, hitting me with two finger guns. "You've done worse."

I manage a tired chuckle. "Thanks."

He clears his throat again, leaning against the cubbies and lacing his fingers together. "It's okay to be nervous, you know."

"Nervous?"

"With Lennon watching. It's natural when someone you have a crush on is—"

I gasp. "A crush? I don't have a *crush* on Lennon. What the fuck? First of all, *Adam*." I rocket to my feet, tearing my boxers down my legs, ignoring Adam's eye roll when my dick springs free. I jab a finger in his shoulder. "I don't *get* crushes."

He grins, looking away to hide it.

I prop my fists on my hips. "What's so funny?"

"Nothing."

Emmett walks out from the shower, looking between Adam and me. "What's so funny?"

"Jaxon just said he doesn't get crushes."

Emmett barks a laugh. "Famous last words, bud." He points at Carter, shaking his hips again, singing "My Girl" as he pulls on his clothes. "Carter said that. Six months later, he proposed."

"Yeah, well"—I jab a finger in Carter's direction before stomping my way toward the showers—"I'm *nothing* like him."

"*You'd be so lucky!*" he shouts after me.

I stay in the shower way longer than I need to, ruminating on why Lennon is here and what I ever did to deserve this misfortune. Sure, it was the best sex I ever had, and yeah, okay, she's the hottest girl I've ever seen in my life. But what am I supposed to do now that I have to see her every day? Be, like . . . *friends*? Yuck, no thanks. I'm barely even friends with my friends.

Look, I know how this goes. I've been down this road before. We hook up, I rock her world (obviously), she wants to be friends, and I reluctantly agree just to get her to stop talking. She winds up in love, and I wind up being the bad guy when she finds out I've been sleeping with whoever caught my eye that weekend. I once had to dump a girl I wasn't even dating because she showed up at my door on a Sunday morning with coffee and bagels, wanting to go to the market for some fucking reason, and the woman I'd been with the night before strolled out of my bedroom ass-naked. Ellen snotted all over my shoulder while I held her in my living room, consoling her as my date slinked back into my room to give us a moment.

Was it Ellen? No . . . Ella? Yeah, it was Ella.

You know what? It *was* Ellen. I remember her clarifying for the barista at Starbucks the morning after we hooked up, after I "sneezed" at the same time I said her name. Damn allergies . . .

Anyway, if Lennon came here hoping for more, I don't have more. Not for her, not for anyone.

If I were being honest with myself—which I'm not, and rarely ever am—I'd say I barely have enough for me.

Still, I drag this out a little longer, having to come face-to-face with the one woman my dick hasn't forgotten as I peek into the hallway, watching as she snaps a few last-minute photos of my teammates as they leave, smiling and laughing with them like they're all longtime fucking friends. When she finally takes off, I heave a sigh of relief, turning to my friends, waiting behind me with exhausted and unimpressed expressions.

"She's gone." I wave them through the door. "We can go now."

"We could've gone at literally any moment," Adam mutters.

"Yeah," Garrett grumbles. "It's not like she's gonna bite you."

"Actually." I chuckle. "She did this thing—" I swipe a hand through the air. "Forget it. The important thing is I don't have to see her again until tomorrow night. I get to relax, have a beer at the bar, and don't have to worry about running into her."

I SEE HER THE SECOND I walk into the bar.

Chestnut spirals piled on top of her head, a few spilling free and framing her face, highlighting sharp copper cheekbones. I'm so fucking irritated when my gaze dips to her heart-shaped mouth, perfect ruby-painted lips turning up in the corners before pulling wide. Her head falls backward as laughter falls from her mouth, and my jaw tics when the rest of the table joins in.

In the center of our table—*my* table—Lennon Hayes sits and laughs with *my* friends.

"Uh, hey, so . . ." Emmett gives me a gritty grin. "Care invited Lennon."

"I'm gonna kill your wife," I mutter, feet cemented in place.

He snorts a laugh, and it takes no time at all for it to spiral out of control. Soon he's wiping a tear from his eye. He claps my back and sighs. "That was a good one, buddy. You make me laugh." He steps toward the table, where Carter, Garrett, and Adam have already raced ahead, pulling their girls from their seats, wrapping them in holds that teeter on the edge of suffocation. "C'mon, Riley. Your fate is waiting."

Rolling my eyes, I stuff my hands in the pockets of my coat and follow along. It'd be awkward if I left now, and Lennon will think I'm scared of her or something. Which is totally and definitely not the case. I just don't want to give her the wrong idea. I'll stay for one beer, then head home to Mittens. He doesn't like when I stay out longer than necessary anyway, not when I'm away from home so much in the first place.

"Jaxon!" Cara pins me with her brightest smile. I see right through it, all those perfect, straight white teeth, the sparkle in her eyes. She might be fooling Lennon, but she's not fooling me. Her picture is in the dictionary next to *conniving* for a reason. "So glad you're here!"

"I'm not staying long," I mumble, gaze fixed on a spot on the far side of the bar. "Gotta get home to Mitts. He's been pretty miserable since I got home from Cabo." I scuff the floor with my shoe. "Missed me a lot."

"He was fine when we watched him," Garrett chimes in. "And he loves staying with Jennie when we're on the road."

"Yeah, well, who knows if Jennie treats him right."

The table goes quiet, and my gaze rises to Jennie's. Her blue eyes are already narrowed on me, and when she arches a brow, I flinch.

"You wanna try that again, Riley?" The quiet way her words carry across the air makes the hair on the back of my neck stand. Fuck, why are all the girls *so* scary?

"You take the most amazing care of him when I'm on the road and he loves you so much that he cries the entire drive home," I whisper, wide eyes hooked on hers.

Jennie checks her nails. "Yeah, I know."

My gaze doesn't flick to Lennon.

Okay, I *glance* at her, and what the fuck? She's acting like I don't even *exist*, looking far too at home snuggled between Cara and Olivia. But this is *my* home. *My* friends. If they're going to be anyone's family, they're going to be *mine*.

I don't know whether to stay and fight for that spot, or call it a night—turn around and go home, accept what was always bound to happen at one point or another. That I'd be replaced.

Because there's always someone better. Someone funnier, someone smarter, someone kinder. Someone who just *fits*, and every time I think that someone is going to be me, I'm wrong. I'm already the odd man out, the one trying to fill the minuscule spaces left in their group. But what if Lennon can do it better?

A finger prods my neck, and I glare down at Cara's amused eyes peeking up at me.

"Why, Jaxon," she murmurs. "This vein right here looks like it may pop."

I swat her hand away, grabbing her around the waist and pulling her in for what looks like a hug. "You sneaky son of a bitch," I mutter in her ear. "I'm gonna—"

"You're gonna what, Jaxon?" Her eerie whisper sends a shiver scattering down my spine, even as I stand here at six foot five, with seven inches on this fierce woman. "Here's what you're gonna do. You're gonna slide your cute little butt in the booth, have a drink, and behave."

"Yes, ma'am."

She wraps her hand around my elbow, pulling me close once more. "Relax, Jaxon. We're not replacing you."

The tension stacked in my shoulders eases as Cara shoves me into the booth, beside the nicest and least scary of the girls.

"How are your balls?" Rosie asks, offering me a deep-fried pickle from her plate.

"Thank you for asking. Nobody ever does."

"Because if you'd just sleep with underwear on, you'd eliminate the problem of your cat using your balls for batting practice," Adam mutters, and when the fuck did he get such an attitude?

"Free-ballin' it is the only way to live." I crunch a pickle between my teeth. "You're just mad 'cause you got a toddler at home that prevents you from sleeping with your dick out."

"Not me," Carter boasts. "I sleep naked."

"Ireland is still in a crib," Olivia reminds him. "She can't very well walk into our room at the crack of dawn and find us having sex."

Carter tears at a chicken wing. "So we keep her in da cwib fo-eba." He swallows, chucking the cleaned bone to his plate. "Problem solved."

"I'm not even going to entertain that with an answer, Carter."

"Message received." He winks at her. "You'll entertain me later."

Olivia rolls her eyes, turning her attention to her other side. "So, Lennon, you said you just moved here?"

Rosie reaches for a pickle, but I yank the plate away from her, staring down at it as I shove the deep-fried goodness into my mouth, not even bothering with the sauce, which is my favorite part. She gasps, looking up at me with wide, betrayed eyes, and I roll mine, handing her a pickle as I tune Lennon out.

"Just got in a couple of days ago," she says, and I distinctly remember her voice being ten thousand times more annoying when she was yelling at me from her villa.

"Where from?" Olivia cocks her head. "You've got a bit of an accent, and I can't place it. Southern, almost."

I tilt my head, angling my ear toward the conversation. I'm positive I remember that accent, slight and barely there, a few drawn-out words and this throaty rasp that made my cock jump when she paired it with my name.

"I grew up in Georgia, but I was born in Toronto. I always say my Canadian dims my Southern. My dad took a job in Georgia, where he was born, so we relocated to Augusta when I was a kid to be close to family."

"Oh, wow," Adam says. "A big move, Georgia to British Columbia. What made you want to come out here?"

"Yeah," I murmur, and why am I speaking? My gaze collides with Lennon's, and my mouth opens again. "Have a thing for hockey players?"

I see it, for a fleeting moment. The race of the pulse in her neck, the flare of her eyes. And then it's gone. She picks up her glass, swirls the pink cocktail, holds my gaze. "Never met a single one that did a thing for me. I find most of them entirely . . ." Her eyes move over me. "Underwhelming." She tosses her drink back with a single gulp, then places her hand on Cara's arm. "Excuse me, Cara. I'm going to grab another drink."

I'm on my feet the second her ass graces my vision, bouncing side to side as she strolls across the bar.

"Sit the fuck down," Adam mutters.

"I'm just getting a drink," I lie, yanking at the tie still around my neck.

"I say go for it," Carter offers. "I like her."

"I'm not going for anything." *Right?* I don't think so. No, of course not. I don't need to hear that she's lying to save face, that I actually rocked her world. I definitely don't need to *remind her* how good it was.

. . . Do I?

"I'm just getting a drink," I lie again.

Garrett crunches a nacho chip. "You're a bad liar."

"Horrible," Emmett agrees, then points at Carter with his beer. "But—and it pains me to say this—I agree with him."

Carter woops a fist through the air. "I always have amazing ideas!"

"Not at all what I said." Emmett looks at me, lifting his brows. "Tell me you're not going for it again, and I'll point out that you pulled off your tie, popped the first three buttons on your shirt, and are currently running your fingers through your hair."

"What? No, I'm—" I grip my hair in my fist, my tie dangling from the other one. Buttons? One, two, three, popped. *Shit.* Smashing my tie on the table, I point to the bar. "I'm going to get a drink. Then I'm gonna find someone hot, take them home, and enjoy the fuck out of my night. And you know who it's not gonna be?"

"Lemme guess," Adam drawls, uninterested, or maybe it's exhausted. "Len—"

"Lennon." Standing, I tug at my shirt. It feels too tight, and I want it off. "Now sit back and watch me work."

"Have fun with Mittens," Cara calls after me, and fuck her, because nobody cuddles like Mittens does.

I prop myself up at one end of the bar, as far from Lennon as possible. Her eyes narrow on mine, and I swear to God the little shit lifts her hand, scratching her nose with only her middle finger.

"Hi," someone breathes on my neck. It's hot and moist and I

hate that word so I automatically hate them. The pretty redhead swings around me, seating herself on the stool that's practically between my legs. "You're Jaxon Riley."

I see Lennon's eyes roll from across the bar, so I turn the charm on, grinning down at my new friend. "The one and only."

"I'm Theresa. And you're my favorite player."

"You're a hockey fan? Gorgeous girl like you?" I brush a strand of hair off her cheek as she bats her lashes. "How about that second inning, huh? Did you see when I scored from the fifty-yard line?"

"*Yes*, oh my *gosh!*" She leans into me, squeezing my forearm. "That was *amazing!*"

I close my eyes so I can safely roll them straight to heaven, and Lennon's snort of laughter is unmistakable. It makes me want this so much more, even if I'll have to swallow a fuckton of pride to take home someone who's just confused hockey, baseball, and football in a single minute.

"You must not have been at the game," I murmur, tracing the infinity symbol on her bracelet. It's clunky and silver, like I could hook it to my bed post while I fucked her and it wouldn't budge. Nothing like the delicate gold chain Lennon's allergy alert hung from. I had to twine my fingers through hers just to keep from accidentally ripping it off. "I'd never miss such a stunning creature."

Another giggle, and Tessa beckons me closer, bringing her lips to my ear as my gaze locks with Lennon's. "You should see me naked."

My brows skyrocket. Lennon's pull down.

I grin. Lennon scowls.

Trisha grips my biceps, pulling back to look me in the eyes while she licks her lower lip. "Sixty-nine is my favorite number."

I look back to Lennon to gauge her reaction, because she suffocated me with her pussy while I fed her my cock in Cabo, but she's not listening anymore. She's turned away, looking through a menu, and what the fucking fuck, I want her attention.

I pry off the hand wrapped around my arm. "Not interested, Terry."

"It's fucking *Theresa*, you asshole," she growls after me. "And I don't even *watch* hockey!"

"Shocking," I mutter, stopping behind Lennon, tugging the menu out of her hand. "Hi, honey. I've missed you."

"*Jesus*—" Her hands curl into tight fists, eyes squeezed shut. Then she spins around, shoving my arms away from her, and those same eyes zero in on me.

They're exactly how I remember them. Deep and rich, cinnamon and spice. Intoxicating then, fucking intoxicating now.

I hate it.

She flings her arms across her chest and arches a brow. "Can I help you?"

"Now, honey. Is that any way to greet your husband after you slipped out of bed in the middle of the night? I've been worried sick about you." I catch the bartender's eye. "Two Bahama Mamas, please. They're her favorite."

Lennon's jaw tightens, nostrils flaring. She clears her throat. "Sorry, I didn't catch your name. Jason, was it?"

My mouth dips to her ear. "You and I both know you know what my name is. Your throat was raw from screaming it all night."

"Hm. Nope. Couldn't be me." Her gaze moves down, then back up, top lip curling with what must be disinterest. It certainly couldn't be disgust. "Fuckboy isn't my type."

"No?" I slide a twenty to the bartender when he drops our drinks in front of us. "Weird. It was your type when my cock was down your throat and my tongue was buried in your sweet cunt."

Her eyes widen, and the way she chokes on her slushy drink is so damn similar to the way she choked on my cock. *"Jaxon."* Her gaze darts around the bar. "Shut up or I'll *shut* you up."

I grin, stepping behind her when she twists away, focusing on her drink. With my arms on either side of her, I drop my chin to her shoulder. "Don't tempt me, honey. I like the way you shut me up, and you know you do too. Don't you, Lennon?"

"Oh my *God.*" Her curls whip me in the face when she spins around. "You can't remember the name of the date you took on *vacation* with you, but you remember mine? Come on."

"You're welcome."

Her brows jump. "You're welcome?"

"It's a compliment, isn't it?"

She chuckles, the sound so dark I wonder if Cara taught her. "You really think you're all that and a bag of chips, don't you?"

"I—" I drop my face, cackling. "'All that and a bag of chips?' Who are you, my gran?"

"If your gran also thinks you're an egotistical ass, then yes."

"My gran thinks the sun shines outta my ass, Len, and I think it just might."

She rolls her eyes, gulping down her drink, flicking that tongue across her lower lip. She misses the sugar from the rim, and when I reach forward, dragging my thumb across that plump lip, gathering the sugar and sucking it off, her breath hitches, eyes glossing over.

"Did you come here for me, Lennon?"

"For fuck's sake," she mutters, spell broken as she shoves at my chest. "If you're good at two things in this life, it's picking fights on the ice and eating pussy; I'll give you that."

I run my palm over my proud chest. "Thanks."

She sticks her finger in my face. "I needed this job. If I'd known it would, somehow in this godforsaken world, lead me back to you a second time, I would've run the other way." She finishes her drink, slams the glass down, and picks up the menu I threw down earlier. "Mmm, that sounds good," she murmurs to herself, tapping on my favorite raspberry lemon cheesecake.

"It's delicious," I say, pulling the menu away again, because I want her attention. "But you can't have it. There are almonds in the crust."

"I—" She blinks up at me for a quiet moment, then shakes her head. "I can't believe I'm about to say this, but I'd rather be wine-drunk and trying to read Swedish instructions right now."

"Huh?"

She hooks her purse over her arm, pushing by me. "Bye, Jason. It's been a time."

"Wait," I call after her, and I don't know why. I scratch my head, because this isn't . . . I mean, I thought . . . Well, to be honest, I thought this was gonna go in a totally different direction. "But, like . . . you don't wanna be . . . friends?"

Her face twists in—*motherfucker, again?*—disgust. "I'd rather get my period while wearing white pants and not have a single tampon on hand."

She turns to leave again, but pauses, hitting me with a patronizing smile over her shoulder.

"In case that wasn't clear enough, that's a fuck no, fuckboy."

7

LENNON AND THE TERRIBLE, HORRIBLE, NO GOOD, VERY BAD DAY

Lennon

I KNOW THE MOMENT I open my eyes.

They crack open, immediately blinded by the flurry of white falling outside my window, the curls I forgot to wrap last night a tangled mess, and I just know.

Today is going to be a terrible, awful, shit-ass day.

There's a chill in the air I'm not used to, because despite spending six winters in Toronto, I don't remember a single one. Every visit back to Canada was spent lakeside in cottage country, basking on the dock in the blazing sun. Sure, I saw the occasional snowfall in Augusta, but I could probably count the times temperatures dipped below freezing on both hands.

And that's strike number one for Vancouver. Google said the Canadian west coast was mild. Promised me, even. But the coat that religiously got me through those Georgia winters has done nothing but fail me this week as Vancouver's been hit with snow, rain, and sleet, day after cold, wet day that leads to bone-chilling night.

When I finally sit up in bed, my nose runs and drips, because it, too, hates the cold. Strike number two.

No, wait. Strike one was that I forgot to wear my silk wrap to bed last night, and now I'm going to have to spend forever detangling my curls.

Strike three, nose.

Strike four . . . ugh, fuck, I don't even want to talk about strike four.

Okay, fine, you twisted my arm. I'll talk about strike four.

Strike four is this little red clit-sucking vibrator, the one currently giving me the stink eye from the floor, where I chucked it last night in a fit of rage.

Okay, it wasn't a fit of rage, but I'll tell you what else it definitely wasn't: an orgasm. Because my little *buddy* died on me in the most crucial moment, when I was *right there*, on the cusp, ready to free fall into oblivion, with somebody's name on my lips that definitely doesn't start with J.

You know what? This is *all* Jaxon Riley's fault. If he hadn't made me so frustrated last night, which in turn made my body so damn *hot*, I wouldn't have ripped off my coat a mere ten feet from my car. If I hadn't ripped off my coat, I wouldn't have a runny nose this morning. And if I hadn't *still* been so hot by the time I got home, I wouldn't have had to pull out that clit sucker, torn off my clothes, and spread my legs on my bed. And if that clit sucker hadn't died, I would've had an amazing, incredible, wonderful orgasm. I would've happily skipped from bed to the bathroom, washed my face, and wrapped my curls in my silk scarf to protect them.

But I didn't. And now it's morning, it's cold as balls, my nose is running like a faucet, and I'm still so horny I'm debating pulling out my dildo, but I don't want to do any of the work, only reap all the benefits.

This is a horrible, terrible start to my day, but I suppose the bright side is there's no way it can *possibly* get any worse. With that knowledge, I finally drag myself out of bed and to the kitchen, because coffee fixes 99 percent of problems. That's a fact; look it up.

I stop when I see the offending Keurig machine on the counter, glossy white exterior stained with brown splatter. It reminds me of that time Ryne got food poisoning in Saint Lucia. He spent all three days of my birthday weekend getaway locked in the pristine white bathroom, and threw a hissy fit when I went to the beach without him.

God, I fucking hate him.

"Shit," I mutter, arms crossed, foot tapping as I stare at my coffee machine. I don't know that it's even broken, so much as the entire debacle was, like . . . *potentially* a user error, but I do know this: I'm not using that machine again. My birthday is coming up; I'll start dropping hints to Devin. And by dropping hints, I mean I'll send him weekly links to the espresso machine Ryne and I had and follow it up with an *oops, sorry, meant to send that to someone else!* The espresso machine is no easier, but I can probably convince my brother to walk me through a latte on FaceTime every morning.

My phone pings as I'm contemplating ~~my existence~~ braving the snow for caffeine, and I scream, chucking it across the room when I see the name lighting it up.

"Okay, Len," I mutter to myself, hand over my racing heart. "It's okay. You're probably seeing things." I creep across the kitchen, into the living room—wow, what an arm on me—and nudge my phone with my toes. It doesn't light up, and I kinda hope it's broken. Sinking to my knees, I crawl closer, waiting to see what it'll do. When it does nothing, I hesitantly pull it toward me, sighing when nothing happens as I press on the screen.

And then it pings again, and another scream leaves my mouth as *PIECE OF MOTHERFUCKING SHIT* scrolls across my phone.

That's Ryne, my ex-fiancé, in case it wasn't clear.

PIECE OF MOTHERFUCKING SHIT: I hate
waking up without you, angel.

PIECE OF MOTHERFUCKING SHIT: Every
morning, I'd open my eyes and look at you,

so beautiful and peaceful next to me, and
I knew I'd be able to get through even the
hardest days with you by my side. It feels
like I'm dying without you. I miss you, Lenny
Bean. You belong here with me. Please
come home.

There's a lot I want to say here, but it would probably take
me years to unpack in therapy. The first is *don't call me Lenny
Bean*. I've hated that name with every fiber of my being from
the moment he coined it. And the rest of it? Don't even get me
started.

Look, I get it. It sounds nice. Great, even. Everyone wants to be
missed, to be needed. But this is the kind of shit that lived in the
back of my brain for years, the things I reminded myself of every
time I wondered if I was better off without him, if he even loved
me at all. I've been through this. Told myself the sweet moments
were worth the bitter ones, that the hard days would pass, and one
day we'd be carefree and happy. I've let him convince me he loved
me, trusted him when he apologized, promised he'd be better, an
attentive husband.

And after every *I love you*, every apology date, every night
spent with his hands and mouth on my body, I've watched him
slip right back into the man I should've left long ago.

PIECE OF MOTHERFUCKING SHIT:
How long are you going to pull this silent
treatment bullshit on me, Lenny?

PIECE OF MOTHERFUCKING SHIT:
Come on. It's immature.

I gasp. "Immature? How fucking dare you? I'll show you
immature, you son of a . . ." My fingers fly furiously across the

screen, typing out a giant FUCK YOU, among some other colorful insults, but then another text comes in.

PIECE OF MOTHERFUCKING SHIT: My grandmother says you moved to Canada. Is this true? Fucking Canada? How old are you? Grow up and come home. You have no one and nothing out there for you.

My jaw clenches, teeth clacking together. My hands shake and tears sting my eyes as I swallow against the burning in my throat. I've cried enough over Ryne, over a relationship that sucked me dry, even if I spent years denying it, years trying to convince myself the red flags were hiccups every relationship had, years telling myself that the good outweighed the bad. I don't know if I have anything left to give, but if I find more, the last person I want to give it to is him. He doesn't deserve it, and he certainly doesn't deserve me.

Rolling onto my back, I collapse on the living room rug and delete his messages. With my phone pressed to my chest, I breathe slowly, in and out, until the rapid rise of my chest slows, the angry patter of my heart quieting, the urge to cry waning.

And then my phone pings again.

"Are you fucking—oh." I sit up, blinking at the brand-new message thread, all the names I learned only yesterday staring up at me from my phone.

Cara added you to a group chat.
Cara changed the group chat name to Penis Cozies.

Olivia: Cara, we are not naming this group chat Penis Cozies. I have to draw the line somewhere.

Jennie: I support Penis Cozies.

Rosie: I'm with Ollie.

Cara changed the group chat name to Cock Suckers.

Olivia: If Penis Cozies was my line, what makes you think Cock Suckers is any better?

Jennie: I also support Cock Suckers.

Cara: Oh, c'mon, Ollie. You're the biggest cock sucker I know.

Rosie: *surprised emoji*

Rosie: But wait, do you mean "biggest" because she likes to suck cock, or "biggest" like . . . <=========8

Rosie: Because, I mean . . . we all know Adam's the biggest.

Jennie: This just in, Rosie's the biggest cock sucker!!!!

Olivia changed the group chat name to Gouda Friends.

Jennie: . . .

Cara: OLIVIA?!?! WHERE HAVE I GONE WRONG WITH YOU???

Jennie: I'm calling Carter. He needs to sort you out. This is disgusting behavior.

Rosie: Surely we can find a happy medium between Cock Suckers and Gouda Friends.

Cara changed the group chat name to Coochie Gang.

Olivia: Hmm . . . I might be able to get on board with Coochie Gang.

Cara changed the group chat name to Coochie Gang: The Chamber of Secrets.

Olivia: Now I know you didn't just call my coochie a chamber.

Cara: Everyone for Coochie Gang: The Chamber of Secrets, say "I suck cock."

Jennie: I suck cock!!! *tongue emoji* *eggplant emoji*

Rosie: I suck the biggest cock *blushing emoji*

Snickering, I cross my legs, getting comfy on the floor as I type out my first message.

Me: I suck hockey player cock when I've been drinking.

Cara: YEAH YOU DO, BABY!!!

Jennie: My girl!!!

Rosie: It happens to the best of us, Lennon.

Olivia: Sigh . . . I suck the most cock.

Clicking out of the thread, I navigate to the only other group chat I use regularly: *Mimi's Favs.*

> **Me:** Guess what???

Devin: chicken butt

Serena: Guess how?

Devin: chicken cow!

> **Me:** Can I say my thing now???
>
> It's exciting.

> **Me:** I MADE FRIENDS!!!

Devin: *clapping emoji* *dancing emoji* atta girl!

Serena: *happy tears emoji* Baby's 1st friends in her new home

Serena: Don't be replacing me though or I'll be coming up there *sword fighting emoji*

Devin: u makin friends with hockey players?

Serena: Yeah, Len. You making friends with hockey players? *winking emoji*

Devin: whats she talkin about??

Faster than I've ever done anything—aside from call off my wedding—I exit the chat, pull up a separate message with Serena, and send her a single text.

> **Me:** Don't. Don't you dare.

Serena: Don't what???

My phone pings before I can spell it out for her, even though I know I don't have to, and the text I see makes me giddy.

Cara: You free tomorrow night, Len? We can
bring takeout, wine, and junk food, and by
the end of the night your IKEA furniture may
or may not be assembled.

Rosie: Adam's already said he'll finish/fix
whatever needs to be finished/fixed when
we're through.

I look at the boxes stacked against my living room wall. There are . . . *so many.* A dresser that comes in three boxes, which, why? Is the goal to intimidate me into never building it? A bedside table to ~~hide my dragon dildo~~ plug my phone in. A coffee table, two bookshelves, and a TV stand. It's so much, and the thought of doing any of it makes me want to curl up and cry.

I want my daddy. He's so good at the furniture-building thingie.

Me: That's really okay, guys. I appreciate
the offer, but I don't expect you to help
me put my furniture together. Thank you
though!

Cara: That's cute.

Jennie: *laughing emoji*

Olivia: We'll be there at 4.

Rosie: I only recently figured this out myself,
Lennon, but nobody does things alone here.
It's everyone or nothing.

Rosie: Sorry, to be clear, it's everyone,
period. There's no other option, because it's
Cara's world and we're all just living in it.

Cara: *happy tears emoji* You know me so
well, Rosie. Lennon, we'll be there at 4.

Buzzing, I send along my address, mentally cataloguing a list of ingredients to make my mimi's famous banana pudding. "I'll need a big trifle dish," I mumble, pulling myself off the floor when my bladder reminds me I haven't peed yet this morning. "So it looks pretty. But what if they don't like bananas? Should I make Mimi's famous key lime pie too?"

I navigate back to the chat with my brother and cousin, groaning when I see the texts there.

Serena: lennonfuckedahockeyplayer

Devin: WHAT

Devin: LEN???

Serena: She's still in denial, but it was the
best sex she's ever had.

Devin: i mean, get it i guess. don't need
to know how good it was though. oh but u
know who u should tell, just for fun??? ryne.
can i tell him???

Me: Gotta go, bye!!!

Racing to my room, I pull my clothes off, dumping them on my bed along with my phone. Rifling through the luggage I've yet to unpack, I find everything I need for wash day, because these curls are too damn gorgeous to let the frizz and tangles caused by last night win today.

This day may have started out shit, but it's on the up and up now. I'm feeling positive. About today, about this new city, this new life. I've got new friends, I'm in a group chat with people who aren't required to love me, I've got plans tomorrow night, and—

"What the shit?" I stop at the edge of my bathroom, water pooled in center of the floor. The steady *drip drip* from somewhere inside makes my heart race, and the damp chill in the small, windowless room sends a shiver through me.

I look from the sink on the left, to the tub on the right, and back to the puddle of water in the center of the room. The floor around it is bone-dry, like the water simply appeared there, which makes no sense.

My eyes zero in on a drop as it hits the puddle, sending ripples through the water, followed by another drip, then another.

The blood in my face drains, leaving me lightheaded when I step fully into the room and the ceiling comes into view.

My jaw drops when I spy that giant bubble, right there in the plaster, making my bathroom ceiling hang a good two feet lower. Water beads on the surface, dropping quickly to the puddled floor, and when it feels like the entire building groans, I dive back into the hallway, landing on my ass.

Right in time to watch the bubble in my ceiling burst, flooding the bathroom in my brand-new apartment.

I sit there on the floor, water lapping around me, drenching my pajama shorts, and I soak up this absolute shit show of a day.

Don't think it, don't think it, don't think it.

. . .

There is *no way* this day can *possibly* get any worse than this.

Damn it, I thought it. Fuck.

Well, can't wait to see how this bitch will level up.

8

I'M HOTTER THAN ADAM . . . RIGHT?

Jaxon

"Would it kill you to smile?"

My gaze slides to Adam, wide grin pasted on his face despite his sour tone, eyes moving around the room even though it's me he's speaking to.

I toss my arms over my chest, jaw tightening as I really solidify my frown, forehead crumpling. "Yes."

Adam sighs, but the corner of his mouth quirks. "Thought we only had room for one drama queen in this group. You know Carter doesn't like to share anything, especially titles."

My gaze narrows on the man in question. He's talking with my archnemesis.

No, talking is the wrong word. He's *laughing* with my archnemesis.

"What the fuck are they laughing about?" My gaze tumbles down Lennon, from the top of her head right down to her feet, and for some reason, I think back on those awful fucking Crocs she was wearing that night in Cabo. Tonight, she's in a pair of black leather boots and matching skintight pants, a baggy caramel sweater, with a white long-sleeve button-up peeking out. Her tight curls are pulled back from her face with a silk scarf the color of cinnamon, and she's so effortlessly pretty it pisses me *the fuck* off. "She's not saying anything funny. *No way* she's saying anything funny." I shake my head. "She's not funny. She's annoying. I'm way funnier. I'm arguably hotter too," I lie, shrugging. "Dependin' who you ask."

Garrett stops in front of us, looking from me to Adam, back to me, then settling on Adam. He thumbs in my direction. "Jaxon on about Lennon again?"

"No," I answer at the same time Adam says, "Yes."

"Look," Adam starts, finally turning toward me. His gaze moves over my shoulder when Rosie's laugh sounds behind us, and the corner of his mouth hooks up the way it always does. He's head over heels, and it's, like, whatever, 'cause now I'm the only single friend in the group, but I'm happy for him. Plus, I wouldn't have Mittens if it weren't for Rosie, since I found him at the shelter she works at.

Adam's eyes come back to mine, and his brows lift the way they always do when he's trying to convey how serious he is. "This is a community event. We're supposed to be happy, smiling, and friendly. Can you do that?"

I grit my teeth and grin, because if I'm one thing, it's a team player. Adam grimaces, and Garrett's expression transforms to one that can only be described as horrified.

"What the fuck is that?" he mutters.

"I don't know," Adam breathes out. "But it's terrifying."

Garrett flaps a hand around. "Go back to frowning, please."

Emmett strolls over, hands in his pockets, easy, crooked grin on his face. "What are we—*ah!* Jesus Christ, Riley, Halloween was three months ago. Stop trying to scare the kids."

I drop the forced smile, shoving my hands in the pockets of my jeans, eyes narrowing on Lennon as she snaps a photo of Carter and a group of kids before pulling her phone out, frowning at the screen. "Whatever. I gotta go take a leak."

I, in fact, do not have to take a leak. Instead, I swipe a water bottle from the snack table and shove a powdery doughnut in my mouth, suppressing a moan when it explodes, raspberry jelly coating my tongue. I lick my lips and fingers clean, slowly tracking the perimeter of the room. Lennon is focused on her phone, head down as she wanders aimlessly, looking up every once in a while to smile and offer an apology to anyone she nearly bumps into.

I don't have a fucking clue why I'm watching her, why my eyes track her every step every time we're in the same room. The guys think I'm obsessed with her because she's acting like she doesn't know me, but that couldn't possibly be it.

She knows me. She knows that one of my fingers inside her makes her moan, two make her whimper, and three make her breathless. She knows that my hand wraps perfectly around her throat, leaves the most addicting marks on her ass. She knows the way my tongue tastes after it's been soaked in her. She knows the shape of my cock, and the home it carved out in her tight, wet pussy.

She knows me.

So why is she acting like she couldn't possibly care less? She should be pining over me, desperate for another dance with Magic Mike, and instead she keeps calling me Jason like she wasn't screaming my name for hours on end, until her voice grew so hoarse I had to pause to get her ice chips.

"Fuck," she murmurs, taking her lower lip between her teeth, gnawing it. Her fingers drum against her phone, and when she takes off down the hallway, my feet force me in the same direction.

"Any size bed will do," she's busy pleading into her phone when I catch up to her, pacing the dim hall, the heel of her palm pressed against one eye. "Please. No, I've called everywhere else. Everywhere is sold out. I need—" She huffs, hanging her head. "Okay. Well, thanks anyway." She reaches into her top, shoving her phone in her . . . bra?

When she looks up, I spin away, reaching for the first door I come in contact with.

"Jaxon?"

"Huh?" I look over my shoulder, not missing the dangerous slant of her eyes when they narrow on me. "Oh. You."

"Were you spying on me?"

I scoff. "Spying on you? Me? On you?" Another scoff, and I point at the door. "I'm going to the bathroom. Quit being so full of yourself. It's not an attractive trait." Propping the door open, I lean my hip on the frame, crossing my arms over my chest and smirking at her. "Plus, honey, you know if you want me to watch, all you have to do is ask. I'll even be a willing participate if you want some help. I'm selfless like that."

A slow smile spreads across her face, but it's the way she drops her head and chuckles, a sound so much darker than this hallway, that really spikes my blood pressure. She stalks toward me, licking her lips, one hand on the camera that hangs from her neck. When she stops in front of me, my chest puffs, and I reach for the door frame above my head. I rarely swing and miss with women, and Lennon is no exception. She wanted nothing to do with me a week ago, and look how that ended for her. That Cabo hate-fuck was the best sex of my life, hands down, and I'm willing to fuck the hate out of her once more if that's what she wants. I just hope she doesn't get attached this time.

"So handsome," she murmurs, fixing the button on my shirt. "Can I take your picture?"

"You gonna look at it later?"

Her grin widens. "You have no idea."

She points her camera at me, snaps a single picture, and looks down at it like it's her favorite thing in the world. God, she's obsessed with me. I knew it. I can't wait to fuck her later tonight, make her admit she's been thinking about me all this time.

But then she pats my chest, turns, and walks away.

"Oh, Jaxon?" She glances back at me, batting her lashes. "That's the women's bathroom."

"I FUCKING HATE HER."

"*Hate* is a strong word, Jaxon." Jennie shoves me out of the way, leaning over the tray the server offers us. She hums and haws before picking something smothered in chocolate.

"Well, I feel very strongly about my hatred for her." I shake my head at the server, only because I accidentally got lost five doughnuts deep while obsessing over the attention Lennon refuses to give me even though I don't really want it.

Jennie stares at me for a long, silent moment before snorting with laughter.

Carter looks me over, tossing a mini cupcake in his mouth. "I'm calling it."

"Calling what?"

Another mini cupcake. "Lennon, at the end of the season, wearing your last name on her back."

With a guffaw, I swipe his last cupcake, shoving it in my mouth. "Dat's abso-wute-wee widic-a-wous." I lick my fingers clean, gaze locked on Lennon across the room as she examines a tray of treats too. She picks one, our eyes meeting when she looks up. When she tosses the treat in her mouth, she gives me the finger. "I can't stand her. She talks too much, and she has an attitude problem. Also, she wears Crocs."

"Crocs are comfy," Jennie argues.

"You fucked her even though she was wearing Crocs?" Carter shakes his head. "You're a goner."

"She lost the Crocs before I fucked her."

"Was she wearing them when you first kissed her?"

I scratch my head, sifting through Bahama Mama–infused

memories. "No, she took them off to feel the sand on her feet, and I carried them for her."

Jennie and Carter share a look.

"What? What was that?"

"What was what?" Jennie asks.

"That look." I point between them. "You two just shared a look."

Carter avoids my eyes. "Did we?"

I roll my eyes, and because they've both pissed me off, I say, "Hey, Carter. Garrett's fucking your sister."

The flash in Jennie's eyes is the only warning I get before she pulls her fist back and socks me in the shoulder. She's fucking ferocious for someone whose dimples make her look downright angelic, so I clutch the sore spot, spinning away from her when she pretends she's going in for a second punch. Carter looks like he's considering doing the same thing, so when he takes a single step toward me, a tiny shriek escapes my throat before I dash away, finding safety with a group of kids playing ball hockey on the opposite side of the room. And also, Adam. Adam will protect me.

"Look who came to play!" He points at me from where he's kneeling on the ground in the tiny hockey net. "Go get him! He loves to be tickled!"

"What? No, I—ah!" Tiny spawn attack my legs, going right for my weak spot—the backs of my knees. Shrieks of involuntary laughter come tearing up my throat as I struggle to protect myself. "Stop, stop! Adam! Adam! Help!"

Does he help? Of course not. Instead, he tells them, "I've heard his tummy is ticklish too."

They don't stop. They don't fucking stop until tears are streaming down my face, until my throat is raw from all the pleas, until my limbs give out and the teensy semen demons drag me to the ground, piling on top of me.

"All right, all right." Adam laughs, but it's not strangled and high-pitched like mine was two seconds ago. "Let's give Jaxon a break."

The kids climb off me, and I continue to lie there, fighting for air and wondering why Adam wants a whole house full of these things. I mean, sure, Connor's cute as fuck. And Lily, the reason Adam and Rosie are currently training to be foster parents, is, like, the sweetest little thing alive. But a whole house full? It seems like a lot of responsibility, nights in, and snotty noses. And plus, when are Adam and Rosie gonna find time to fuck? He's happier than he's ever been since I've known him, though, and the dazed smile on his face each morning after returning from a trip says he's extremely satisfied, so I think about asking him, but it doesn't really seem like the opportune time.

I pull in a deep breath, letting it go with a long, loud huff, and sit up. There's a small girl at my side, grinning widely at me, and I nearly shriek again, but manage an "Uh, hi" instead.

"Hi." She snickers, tucking her hair behind her ear. "You're cute."

Oh. Well, then. "I know." I lift my shoulders in a lazy shrug. "Some might even say I'm the cutest boy here."

"Hmm . . ." She glances behind me, batting her lashes at fucking Adam. When she looks back at me, her round cheeks are extra rosy. "Sorry, but he's cuter." She reaches forward, patting my head. "Don't be sad. Someone will choose you to be their boyfriend." She tosses another look at Adam. "Just not me."

"Whatever," I grumble. "I don't wanna be anyone's boyfriend anyway."

She pins her arms across her chest, face scrunched. "Good, 'cause ain't no one gonna wanna be your girlfriend with that attitude." She scrambles to her feet, tossing another unimpressed look at me. "You'll probably just be a lonely old cat man for the rest of your life."

I gasp, looking to Adam when she scurries off. He's got his head dropped between his shoulders, his entire body shaking with laughter.

"You already . . . are . . . a-a-a—" He pauses, scrubbing at the tears running from his eyes, "—*lonely old cat man!*"

I pick up a foam hockey puck, chucking it at his head. It doesn't stop his laughter. In fact, it spurs more on. From him, as he collapses to his back, hands on his trembling belly. From the girls, watching us across the room. From Garrett, Carter, and Emmett, high-fiving my newest archnemesis—*why are they all girls, by the way?*

And from Lennon, who happens to be alternating among being keeled over with laughter, swatting at her tears, and taking pictures of me on the floor.

"It's not funny!" I leap to my feet, scooping up more foam pucks along the way, chucking them at all my friends. "I gave Mittens a home! He needed me!"

"Lennon!" Carter points at me while he deflects a puck. "Did you get that one? Mid–hissy fit?"

"I got it!"

"Post it on Instagram!"

"I hate you!" I shout. "I hate you all!"

Rosie appears at my side, lips clamped tightly. She grips my elbow, gently leading me away. "Shhh. They tease you because they love you. Here." She hands me a doughnut, then points at a board. "Does it make you feel better to know that you're the top pick right now for 'Who Would Win in a Standoff with a Moose'?"

My breath evens out, the frantic rise of my chest slowing as I examine the board. Everyone's pictures are up there, along with our names, numbers, and stats. One or two moose stickers fill the space beneath each player, but it's my space that's overflowing.

"Yeah. Yeah, that does make me feel better." I sniff, stuffing the doughnut in my mouth. "I'd definitely win in a standoff with a moose, wouldn't I?"

Rosie pats my shoulder. "You sure would, champ. You sure would."

I shoot a narrowed look at my friends. "You guys wouldn't last thirty seconds." I shove a finger at the board. "Everyone knows it."

Emmett dips his mouth to Cara's ear. "Someone needs to get laid."

And while I don't necessarily disagree with him, I decide to take a break, escaping to the bathroom, washing all the powdered sugar off my fingers, checking myself out in the mirror. That little girl has lost it if she thinks I'm not as cute as Adam. I'm *so* fucking cute. Plus, the split down the center of my lower lip from my fight last night lends a certain *je ne sais quoi* to the whole look.

I splash some water on my face, waking myself up before I head back out there to be picked on by kids a quarter my size. Everyone has dispersed, interacting with kids and families throughout the room, and I'm just looking for a spot to fit in.

This isn't new to me, these types of community events. Every team I've played for does them occasionally. But Vancouver, by far, gives back to the community more than any other team I've been a part of. I hated going to them at first. Hated looking around at a community I wasn't really a part of, one I'd never fully fit into.

One I'd be forced out of someday, just like the last one.

Teams always want the enforcer. The defender who'll stop at nothing to protect his goalie, to go to bat for his team.

But at some point, they become a burden. Someone who racks up penalty minutes, who sits helplessly by and watches as their team struggles to keep up with one less player on the ice. Someone whose absence becomes the reason behind one goal, and then another, and another, until the best plan of action is to trade them. Uproot their life, ship them off to another team, make them someone else's problem.

That's my experience, at least.

When I was first traded here last season, I was hellbent on hating these events. These guys have played together for years, built a family, and they're embedded into this community. Why even bother trying to be part of it?

But then Carter turns around, his gaze moving around the room, lighting when it lands on me. "Jaxon!" he hollers, waving me over. "Come here!"

I meet Lennon's gaze as I stuff my hands in my pockets and head over. She looks away quickly, rushing over to the snack table, giving it all her attention.

Carter tosses his arm over my shoulder, gesturing at the man in front of us. "Tim runs the Junior Vipers Training Camp. He wants to start a defense camp this summer."

"Is that right?"

"We're looking at developing an advanced program for elite players with a real shot of getting drafted," Tim tells me. "Focusing on body contact and positioning, one-on-one play, defending against multiple attackers, gap control, that kinda thing." He gives me a smile, half hesitant, half hopeful. "We could really use some help, though."

"Told them there's no better d-man than you," Carter says. "They'd be lucky to have you hop on board."

It's funny what a few words of affirmation do, the way they lift an invisible weight off my chest, even if I'd never admit there'd been one in the first place. I'm a protector. A defender. I'll always have my team's back, every guy on that ice. I'm good at it, when it doesn't lead to failed penalty kills or injuries that have me riding the bench, but that's about all I've ever felt good at.

And no one's ever said they were lucky to have me.

"I'd love to help out. Got lots of time this summer. As long as Vancouver doesn't ship me off before then." I add on a chuckle, rubbing the back of my neck.

Carter frowns, squeezing my shoulder. "No way that's happening. You're stuck with us, bud."

Heat creeps up my neck and to the tips of my ears as I fight against the relief that wants my shoulders to collapse, the hope that inflates my chest like a hot-air balloon. It's been . . . a long time, if I'm being honest. Since I've had a place, a *real* fucking place with anyone. These guys, their girls . . . they're the closest I've come since I was a kid. I don't fit, not really. I shouldn't. They've got everything, the families, the houses, the love. They've got each other, and I just try to creep a little bit further in each day, because maybe they'd rather have me fill the spaces than deal with the gaps.

"I think I speak for all the Vipers fans when I say we sincerely hope you'll be here a long time," Tim says. He turns around, thumbing at the back of his jersey, where my name and number look back at me. "I've been a huge fan for a while now, even when you played in Nashville. My wife hates when I wear sixty-nine out in public, though."

I bark a laugh, covering the sound of someone's sudden, hoarse cough behind me. "My gran's still mortified I picked that number. Refuses to wear the jersey."

"Can't believe I didn't think to pick it," Carter mumbles. "What a missed opportunity."

"Ollie would make you change it," I tell him distractedly, looking over my shoulder for the culprit of all that coughing.

"Ollie isn't in charge." He crosses his arms over his chest, then drops them just as quick. "Okay, Ollie's a little bit in charge." He frowns, head swiveling. "Who the hell is coughing so much?"

"I don't know . . ." My gaze lands on Lennon, her hand splayed over her chest as she hacks up a lung. She waves off a server who approaches with a bottle of water, and I try to bring my attention back to Tim. "Uh, anyway, Tim, I'd love to, uh . . ." My eyes ping back to Lennon as her coughing turns to wheezing, and when she yanks her camera off her neck, clutching at her throat, wide eyes finding mine, my legs move without thought, eating the distance between us.

"Hey." I grip her biceps, forcing her to look at me as color pools in her cheeks, staining her flawless copper skin a deep, furious red. "Breathe, Len. Breathe."

She claws at my shoulders, gasping for air as people gather around us, but it's the fear swimming in her rich brown eyes that brings the unwanted memories I've spent years trying to bury.

A shock of messy red hair. A face full of freckles he always hated but his mom always loved. A pair of Nikes he refused to take off, and blue jeans with perpetual dirt stains. Two brown eyes that begged for help.

Two brown eyes that begged for help.

My hand closes around Lennon's wrist, feeling the cool kiss of her allergy bracelet. "Shit, Lennon. Fuck. What did you eat?" I grip her waist, then her hips, hands roaming, searching for a bag that should be here, housing what I need. What *she* needs. "Where's your EpiPen?"

She opens her mouth, but the only thing that leaves it is the crackle of her quickly dimming voice. Frantic eyes pinball around the room, and she panics, clawing at her throat. "J . . . Jax . . ."

"*Lennon.*" I take her face in my hands, heart jackhammering against my chest as I force her eyes back to mine. "Where's your EpiPen?"

"What's happening?" Carter asks, laying his hand on Lennon's back.

Adam squeezes my shoulder. "How can we help?"

"Nine-one-one," I bark out. "Call nine-one-one."

"Rosie's already got them on the phone," Olivia says softly. "What do you need, Jaxon?"

"I need someone to find her fucking EpiPen. She's going into anaphylactic shock."

Olivia, Cara, and Jennie spring into action, racing around the room while Rosie's firm voice tells the emergency operator on the phone that we need an ambulance immediately.

"Jaxon," Rosie calls. "They want to know what she ate."

"I don't know," I murmur, looking into Lennon's eyes. "But she's allergic to peanuts and tree nuts." My gaze slides across the room, locking on a panicked server. "I need a list of everything that was served tonight, and all the ingredients."

He nods, dashing into the kitchen, and I scoop Lennon into my arms.

"Clear the table," I order, carrying her toward it.

Garrett and Emmett sweep it clean, and Carter whips off his sweater, shoving it under Lennon's head as I lay her down. Her head lolls to the side, eyes going to her camera bag, sitting on a table in the corner of the room.

"Adam, hold her here." I let go of her, stepping toward the bag, but her hand shoots out, fisting my shirt. Her chest heaves, tears pooled in her terrified eyes, and she shakes her head as she tries to drag me closer. Blood thunders in my ears as I take her hand in mine, clasping it tightly. "Okay, honey. It's okay. I'm not going anywhere." I point at the bag. "Over there. The camera bag."

Olivia gets there first, tearing the bag apart on her way over to us. She shoves the EpiPen into my hand, stopping at Lennon's side, pushing her curls off her neck. "Jaxon's got you," she murmurs, but her voice shakes and tears gloss her eyes, like she's not sure if she's lying.

I guess that's the thing, though. I failed at this once, so many years ago. And after you fail once, you vow to never, ever fail again.

"You're doin' so good, honey," I whisper to Lennon as I pull off the blue cap. "So fuckin' good."

Tears spill from her eyes, streaming across her temples as she watches me, everyone in the room holding their breath as I slide my hand over her thigh. Her chest heaves, up and down, up and down, a vicious pattern that leaves me fighting the desperate urge to shake. Her eyelids dim and flutter, and fear wraps itself around my throat, squeezing until I can barely breathe.

"Hey." I squeeze her thigh as I jam the orange tip against it. "Look at me, honey. You're gonna be okay."

I depress the EpiPen, holding it firmly against her thigh as I count to ten in my head. Sweat trickles down my brow, and I wipe it on my shoulder as someone shouts out the ambulance's arrival outside.

Tossing the EpiPen aside, I clamp my hand over her thigh, rubbing the spot as the tremors win, making my hands quiver. I paste on a smile, pretending like I didn't just nearly watch the life drain from another pair of brown eyes, and tell her, "So fuckin' good, honey. Gonna be right back to annoyin' me in no time."

But she's already passed out.

9

HEY, REMEMBER WHEN
YOU FUCKED MY THROAT?

Lennon

STATISTICALLY, THE DAY COULDN'T GET worse.

It *shouldn't* have gotten worse.

There was no way in hell the day had potential to get *any fucking worse* than it already had.

But then Jaxon caught me looking at him, so I ran to the snack table—*the only logical choice*—and then the server came over with his shiny tray and set down these teensy little lemon-cherry tarts, and they reminded me of my mimi, and thinking about my mimi reminded me of home, and thinking of home reminded me that my new home was flooded and unlivable, and thinking about my unlivable home reminded me that every single hotel within a sixty-mile radius was fully booked—*thank you, Harry Styles*—and thinking about the fact that I had no idea where I was going to sleep tonight, or tomorrow, or the next day, made me anxious, and if there's one thing about me? I'm gonna eat when I'm anxious.

"The crust was made with almond flour," the doctor tells me, because of course it was.

"That's not how Mimi makes it," I whisper, picking at the blanket covering my lap. It's blue and scratchy, and the only thing I hate more is the hospital gown I'm wearing. And also, the fact that I'm alone, that all of my family is at least one plane ride away, which really fucking sucks when all you want is a hug that makes you feel like everything's going to be okay.

At least I have a bed for tonight.

"Anyway, Miss Hayes, everything looks good so far. You're fortunate that your friend administered your EpiPen as quickly as he did. We're going to keep you another hour to make sure you continue improving, but the good news is you should be able to go home soon."

I shoot up in bed so fast my head spins. "An hour? But-but . . . but I can't . . . shouldn't I . . . An hour?"

The doctor tilts her head, smiling. "Most people are eager to get home after something like this."

I bet most people also have homes that aren't submerged in water.

"We typically keep a patient for four to six hours following anaphylaxis, so long as everything is going well. You've been sleeping for the last three hours, and your numbers are looking great. Like I said, you should be good to go in the next hour."

I scratch at my throat, trying to rub away the dryness. "I can't stay overnight?"

"I'm afraid not. We're extremely low on emergency beds. Get some rest, and one of the nurses will be back shortly with your discharge papers."

"But—" My mouth hangs open as I watch her leave. I don't know what to do. Despite my three-hour nap, I'm so exhausted my brain feels like it's decaying. Everything is foggy, and my limbs feel like they're tied to anchors. I want to go home. Home to Augusta, to my parents. I want Mimi to make my favorite sausage and biscuits, and I want to curl up on the couch with my mom, lay my head in her lap while she twirls my curls around her fingers and we watch *The Real Housewives of Atlanta*.

I want to remember what it feels like when someone takes care of you.

Instead, I lay my head back down and force the heavy feelings away.

An hour later, I'm post–nap number two and feeling no more refreshed as I shuck my gown and pull on my clothes, the nurse prattling on about the signs of biphasic anaphylaxis, which is a second round of anaphylaxis.

"Where's my phone?" I ask, looking around the room. "My purse?" Panic brings a shaky hand to my mouth. "Oh my God. My camera. Where's my camera?"

"I believe your friend has all of your things out in the waiting room."

I blink. "My friend?"

As if on cue, the door opens, and Jaxon stands there, wearing a blank expression, all of my possessions in his hands. "You ready?"

"Ready?" I look from him to the nurse. "Ready for what?"

"You shouldn't drive for the next twenty-four hours or so, just to be safe," the nurse answers with a smile.

"Can't drive? But who will drive me—who will take me—but where will I—" I look between Jaxon—his expression still alarmingly blank, like he doesn't feel a thing—and the nurse, and I shake my head. "No, but I . . . I don't wanna." I . . . can't. Not after tonight. After he rushed to my side when he realized I could barely breathe. Not after he held my hands tightly in his, promised me it'd be okay. Jaxon Riley is the reason I'm still breathing, and I don't know how to face him. Not when it feels like he's seen me at nothing but my worst. "You can't make me."

His brow quirks, the tiniest twinkle of humor flashing in his eyes the only sign that he's not a robot right now. "I'm extremely persuasive, and you're extremely willing. There's a fading hickey right here"—he jerks down the neck of his shirt, pointing to a barely-there bruise on his collarbone—"to prove it, and if I had to guess, there are at least five just like it on your body. We both know you're getting in my car, honey."

My mouth gapes, heat clawing up my neck, burning the tips of my ears, and I hate, hate, *hate* that my hand goes to my right hip, right where one of those hickeys still clings to my skin. I hate his satisfied smirk even more.

"Well, then." The nurse rocks back on her heels, clasping her hands together, awkward grin as she watches us. "This is an odd dynamic." She points at the door. "I'm going to head out. Lennon, be well."

Jaxon holds the door for her, not taking his eyes off me as she passes. He's back to being an asshole, I see, which is nice. I can handle asshole. What I can't handle is all the innuendos, him joking that he's willing to *help me out*, because I'm emotionally fragile enough that I might accidentally repeat what was a mistake in the first place, just to forget about all the other mistakes I've made, like nearly marrying a piece of shit with brains as big as his dick (minuscule), and eating a tart made with killer almonds.

I cross my arms over my chest. "What are you doing here?"

"I rode in the ambulance with you."

"Why?"

"Because you wouldn't let go of my hand."

"I don't remember that. Musta been out of it." I was most certainly not. I came to when the paramedics were shifting me onto the gurney, at which point I flew into a panic, latched on to Jaxon, and begged him not to leave me.

His gaze moves over me, cool and disinterested. "Musta."

"Well, let's go, then." I reach for my things, my camera, tucked neatly in its bag, hooked over Jaxon's arm. My coat, my purse. My beanie, stuffed in the pocket of his coat. But he twists out of reach.

"I'll carry it."

"But I—"

"Can you just fucking relax?" he barks out. "For fuck's sake, Lennon, you nearly died today."

"I did not," I argue, embarrassment making my palms itch. There's something there, something dark dancing in his hazel eyes that makes me want to step back. But as he steps toward me, I force myself to stay, to hold his gaze as he looms above me.

"I watched you choke. I watched you gasp for air. Saw the fear in your eyes as your goddamn life flashed before them while you held my hands like I was your only lifeline." His chest rises sharply, and the slightest tremor runs through him before he clenches his jaw. "And then you passed out, and I thought you were going to die in my arms. So forgive me, Lennon, if I'd rather carry your shit for five minutes so you can take it easy." He flicks his head at the door. "Now march your ass down the hall and out to the parking garage."

My fists ball at my sides, tears stinging my eyes. I haven't had an allergic reaction since I was eight. I was careless today, lost in my head, the same place I've been since I walked away from Ryne not even three weeks ago. And now Jaxon has this hanging over his head, the knowledge that for a few minutes, someone's entire life was in his hands. But the last thing I want to give him right now is my humility, my hurt, my tears.

That must be why I snarl out, "Yes, *Dad*."

"You can call me Daddy, honey. My only stipulation is that I'm buried eight inches inside you while you do it."

I gasp, and when he grins, I stomp past him.

"Len," he snickers out. "Wait."

I spin around, expecting some sort of an apology. He throws my coat over my face.

"Put this on. It's cold out."

If I thought I was angry before, it's nothing compared to when we climb into the elevator, joined by a nurse who is, apparently, a big fan of Jaxon's. She's got him backed into the corner while she twirls her long blond ponytail around her finger, asking him about his tattoos.

"I've seen them on your Instagram," she tells him. "I'd love to get a good look in person, though."

"Yeah?" he murmurs, and I swear to God he's only entertaining her to piss me off.

"Show me yours, I'll show you mine." She winks, the tip of her tongue poking the corner of her mouth, and I decide if I have to go into biphasic anaphylaxis, there would be no better time than right now.

Instead, I offer coolly, "Hospital doesn't really seem like the best place for that." But what the fuck do I know?

She doesn't take her eyes off Jaxon. "I know a room."

"Hear that, Len?" Jaxon grins at me. "She knows a room. Should we take a detour?"

"Better yet, *Jax*, you should take her to Cabo. I hear girls love that."

"Speaking from experience, huh?"

"Extremely *underwhelming* experience."

Our elevator friend steps to the right, trying to block me from Jaxon. "Do you have any tattoos the pictures don't show?"

"Yeah, actually, he does." The doors pop open, and I grab Jaxon's wrist, yanking him forward, pushing him out ahead of me. "He's got an arrow pointing to his giant cock, and I traced it with my tongue before he fucked my throat."

Howls of laughter bounce off the walls of the parking garage as the shocked nurse disappears behind the elevator doors, and I storm ahead of Jaxon, no idea where I'm going or what kind of car I'm looking for.

"You jealous, honey?"

"As fucking if. It's rude as fuck to flirt with you when you're with someone else. I could've been your girlfriend for all she knew."

"I've never found jealousy hot, but I gotta tell ya, honey, I've got half a mind to yank down those leather pants, bend you over the hood of my car, and remind us both how good it feels to have that tight little cunt strangling my cock."

"*Jaxon!*" I spin around, crashing into his chest, because for some reason he's *right* behind me. "Stop saying that word!"

"Cock?"

My eyes dart around the garage before I whisper, "*Cunt.*"

"Hmm . . ." His lower lip slides beneath his teeth as he thinks. "Nah, don't think I will. Filthy word for my filthy girl."

"I'm not your—*ugh*, forget it. Where are we going? Is your car even here? You rode in the ambulance with me."

"It's right there." He points down the row to a bright blue two-door Porsche, because *obviously.* Arrogant, ostentatious car for an arrogant, ostentatious man. "Garrett and Jennie dropped it off. So I guess two scary things happened today."

I raise my brows.

"You nearly died, and Garrett got behind the wheel of my baby." He pats the hood of his car, grinning as he opens the passenger door for me. "Now c'mon, honey. Come sit that pretty little cunt in my car."

I roll my eyes, smacking his arm out of the way as I climb inside. "If your mission is to finish what the almonds started, congratulations. You're well on your way to annoying me to death."

He chuckles, but it's a quiet sound, and when he tucks my things into the front trunk and climbs into the driver's seat, all traces of humor seem to have disappeared. He's tense as he pulls out of the garage, withdrawn, and the sudden iciness makes my skin crawl.

He clears his throat as he turns onto the road. "Where to?"

"Oh. Uh . . ." *Fuck.* Pulling out my phone, I review my earlier message thread with my landlord. His only response to me asking if it was safe to sleep in the living room since the collapsed ceiling was in the bathroom was *u fuckin serious????*

Rick has clearly never struggled, and it shows.

But it's nearly midnight, and I have no clue where I'm sleeping tonight.

"Lennon? What's your address?"

"Um, could you actually . . . could you take me to my car? I have some stuff to get."

He doesn't answer, just shifts into the left lane, checks to make sure the road is clear, then pulls a U-turn. The drive back to the community center is painfully silent, and the exhaustion of the past month fully sets in the longer I sit here in the dark next to a man who has probably second-guessed jabbing me with my EpiPen at least once tonight.

I just want a place in this world. Friends I make all on my own. I want to build a life that's all mine, my hopes and dreams, my failures and my lessons. I want to grow into the person I was always meant to be, and I want to do it all on my own without someone else's hand forcing mine.

And here I am, trying, and it's all gone to shit in a matter of days.

What am I doing? Where do I go from here? I don't know the answers, but I want to find them, so as I close my eyes, I remind myself that tomorrow is a new day, and I can start over as many times as I need to.

The car rolls to a stop, and when I open my eyes, we're parked beside my car. I unbuckle my seat belt, climb out of the car, and look back at Jaxon. His eyes are—

"Unbelievable. Were you looking at my ass?"

His gaze flicks to mine. "You're wearing skintight leather pants, honey. Don't know how the hell you got 'em on. Make your ass look gorgeous, though." He cocks his head, eyes on my jutted hip.

"Second-guessing whether I would've been able to yank 'em down in the parking garage."

I swear, my eyes are going to have a permanent place rolled to heaven. "You're a pig." I swallow my pride. "But thanks for saving my life, and thanks for the ride. See you around."

I shut the door behind me, pop the front trunk, and yelp when it slams before I can grab my things.

Jaxon's hands come down on the hood on either side of me, his chest pressed to my back as he cages me in. Warm breath tickles my ear, rolling down my neck. "What the fuck do you think you're doing?"

"Getting my stuff." I swallow. "Getting in my car."

"Ah. And then? What was your plan after that?"

Finding the closest Walmart, because according to the couple I follow on Instagram who have been road-tripping through North America for the last eight months, Walmart allows overnight camping in its parking lots. "Driving myself home."

He curses under his breath. "You were there, right? When the nurse told you not to drive for twenty-four hours? Or are you purposely choosing to be careless with your life?"

There it is again, all of it. Humiliation, anger, frustration at the way my life has taken such a sudden turn. All of it bubbles to the surface, making my blood run hot. I turn in his arms, pushing against his chest, but he doesn't budge. Doesn't even blink.

"What happened tonight was an accident. That's the reality when you live in a world where there are traces of tree nuts all over the place. Sometimes things slip by you. But I'm fine. I *feel* fine, and I don't need you on my heels just to make sure I get tucked safely into my bed tonight."

He makes no move to leave, to get out of my way, so I slip under his arm, heading for my car. I'll get my things at the arena. Surely he won't keep them from me forever.

Jaxon's one step behind me the entire way, and the second I open my door, I know it's a mistake. The interior lights up, illuminating the shit show inside. A matching set of berry-pink luggage, all of it opened, clothes spilling out. A garbage bag full of hair products. Several pairs of shoes strewn about, and every blanket I own on my passenger seat.

Jaxon steps closer, his eyes moving over the mess, and my heartbeat pounds in my ears as I wring my hands, frantically trying to build a story in my head. "What the fuck is this?" His gaze comes to mine, and I panic, blurting out the truth.

"It's-it's-it's—" My chest tightens, and Jaxon watches as I place my palm over my thrumming heart. "A pipe burst, and now my upstairs neighbor's bathroom is in my bathroom, and every goddamn hotel in this damn city is booked because"—I laugh so I don't cry—"that's how life is going for me lately."

His eyes ping to my phone, screen still lit up, *Walmart* typed in my Maps search bar.

"It's only for tonight," I rush out. "A couple days, at most. Until I can find a hotel. Or a new apartment."

He's not saying a damn thing, just standing there, staring at me, watching me fumble through this. It only serves to heighten this utter humiliation, because really, how could it get any worse? First, he finds me on my honeymoon, sans husband. Then he finds me at *his* workplace, where I run from the room to vomit. Then I nearly kick the bucket in front of him over a fucking *tart*. And now this. Me, standing here, no husband, no friends, and nowhere to sleep tonight but my cold car.

Finally, he blinks. Turns back to my car, slams the door, and yanks my keys from my hand. Aims the fob over his shoulder as he heads back to his car, locking mine, and opens his passenger door. "Get in the car."

"What? No, I'm not—"

"Get in the fucking car, Lennon. I'm not standing here in the middle of the night, arguing with you over whether you're gonna sleep in your car in the middle of winter or in a warm fucking bed."

"It's just one night. I'll be fine. I have my blankets, and I'll—"

"Get in the fucking car."

"But it's—"

"The car." He jabs his finger inside, his chest lurching. "You. Right now. I fucking get it, okay? It's a series of unfortunate events. It's not your fault, none of it, but for fuck's sake, Lennon, accept the help when it's offered to you. You can continue hating me while you do it, and I'll make it easier for you by driving you up the fucking wall." His rapid breathing slows as his frustration wanes, like he sees my fight dimming. "C'mon, honey," he murmurs, the soft words carrying across the frigid air, warming parts of me that have no business being warmed. He holds his hand out to me. "Get in the fucking car."

My heart tells me to keep waging this war, to refuse, insist I don't need him. My brain begs me to give it up, to take the help, the warm bed. Reminds me that accepting help doesn't have to equal giving up my independence.

So I slip my hand into his, letting him help me back into his car. "Fine." I narrow my eyes at his triumphant grin. "And *don't* call me honey."

"I'll try my best," he says, hand above my head on the shell of the car as he bends to look me in the eyes. "My best's never been all that good, though, honey."

HE WANTS ME TO BE impressed that he's somehow managed to wrangle all my shit in his arms without me having to lift a single finger on the way from his condo parking garage up to his—you guessed it—penthouse. I can tell by the self-satisfied expression living on his face, and also that he keeps pumping his brows at me, then my stuff, and saying, "Eh?"

"I'd be more impressed if we hadn't had to leave my biggest piece of luggage in my car."

"Okay, well, the frunk only holds so much. Sorry it's not big enough to accommodate all your shit."

My brows rise as he keys in a code outside his door. "Frunk?"

"Front trunk. Keep up, honey." He opens the door, grimacing at the screech that sounds from somewhere deep inside his condo, followed by a thud. "Uh, I have a cat. He's got an attitude problem, and he's gonna be extra pissed since I'm home late."

"Oh, I love cats." I crouch down, smiling at the big white-and-orange chunk as he skids into the room at full speed, floofy belly swinging back and forth. "Hey, baby," I murmur, holding my hand out. He slows, approaching me cautiously, orange paws pattering closer as he sniffs me.

"Yeah, well, he doesn't like women, so don't expect him to—"

His words die as the cat drops to his back, belly up, paws in the air, screeching at me for rubs. It's my turn for a triumphant smile as I scoop him up, snuggling him close, enjoying the way Jaxon's eyes narrow as I shower his cat with affection.

"Oh, you're so handsome, aren't you? Yes, you are. You're Lennon's handsome boy."

"He's *Daddy's* handsome boy," Jaxon argues, reaching for him. The cat smacks his hand away, hissing, then nuzzles his head into the crook of my elbow. "You little shit. I gave you a home!"

I snicker, stepping farther into the condo, taking in Jaxon's space as he disappears down a hall with my things. It's beautiful, a gorgeous open space with exposed ceilings, brick walls, and floor-to-ceiling windows that are perfect for storm-watching. But it's alarmingly sterile. There's furniture, yes, but the only hint that someone lives here is the cat toys piled in a basket, the several extravagant cat beds that seem to be placed strategically through the space. There's a large bookcase on one side of the living room, bare and begging to be filled with something more than the three photo frames and dying aloe plant.

If I had to guess, I'd say Jaxon isn't planning on being here long. When he returns, I focus my attention back on the cat who's currently kneading my boob. "What's his name?"

"Mitts."

"Mitts?"

"That's what I said."

"Like Mittens? Why?"

Jaxon blows out an irritated sigh and holds his hands up, wiggling his thumbs. "'Cause he's polydactyl. He's got extra toes, and it looks like he's wearing fucking baseball mitts."

I pick up a paw, examining his little jellybean toes. Sure enough, there's an extra one. "Oh my God," I coo. "It's so fucking cute."

"Right? Obviously I had to bring him home with me."

"You adopted him?"

He nods. "In September. Rosie works at a shelter. I found him there." He looks from me to the kitchen, and when he tears off his beanie, the pretty mop of brown waves sitting on top of his head springs free. He runs his fingers through them, and I ignore the memory that chooses that moment to surface, my fingers tangled in those waves, his hands on my thighs, spreading me wide as he gorged on me like I was his last meal. "Anyway, uh, I'll show you to your room." He shoots a look at Mittens. "He can't sleep with you. He likes to sleep on my pillow. Right by my head. Keeps his belly warm."

I press a kiss to Mittens's head. "Sorry, Mitts. Daddy says you're not allowed to sleep with me."

He meows his protest as I set him down, and when I follow Jaxon down the hall, the pitter-patter of his paws chases behind us.

"There's a bathroom there," Jaxon says, pointing to door number one. "But there's one with a tub and shower in your room too." He stops at door number two, stepping aside, scrubbing the back of his head as I creep inside. "I threw your bags in the closet. There's lots of hangers and crap." He points at a small dresser beneath the window. "Drawers." Looks at the queen-size bed. "Bed."

I follow him into the en suite bathroom, where he continues to point out every piece of furniture.

"Tub. Shower. Vanity. T—"

"Toilet. Got it. Thank you for labeling everything." He's clearly out of his element, which is both interesting and not at all shocking. He's obviously quite the ladies' man. If Google didn't tell me that much, every moment I've spent around him has told me so. He must be used to entertaining women. I'm just not so sure he's used to having one in his space. "Thank you, Jaxon. I'm going to take a shower, if that's okay. That's what I was about to do when hell decided to rain down on me."

The corner of his mouth hooks in what *appears* to be a smile, but he quickly wipes it away with his thumb. He scoops up Mittens, draping him over his shoulders. "'Kay. Um, well, I'm the last door if you need anything. Just knock first, unless you wanna get reacquainted with Magic Mike, 'cause I sleep naked."

My brows jump. "Sorry, what?"

"I sleep naked."

"Yeah, I got that. Back up for me real quick. Did you just call your dick Magic Mike?"

Jaxon smiles, running a palm down his proud chest. "Yeah."

"Uh-huh, and—" I pop my chin on my fist "—why have you done that?"

"'Cause he likes to dance, Len, and he's magical and incredible, like a mythical creature. You know that, honey."

"Oh, God." I bury my face in my hand before ushering him out of the room. "Out. Get out. See if your magical cock can pull a disappearing act." I slam the door in his face, but his laughter follows me into the closet, where I pull out everything I need to take a bath, because the brief glance I caught of it revealed at least four jets, and I'm all about a little massage in the tub.

I dump my things on the vanity as the tub fills, then drop my elbows to the marble and my chin to my hands as I stare at myself in the mirror and immediately wish I hadn't.

The exhaustion that runs straight through to my core shows in every imaginable way. The slight pout of my lips, the small crease between my brows. The bags beneath my eyes, heavy and puffy. My normally glowing brown skin is dull and dry, and all I want to do is bury my face in my pillow and cry.

Instead, I peel off my clothes, climb into the bath, close my eyes, and turn off my brain. I soak until the pads of my fingers are wrinkled and the water is lukewarm. I soak until my stomach grumbles, reminding me I haven't eaten in hours, until the silence is too loud. All I want is a friend, even if that friend is Jaxon.

I slap on some moisturizer, a bit of lip balm, pull on my cutest pair of pajamas, and creep out of my room. The hallway is dark, and at first I think Jaxon's asleep. But then I see the warm glow of a light coming from the kitchen, and hear the rustle of bags.

Pausing at the edge of the hall, my chest pulls taut as I watch Jaxon, sorting through the contents of his fridge and pantry.

"Goodbye, peanut butter," he murmurs, dropping the jar in the trash. "Goodbye, honey-roasted nuts. Goodbye, white chocolate macadamia nut cookies." He pulls out a box of Reese's Puff cereal, and this giant, grown-ass man before me actually fucking *whimpers*. "Goodbye, sweet, sweet heaven."

And when he's done tossing his peanut and tree nut products? He opens the cupboard beneath his sink, pulls out a disinfectant, and wipes down the inside of his fridge, the countertops, and every single handle in his kitchen.

I stay in the shadows, watching him curiously, until he grabs the garbage and leaves the apartment. Mittens runs out to greet me when I step into the light, and I scoop him into my arms as I find the cups and pour myself some water. When Jaxon steps back inside, he stops short.

"Oh. Thought you were sleeping."

"I was thirsty." My stomach chooses this moment to grumble, and I grin. "And hungry."

"I can make you something," he says, opening the fridge. "I don't have much, 'cause I gotta go grocery shopping." That and he just threw out half his food. "Um . . ." He scrubs his jaw. "You like grilled cheese?"

"Who doesn't?" I take a seat at the island, letting Mittens lick my wrist as Jaxon preps the frying pan. "Where did you go just now?"

"Thought I forgot something in my car," he lies, buttering the bread. "The secret is sprinkling a little powdered sugar on the bread before you fry it. It sounds wack, I know, but trust me. Gran made one for me every day after school. Two when I turned fifteen and was eating, like, six meals a day." He stops short, looking at nothing. "Shit. Is powdered sugar nut-free?" He pulls the bag from the cupboard, reading the ingredients. "Yup."

He rambles on while he cooks, talking more than I've ever heard him speak, but I can't focus on a thing other than the fact that this man who everything in my entire body tells me to *hate* remembered what I'm allergic to even though I've never actually told him. That he recognized the signs of anaphylactic shock and rushed to my side. That he stayed there for four hours while I slept in the hospital. That he brought me home, gave me a bed, threw out all his nut products, and fucking *sanitized* his kitchen.

That in a single day he's done more for me, *cared* more for me, than my fiancé ever did.

And it's so heavy and freeing all at once.

"There." Jaxon slides the sandwich in front of me, a beautiful shade of golden brown, and when he slices it in half—diagonally, just the way I like it—cheese oozes from inside. "Bon appétit, or whatever."

I swallow, slowly bringing the grilled cheese to my mouth, taking a careful bite.

Jaxon grins. "Good, right? I dunno what it is about the powdered sugar, but it just levels it up. Gran knows best."

A tsunami of emotions crashes into me head on, and my chest aches as I struggle to keep everything inside of me.

"Mimi makes her sweet tart crust with all-purpose flour," I mumble.

"Huh?"

"The lemon-cherry tart. My mimi makes them. That's why I had one tonight. But she uses all-purpose flour, not almond flour. One and a half cups. Quarter cup powdered sugar. Stick of butter. One egg. Sprinkle of salt." My chin quivers, and I sniffle. "Splash of vanilla. The real kind, not the fake shit." My voice breaks, my chest cracks wide open, and I scrub at my eyes as tears free fall down my cheeks. "I'm sorry. It's been a hard month."

Jaxon doesn't respond. In fact, he's so silent, I consider that he's left the room. But then I hear the tap of his fingers against his phone, and I barely resist the urge to roll my eyes. I want to hide in my room, but I'm too embarrassed to run away after he's made it clear he'd rather be texting than dealing with my emotions.

His phone pings, and a few seconds later I hear the shuffle of his feet behind me, feel the heat of his body when he stops at my back. Then, slowly, his arms slide around my waist, pulling me gently into his chest.

"What are you doing?"

"Hugging you. That's what the girls said to do."

"What?"

"I texted the girls. They said you probably needed a hug, so I'm hugging you."

God, I want so badly to laugh, but instead it comes out a horrible, choking sob. "You texted your girlfriends for advice because I'm crying?"

"I don't know how to do tears."

Another sob, and Jaxon softly squeezes me closer, like he's afraid to do it but thinks it might help. I hate that it does. That, somehow, it shifts the pain of the last month, the anger and confusion. That it gently nudges aside the desperate longing for acceptance and says, *Hey, I'm here. You're not alone.*

"I'm not good at the whole talking-about-feelings stuff," Jaxon starts softly, "so be quiet and listen for once in your life, because I'm not gonna say it again. I don't know why you were alone on your honeymoon, but I'm sorry if the reason hurt you. I'm not sorry I got to spend your last night there fucking you speechless. It was spectacular, and I've been thinking about your pussy ever since."

This time, my sob somewhat resembles a laugh. At the very least, the snort of a dying animal. "It's a great pussy," I cry.

"It really is." He rests his chin on my head, his chest deflating on a long, low breath. "I'm sorry you had to leave your family behind to get a fresh start. I'm sorry you feel alone in a new place. It never gets easier, no matter how many times you do it. I'm sorry your apartment fell apart, and I'm sorry you had to go to the hospital tonight."

I sniffle. "And my hair."

"Huh?"

"My hair. I forgot to wrap it last night, so when I woke up this morning it was all tangled."

"Oh. It looks pretty to me."

I stomp a foot. "Because I spent an hour detangling it and then hid half of it under a scarf!"

He hugs me tighter. "Good job."

I open my mouth to tell him praise is the last thing I'm looking for, but he slips his hand over it, stopping the words before they can come.

"What did I say two minutes ago?"

"'Be quiet and listen,'" I grumble from behind his palm.

"Very good, honey." His hand slides down my throat, splaying over my collarbone. "It's going to get better. I promise. You'll realize you're better off without your ex, and you'll really like it here. You'll make friends and . . . I'm glad you didn't die tonight."

One last squeeze, and then he releases me, strolling across the kitchen. He pauses at the edge of the hall, glancing over his shoulder. Hazel eyes move over me, and the corner of his mouth pulls up with that signature Jaxon Riley arrogance.

"Waste of a perfectly good mouth."

10

IS THAT YOU, MAGIC MIKE?

Lennon

"*Ah! Fuck me! I've been shot! I've been fucking shot! Man down!*"

The high-pitched screech cuts through the thick fog of sleep that has me facedown in a pillow, a pile of drool warming my cheek. I scramble out of bed, a tangled mess of limbs and sheets that sends me to the floor with a *thud*.

"Jaxon!" I scream, clambering to my feet. "*Jaxon!*" I launch myself through the door, slipping on the hardwood floors, my fuzzy sock-covered feet coming out from under me, pulling my ass to the floor, legs in the air. Flipping onto my belly, I army-crawl across the floor, find the handle on Jaxon's bedroom door, and hoist myself up before I throw myself through it. "Are you o—"

"*Ah!* I'm naked!" Jaxon claps his hands over his cock from where he's rolling around on his back on the rug.

"*Why are you naked?*" I shriek.

"*I told you I sleep naked! I told you to knock unless you wanted to get reacquainted with Magic Mike!*"

"*You said you'd been shot!*"

"*Did you hear a fucking gunshot, Lennon?*"

"*Then why did you say it?*" There's so much screeching, and I don't know what's happening. My throat hurts, and now my head does too. Then Mittens wanders out of the bathroom, looking smug as fuck, and when he hisses at Jaxon, the giant of a man covered in tattoos actually *cowers*. "What's wrong, angel?" I scoop my new favorite kitty up when he twines himself around my legs. "Did Daddy make you mad?"

Jaxon points a shaky finger at Mittens. "He's no angel. Goddamn fucking . . . *demon* cat." He clutches the edge of his mussed bed, hauling himself to his feet, not bothering to cover his junk. "Motherfucker batted at my balls like it was the last inning in the World Series and a home run would clinch the win." He cups said balls in his hands, showing them to me as Mittens licks my ear. "Look! He got me!"

There's a drop of blood on his left ball, no bigger than a pinprick, but it's the raging erection I can't look away from. Huh. My memories didn't do Magic Mike justice. Was he always that big? That veiny? That angry purple head looks desperate for release, and my vagina screams *We could take care of that!* at my brain, which sends a signal to my legs to walk themselves over to him and spread myself wide.

Goddammit, no. No, vagina. Keep it together, girl.

I flick an uninterested glance at Jaxon. "Want me to make it better?"

The frustration in his face melts, and he tries so damn hard not to grin, stretching his arms over his head in a big, obnoxious way that lets his dick bob, nearly touching his belly button. "Yeah, that could be nice."

"Okay." I turn, heading for the door.

"What? Wait! Len!" His feet slap against the planks behind me, and when I spin back to him, he buries a hand in his mussed waves. Christ, the man is damn near perfect naked. Broad shoulders lead to sinewy arms painted with art that only makes him more beautiful. A torso I swear was hand carved by God himself, veins on either side of his hips that beg me to drop to my knees and open wide. "Where you goin'? I thought you were gonna . . .

you know." He aims a pointed glance at his crotch. "Make it better."

"I am." I tip my head toward the kitchen. "Gonna get a knife. That's a bad scratch. Don't think your ball can be saved. Best we amputate."

Mittens and I head down the hall as the door slams behind us, and Jaxon's frustration returns, boiling over.

"I *hate* you!" he shouts, and I smile.

"Love you, too, honey!"

In the kitchen, Mittens leads me to his food, and when I dump in one scoop, he convinces me via screeching that he requires a second. As I'm dumping it in, Jaxon screams, "You better not be giving him two scoops! He's on a diet!"

"*I only gave him one; stop yelling at me!*" I yell back, opening his pantry. He's got at least seven different types of cereal in here, all sugar-laden, my favorite type. I pull out the Trix and Lucky Charms, dump an equal amount of each into two bowls, and top them off with milk.

When Jaxon walks in two minutes later, his hair is wet, his dick is exquisitely highlighted in his gray sweats, and he's pulling a T-shirt over his spectacular abs.

I slide one of the bowls across the counter to him. "I made you breakfast."

"A-plus for effort," he murmurs, cocking his head. "Did you . . . *mix* two kinds together?"

"Yep. It's incredible."

He dives in with his spoon, closing his eyes and humming as he chews. He devours the bowl in thirty seconds and then promptly refills it with both cereals. "Fanks," he manages between bites. "I hung-wy."

When I'm done, I drink the milk from the bowl, rinse it out, and put it in the dishwasher. It's an absolute mess in here, dishes all willy-fucking-nilly without any thought given to their placement, so I rearrange it to keep my eye from twitching.

"What was wrong with the way I did it?"

"Everything." I pour myself a glass of water and drain it quickly while Jaxon watches through narrowed eyes.

"Got any plans today?"

Besides wallowing in self-pity? "I was supposed to have the girls over tonight."

His brows jump. "The girls? Like . . . my girls?"

"I didn't know they belonged to you."

"Well, they're *my* friends."

"And according to our group chat, they're *my* Coochie Gang."

"What the—" He shakes his head. "Never mind. That tracks. Cara probably named it."

"Well, anyway, they were going to help me build my IKEA furniture. There was going to be wine, so I'm not sure how successful we would've been, but it would've been nice nonetheless to have someone to talk to. Plus, I was gonna make Mimi's famous banana pudding and her famous key lime pie to ensure their allegiance to me over you."

He ignores the last part, which is annoying since I only said it to piss him off. "Mimi's famous lemon-cherry tarts, Mimi's famous banana pudding, Mimi's famous key lime pie . . . how many famous recipes does Mimi fucking have?"

"Well, Jaxon, one thing about Mimi is all of her recipes are famous, so jot that down." I count it a personal achievement when he chuckles, and I look down to hide my own smile. "Anyway, girls' night is obviously not happening now that my apartment is underwater. So I'm just gonna grab a shower and then I'll be out of your hair."

"Didn't you have a shower last night? Why do you need another one this morning?"

"Because I need to wash my hair."

"Why didn't you wash it last night?"

I scoff. Typical man. If I hadn't seen it with my own eyes twenty minutes ago, I still would've guessed that he just wakes up like that, his hair in perfect disarray. "Because, *Jaxon*, washing my hair is a commitment, one I didn't have energy for last night. Beyond that, I'm absolutely *not* sleeping on a fresh style. Honestly, get it together."

Eyes wide, he mouths *okay* at his cereal. "So, uh, what's your plan?"

"My plan?" I touch my coarse curls. I didn't bother wrapping them last night, knowing I'd give them some TLC this morning, so they're tangled, frizzy, and have lost a significant amount of bounce, hanging halfway down my back. "The usual. I like to stick with my natural curls on wash day when they're fresh, so I'll just diffuse them and wear them down."

Jaxon drops his face as a snort of laughter barrels up from his throat. "Your plan for where you're going to sleep tonight, Lennon, not your fucking hair."

Oops.

"Did you manage to book a hotel?"

"I haven't called yet but Harry Styles has officially left the province. Surely the girlies have dispersed. There must be some availability." I'm trying this new thing this morning where I speak things into existence. "Just have to call my landlord, see how long I need a place for. What do you think? Will the bathroom be fixed tomorrow? Midweek, maybe?"

The way Jaxon looks at me makes me want to reach out and catch all those words in my fists, shove them back down my throat. "You think they're gonna fix the pipes, check for further water damage—and mold, which has probably been growing in there— fix the ceiling, and rebuild both bathrooms in a day or two?"

Okay, I hear how it sounds.

My phone dings, and my stomach somersaults. "It's my land-lord."

Jaxon rounds the island, chest at my back, chin dipped to my shoulder as he peers down at my phone.

I glare up at him. "Must you stand so close?"

"No, but it pisses you off so I like doing it." His hand closes over mine, jerking my phone up high enough that I can't read. Instead, I watch his lips move, then stop, the drop of his gaze to mine, and the slow, cringey smile he gives me. "So, heyyy, your landlord can't get someone in until the spriiing."

"*Spring?* But it's still January!" Spinning away, I press my hand to my forehead. Shake both hands out. Breathe deeply, then fail and panic. "Okay, okay. It's okay, Lennon. It's fine." I shrug, popping a fist on my hip. "Yeah, it's totally fine. I'll grab a hotel for a couple nights and look for a new place for February first, and, um . . . yeah, it's totally fine. Not a big deal. That's life, ya know? Hiccups. Like Dad always says, 'Life throws you curveballs. You have to learn how to knock 'em out of the park.'" I laugh so I don't cry, and it only comes out a little hysterical. It's also at this point I realize I've migrated to the living room, have fluffed every single cushion on the couch, and am shaking out the throw blanket. I lay it back over the chaise lounge and stick a hand in my hair. "Um, so, I'm gonna go shower."

I march across the apartment with my head held high, because everything is totally fine and I'm gonna figure it out because I'm an independent woman and so the fuck what if I've had a terrible string of luck this month. It's whatever and not important and I'm gonna bounce back so hard everyone's gonna get whiplash watching me.

"You could stay here."

I stop at the edge of the hall, tugging on my ears. They must be waterlogged, because no way I heard that right. "What?"

"You could stay here," Jaxon repeats, slowly, like he's not sure how to put the thought into real words. He doesn't move, and I think it's more for his benefit than mine. He doesn't know what he's doing, inviting a girl to stay with him. His brain has probably just sent alarms sounding in every crevice of his body, and all his major organs are panicking. All of mine are. "I've got space. No need to waste your money."

Oh my God, what do I do? *What the fuck do I do?* I need Serena. I need the Coochie Gang.

"I . . . I'll look for apartments. So I don't put you out for long." *What the fuck, Len? Are we* agreeing *to this?*

"Sure. If you want."

If I want? Surely he's not suggesting I stay *here* until my apartment is ready *in the spring.*

Jaxon makes no move to leave the safety of the kitchen, to come any closer, and I don't dare turn around. It would mean having to look a horrible decision in the face. Because that's what this is, isn't it? We met on vacation, got drunk, and fucked so hard I saw stars. We were never supposed to see each other again, and then I took a job with his hockey team. And now? Fuck. This is a horrible, awful, no-good idea.

"Let's not make this a big thing," he finally says. "It's just a room."

"What about your Reese's Puffs?" I whisper.

"What?"

"Nothing. Are you sure about this?"

"Literally not at all. I planned on avoiding living with a woman for the rest of my life, and the life after that too."

"Then—"

"Go take a shower so I can freak out over this in peace, please. Just promise me you won't, like . . . make everything pink in here."

"Oh, Jaxon . . . I can't promise that. Pink's my favorite color."

I dash to my room, pull out my suitcase, and dump it on the bed before he can rescind the invitation. I can hear the regret in his long, loud sigh, but then Mittens strolls in, jumps on the bed, and flops down on my clothes. "Hear that, little marshmallow? We're gonna be best friends!"

"No!" Jaxon shouts. "Mittens is *my* best friend!"

"We'll see about that," I whisper, letting him boop his head against mine.

"I can fucking *hear you!*"

"Well, stop *eavesdropping!*"

Rolling onto the bed, I curl up next to Mittens while I check my phone.

Serena and Devin have already recovered from my near-death experience after keeping me on FaceTime for an hour in the middle of the night, and Devin wants to know if I have full use of my airways this morning. Serena has responded with: *Probs not. If it's not nuts she's choking on, it's hockey player cock.*

There are more than twenty messages in our Coochie Gang thread, the girls checking in at various points throughout the night and early morning. The latest message is from Cara, threatening to break in and steal Mittens, because she's concerned Jaxon annoyed me to death and that's why I haven't responded yet. I shoot off a text, letting them know I'm okay but that I'll have to cancel our plans tonight. It's particularly gutting, because the love that immediately lights up my screen when all four of them respond is exactly what I need in my life right now.

I skip off to the bathroom, finding homes for all my necessities in the shower, where I spend the next thirty minutes, massaging clarifying shampoo into my scalp, detangling my coils, soaking them in my favorite curl cream, the coconut hibiscus scent infiltrating every nook and cranny in the bathroom. When I'm done, I decide the countertop is way too small a space for me to do my thing, so I scoop everything into my arms and head across the hall to the other bathroom. It's the same size, and when I hear the TV playing in the living room, I poke my head around the corner, spotting Jaxon sprawled out on the couch, Mittens on his chest.

Quietly, I tiptoe down the hall and creep into his bedroom, the heavens opening up when I get a look at his bathroom. A shower three times the size of mine, a ginormous window that lets in just the right amount of sunshine and makes this the perfect place to apply makeup, and a double vanity plenty big enough for me to spread ~~my wings and soar~~ my beauty products out.

So that's exactly what I do.

Like Jaxon has some sort of sixth sense and knows I'm somewhere I shouldn't be, he finds me five minutes later, combing curl butter through my hair.

He pauses in the doorway, jaw unhinging as he takes me in. Or rather, takes in the bomb that appears to have gone off in his bathroom.

It's me. I'm the bomb.

"Can I help you?" I rake mousse through my hair before flipping my head over and scrunching my curls. "I'm busy."

"What the fuck are you . . . No, but this is . . . It's-it's-it's . . . it's *my* bathroom! You have your own!"

"Yours has better lighting and more counter space."

Oh look, there's that vein in his neck Cara was talking about a couple nights ago.

He steps forward, eyes pinballing around the counter. He picks up my purple tub of curl butter. My pink can of mousse. My bag full of lipsticks in varying shades of deep plums and crimsons. My eye shadow palette. And then, with wide eyes, he backs away, slowly and while shaking his head. His hands come up, clapping over his cheeks, dragging down his face in slow motion. "No. No, no, no, no."

I hold his gaze while I plug in my hair dryer, attach the diffuser, and turn it on. When I lift it to my hair, he turns and dashes from the room.

And that's the story of how I get Jaxon's entire apartment to myself for three hours, along with his phone number, which he leaves on a sticky note on his kitchen island, and a sweet message.

Don't touch any of my fucking stuff. I'll be back.

When he returns in the afternoon, I'm standing at the bookshelf in the living room, filling it with my books.

"What the fuck?" He plucks one off the shelf, inspects the three half-naked men on the cover, then reads the back. "Three guys and one girl? No way. She'd be split wide open."

"Every girl's dream, Jax."

"Don't call me Jax." He holds up a book with two women twined together. "And this?"

"I like men and women, therefore I read sexy books with both men and women."

He sifts through the books, panic setting in when he finds a *why choose* dark romance that involves stalking. "You can't put these here."

"Ah, yes. I can see why having books on a bookshelf would be an issue."

"And where's my algae plant?" He points to the empty spot, where a ring of dust is. "I had that for ages!"

"It certainly showed, Jaxon. It was dead and the roots were rotted, which is why I threw it in the trash. And by the way—" I tap the corner of his mouth, right where it's pulled down. "It's an *aloe* plant, not an algae plant. Algae isn't a plant, and it lives in water."

"Like your apartment," he grumbles, arms pinned across his chest as he watches me inspect the photos on his shelf, starting with a group shot of him and the boys. Nobody looks prouder than Carter, dressed as Posh Spice. "That was from last Halloween, and don't you fucking say a word, because I know I looked hot as fuck as Ginger Spice."

He's not wrong, which is a little alarming, but then Ginger was always my favorite Spice Girl.

The next photo is Jaxon with his lips pressed to the cheek of an elderly woman wearing a red sweater with a Christmas tree on it. She couldn't look happier to be with Jaxon, who happens to be wearing a horrible, *awful* red vest, bedazzled to shit, covered in patches of stars, snowmen, and— "Are those real bells on the hem?"

Jaxon yanks the photo away. "That's my gran. She crochets me a new vest for every holiday and important occasion, and she's a real-life angel, so shut up."

I fold my lips into my mouth, humming to keep from laughing in his face. This would make excellent content on the Vipers' Instagram page.

"And this?" I pick up the final frame, cheap, cracked plastic with an old picture, the colors dull and muted. Though the two boys in it can't be more than twelve or thirteen, it's clear the one on the left is Jaxon. He's got the same twinkle in his eyes, the one that reeks of trouble, and that smirk says he's about to get into it. The boy he's got his arm around wears a matching smile, the shock of red hair on his head a mess, like he just tore off his hockey helmet. Judging by the equipment at their feet, I'd guess he did. "Who's this?"

Something changes in Jaxon. Shuts down, maybe. His eyes dim and shutter as he takes the photo from me, and when he sweeps his thumb over the face of the red-haired boy, his throat bobs. "Bryce," he whispers, setting the frame on the top shelf, out of my reach.

"You played hockey with him?"

"Yeah."

"Does he still play?"

Jaxon turns away. "No."

It's only two letters, a single syllable, but there's so much weight in that word that it slithers up my back, creeps across my shoulders, settles on my chest. If heartache were palpable, it would be the crushing weight of that simple word, the way Jaxon murmurs it, the flex of his fists at his side, the slight curl to his shoulders.

We may not be friends in the usual sense of the word, but everything in me longs to make this right, to take the hurt and replace it with something better, something that brings him back to this moment.

"Do you keep all the vests your gran crochets for you?"

Jaxon's spine snaps straight. "No."

"Hm."

He twists toward me, approaching me slowly, his hands up in surrender as I back up toward the hall. "Lennon," he warns, and I take off. Dash down the hall, throw myself into his bedroom.

His feet pound behind me, and the moment I get my hands on his closet doors, he wraps his arms around my middle, tossing me on his bed. He's on top of me before I can take my next breath, fingers wrapped around my wrists, his heaving chest pressed to mine.

"Don't you fucking dare."

"I wanna have a fashion show," I murmur, bucking my hips. His nostrils flare, and he closes his eyes. "Oops. Did I wake Magic Mike?"

His eyes pop open, taking in my hair before they roam my face. "Honey, I'm this close to burying my hands in that pretty hair you spent so long on this morning and fucking *ruining* it." He runs his nose along the column of my throat, up to my ear. "The only fashion show that happens in this room between me and you is your naked body sprawled over mine while I bury my tongue in your sweet cunt and my cock in your throat."

Shit. Shit, shit, shit. Heat tumbles down my belly, rolling to an abrupt stop at my clit, where it thuds like it's got its own heartbeat, and I moan. I fucking *moan.* That . . . that wasn't supposed to happen.

Jaxon grins down at me as my face floods with heat, the triumph clear.

"We can't . . . we can't sleep together," I tell him. "Not again. Not now. Not if I'm staying here."

"Of course not. Then you'll never leave." He hooks his arm under my thigh, spreading it wide as he gets off me, strategically rubbing his cock against me one last time in a move that has every coherent thought leaving my brain.

When he stands, his eyes go to my crotch, and the corner of his mouth hooks. "Go put on a new pair of pants, honey. We're going out."

I look down at my pants.

At the small wet spot, right there in the crotch of my gray yoga pants.

Fuck. That was *not* supposed to happen.

"You still mad at me?"

"I don't know what you're talking about." I smash my fingers against the seat belt release seventeen hundred times over, holding my breath when Jaxon leans over, releasing it on the first go.

"You started it," he reminds me as I march up the steps to an extravagant house with the mountains as a backdrop. I don't even know where we are or whose house this is. I wanted to ask on the way here, but I was too busy giving Jaxon the silent treatment. The only time I opened my mouth was when we got out of the elevator and I found my car next to his in the parking garage. Apparently, he stole my keys when he went out earlier and Adam had taken him to get it.

I hate that he's way nicer than he lets on. In an alternate universe, I think we'd actually be great friends, because he also makes me want to laugh. But I've fucked him, and it's not that I can't be friends with someone I've been intimate with. It's that my pussy still weeps at the sight of him. *That's* why we can't be friends.

I ring the doorbell, and a chorus of barking and screeching ensues within the house.

Jaxon steps up behind me. "If you wanna waive the no-sex rule for one night, I could probably rock your world so hard later you'll be satisfied for the next six to twelve months." He leans over me, reaching for the door handle. "We just let ourselves in here, honey."

The moment the door opens, three ginormous dogs crash into me, followed by Cara.

She wraps her arms around me, tugging me tight against her as the dogs nudge at my hips, my ass, anywhere they can reach. "We're so glad you're okay, Lennon," she murmurs, and a moment later, three more women wrap themselves around us.

"No one greets me like that," Jaxon grumbles, but then a small boy toddles into the hallway, and his eyes light like a Christmas tree.

"Unc'a Jax!" the little boy shouts, racing toward him.

Jaxon scoops him into his arms, tossing him above his head. "Hey, buddy! I missed you!"

The little boy looks at me, green eyes dancing as he points proudly to his chest. "Unc'a Jax miss Conn'a."

"Oh, are you Connor?" I take his tiny hand in mine. "I'm Lennon. It's so nice to meet you." I look to Rosie. "God, he's your twin, isn't he?"

She opens her mouth to answer, but a screech from farther in the house stops her.

"*Ireland! Wait!* You need your helmet!"

"Oh, shit." Olivia pushes by us. "*Carter!* She doesn't need a helmet!"

Jennie rolls her eyes. "Ireland's ten months old and standing on her own. She's started taking a couple steps here and there."

"But . . . a helmet?"

"Oh, sorry. Were you not aware that my brother is extremely over the top to his core?"

"Really? I mean, yeah, ostentatious for sure. I see that on the ice and the way he eats up camera time. But surely he's not *that* . . ." My words die as a tiny brunette waddles into the room, one slow-motion, wobbly step at a time, dark curls pulled into two teensy pigtails, huge emerald eyes alight with wonder. She's a perfect mixture of Carter and Olivia, like she was split right down the middle. That's not what stops me in my tracks, though.

It's that teensy little Ireland has strips of Bubble Wrap around both knees, and her elbows.

My jaw hangs, and Jaxon shrugs.

"You wanna be part of this friend group, you better be willing to get on board with a lot of weird shit."

Cara swats him away, shoving him toward the boys, who are actively watching and enjoying as Carter short-circuits, clutching a teensy hockey helmet in his giant hands while Olivia holds him back from going after their daughter.

Cara loops her arm through mine, pulling me into the kitchen. "Rosie made key lime pie, and I made banana pudding."

"What? You did? Why?"

"Jaxon said you wanted to make them for us tonight, so we thought we'd give it a whack."

"We pulled the recipes from Pinterest, so they're probably not as good as your mimi's," Rosie tells me.

"And also, I can't bake worth shit," Cara adds.

Rosie rubs her arm. "Anybody could've mistaken that salt for sugar, Care."

Something thick clogs in my throat as they present the desserts to me. Cara wraps her arm around me. "They look like shit."

"They really do," I cry, my voice cracking. "But it's the effort that counts, and they smell amazing."

Garrett raises his hand from the living room. "Can confirm they taste amazing. I licked both spoons clean."

"Thank you, guys. I appreciate it."

"You're gonna need all the help you can get if you're going to survive living with Jaxon for any amount of time."

Jaxon throws his arms in the air. "Jennie, what the fuck?"

"Why is nobody telling her what she *really* needs to survive?" Emmett asks, cracking the lid off a beer before he pulls me in for a hug and claps a hand to Cara's ass.

"What?" I ask as Olivia pulls me to the couch in the living room. Jaxon has freed Ireland from her Bubble Wrap kneepads and is now playing peek-a-boo with her and Connor from behind a chair, which is an alarmingly attractive sight. It also seems to have relaxed Carter, who is now setting something up on the TV. "What is it?"

"Now, Lennon," Carter says, his back to me as he rummages through a drawer. "I'm a Disney man myself, but Ollie said I should start slow so I don't scare you off. So I'm giving you one song before I dive headfirst into *Frozen*, because Anna and Elsa are my queens."

"One song? What are you—oh my God."

Carter twirls around, brow arched, charming grin in place . . . microphone in hand. "Welcome, everyone, to another iconic night of Karaoke with Carter."

That's all the warning I get before music explodes through the speakers, and Carter launches into a rendition of "Dancing Queen" by ABBA.

"Holy motherfucking tits," I murmur, a shaky hand coming up, covering my mouth.

"Tragic, isn't it?" Olivia says, and yet she looks like she's about to ask him to put another baby inside her.

"It's . . . it's like if one of my playlists were a movie."

"What playlist?"

I can't take my eyes off Carter as he does what I'm sure he thinks is a beautiful, provocative dance, but is really just him gyrating while rubbing his left ass cheek. And I sigh.

"Songs That Get White People Turnt."

11

TIDBITS AND TESTICLES

Lennon

IT'S BEEN . . . A WEEK.

Literally and figuratively.

Literally, it's been a week since I moved in with Jaxon. Figuratively, it's been the longest, most aggravating week of my life.

Of our first seven nights together, three of them were spent on the road, from Dallas to San Jose. Watching Jennie answer her FaceTime calls with the roll of her eyes before she sets her phone up in front of Mittens so Jaxon can check in with him over team breakfast. Listening to him sigh and talk about how hard life as a single father is when you're on the road as much as he is. Snapping picture after picture of him crushing players into the boards, taking someone out moments before they can take a shot on Adam.

The other four nights, the ones spent tucked into his apartment . . . testicles. *Testicles everywhere.* The man has made it his mission to annoy the living hell out of me, and apparently, the best way to do so is to walk around naked first thing in the morning.

I sleep naked, Len, I fuckin' told you that on day one. I don't get dressed until after I've had my morning coffee, and I like it that way. I humored you for one morning, but I can't change my whole life for you.

I'm not asking him to change his whole life. I'm asking him to stop swinging Magic Mike and his two backup dancers in my goddamn face first thing in the morning.

Apparently, though, doing so would ruin his life.

Jaxon is everywhere. And I hate it.

And yet . . . I don't. It pains me to say it, but if I'm going to be stuck with someone in a place where I know no one, Jaxon Riley is . . . okay. He turned the heating up two degrees to 72 without me asking, because I was walking around wrapped in a blanket. I made an offhand remark about the single shelf in the shower not being big enough for all my products, and even though he said *maybe that's a sign to use fewer products*, when I came home from lunch with the girls, there were brand-new floor-to-ceiling shelves in one corner of the shower. A step stool magically appeared in the pantry a day after he walked into the kitchen to see me scaling the counters so I could reach the mugs on the top shelf, and even though he explicitly said Mittens wasn't allowed to sleep with me, when my emotions got the best of me one night, the door creaked open, Mittens was tossed inside, and then the door was promptly shut again.

Jaxon doesn't need to know I was only crying because I had just realized—knee-deep in *Red (Taylor's Version)*—that Taylor Swift will, one day, stop making music, and I'll no longer have a soundtrack to my life.

Yes, I was on my period, thank you for asking.

I flop onto my side when my bedroom door creaks, and my best pal waddles in, floofy belly swinging back and forth. Mittens lets out one of his famous screeching meows before leaping onto the bed. I roll onto my back, letting him climb aboard my chest, nuzzling his face against mine.

"Hello, little marshmallow. How's the handsomest boy in the whole wide world? Yes, you're so handsome and floofy." He purrs his agreement, and I press a kiss to my favorite orange splotch around his left eye. "Don't tell Daddy I'm your favorite. It makes him feel bad about himself."

"Goddammit, Lennon! *I can hear you!*"

"Well, why are the walls so fucking thin?" I scream back, and Mittens turns his face toward the door, meowing what I imagine to be a *Yeah, Dad!* "Did you get Daddy's balls this morning? Did you make sure your claws were out?"

"Fucking . . . women." Somewhere, a door slams. Ten seconds later, the toilet flushes. "Why the fuck did I think this was a good idea?"

I've been asking myself that all week. I've come to the conclusion that I'm extremely pretty and an utter joy to be around. Jaxon's subconscious couldn't resist the pull to have me near, forcing the words from his mouth before giving him a second to think about it.

"What, no cocky comeback, honey?"

I sit up, scooping Mittens into my arms for a kiss before I deposit him in my spot and tuck the blankets around him. Then I slip my heart-shaped sunglasses on him, take a picture, and send it to Jaxon. "We both know you're in love with me and that's why you asked me to stay, Jax."

"*Ha!* You're gonna be waiting a long time if you're—Lennon, what the fuck! He's gonna get too hot tucked in like that! And I don't want him getting comfy in there! Then he'll think he can sleep there whenever he wants! And take those sunglasses off!"

I roll my eyes, but before I have the chance to deliberately disobey him, he opens his mouth again.

"Wait, can you get one of him with your sleep mask on?"

I swap the sunglasses for my purple silk sleep mask, *wake me for snacks* embroidered in loopy letters. Jaxon's chuckle when he gets the picture a moment later has no right making me smile the way it does.

Five minutes later, with a fresh face and sparkling, perfect teeth, I amble out of the bedroom in my sleep shorts, tank, and fuzzy socks, Mittens at my heels. The apartment is still dark, so I wander through it, opening the shades, letting in the morning sun. It warms me from my head to my toes the moment it kisses my skin, and for a second, I'm transported back to Cabo. To a blazing sun, warm sand, the sound of the ocean just outside my door.

My honeymoon might not have been the happy occasion it was meant to be, but truth be told, it was the first time in a long time I'd felt so *me*. Maybe it was because I was able to listen to my audiobooks without Ryne looking over my shoulder, telling me how romance books only created unrealistic expectations. Maybe it was because I spent hours lying in my hammock after dark, staring at the stars, appreciating their beauty, how small they made my problems feel. Maybe it was the sunrises I watched paint the sky each morning, Mother Nature's reminder that each day is a chance at a new beginning.

Cabo wasn't my honeymoon. It was my new beginning.

Footsteps slap against the hardwood, and a bowl clangs against the countertop. I close my eyes as Jaxon dumps a fuck-ton of cereal into his bowl, same as every morning.

"You wan' some waff-ows dis mornin'?" He pauses, and I pray to God he's swallowing. "I'm starving today."

"Sure, I like waffles." I turn toward him, sighing when I see it. All eight inches of it, to be specific.

"Bananas and chocolate chips? Or blueberries and cinnamon?" He stares at the contents of his fridge, shoveling cereal into his mouth. "Know what? I'm gonna do half and half. 'Cause I can't decide, and both sound good." He looks at me, I think. "Len? You listenin'?"

"No."

"Huh?"

"I said I'm not listening."

"Well, that's rude. I always listen to you, even last night when you were telling me about how Justin and Henry tag-teamed Giselle in the parking lot." Another spoonful of cereal, and the man doesn't even blink as he goes on about the book I was listening to last night while he was playing a video game. "It was her first time doing double penetration, and now she's worried nothing will ever stack up again. I said she should just get a DP toy, and you said, 'That's a good idea, Jax. I didn't know you had those.' And I said, 'Don't call me Jax.'"

"I . . . Jesus Christ." Squeezing my eyes shut, I wave a hand in front of my face. "I genuinely can't believe that this moment right here is my life."

"Well, excuse the fuck out of me for taking an interest in your books and offering to make you two kinds of waffles."

"You're naked!" I shout, arms wide. "You're fucking *naked*, Jaxon! And while Magic Mike and his backup dancers are swinging about, you're standing there, casually eating your cereal and talking about a fictional character getting DP'd in a parking lot!"

He sets his bowl down and gestures aggressively at his junk. "This is who I am, Lennon! If you can't appreciate *us*"—another jab at his crotch, followed by one toward the door—"then there's the door! Don't let it hit your ass on the way out!"

"Oh my God," I murmur, running a hand over my mouth. "You are so fucking weird. Why do I like it so much?"

The crease between his brows disappears. He lifts a lazy shoulder. "Gran says I'm endearing."

I'm beginning to think there's a good chance Gran might be smoking something, but she also might be onto something. I've wanted to hate Jaxon with every bone in my body from the moment I heard him call Brielle Breanne. Every day the four-letter word loses more and more meaning. Dare I even say it, I'm beginning to . . . *look forward* to what each new day will bring me with Jaxon's antics, and what I'll learn about him in the process.

Jaxon picks his bowl up, eyes locked on me as he drains the milk. He wipes his mouth with the back of his hand. "Still too cold in here for you?"

"No, it's perfect. Why?"

"You seem cold, that's all." He aims a pointed look at my tits, sipping his orange juice a little too smugly for my liking when I follow his gaze to my rock-hard nipples.

I tilt my head, staring at his cock. "Is that why Magic Mike looks like that? Because you're cold?" Swiping his orange juice, I lift it to my mouth, hiding my smile. "I don't remember him being so small and shriveled, but then again, I was five Bahama Mamas deep when I fucked you."

"You're fucking annoying. And also, *I* fucked *you*."

"Mmm. Well, annoying must be your type."

"Must be. Only way to explain how I went from Breanne to you in the same day."

I gasp, setting the glass down. "Don't you *dare* compare me to Brielle."

He shrugs. "If the shoe fits."

"It doesn't. The shoe doesn't fit."

Another shrug, and Jaxon heads down the hall, leaving me staring after his *unbelievable* hockey ass, so damn firm, and why is his back so hot? Knots of muscles framed by tattooed arms, two little dips above his bubble butt, thick thighs, powerful enough to pin someone to a mattress, or a wall.

Someone, but not me.

Again. Not me *again*.

"Jaxon! Take it back! Take it back right now!"

He pauses at his bedroom door, having the *balls* to look me over before lifting his shoulder one last time and offering an "Eh."

I march toward him, pointing at his door. "Don't you dare go in there." He reaches for the handle. "Don't you dare touch that handle." He touches it. "Don't you dare turn it." He turns it. "Jaxon, I swear to God, if you—" He opens the door, and I halt, head tilting as I give him the eyes, the ones that tell him he needs to think *very carefully* about his next move.

But what does the little shit do? The little shit smirks, stepping inside his bedroom, and it must be my imagination, because there's no way in hell his cock is actually getting *hard* right now.

"Take it back," I whisper.

"I'd love to, honey, but I can't right now." He aims a pointed look at Magic Mike, growing firmer by the second. "Gotta take care of something."

The door slams in my face as my jaw drops, and Jaxon calls out, "I'll tell you one thing, though, honey. Arguing with Breanne never got me hard."

"What the—I don't—fuck." My fists ball at my sides, and my belly tightens way down low. "Not now, coochie," I mutter. "We're mad at him." Splendid timing too. I'd really love to start my morning off with a gingerbread oat latte—Jaxon has all the fancy syrup flavors—but ever since he caught me pressing three different buttons at one time on his espresso machine, he's been making all my coffees for me. "I guess I'll make my own coffee," I call toward his room as I head back to the kitchen. "I just hope your espresso machine doesn't blow up!"

"You're gonna do great, honey!"

He and I both know that's a lie, which is why I head to the living room windows so I can survey the weather. It's a nice, bright morning, and the closest Starbucks is only a five-minute walk away. I could go get my gingerbread oat latte, come back here, pour it in a mug, and pretend I made it.

I briefly consider how long it'll take Jaxon to jack off. Probably only thirty seconds. Not enough time. Ugh.

Making my way into the kitchen, I pull my favorite mug down. It's Jaxon dressed as Ginger Spice. Apparently, Cara had it made for him for Christmas. I set it down next to the espresso machine, line up all the ingredients beside it, and then get overwhelmed. I like annoying Jaxon, but I've been known to cry when in trouble. If I break his expensive machine, I'll turn into a blubbering mess, because, secretly, I'd prefer he doesn't hate me. So I gather everything in my arms and move to put it away.

Except right there, to the left of the machine, is a small notebook that wasn't there yesterday.

I pick up the small green book, and something thick and foreign settles in my throat, something I can't swallow down as I read the words scrawled over the cover.

Lennon's Guide to Making Coffee

The tightness in my throat expands to my chest, pulling it taut as I flip through the pages, directions on how to use the machine, recipes for different drinks. He's even added a section that tells me which cereal pairs best with each drink.

Somewhere behind me, I'm conscious of a door opening. Of footsteps on hardwood, the jingle of a bell as Jaxon pauses to scratch Mittens's chin, tell him how much he loves him, and that he's Daddy's bestest boy. I feel him when he enters the kitchen, feel the heat of his body as he moves about around me, hear the murmur of his voice as he rambles on about God knows what.

But all I can focus on is this damn notebook in my trembling hands.

"Len? Did you hear me?"

My gaze rises to Jaxon's, and I clench my jaw to keep my chin from quivering. "You made me an instruction manual," I whisper, and goddammit, there goes my chin.

"Oh. Yeah. That. I mean . . ." He scrubs the back of his neck, searching for his words. "It's not a big deal. You didn't know how to use it."

"There are recipes."

"Yeah."

"And cereal pairings." *Oh, shit. Shit, shit, shit. Not the tears. Hey, God? Are you there? It's me, Lennon.*

"'Cause you like to eat cereal when you have your morning coffee," he mutters, and oh my fucking *God*, is Jaxon Riley *blushing* right now?

"You made me an instruction manual," I cry out, and as the tears tip over the edge and stream down my cheeks, I lose my grip on reality and launch myself at his chest. He stands there with his arms above me, and the frantic beat of his heart beneath my ear tells me I've just overloaded his system, all his signals are misfiring, and he has no idea what to do.

"I don't know what to do right now," he whispers. "And I can't reach my phone to text the girls."

I squeeze him tighter in response. Slowly, his arms come around me, one hand gliding over my back, the other tangling in the curls at the base of my neck, and any chance I ever had of hating this man flies out the window. How can you hate someone who's hiding all this adorable beneath his arrogant, blasé exterior?

"Meow!"

The tiny, angry screech startles us, and we jump apart. Jaxon scoops Mittens up, letting him lick at the scruff on his face, his eyes bouncing from me to any other place in the kitchen while he tries to think of something to say to ease the sudden tension.

"Your face is all wet."

That was it, huh? That was the best he could come up with?

I grab a fistful of his hoodie, drying my eyes on it. "Thanks."

"For the instruction manual, the hug, or letting you use my hoodie as a towel?"

I pat his chest. "All three. You're so generous."

He rolls his eyes, pressing a kiss to Mittens's nose before laying him on the chaise lounge in the sunshine. He heads to the front closet, steps into a pair of boots, slings his gym bag over his shoulder, and tugs a beanie over his hair. "I'm heading to the gym with the guys. Want me to grab anything while I'm out?"

"No, I don't think—*oh!*" I clap my hands excitedly. "Could you go through a Tim Hortons drive-thru and get me some Tidbits? I've been dying to try them! People are always walking around with those cute little boxes. It feels wrong that I was born in Canada but have never tried them before."

Jaxon stills. Slowly, his eyes come to mine. "What did you say?"

"Tidbits. You know, the little doughnut hole things? I'm not picky about flavors. What about a variety pack?"

He stares at me. For so long, and just as I'm about to ask if something is wrong with his eyes, he keels over, howling with laughter. "*Tidbits! You called them Tidbits!*"

I pin my arms over my chest, because I fail to see the problem.

Jaxon stalks toward me, still laughing—*is he crying?*—and scoops his keys off the counter. He drops his forehead to my shoulder, holding me as he shakes with laughter. "Tidbits." He snickers, tears coating the crook of my neck, and when he pulls back, grins down at me, I'm too thrown by the sheer beauty of the man wearing a smile as bright and light as that to be angry with him. "Sure, Len. I'll get you your Tidbits."

His laughter follows him out of the apartment, and I turn toward the speaker in the living room.

"Hey, Google!" I shout. "What are the doughnut holes called at Tim Hortons?"

"*Timbits. Tim Hortons, a popular fast-food chain in Canada, makes Timbits, similar to doughnut holes.*"

"For fuck's sake." I march to the door, throwing it open as Jaxon climbs into the elevator. *"I hate you!"*

He winks at me. "No, you don't, tidbit."

I wish he was wrong. I wish more than anything that he was wrong. And when he comes home three hours later without Timbits, for a moment I think he just might be.

"Hey, tidbit." He kicks off his boots, drops his gym bag to the floor, a grocery bag to the counter. "I didn't get you Timbits because they're not tree-nut-safe. I got you these instead."

He opens the grocery bag, pulling out two boxes of cereal with tiny Timbits on them.

I pick up the boxes, my heart pattering as I read the names.

Timbits Birthday Cake and Timbits Chocolate Glazed.

"They're nut-free," he says, and fucking shit, there goes my goddamn chin *again.*

12

MARVELOUS MITTENS AND HIS . . . MOMMY?

Jaxon

"YOU'D BE, LIKE, SUPER PRETTY if you were a girl."

"I'm super pretty as is," I remind Sarah, and everyone else within earshot.

She stops everything she's doing, frowning. Or maybe it's a grimace. Whatever it is, it's definitely unimpressed, which cannot possibly be right. She pops a fist on her hip, tossing her jet-black hair over her shoulder, narrowing her dark brown eyes. Fuck, there's no attitude like that of a twelve-year-old girl. "Ya know, Jaxon, I think it's really important and great to be confident."

"We love a confident king!" Carter calls from across the table, where he's currently stringing together a friendship bracelet for Olivia. That's what he's calling it, at least, but the letters he's lined up in front of him are L E T S F U C K, and I'm not sure that spells friendship.

"As I was saying before Carter *rudely* interrupted, being confident is great and all, but sometimes"—Sarah grants me a once-over—"a dose of reality is needed too."

"What the fu—rrrck." I throw my hands up, and before I can drag them down my face, Sarah gasps.

"*Don't touch your face! I just did your makeup!*"

"Why do I even come here? Nobody appreciates me. I let you

do my hair, I let you do my makeup, I even let you do my nails"—I tick each one off on my fingers—"and I'm supposed to just *sit here* while you tell me I'm not *pretty* enough?"

"Do you even listen? I simply said you'd be super pretty *if* you were a girl. Now sit still." She dabs her brush in a pot of sparkly pink powder. "I wanna do your eye shadow. And, oh!" She grins, holding up a sheet of star stickers. "Look what I got. They'll look *perfect* in the corners of your eyes."

I roll my eyes before I close them, letting Sarah work her magic. We come here to Second Chance Home as often as we can to spend time with the kids. That means a lot of arts and crafts, hot mess makeup, weird hairdos, and sometimes baking, which is my personal favorite. I also enjoy getting manicures, but I pretend they're the worst so Sarah won't catch on and stop doing them. I enjoy it a lot more than I thought I would, and the first time I walked in here, over a year ago now, Sarah dubbed me her *special project.*

A small hand clasps my arm, and I crack a lid in time to see Lily tug on my elbow.

"Hey, Lil. How's it goin', angel?"

"Hi, Jaxon," she whispers, tucking her brown hair behind her ear, looking around the room. She's only five, a quiet little thing who, like most, prefers Adam to everyone. "Um, is Adam coming today? He's not here." She wrings her tiny hands, lower lip trembling. "Did I do somethin' to make him mad? I didn't mean to."

Christ, my heart. I hold my hand out to her, and she slips hers in tentatively, letting me pull her closer. "Dinosaur ripped up all the toilet paper in the bathroom and made a big mess," I tell her about Adam and Rosie's kitten. "Adam will be here soon, he's just running late."

Lily's shoulders uncurl, brown eyes lighting. She snickers, covering her mouth. "Dinosaur's such a silly kitty."

A menace, really, so when Adam and Rosie told us a month ago they were beginning foster and adoption training, with the goal being to adopt Lily, my first thought was *holy fuck, their house is gonna be a zoo*. On top of their brand-new kitten, they've got two dogs, and Connor. Except a single look at the four of them together tells you the only thing you need to know: Lily was made for Adam and Rosie and Connor. If families are puzzles, Lily is their missing piece. I just wish she didn't have to wait to find that out.

She laces her fingers through mine, plastering herself against my side. "Can I stay with you until he gets here?"

"You can sit with me, Lil," Carter calls. "I'm making Ollie a bracelet." He holds up the monstrosity. "I used these shiny brown beads 'cause they remind me of her eyes. And these star beads, 'cause I love laying on the balcony and watching the stars with her. And these pinkish ones, 'cause they're the same color as her nip—" He mashes his lips together, eyes huge.

Lily looks up at me with wide, begging eyes. "Please don't make me sit with him. He talks so much it makes my ears hurt."

Carter gasps, and Emmett and Garrett high-five Lily.

"Hey, Jax?" Garrett calls, and when I look up to tell him not to call me that, he snaps my picture.

"What the fff . . . rick?" I spread my arms wide as he grins down at his phone. "What are you doing, you donkey?"

"Sending it to Jennie. She's with Lennon."

"What? No! Don't send it to her!"

"Fine." He tucks his phone away, crossing his arms. "I won't."

"Thanks." My phone pings in my pocket, and I pull it out.

Tidbit: How's my prettiest girl doing???

"You fucking liar!" I scream at Garrett, and when everyone yells at me for swearing, I pull up his contact, type out a message, and glare at him while I wait for him to read it.

Me: Ur a dirty fuckin liar.

Garrett: Sorry. Jennie said I had to.

Me: Ever try saying no????

Garrett: LOL

He grins, giving me two thumbs up. When I don't smile, his falls. He taps at his phone.

Garrett: Oh, you were being serious??

Garrett: I never say no to Jennie. She's scary and powerful and beautiful.

I roll my eyes, navigating back to my message thread with Lennon as Sarah dusts blush over my cheekbones.

Me: Good, thx. And how's my wife?

Tidbit: OMG! Brielle's gonna be so happy to hear you call her that *heart eyes emoji*

"You have a *wife?*" Sarah yells. "What the heck? When did that happen?"

"No, it's not—Lennon's not—" I shake my head. "I don't have a wife."

"Yet," Carter says, threading a heart bead onto his bracelet.

"What did you just say?"

"I said yet. As in, you don't have a wife *yet.*" He looks to Sarah. "Lennon's his roommate, but I give it six months."

"*Six months?* Six months till what? She'll be gone in six months! She'll be gone, like, tomorrow!"

"She's moving out?" Emmett asks. "Surprised she found a place so quickly. That's great."

"Well, no . . ."

"No what?"

"She's not moving out. Yet. But she will."

He smiles. "Okay."

"What? Why are you smiling at me like that?"

He shrugs. "No reason, buddy."

"I don't have a wife," I reiterate. "I'm not even having s-e-x right now, in case anyone cares. In fact, it's been so long I'm practically a born-again virgin."

"What's a virgin?" Sarah asks.

"Definitely *not* what Jaxon is," Emmett assures her.

"I think it's nice you have a girlfriend, Jaxon," Lily tells me. "I bet all the hugs feel nice and warm. Adam says huggin' Rosie makes him feel like sunshine. Is that how it feels when you hug your girlfriend?"

"Yeah, Jaxon," Garrett muses. "Does it feel like sunshine when you hug Lennon?"

"Your literal nickname for your girlfriend is sunshine!" I shout at him.

"Because she makes everything bright and warm like sunshine!" he shouts back at me. "And she's my fiancée, not my girlfriend! Get it right!"

"She was my sister first!" Carter chimes in, because why the fuck not.

"Jesus," a voice murmurs from behind me. "Can't leave you guys alone for a half hour without a fight breaking loose."

"Adam!" Lily scrambles out of her seat, tripping over her feet on the way. She sprawls out on the floor, and Adam scoops her up, clutching her to his chest, where she throws her arms around his neck. "I missed you," she whispers, and he closes his eyes, squeezing her tighter.

"I missed you *so* much, Lily-bug."

She reclaims her seat beside me, grinning at Adam when he

flanks her other side. Then she turns her beam on me. "It feels like sunshine when I hug Adam. All my dark spots feel bright and happy again. I hope it feels like that when you hug your girlfriend."

"She's not my girlfriend," I grumble, hanging my head as Sarah starts yanking the hair there into a ponytail.

"Yet."

It's not Carter this time. It's Adam.

"WHAT IN THE FUCK IS this?"

I stop inside my entryway, arms out wide as I take in my condo. The question is a loaded one, because:

a) there are five girls in my living room, spread out on my furniture;
b) there appears to be a porno playing somewhere, judging by the sounds coming from my speaker; and finally
c) my entire apartment is covered in pink.

Lennon looks up from her spot on the floor, grinning. "Jax! You're home!"

"He lets you call him Jax?" Cara stares at me from where she's hanging upside down on the couch. "What the fuck, Jax? You yell at me when I do it."

"I yell at her too." I stalk toward them, ignoring the way Lennon, Cara, Olivia, Jennie, and Rosie all watch me with a smile. I circle my hand around them. "What the fuck is this? Some sort of girls' night? In my apartment?"

Jennie winks. "Nailed it."

"And this?" I point toward the ceiling, eyes roaming as I listen to the words drifting around us.

"Her tongue circles my nipple before trailing down the center of

my torso, around my belly button. She settles herself between my thighs, a playful glint in her eyes that has my hips bucking, a silent beg for more. She laughs softly, her breath tickling my clit. 'Want my fingers first, or my tongue?'"

"Sounds like a porno, but there's nothing on TV!"

"It's book club," Olivia tells me. "Audio version. My first sapphic romance! I'm *obsessed.*"

"And *this*?" I sweep my arms out wide, perhaps a little aggressively, gesturing at all my brand-new pink décor. "What in the *fuck* is this?"

"Valentine's Day decorations," my *roomie* answers, the *duh* hanging heavy in the air. "We went shopping today."

"It's not Valentine's Day!"

"It's February first, Jaxon! *Excuse me* for trying to brighten up the place with a bit of festive fun!"

"It doesn't need brightening up!"

"Not anymore it doesn't!

"I *explicitly* said no pink! Do you remember that?"

"And I *explicitly* said pink was my favorite color! Do you remember *that*?"

I groan, dragging my hands down my face. That's when I spot Mittens, sprawled out on his back in the middle of this pack of wild animals, a pair of glasses, a scrap of plaid fabric—for some fucking reason—and a book with three naked men on the cover sitting next to him. I point at him, at the whole . . . *scene*, but no words come out, so I just raise my brows in question.

Lennon gives me a teeth-gritting grin. "Yeahhh, sooo . . . We had a bit of a photoshoot." She hands me her phone, and I flick through at least twenty photos of my cat in various positions, wearing reading glasses and a kilt, reading a *why choose* romance.

"Len, what the fuck? You can't just take pictures of my cat in vulnerable pos—"

"The one where he's looking over his shoulder has over ten thousand likes on Instagram already."

My brows skyrocket. "Ten thousand, you say?"

She glances at her phone. "Thirteen now."

"Where are you posting these?"

"I made him an Instagram."

"What? Lemme see." I sprawl out next to her on the floor, scooching close as she pulls up the app. "Marvelous Mittens," I murmur, reading his handle. "That's good. I like that." I point at a picture of him at the kitchen counter, wearing a tiny chef's hat and positioned in front of a mixing bowl. "What's that one? Lemme see. That's so good." I chuckle. "He's so fucking cute. Twenty thousand likes? Holy fuck, my son's a star!" I roll to my side, chin propped on my fist, elbow on the ground so I can look at Lennon. "Hey, you should get one in the morning when he's on the chaise lounge. He looks so majestic when the sun rises on him through that window."

I scoop Mittens up, collapsing onto my back as I hold him above me. "That's my famous boy. Everyone loves you, don't they? Yes, they do, squishy, handsome boy." I clutch him to my chest, his face squished against mine. "Len, honey, get this shot."

She rolls her eyes but complies, snickering.

"Should we get him a manager?"

"Oh my God." Lennon claps her hands to the floor, shoving her excited face in mine. "What if we get him a spot on a commercial? That toilet paper—"

"—that does commercials with fluffy kittens!" I shoot up to sitting, nearly hammering her face in the process. "Yes, Len, amazing idea! He'll be the new face of the Royale brand!"

"Well," someone says, and *oh shit*, I totally forgot there was other people in this room. Rosie stands, stretching her arms above her head. "Ladies, I think this is our cue."

Olivia scoops up her bag. "Yeah, I feel like we're interrupting an intimate moment."

"What intimate moment?" My pulse races, which is the only reason I ask again, "What intimate moment?"

"They're joking," Lennon says, but the way she jumps to her feet and puts distance between us, fixing her hair even though it's already perfect, tells me she's as uncomfortable as I am.

"I'm not joking," Jennie says, following Olivia and Rosie to the door. "It's giving *we're about to fuck* vibes in here, and I don't want to be here when that happens."

Cara stands, tucking her things into her purse. "I, personally, could get behind some voyeurism, but I draw the line at my friends." She stops before us, smiling her famous Cara I-could-fuck-you-up Brodie smile. With two fingers, she points at her eyes, then us, and whispers, "The Coochie Gang sees all."

Lennon looks at me, but I'm already looking at her, so she quickly schools her scared expression into a glare. "You wish, fuckboy." She follows the girls to the door, pausing only to toss the middle finger at me over her shoulder, but I barely see it because she's wearing those tiny sleep shorts she loves, the ones that crawl up her ass, let the bottom of her plush cheeks peek out. When Destiny's Child wrote "Bootylicious," they were talking about Lennon's ass, I'm certain of it.

I turn away as the girls take turns hugging Lennon. She seems so at home with them, like she's always been part of the group. Part of me is envious of her confidence. How does she do that, so easily accept that she's one of them, that her place is permanent? I don't know what permanent feels like. I'm well-versed in temporary, though.

A hand closes around my elbow, and I turn around, finding the girls lined up behind me.

Rosie smiles, kissing my cheek, then Mittens. "Bye, Jaxon. Love you."

Olivia is next, pulling my face down so she can reach my cheek. "Bye, Jaxon. Love you."

Jennie pecks my cheek and rubs Mittens's belly. "Love you, Jaxon."

Cara tugs on my earlobe. I swat her hand away. She presses a kiss to my cheek, which is, by the way, now warm as fuck, and I hate it. "Love you, Jax."

"Don't call me Jax," I whisper, swallowing down the panic that doesn't know how to respond, the same panic that's afraid that love will be taken away if I don't do something and do it fast. "Love you, too, I guess," I say quietly, and when they smile back at me from the door, it's like the fist squeezing my heart eases its grip just a touch.

The door closes, and I'm left alone with Lennon, my superstar son, and the sex scene that's currently playing through the speakers in my living room.

Lennon shuts off the audiobook, avoiding my gaze. She's got her hair tied back today, two braids that start at her hairline and meet at the nape of her neck, where her curls are wrapped in a bun. She's always pretty, but there's something about her like this, showing off her high cheekbones, her wide, dark eyes, the golden glow of her brown skin, and her full, heart-shaped lips, the perfect bow that sits at the top of them.

Cautious eyes lift to mine, and she runs her fingers along one of her braids. "Um, I'm just gonna use the bathroom, then I'll clean up in here."

She takes off before I can respond, and I wander through the apartment, checking out the décor that's been barfed up all over it. There's so much pink, a zillion different shades of it, and at least 75 percent of it is shimmering. Tinsel draped along the edge of my kitchen island, wrapped around the window frames. Red hearts with pink scalloped hems hang from the ceiling, and there's a wooden bowl on my kitchen counter with knitted *x*'s and *o*'s. Why they're in my kitchen I've got no fucking clue. Last time I checked, yarn isn't edible.

Mittens crawls up my chest and drapes himself over my shoulders, and I reach back, keeping my hand on him as I amble over to the bookcase. Red and pink heart garland lines each shelf. There's a small vase with fake pink flowers, a heart-shaped dish with red, purple, and pink Smarties in it, which I immediately shove my hand into, grabbing a fistful and stuffing it in my mouth, and a small picture that says *be mine* on it in fancy, curly letters. On the bottom shelf, there's even a heart-shaped cat bed, one Mittens eagerly curls up in when I place him in it.

My gaze rises to the top shelf, and my heartbeat slows to a crawl. Right in the center is the photo of Bryce and me, my childhood best friend, but instead of the same broken frame it's been in for more than fifteen years, it's now tucked safely inside a stunning wooden frame.

I pick up the rustic walnut, running my finger over the divots, the imperfections that make it what it is, and my heart stops altogether when I see the words etched into the bottom of the frame, right below the picture. My name and his, side by side, mine in my messy writing, his in the scrawl that was always neater than mine.

Blood drums in my ears as I pull the backing off the frame, finding the same writing there. I trace the blue ink, the letters of his name, and angry, heartbroken tears gather in my eyes. Because it should be him living out his dream, a star goalie in the NHL. Because he would be if it weren't for me.

Because if it weren't for me, he'd still be here.

I don't hear Lennon enter the room. I don't see her as she approaches me. But I feel her the second she's beside me. The air around me changes, thick and heavy somehow. Maybe it's all that heartache I've been keeping locked up all these years. My gran always said one day it would come pouring out of me, that I wouldn't be able to hold it on my own anymore, that I'd need someone else to help me carry it.

The thing about needing someone else is that there will inevitably come a day when they're not there. In my experience, that day is most often the one you need them most.

Like when you're looking down at your best friend, lifeless and wearing his best suit, the one he used to wear on game days. And your tie is on all wrong, because you never could quite figure out how to loop the two ends properly, and today is really fucking important and you just want to get it right and look nice for him.

But the person who always fixed it for you is the same person who can't now.

"You two look like you were trouble."

The corner of my mouth hooks up as I glide the pad of my thumb over Bryce's heart, like I might be able to feel it beat through the picture. "I was the bad influence, and he was the faithful friend who went along with every one of my bad ideas. Never let me take all the blame, either."

"I just knew you were the bad influence," Lennon murmurs, eyes on a ten-year-old me. "That smile just screams trouble." She smiles up at me, a sight so unexpectedly soft it knocks me back a half step. "Same as it does now."

She gives my bicep a gentle squeeze before she leaves me with the photo, cleaning up the living room from the aftershock of girls' night. I stare down at Bryce a moment longer before I tuck the frame back on the shelf, whispering a barely there, "Miss you, buddy," before I help Lennon put the room back together.

When we're done, I follow her into the kitchen, where she pulls out cheddar cheese, mayo, and pimentos. I feel the way my eyes light, and I know Lennon can see it, because she chuckles.

"Pimento cheese?" I ask excitedly, hands clasped at my chest. When she nods, I race to the pantry. "I have a fresh loaf of bread!"

Another one of Mimi's famous recipes, and if they're all as good as this one, I can see why they're famous. Lennon first made it for me two weeks ago, and I loved it so much she now keeps the fridge stocked with the ingredients so she can make it whenever I'm in one of my *moods*, as she calls them.

Okay, *I* keep the ingredients stocked in the fridge, and sometimes I fake my moods just so she'll make it.

She hands me a grater and the cheddar, and I get to work shredding it as she measures out the ingredients.

The silence we work in is comfortable, so maybe that's why I swallow down the reminder that I don't do this, that I don't talk about personal things with anyone, let alone a woman I slept with once, and quietly ask her, "Did you ever have a friend like that?"

"I *was* that friend," she says with a laugh. "My cousin Serena was the bad influence. She *is* the bad influence."

"Where is she now?"

"Serena? At home in Augusta." Her eyes come to mine, and I see the question there, the hesitation that keeps her from voicing it. She wants to know where Bryce is, and maybe deep down she knows. Maybe that's why she chooses not to ask. Whatever the reason, I'm glad. "I wasn't ever that person with a ton of friends."

"I thought you were in a sorority?"

"I was, but—and I don't know, maybe other people have different experiences—those people weren't my friends. When it was convenient, sure. But none of them were there for real problems, for any of the hard shit. Hell, not a single one showed at Gramps's funeral when he passed in junior year." She shakes her head, a tiny furrow between her brows as she sniffs. "Show friends, not real friends. That's what my brother called them when he found me crying behind the church, wondering why no one came to support me." She pastes on a smile, every bit as bright as it is fake. "You're lucky to have your friends. They're the kind you hold on to, that always show up for you."

They do always show up for me. But how long will that last? If I were traded tomorrow, would they show up for me next year if I needed them? Past experience dictates that answer.

No.

But instead, I tell Lennon, "They're your friends too."

She shrugs. "I'm just passing by, and they're being nice."

I cock my head. "You can't seriously think that. They love you. And sure, they're all nice, but they don't just pull in any random person and give them a spot in their chosen family."

She lifts a brow, all parts amused. "And *you* can't seriously think you're not a part of that family."

"What? I didn't say that."

"You don't have to say it, Jaxon. Your actions do it for you. You think you're not really one of them. That's why you were so embarrassed and thrown when the girls told you they loved you tonight."

I don't know how to respond, and I don't really want to, so I turn away, hiding the heat staining my neck, creeping into my ears. I find the spatula, handing it to Lennon, standing by as she mixes it, and when my phone rings, my gran's name lighting my screen, I panic.

I bury my head in the pantry, answering the video request with a hushed whisper. "I can't talk right now, Gran. Can I call you later?"

"Oh, I see how it is. I give you the world, all my love, and the secret to the best grilled cheese sandwiches, and you repay me by not having any time for me?"

"What? No. I always have time—I don't—ugh. Gran, I—"

"Are you talking to yourself in your pantry, Jaxon?" Lennon asks. "Just when I think you can't get any weirder."

"I'm not—no, I—"

"Jaxon Eugene Riley," Gran gasps. "Is that a *woman*?"

"*Eugene?*" Lennon squeals, and my life ends as I hear the tap of her fingers against her phone. "Taking this straight to the Coochie Gang. The girls are never going to believe this, Eugene."

I roll my eyes and groan, smacking my forehead off the cereal shelf in my pantry. This is exactly what I was trying to avoid, introducing the two women in my life who live to annoy me. When I glance at my phone, my gran is waiting there, sitting at her old Formica kitchen table, her crossword in front of her, and that damn eyebrow raised so motherfucking high.

Suddenly, Lennon appears over my shoulder.

"Oh my God, you must be Gran! I've heard so much about you!" She tears my phone from my hand, taking Gran to the counter, propping her up against a cup. "I'm Lennon. You've probably not heard a word about me." She drops her elbow to the counter, her chin to her fist. "Hey, has it always been like pulling teeth to get Jaxon to open up?"

Gran's blue eyes light, and she grins. "Oh, Lennon, honey. How much time do you have? We have so much to talk about."

I groan again, this one extra dramatic, super long and loud while I fold my entire upper body over the counter, pressing my cheek to the cool marble. "Fuck my life."

"Watch your language, young man."

"Yes, ma'am," I mumble into the counter, but no one's listening. Gran's busy telling Lennon about the time I found her period pads and attached them to the inside of my T-shirt, over my nipples, insisted on wearing them to the grocery store, and then proceeded to tell everyone there that my nipples were menstruating. I was only six, but apparently that detail doesn't matter to Lennon, because she's laughing so hard she's crying.

I cross my arms over my chest. "Don't get your tears in my pimento cheese."

"Oh, watch out, honey," Gran says. "If you start feeding him, you'll never be rid of him."

"*I'm* the one housing *her!*" I reach for the dip when Lennon finishes mixing it, but she smacks my hand away, snapping the lid on.

"Jaxon, it needs to chill."

"I just wanna taste it! Make sure you got the ratios right and shit."

"Please. You know I never miss." She tucks the bowl in the fridge, then carries Gran into the living room. I follow, my jaw hanging, watching as she snuggles in on the couch with my cat, chatting with my gran over FaceTime like they've known each other their whole lives. I sprawl out next to her, poking her thigh with my toes, because I want attention and I have none. Lennon lays her hand over my ankle, squeezing gently, and I don't know why, but my chest tightens.

By the time Gran is saying good night, her daily crossword is done, they've made weekly plans to video chat, and she's got Lennon's measurements for a special crochet project, which is exactly as terrifying as it sounds.

Lennon and I set up shop on the couch with the cooled dip, Mittens snoring quietly between us as we argue over what to watch. We settle on some dramatic show about hot firefighters, mostly because Lennon nearly knocked me out cold with a knee to my face when she dove for the remote. She ends up crying through two episodes straight, then yells at *me* for picking an emotional show.

It's nearly midnight when I follow her down the hall, Mittens clinging to her chest, and I swear to God the cat is wearing a shit-eating grin as he stares at me from over her shoulder.

"You can't sleep with her," I remind him when she sets him down outside her door. He glances at me, seems to size me up, then turns his back on me and struts right through her door and into her room. "Fucking asshole," I mutter. My gaze falls to Lennon, who happens to be failing at hiding her smug amusement. "Listen, if Mitts is gonna be Mr. Worldwide, we'll have to make sure the fame doesn't go to his head. You know what can happen to a cat with unsupervised access to fame. I won't let him be a statistic."

She works so damn hard to hold back her laugh, tongue in her cheek, lips pressed together. But it's the sparkle in her brown eyes, the way they seem to come more and more alive the more I give her, that's what gives me this strange sense of pride. Someone wants to know me, and the more she learns, the more she seems to want to stay. I'm not sure I've ever felt that before.

"You weren't lying about your gran. She's fantastic."

"The best."

Lennon smiles up at me, and because I know what she wants to ask, what's stuck in her throat, because giving her pieces of me feels nicer than I thought it would, I tell her, "I never met my parents. They died in a wreck. My mom was thirty-seven weeks pregnant, and they were able to save me. Gran stepped in and raised me."

Lennon's eyes are saucers, gigantic and soft, and I watch them fill with compassion right before my own eyes. She opens her mouth, and I hold my hand up, stopping her.

"It's okay. I couldn't have asked for a better gran. Not a day went by that I didn't feel how much she loved me, and she made sure I knew how much my parents loved me, too, even though we never got to meet. I'm okay."

Her eyes move between mine, and she nods, a silent understanding. I've said as much as I want to say about it.

And then Lennon steps forward, wrapping her arms around me, and because I'm not used to all these displays of affection, my mouth drops and my arms hang awkwardly in the air. "Thanks for letting me have girls' night here."

"You didn't ask me. I just came home and they were here and there was porn playing through my speakers."

"It was really fun."

I chuckle, finally letting my arms come around her while my heart patters in my chest. She feels warm, and it makes me feel warm too. I breathe her in, soak in the way she wraps herself around me, makes me feel worth a little more than I felt yesterday, the way the dark spots feel a little brighter now that I'm not sitting in them all alone.

"Thank you, Lennon," I whisper. *For the picture frame. For Gran.*

For the hug.

"You're welcome, Jax."

"Don't call me Jax."

She pops up on her toes, pressing a soft kiss to my cheek. When she backs into her room and Mittens meows his demand for her to hurry, the sparkle in her eyes turns evil, same as her smirk. "Pretty soon, your cat's gonna be calling me Mommy."

My outraged gasp is lost to her cackle and the sound of the bedroom door slamming in my face.

13

ABOUT FUCKING TIME

Lennon

ONE OF THE BEST PERKS of this job is, by far, that I get paid to listen to porn.

Okay, so, it's not exactly like that. First of all, it's not porn. It's romance with explicit, dirty, downright filthy sex. Second, I get paid for plane travel, and that time is mine to do with it what I please.

Sometimes, like tonight as we fly home to Vancouver, that means apartment hunting on my laptop, while the grumpy mafia don, playing through my headphones, shouts at everyone to get out of his office so he can bend his mouthy wife—an arranged marriage, obviously—over his desk and fuck the submission into her because she came to his office wearing a low-cut top and miniskirt just to piss him off.

"This one's nice," I murmur to myself as Dante grips a fistful of Gia's hair and tells her to get on her knees. I click through the one-bedroom apartment, pretending my nose doesn't wrinkle at the brown water stains on the walls in the bathroom, or the one above the bed. Gia takes Dante as far back as she can as I find another apartment, this one more expensive but somehow worse than the last.

Out of the corner of my eye, I catch someone stand, their wide frame taking up the aisle. My gaze rises to Jaxon as he strolls toward me. Hazel eyes lock on mine, and when he flicks my shoulder, I jam my elbow into his thigh. It's a weird game we play on road trips, like we barely know each other. Sometimes we don't speak at all, just share these little moments of peace. Many of them occur postgame in the local bar, where I watch him get hit on by woman after woman, and he watches me flirt with whoever I feel like flirting with just because I kinda like having all of Jaxon's attention, and that always ensures I have it.

The weirdest part, though, is having a space all my own for those couple of days. The only time I've spent living by myself is the single week in Vancouver before my apartment turned into the Lost City of Atlantis. I'm supposed to be learning how to be by myself, being totally and completely independent. Lately, though, I'm struggling with the notion of whether it's more important to be able to stand on your own, or to have someone at your side you rely on, someone to step in, hold you up when you need it. Ryne held me up when I needed it, but as the years went on, he started throwing it back in my face as often as he could. If I could've done it on my own, I would have. I *needed* him.

I turn the volume up on my headphones, because I'd rather listen to Gia ask Dante for permission to swallow his load than think about Ryne.

"Oooh," I hum, clicking on a listing for a one-bedroom plus den apartment in a duplex. It's a little outside my budget, and farther than I'd hoped, but the kitchen is roomy, there's space for me to spread out my photography, and the bathroom has a ceiling. I start typing out a request to view the apartment, but stop when an exceptionally large shadow falls over me.

One perfect, corded, tattooed arm grips my thigh, and I slip out an AirPod as Jaxon's chin dips to my shoulder, his tongue flicking over the split in the center of his lip. He got in another fight tonight. I thought my heart stopped when I watched him fall to the ice after taking a dirty hit from behind, but then he leapt to his feet, chased after the jerk, and three minutes later when Jaxon skated off the ice, knuckles and mouth tinged red, I had to stop by the beer kiosk for a cup of ice. I seriously don't know what's wrong with me. Watching Jaxon turn into an animal on the ice does something filthy to me. And the bruise forming beneath his left eye? The icing on the cupcake.

"What are we looking at, tidbit?"

God, this new nickname is driving me up the wall. I never thought I'd see the day I'd be begging for *honey*.

"New apartments, so I don't have to hear you call me tidbit one more time, or see *your* tidbit again." I aim a pointed look at his crotch.

Something flits through his eyes, and he spins my laptop toward him, ignoring my funny joke about his tiny cock, which is actually not at all tiny; he knows it and I know it. "Lemme see."

"Can you just—*ugh*." I scowl, jerking my laptop back. "You're so bossy."

"Yeah." He slips by me, plopping down in the empty seat next to me, scooping up my cheetah-print neck pillow and slinging it around his neck. "Show me." He steals my Sour Keys off my tray, winking at me as his sucks one into his mouth. "Don't make me wait, honey."

I narrow my gaze, and when I open my mouth to tell him to fuck off, he shoves a Sour Key between my lips. I hook my pinky through the little hole, sucking on the treat as I flip back to the apartment listings, starting with the shittiest one so the best one looks like a dream by the time I get there.

"So, there's this—"

"No."

"Jaxon, you can't—"

"Len, are you kidding me? There are fucking *brown stains* on the ceiling! You'll be back living with me in a week when your ceiling collapses all over again!"

"Okay, well—" I navigate to the second one. "This one's nicer."

"It's worse. How is it worse? It's more expensive; that makes no sense." He jabs my screen. "There's a literal *hole* eaten through the wood of this cupboard. You like mice? 'Cause Mitts isn't gonna be there to save you from them."

A growl rumbles in my chest, so I go for the big guns, the best one. "Here. There's nothing wrong with this one, and there's even a little office space for me."

He scans the screen, looking for something to complain about as he covers my hand with his, forcing my finger to click through each picture. Then, he sits back, and simply says, "Nah."

"Pardon me?"

"It's too far from the arena."

"You know, it's the oddest thing but they have these things called automobiles. Invented way back in the eighteen hundreds. Yeah, they're super great for getting around."

Jaxon watches me, knees waving in and out as he sucks on his Sour Key. "There's mold."

"No there isn't."

"It's small."

"It's cozy."

He rolls his eyes. "Another word for small."

"I don't need a big space, Jaxon. It's just me."

He taps his finger on my tray. Instead of arguing with me, he asks, "What are you listening to?" and then promptly steals my AirPod, sticking it in his own ear. *"Jesus fuck,"* he screams, tearing the bud out, leaping to his feet. "That's-that's-that's—" He points at me with a shaking hand. "Gia . . . Gia . . ."

"Gia's getting fucked six ways to Sunday." She's also got a thumb in her bum, because Dante just told her every single one of her holes belongs to him, but that's neither here nor there.

"You were sitting next to me, on a plane filled with people, looking at apartments, while listening to *that*?"

"Multitasker is on my résumé."

He presses the heels of his palms to his eyes. "I have to scrub my eyes out."

"Why? Did they figure out how to hear sound?"

Hazel eyes narrow. "You're so fuckin' annoying, I swear to God."

"Like I said before, Jax, annoying must be your type."

He shakes his head, climbing out of the row. Halfway up the aisle, he stops and turns back to me, scratching the back of his head. "I'm just . . . I'm not kicking you out or anything. 'Kay?"

My eyes move between his, searching for the lie. When I don't find it, I nod. "'Kay."

"Jaxon!" Carter shouts from his seat, holding up a deck of cards. "You coming?" His gaze comes to me. "Actually, Len, you know how to play euchre? Jaxon sucks; we can ditch him for you."

I do, actually, but I'm 99 percent sure Jaxon has a complex about being replaceable, so I pout, shaking my head. "Sorry."

"You can still hang with us if you want."

"Thanks, but—" I hold up my laptop, hoping it's answer enough. I've infiltrated every part of Jaxon's life, and he's handled it relatively well. I'd rather not take this time from him. Plus, I like watching him interact with the guys.

Like right now, as he takes a seat with Carter, Garrett, and Emmett around a table, starts bickering with Garrett about who has to partner with Carter, leans over to check in with Adam about what book he's reading tonight. There isn't a single conversation he doesn't try to participate in, and he's not shy about starting them either, like he's trying so hard to get to know them, to make himself a permanent fixture in their lives. And yet, when the questions come back to him, he offers next to nothing, shaking his head, shrugging, playing it off like his life is boring.

I watch him for a moment, his grin so big as he takes the first euchre hand, pulling the cards in front of him, high-fiving Emmett. There's something so boyish about him like this, an innocence that pulls me in. It lives in the light of his eyes, behind the giddiness of his smile, like he's just . . . *grateful* to be included. It makes me as happy as it does sad.

He looks up, catching my eye, and I'm almost irritated at the way he immediately looks away, picks up his phone.

Until an iMessage pops up in the center of my laptop.

Magic Mike: Take a picture, honey. It'll last longer.

I look up, flipping him the bird. His grin widens, and when he winks, I hide my smile behind a Sour Key. Navigating back to my email, I stare at it for a minute, contemplating Jaxon's words.

There's no rush.

But isn't there? He hasn't left with a single woman postgame, despite all the women that try with their whole chest. And he's certainly not bringing anyone home. The bottom line is I'm cramping his style. Isn't it best I leave before I overstay my welcome?

The thought alone makes my head hurt, but since Jaxon promised he's not kicking me out anytime soon, I close the email, then the apartment listings. At the very least, I have a little more time to find something better suited and within my price range. With that in mind, I recline my seat, pop my AirPods back in, turn the volume up, and google *where to see the Northern Lights near Vancouver.* I open the number one hit, but before I have a chance to appreciate the stunning hues of deep blues, teals, and greens, a FaceTime request from PIECE OF MOTHERFUCKING SHIT takes over my screen, and I scream, throwing my laptop to my feet.

"Len?" Jaxon's on his feet in a heartbeat, the other boys following.

"It's fine." I wave my arms around, shooing them back to their seats. "I thought I saw a spider."

"Spider?" Garrett shifts himself behind Adam. "I don't like spiders. Nothing needs that many legs."

Carter's chest puffs. "I can get it."

"Nope, it's totally fine." I force a smile, hitting the decline button as I scoop up my laptop and sit back down. "It was just a piece of garbage."

The boys fall back to their seats, but Jaxon hesitates. I give him a thumbs-up and another forced smile before looking away, because sometimes I think he's secretly really great at reading me, and I'd rather he didn't right now.

So when PIECE OF MOTHERFUCKING SHIT calls again, I decline it in an outwardly calm manner while the fiery depths of hell boil and rage inside me.

The third time, my eye starts twitching, and the fourth time, my fingernails leave gouge marks in my palms.

The fifth time he calls, this time audio only, I smash the accept button and whisper-scream, "*What?*" at my laptop.

"Oh, wow," Ryne's whiny voice murmurs through my ear buds. "The queen has finally graced me with her voice."

"I'm gonna grace your balls with my fist if you don't stop calling me."

He chuckles, and it's as patronizing as it's always been. "You always did beg for rough sex."

I grit my teeth, then run my palm over my face when Jaxon's eyes flick to me. "Goodbye."

"Are you on a plane right now?"

"Did you not hear me? I said goodbye. That means this conversation is over."

"I heard you took a job with a hockey team."

"So you heard that but you didn't hear me say goodbye?"

"You fucking the players, Lenny?"

My knee bounces, and I curl my shaking fingers into a fist. "Yes. All of them. Sometimes at the same time. You fuck the wait staff at our wedding?"

He chuckles, and I imagine his head imploding so that I don't. "I didn't fuck her that night."

That night. I didn't fuck her *that night.*

"You're a piece of shit," I whisper, and for fuck's sake, will Jaxon stop fucking looking at me?

"Was I supposed to sit by and wait for you to come to your senses and come home after your little hissy fit at our wedding rehearsal? Real mature, by the way, Lenny. My partners were there."

I scoff, loud and disbelieving, because *be for fucking real.*

"You're mistaken," I mutter, hiding the words behind my hand when Jaxon's eyes flare. "I don't give a shit what or who you do. What you do with your life isn't my business, because it's not my life anymore."

A message pops up on my screen, forcing me to breathe.

Magic Mike: U ok?

"Lennon. You're my *wife.* You're *supposed to be* my wife. My whole damn firm was there, watched you walk out on me like some melodramatic preteen. You *embarrassed* me. You can hardly blame me for seeking comfort somewhere else."

Magic Mike: Len??

Magic Mike: Who u talkin to?

Magic Mike: Do I need to come back there
and make heads roll?

Magic Mike: Fuckin answer me honey or I'm
coming back there.

"If you're ready to apologize, sweetheart, I think we can move past this. We can get married at the courthouse, tell everyone we made up and eloped, and Grandmother's said she can host an intimate celebration of one hundred guests until we can have a proper wedding in the summer."

This entire thing is ridiculous, but it's that his grandmother thinks a hundred people is an intimate celebration that tips me over the edge. "You've really lost it, haven't y—wait a second." I hold up a finger, replaying his words in my head. "If *I'm* ready to apologize? And just what the fuck do I have to apologize for?"

There's movement in the cabin, sudden and heavy, and I glance up in time to see Jaxon leap to his feet. I appreciate the hell out of the fact that my frenemy roommate cares enough to come to my rescue, but goddammit, I'm so sick and tired of not being able to rescue myself.

I hold my hand up, stopping him in his tracks.

"Jesus, Lenny, you really don't see that what you did was wrong? How immature and selfish it was of you?" Ryne chuckles, a sound of utter disbelief, absolutely flooring me with just how out of touch with reality he is. "I told you, those books you listen to only serve to plant unrealistic ideas in your head of what romance really is, of what it means to be a partner."

"I've not ever been a partner," I bite out. "I've been the pretty trophy on your arm. The story you tell to make you look like a family man. I've played every damn part you asked me to play to make you look good to people whose opinions shouldn't matter, and somewhere along the way I forgot who I was, who I was supposed to be. So excuse me for chasing romance on paper when real life showed me none. Excuse me for escaping to a fantasy world where the idea that someone might love me so wholly, so obsessively, isn't far-fetched." I pause. "No, actually, excuse *you* for being such a selfish prick and depriving me of that. You're a piece of shit, Ryne. Goodbye."

I snap my laptop shut and tear my earbuds out, chest heaving as adrenaline courses through me, the words I've been dying to scream at him finally set free.

Jaxon hovers in the aisle, fists flexing at his sides. I'm too angry to talk to him right now, to reassure him that I'm fine, that he doesn't need to fight anyone. He overheard more than I'd like, and it's not something I'd ever planned on discussing with him.

The woman you fucked in Cabo was alone on her honeymoon because her fiancé, as it turns out, had no intention of being faithful to one woman for the rest of his life.

I'm not generally a self-conscious person, but being cheated on certainly has a way of bringing all your perceived flaws to the forefront of your mind, of making you feel more worthless of love than you've ever, *ever* felt.

That's how I felt, at least, when Ryne accidentally butt-dialed Serena the night of our wedding rehearsal. Serena, whose phone was connected to the projector in the dinner hall, casting onto the giant screen as she prepared to share a slideshow of me from birth to twenty-six.

Except instead of photos of me, the fifty people enjoying their dinner at our wedding rehearsal got to listen to Ryne tell one of the waitresses that she was such a good girl for taking his cock so far back.

IT'S NOT JAXON I'M MAD at. It's not Jaxon I'm mad at. It's not Jaxon I'm mad at.

The words have been on repeat in my head from the moment I slid into his passenger seat fifteen minutes ago, after stepping off the plane.

He hasn't said a word to me, but I feel his eyes on me the entire drive home.

"Wanna watch the road?" I bark out.

"Sorry," he murmurs, and I close my eyes.

It's not Jaxon I'm mad at. It's not Jaxon I'm mad at. It's not Jaxon I'm mad at.

"Lennon?" Jaxon whispers into the dark car. "You okay?"

"Nope."

"Do you wanna t—"

"Nope."

"'Kay." He drums his fingers on the steering well, whistles what I'm almost certain is the tune of "Soft Kitty" from *The Big Bang Theory*. "So, listen, I'm normally really good at minding my business, but—"

"He called to remind me I made the right decision."

Jaxon pulls into his parking space. "And what's that?"

"Starting over as far as possible from him." I grab my bag, slam the door, and stalk toward the elevator. We ride in silence, greeted by more of it upstairs, and I hate every second of it. It's after one a.m., so we can't pick up Mittens until the morning. Right now, I'd like nothing more than to climb into bed and angry-cry myself to sleep with my face stuffed into the softness of his belly. Instead, I ditch my shoes at the door and march down the hall with Jaxon in tow.

"Lennon?" He pauses in his door, right before I can shut mine. "I think you're funny and cool and you're definitely the most beautiful girl I've ever seen in my entire life. You're also strong and brave, and nobody is worth you feeling worthless." Hazel eyes move over me, and the warmth that softens their edges heats me from my head to my toes, sends my pulse racing. "Don't give him that power."

He's right. I know he's right.

Power is something I rarely felt I had in all my years with Ryne. At first, I liked it. For a while, I even convinced myself it was what love was supposed to look like, feel like. Someone to look after me. Someone for me to follow. Giving Ryne the power he wanted felt like being shrouded in a safety blanket.

And then my feet got tangled. I lost my footing, stumbled my way through years of uncertainty, trying to remember who I was, becoming who I wanted to be.

Then I decided I wanted to take it back, all that power. And I did.

I took back my power when I left him, right then and there at our wedding rehearsal, in front of fifty guests, after catching him getting a blow job from one of the wait staff.

I took back my power when I fucked Jaxon in the bed I was supposed to be fucking my husband in.

I took back my power when I took this job and started all over again in another country.

Now I've had a taste for it, I want more. Need more. *Crave it.*

I think that's the thing about power. You have to consciously decide you want it. That you want to feel it coursing through your veins as you take control of your life, your destiny. And you have to go after it.

Because this life is mine. The decisions I make are mine. I get to decide the way this life plays out. I get to decide what I want and how I chase it.

I throw open my bedroom door, heart slamming against my chest.

I don't think twice before I fling Jaxon's door open.

He glances over his shoulder, pausing in taking his shirt off. Something like understanding flickers in his eyes, and he turns toward me, slowly pulling his shirt over his head.

My throat runs dry at the sight of him, carved and tattooed

muscles flexing as he moves toward me, hooking his thumbs in the waistband of his sweats, dragging them down his thighs. He steps out of them, tossing them over his shoulder in the hamper, all without taking his eyes off me, without faltering in his stalk toward me.

Fuck, he's gorgeous. One of those people so beautiful it hurts to look at them.

But he makes me feel beautiful too. Desired. Craved. I've never once been worshiped the way he did so flawlessly that night in Cabo. It's a high I've been chasing ever since I allowed myself one last glance at him, sleep rumpled in my bed, before I left him there.

My breath comes in uneven spurts, chest heaving, my hands trembling as his steps force me backward. He reaches behind me, and the sound of the door slamming startles me before my back collides with it.

Jaxon looms above me, and I swear I can see his pulse pounding in his neck, racing the same way mine is. One more step, and he's pressed against me, the hard lines of his body grazing the soft edges of mine. He catches my shaking hand, his eyes falling to the connection. There's that signature arrogance, the sharp quirk of his mouth, right there in the corner. He knows how *desperately* I need this. How desperately I want this.

Fingertips dance up my arm, across my collarbone, catching the lone spiral lying there, twirling it softly around his finger before letting it spring free. His gaze rises to mine, sparked with the same feral need buzzing through me.

A rough palm skates up my throat, gripping my jaw, tilting my face to his. "What do you want, honey?"

"You."

He licks the corner of his mouth, right where a grin is starting.

"'Bout fuckin' time" is all he murmurs before his mouth collides with mine.

14

SUDDENLY I HAVE AMNESIA

Lennon

THIS.

This is the high I've been chasing. The scrape of his teeth against my throat. The bite of his fingertips digging into my hips, holding me where he wants me. The ragged exhale, feathering across every exposed inch of skin he tastes as he rips my clothes off. The feel of his swollen cock grinding against me. The heady feeling that rushes through me, knowing he wants me the way I want him. The shiver that tumbles down my spine, following the path of his tongue as he falls to his knees, taking my panties with him. The burn of his palm pressed to my lower back as he holds me against the wall.

Rough hands scrape over my hips, down my thighs, gliding back up, settling on either side of my ass. When I feel the quick, sharp bite of pain from Jaxon's teeth, I whimper, arching my back.

"Fu-u-ucck." The single word crawls up his throat, falls off the tip of his tongue before he uses it to soothe the pain. "Can't tell you how much I've missed this ass, honey." Rising, he presses his chest to my back as he palms one cheek. "Been watching you parade around here in those flimsy shorts every morning, dreaming about shredding them, bending you over my couch, putting my poor cock out of his misery." He licks a path up my neck to the shell of my ear. "He's missed you, honey. Have you missed him?"

I shake my head, fingertips digging into the wall.

Jaxon doesn't look surprised, but he tsks anyway, shaking his head. His hand glides over the curve of my ass, and he dips his fingers, sliding them through my soaked pussy. His other hand tangles in the curls at the nape of my neck, pulling my head back, showing me his dripping fingers.

"Little liar," he purrs, painting my lips before he sucks his fingers into his mouth, his chest vibrating with satisfaction. "My memory didn't do you justice, honey. Knew I'd never tasted something so delicious, but didn't realize a second taste would have me trying to figure out how I can make you my breakfast, lunch, and dinner for the rest of my life." His mouth pauses at my ear, sending shivers scattering through me. "Eating well is the key to a happy life, after all."

"Jesus," I whimper.

"Not Jesus," he murmurs. "But I guess this is my second coming."

He thrusts two fingers inside me before I can form a coherent thought, and I arch off the wall, shoving my ass back into his hand as I cry out his name.

"More," I pant, riding his fingers. "Give me more."

"You want more, honey?"

"I want it all," I beg. His fingers, his mouth, his cock. I want him everywhere, erasing every memory of Ryne on my body, replacing it with something better, something I'd be happy to remember for the rest of my life.

Jaxon isn't my fiancé, or my boyfriend. Hell, I'm not even sure he'd call me a friend. But he's not going to maliciously hurt me either. It's attraction. Chemistry. Off the charts, yes, but nothing more. We can do this, *again*. We can make each other feel good, maybe just for tonight, or maybe as long as I'm here. And then we can both walk away, unscathed and sated, and he'll still be the same man who drives me up the wall, and the one who saved my life and gutted his pantry to keep me safe.

"Fuck, honey. You're making a mess, dripping all over me. Should I lick you clean?"

"Oh, *God*." I toss my head back, grinding against his hand.

"Or do you want my cock first? Huh?" He shoves his knee between my thighs, pushing them farther apart, thrusting his fingers as deep as he can. His thumb puts pressure on a place no one's ever touched, one Ryne begged for access to, and when I moan, leaning back into it, Jaxon chuckles. "You want it all," he murmurs, "and I just want whatever you're willing to give me."

"*Everything.*" I squeeze his fingers, clawing at the hand that wraps around me, finds my clit and strums it like he knows every note to hit. "You can have everything."

"You didn't give him everything." It's a question, but he's not wording it that way. If I gave Ryne everything, I wouldn't have run away.

"He didn't deserve it."

"No." Jaxon's eyes move over me, heated but thoughtful, assessing. "He didn't. And neither do I, but I'm gonna take it anyway." He pulls his fingers from my clit, and just as I'm about to protest, he slaps it, sharp and biting, and I shatter around him without warning, dragging my hands down the wall as I struggle to breathe. "That was quick, honey. You really needed that, huh?"

He wraps an arm around my waist, lifts me off my feet, and tosses me down on his bed. His eyes stay on me as he drops his boxer briefs, letting his cock spring free, fisting it in his hand. He runs a shaky hand over his mouth as he takes me in, bare and spread out before him.

"Christ, I'm gonna enjoy this," he mutters, then grips my hips, jerks me to the edge of the bed, and falls to his knees. Warm breath teases my soaked pussy, and Jaxon spreads me wider, pressing his lips to the inside of my thighs, hot, wet kisses that drive me wild, have me shoving my hands through my hair, squirming, desperate for his mouth where I've been dreaming of it for weeks.

"So eager," he mumbles, trailing the tip of one finger up the center of my slit. He dips it, just barely, enough to gather a pool of wetness and smear it on my throbbing clit. He presses the pad of his thumb there, circling too slowly, too gently. "Here's how this is gonna go, Len. You're gonna tell me what happened. Why you're in Vancouver." I open my mouth to protest, and he pinches my clit. "Not because I asked. Because you need to get it off your chest. You looked like your head was going to explode earlier tonight, and I can't have that. Mittens would be fuckin' devastated, and I'd never hear the end of it."

A garbled laugh leaves my mouth, and he rewards me by sinking a single finger.

"You can be as vague or detailed as you like. Tell it to me in a few words or a lot of words. I don't care, honey, just say it. And when you're done, I'll treat you the way he didn't. Give you what he wouldn't. Fuck you the way he couldn't." His heated gaze holds mine as he pumps his finger, circling my clit, flicking his tongue over the cleft of my thigh. "Go on, honey. Take back the power he stole from you."

I drag my hands down my face, rolling my hips, meeting each of his thrusts. As a general rule, I don't talk about what Ryne did. I don't think he deserves the energy or the time. I gave the girls the short story—*he stuck his dick somewhere else*—and I know I could do the same right now. Six words, and that would be enough for Jaxon. But maybe he's right. Maybe my unwillingness to give it a voice only gives it more power over me. Because it lives in my thoughts instead. It's rooted in my brain, and every time I bury the memory, I only secure its spot inside me, solidify the hold it has on me.

If I give it a voice, will the voice fade?

"He cheated on me," I whisper. "At our wedding rehearsal, sixteen hours before our vows. With one of the waitresses."

Jaxon doesn't say anything, just slides his palm over my thigh, squeezing gently, kneading. He listens silently as I recount the way Ryne's orgasm pierced through the speakers in the room, in front our family and friends. The way he strolled back into the room two minutes later still tucking his shirt into his pants. How he grinned at the crowd, winked at me, called me sweetheart before he pulled me in for a kiss. The way I slapped him so hard not even the gasp of the crowd could drown out the sound. How he had the nerve to follow me home, try to bypass my dad and brother, who were blocking the front door. How he watched me throw my luggage into my dad's car twenty minutes later and told me to *be for fucking real*.

I slapped him again.

"'Atta girl," Jaxon whispers. He bends my knees, pulling me closer to his face, where his eyes glitter. "Such a beautiful pussy, especially when it weeps like this for me." With his gaze on me, he presses his tongue against me, gliding it slowly through my slit. It flicks over my clit before he gently tugs it with his teeth. "So you came here. To Vancouver, to get away from him."

I shake my head, sliding my fingers through his hair, smiling at the way he chuckles when I push his mouth back where I want it. "It wasn't just about getting away from him," I manage, rocking against the lash of his tongue. "It was about finding the pieces of myself I lost along the way. Following dreams I'd tucked away because he made me feel silly for chasing them."

"Like what?"

"Nature. Mountains, forests, skies." I blow out a sigh, fisting Jaxon's hair, riding his face and that perfect, smug grin. "Astrophotography. A perfect life is one where I spend the rest of it stargazing. And fucking," I tack on, breathless, because *holy tits*, his tongue is wild.

Jaxon pushes forward, rising from his knees and gliding me backward at the same time, his mouth suctioning over my clit. He crawls onto the bed, his face never leaving its home between my legs, and I collapse to the mattress as he shows me how much he was holding back while I was talking. He turns feral, a starved man who's been wandering for days and has just been given an all-access pass to the only thing he needs to survive. He laps at every inch of me, spreading me wide, dipping low, thrusting deep. He sucks my clit into his mouth, rolls his tongue over the tight bundle of nerves, sinks his fingers inside me. He pulls one orgasm out of me, then two, and right before number three, he pulls away, leaving me hanging.

"None of that sounds silly," he says, climbing on top of me. "I'm glad you chased your dreams to Vancouver." He brushes his thumb over the corner of my mouth before capturing it with his. "Why you lookin' at me like that, honey?"

"You didn't finish," I whine.

"I finished. Well, you did. Twice." He cocks his head. "Three times if we're counting before I got you on the bed."

Another whine, this one extra dramatic, and Jaxon chuckles, claiming my mouth with his. His tongue glides against mine, and there's just *something* about the taste of myself on his tongue that drives me wild. I come alive, scraping my nails down his back, gripping his ass as I roll against him. His cock slides through my pussy, and I rub myself against it, chasing an orgasm he's deprived me of. And he lets me. He rolls his hips in time with mine, let's his cock glide through my slit over and over, rubbing against my clit. And when I'm right there, standing on the edge of the cliff, he stops. Gripping my knee, he shoves one leg wide and backs away, just an inch, leaving the cool air to lash at the wetness coating me.

"Jaxon." His name is dripped in venom, but he doesn't tear his fixated gaze from the apex of my thighs. Instead, he strokes a single finger up my center, pressing on my clit, pulling a full-body shiver from me as he bites back that arrogant grin.

"Such a pretty, greedy cunt, Lennon."

Another shiver, this one paired with a whimper, because I'll never get used to the way that filthy word sounds leaving such a beautiful mouth.

"You want me to fuck this cunt, don't you, honey?" His thumb works my clit as his mouth slides wet kisses up my torso. "Imprint the shape of my cock inside it?" His tongue flicks over my tight nipple, and he pulls it into his mouth, sucking, rolling, tugging it gently with his teeth before he lavishes the other with the same, well-deserved attention. "Give you everything you need and then some?" Jaxon drags his mouth across my collarbone, showers my throat in kisses, makes certain he's leaving his mark as he works his way up to my ear. His rough breath fans across my neck, sending a wave of pleasure tumbling through me as he holds my head taut and presses his whisper below my ear. "You want me to fuck the memory of him right out of you? Ask me nicely, honey. Beg."

I open my mouth to do exactly as he's asked: *beg*. For everything he's offered, everything he can give me. The attention, the pleasure, the fucking *orgasms*.

But I'm the one with the urge to wield power tonight. And I don't think Jaxon's going to deny me that right.

Fisting his waves, I pull his mouth to mine. "That's not how this is going to work. Not tonight, at least."

With my palms on his chest, I push him down to his back. His cock bounces upright, the poor purple head looking so angry as it weeps with pre-cum. In fact, I feel bad for Magic Mike. He's innocent in all this, after all. That's why I bend, swallowing the head into my mouth, licking it clean before I climb aboard Jaxon

until his cock is nestled snugly between my sopping folds. His
eyes flare, a tiny furrow of frustration between his brows. I smile,
brushing the corner of his frowning mouth with my thumb, same
as he did to me only minutes ago when he denied me. And I say
the same thing he said to me.

"Why you lookin' at me like that, honey?"

His mouth pulls up into a smile, quickly replaced with a pout
when he whines, "You didn't finish." His hands skate up my thighs,
gripping my waist. "You in charge tonight, tidbit?"

"Yes, and I'll be a lot kinder to you if you ditch that nickname."

"I don't need you to be kind to me. I need you to take what you
want, everything you've been too afraid to ask for. I'll give it to you."

It's on the tip of my tongue to ask him if he really means it, but
the steadiness in his gaze tells me he does. Something sparks inside
me, a flurry of butterflies set loose in my stomach. There were things
Ryne wanted that I denied, not because I didn't want them too, but
because we wanted them on different terms. Because I didn't feel as
comfortable as I should be when giving those things to a partner.
Because he made me feel ashamed for an act as simple and harmless
as reading erotic romance, or partaking in self-pleasure.

"What if . . ." I suck my lower lip into my mouth, shaking my
head. "Never mind."

Jaxon tugs my lip free. "What if?"

"If . . . I want to listen to one of my books?"

His brows quirk. "We're acting them out? Fuck, yeah."

"If . . . if I want to touch myself?"

His eyelids hood, and he slides his palms to my hips, rolling
them. "I'll happily tattoo the image of you making yourself feel
good into my brain. Fuck, I'd tattoo it on my body, too, but that's
definitely gonna get me some looks."

I giggle, and it quickly spirals into a moan when Jaxon nearly
slips inside me. With my palms on his chest, I lift myself up, teasing

him, swallowing the head of his cock with my pussy before I pull off again, enjoying the tortured look on his face. "Toys?"

"We can go shopping tomorrow."

"What? *No!* I'm not being seen in a sex shop with Jaxon Riley."

He rolls his eyes, and when I grip his cock, gliding the head from my clit, through my slit, and all the way to my ass, he short-circuits. *"Online! We can go online shopping!"*

Another laugh, one that slowly dies, leaving the room quiet, save for our heavy panting. Uncertainty heats my cheeks, and I look away. Jaxon's hand slides along my jaw, angling my face back to his. I swallow, tracing the mountains etched into his biceps. "If I want to try . . . something else?"

"Then we try. A little bit at a time."

"And if I don't like it?"

He tilts his head. "Then we stop, Lennon. No matter what, no matter when. You say stop, we stop."

It's the bare minimum, isn't it? And yet it still means something to me. It builds trust where I hadn't realized it was so severely depleted. Because every single time I debated letting Ryne somewhere I wasn't sure I'd enjoy having him—or anything—the question wasn't whether he'd stop if I said stop—he would—it was how mad would he be? Would he give me the silent treatment for four hours or four days? Would he throw it in my face in a million different ways? Would he say it shouldn't surprise him that I changed my mind, considering how indecisive I was about everything in my life?

"If you're not comfortable, I'm not comfortable. You drive me up the fucking wall, honey, but I don't wanna break you. Just wanna fuck you the way you should've been fucked all this time. Bonus points if you're too tired to give annoying me your all in the morning."

I smile down at him. "I think it's sweet you dream so big, Jason."

His lips flatten, brows pulling down. "Honey, you better get a condom on Magic Mike and sit your tight pussy on him right now if you wanna be in control tonight."

I slither off him, strolling to his bedside table. There are no condoms in here, just a bottle of lube, and the longer I stand here confused, the more restless I get.

"Just pick one, honey. Pink's for your pleasure."

"I would, but . . ."

"But?"

"But . . ." I glance at him over my shoulder. My thighs rub together with the movement, and I fight the urge to whimper. I'm so fucking horny right now, and I can't possibly deal with the notion that I'm not going to get to come all over his cock tonight.

Jaxon's face falls. "No." He scrambles out of bed, fisting his rock-hard cock, and joins me at the table, shaking his head. "No. No, no, no, *no*." Wide, horrified eyes come to mine. "I-I-I—"

"You're fresh out, Jax."

"Don't call me Jax," he whispers, scratching his temple, looking off into the distance. "Holy fuck. I haven't had sex since . . ." Hazel eyes drop to mine. "You."

"Me neither."

"And you don't have any—"

I shake my head.

"Fuck. I mean, I've never . . . you know." He aims a pointed look at his cock, then my crotch. "Not bare."

I swallow. "Yeah. Me neither."

"Really? Even with—"

"No."

"Oh." His head bobs, and he rocks back on his heels, clapping his fist into his opposite hand. "So I'd be the first. Hypothetically speaking."

I nod. "Hypothetically speaking."

"And hypothetically speaking, are you—"

"On the shot."

"Oh. Cool." He clears his throat. "Cool, cool, cool."

"Hypothetically speaking, are you—"

"All clear."

"Oh. Nice. Yeah, me too."

More head bobbing, and he smacks his lips together over and over, letting the sound *pop*.

Curious, cautious eyes come to mine, and we stare at each other in silence for a moment.

And then I throw myself at him. Toss my arms around his strong neck. Bury my hands in his unruly hair. Wind my legs around his trim waist.

His mouth collides with mine, and suddenly we're nothing but strangled breaths, scraping fingers, rough hands, nipping teeth. He swallows every one of my cries, whispering my name against my lips as we pinball around the room, lost in a delirious frenzy.

He pins me to the wall with his hips, my wrists on either side of my head, and he fights to breathe as he stares down at me. "Fuck, Len. I'm struggling." He drops one wrist, showing me his shaking hand. "Need you to tell me what to do so I don't do it for you."

"Let me go."

He does, stepping back, every inch of him trembling as he fights the urge to take control. With my hand on his collarbone, I walk him backward, forcing him to the edge of the bed, where I sit myself on his lap, his cock standing tall against his torso. I fist it in my hand, stroking it slowly. It's a special kind of power, holding a cock in your hand, feeling the way it strains for freedom, pulses and flexes beneath your hold, the way such a simple touch can pull that bead of cum to the tip. I press it to my clit, coating it with him before I lift myself, line the head of his cock up with my entrance, and slowly seat myself.

"Fu-u-u-ckkk," I groan, raking my hands down Jaxon's shoulders at the stretch, the feel of him inside me with nothing separating us. "God, that feels—"

"Fucking incredible," he murmurs, barely a breath, wide, wonderous eyes locked on the connection. "Jesus, Lennon. I . . . I . . ." He shakes his head, sinks his fingers into the curls at my nape, and pulls my mouth to his for a hungry, rough kiss as I fuck him slowly, rolling my hips, picking myself up and seating myself as deep as I can, over and over. An orgasm builds with no effort at all, desperate for the release it was denied minutes ago, so I push Jaxon back onto the mattress, ripping my mouth away, gasping for air as I chase my high.

He's fascinated as he watches me bounce on top of him, hands gliding over my thighs, hungry eyes roaming my body as my hands cup my breasts, tug on my nipples. As I bury one hand in my hair and dip the other to the cleft of my thighs, stroking my clit.

"Fuck, honey. Look at you. So fuckin' beautiful when you take what you want. That's it. Take it."

"Oh, God," I cry, riding closer and closer. Every nerve ending dances and sizzles, a wick burning fast and furious. I'm not going to last, and I have every intention of being fucked into a twelve-hour sleep tonight.

I capture Jaxon's roaming hand, bringing it to my clit. I'm drenched, soaking his cock, and when his fingers are good and drenched with me, I swallow the uncertainty, guiding his hand around to my ass. Broad fingertips slip over the hole he touched earlier, and his eyes come to mine.

"Sure?"

Am I? It's hard to let go of your body, to take control of it and its pleasure. It's easier to stay inside your box, where you built your comfort zone, even if you dream of stepping outside it.

Ryne was my cardboard box. He looked safe and sturdy, but

instead all he was good for was keeping me contained, from growing beyond my walls.

Jaxon is . . . living. Fresh air. An endless sky dotted with possibilities. He's the deep breath before a scary step, the thundering of your pulse as you close your eyes and jump. He's life beyond four suffocating walls, where stepping outside is like seeing in color for the first time.

So, yes. I'm sure.

Leaning into him, I catch his mouth with mine, spreading myself wider at the back as I grind against him. His fingers glide up and down, from my pussy to my ass, coating the tight hole with wetness, massaging it with gentle pressure. I drag my mouth from his, along his jaw, pausing at his ear.

"I need you to fuck me like it's the only thing you've been dreaming of. Like there's no one else in the world you'd rather be with tonight. I need you to fuck me like I've been missing out for the last nine years. Because I've only been fucked right once in my life, and it was by a stranger on my honeymoon." I close my eyes to the sensation as he adds a little more pressure. "I need you to fuck me like you fucked me on my honeymoon. Isn't that what I deserve?"

Jaxon grips my neck, thumb stroking my cheekbone, coaxing my eyes open. "Obsessed? Feral? Starved? Not a thing less, honey."

"I don't think there's anyone else who can fuck me the way you do."

"Not a fucking chance."

"Then just *fuck me*, Jaxon." I seat myself as deep as I can, moaning as I grind my pelvis against his. "Or I'm gonna fuck myself."

Arrogance spreads across his face, starting in one corner of his mouth, and it's—irritatingly enough—completely justified. Because the man bucks his hips, pushes the tip of one finger past that tight muscle, strums my clit, and I scream his name, folding over him as I come all over his cock.

"Atta girl." Yanking me off him, he flips me onto my hands and knees. "Such a turn-on, watching you take what you want." He grips my ass, spreading my cheeks before he slaps the plump skin. "Fuckin' gorgeous ass, honey. Can't take my eyes off it whenever we're in the same room."

His cock pushes at my entrance, and he sinks inside with ease, groaning, squeezing my ass as I grip the bedsheets. He leans over me, yanking open the bedside table, and pulls out the lube. I gasp when the cool liquid drizzles down the crack of my ass, and shudder when he slides the pad of his thumb over my hole, coating it.

"We stop when you say stop," he reminds me, slowly working the tip of his thumb inside as he rocks his cock in and out of my pussy. "No questions asked."

"Please." I drop my forehead to the mattress, back arching as my body urges to fight the intrusion. "More."

"Relax," he murmurs, sliding his free hand over my lower back, around my hip. He finds my clit, circling it slowly, and when I moan, he pushes his thumb inside. "Fuck. Fuck, fuck, fuck. Len, honey, I think I've died and gone to heaven."

Me too, because as the pressure fades, I'm left with a delicious fullness, and when Jaxon slowly eases his thumb out and then pushes it back inside, my pussy convulses, throwing a fit like she's my own personal cheerleader.

Jaxon grabs my hand, dipping it between my legs, working my fingers over my clit. "Nothing," he rasps, working his cock and his thumb in and out of me. "Nothing in my life has appropriately prepared me for this."

"For what?"

"The sight of you, ass up, pussy soaked, filled with me." Fingertips bite into my hip, and he pounds into me harder, deeper, faster as I struggle to breathe, fireworks sparking low in my belly. "It's doing something bad to me, honey."

"What?"

"Makin' my brain scream *mine*."

Another slap to my ass, and I yank the sheets off the mattress.

"Nobody else gets you like this. Just me. Just you. Say it, honey. Tell me who gets to work this body like this."

"Me," I gasp. "Nobody gets me like this except me." My eyes roll back when he hooks his thumb, and I collapse on the mattress as he fucks me right into it. "And you."

"Good fucking girl."

And then he lets go. Of all control, his grip on reality, and somehow, mine too. He drives himself inside me, over and over, deeper and deeper, making sure my pussy will remember the shape of his cock for the rest of my life.

"*Jaxon*. Oh, *God*. I'm gonna c-c-come."

"You are, honey, and it's a gorgeous fucking sight watching you soak my cock." He holds me in place, hips snapping forward, slapping against my ass, sending a wave of pleasure through me with each push of his thumb. "Let go, Lennon," he demands, and I do, soaking the sheets below me as every thought leaves my head and my bones turn into limp noodles.

Jaxon pulls out, flips me onto my back, and tugs me to the edge of the bed. "How many was that?" he asks, but then he dips his head, buries his tongue in my pussy, and how in the fuck am I supposed to answer? "How many, Len?"

"Th-thr—"

"Nope."

"F-f-four."

"Four." He stands, pushes my knees wide, and grins up at me. "Let's see how many more we can pull out of you before you pass out."

He drives his cock inside me without warning, and I scream out his name.

The answer is five. Another five orgasms, for a total of nine, but I only know because, as Jaxon carries me across the hall two hours later, he won't shut up about it.

"We'll try for ten next time," he murmurs, tucking me into bed. "Double digits."

My eyes flutter closed as Jaxon rummages around my bedside table, and I'm too tired to tell him not to snoop. His fingers move through my hair, and if I could move, I'd slap his hand away.

"Randy only ever gave me two in one twenty-four-hour period," I think I murmur.

"Who the fuck's Randy?" Jaxon chuckles, kissing my nose when I don't reply. "Night, tidbit."

It's not until I hear the door close that my hand is finally able to find my hair, except it's not my hair at all. It's my silk wrap.

Jaxon wrapped my hair before bed.

I don't even have the heart to tell him it was mostly pointless, considering he had his hands buried in it while he fucked my brains out.

This is also the moment I realize I called my ex-fiancé Randy, not Ryne.

Oops.

15

I DON'T NEED A VALENTINE;
I HAVE A CAT

Jaxon

I'VE MADE A LOT OF mistakes in my life, but never has one of them ever been fucking a girl even *remotely* close to Valentine's Day.

I like pussy. *Love* it. Just . . . not that much.

But, um, as it turns out, I fucked a woman in Cabo a month ago, then found her a week later essentially at my doorstep, blah blah blah, long story short, now I'm addicted to her pussy, Valentine's Day is tomorrow, and I'm freaking out because I can't even ghost her.

Right?

I pull up my phone, heading to Google.

Is it possible to ghost someone I live with?

. . .

No, I can't. I mean, Google says I can. But that's just cruel. And sure, I don't wanna be Lennon's boyfriend, but I don't wanna crush her spirit either. I like her spirit.

I'll just act like it's any other day. I'll slap her ass when I wander into the kitchen and find it hanging out of her flimsy jammie shorts. She'll karate chop my wrist and tell me to fuck off. Then she'll catch sight of Magic Mike, I'll smile at the way her eyes widen like she forgets every morning how huge and incredible my cock is, and when she rolls her eyes, I'll remind her of how she did that in my bed, her bed, or on the living room couch the night before, while moaning my name. We have a routine, and routine is good. Routine is important.

But tomorrow, I won't fuck her. Definitely not. Not on Valentine's Day.

"Oh, hey." Carter taps the table, sipping his chocolate milk when he gets our attention, because that's the thing about our attention: he wants it for as long as he can possibly have it. "I'm not gonna be reachable tomorrow, so if you need anything from me, make sure it's tonight." Another sip of his chocolate milk, pausing to blow bubbles in it before draining it. He sighs, long and theatrical, leaning back in his chair, arms overhead as he stretches. "Yeah, I'm gonna be balls deep in my wife all day long."

I didn't know Carter personally before he and Olivia got married, but I'm 99 percent sure one of the reasons behind the wedding was so he could say *my wife* at any and every opportunity that presented itself.

"Don't you have a child?" I ask, cutting Adam's last breakfast sausage in two, stuffing half in my mouth as he frowns. "And doesn't she need, like . . . attention?"

"Yeah, well, I mean . . ." Carter scratches his head. "Okay, well, Ireland naps twice a day, so I'll be . . ." He frowns. "Okay, wait. We're going for breakfast at nine, and then we're going to Maplewood Farms at ten thirty, and then . . ." He trails off, counting out his fingers. When he looks up at us, his expression is bordering on the edge of distraught.

"What?" Garrett asks.

Adam swirls a bite of pancake in syrup. "Looks like he just remembered you can't fuck whenever you want when you're a parent."

"Carter, buddy, you okay?" Emmett watches with a grin as Carter drags both hands down his face.

"I'm only gonna get to be balls deep in my wife two times for Carter's Valentine's Day Extravaganza!"

Why Carter's Valentine's Day Extravaganza? Because it's not just Valentine's Day; it's also his birthday. That's why.

"Oh no," I murmur, drizzling chocolate syrup over my fruit kebab. "You're only gonna get to fuck your wife twice in one day."

"You watch your filthy mouth," he barks. "You're gonna spend the day fucking Lennon."

I snort, stuffing my kebab in my mouth. "No. Nope. Not tomorrow."

"Why not tomorrow?" Adam asks.

"Yeah," Garrett murmurs. "You fuck her every other day."

First of all, I want to clarify that it wasn't me who told everyone we fucked the other week, or that we've been fucking virtually every day since. It was Cara. Well, technically, it was Lennon. She told the Coochie Gang, and even though their group chat subheading is the Chamber of Secrets, everything said there is, in fact, not a secret. Cara opened her big mouth, and two minutes later the guys were blowing up our Puck Sluts group chat.

"Tomorrow's Valentine's Day." Emmett licks maple syrup off his fingers before signaling the waitress for another round of chocolate milk. "Jaxon can't fuck Lennon because then it means he wants to date her."

"Okay." I clap my hands on the table. "Does it? It does, right? I knew it. I fucking *knew it*." Sitting back in my chair, I throw my hands up. "And that's why I can't fuck her tomorrow." I prop my chin on my fist. "But it won't hurt her feelings either, right? If I just, like, pretend it's not Valentine's Day. Don't bring it up at all? 'Cause I don't wanna hurt her or whatever." I've seen her cry more than once, and it feels like someone's ripping my heart from my chest, that the only remedy is to hand it over to her if it'll help. "Yeah, hurting her feelings is not something I'm on board with, like, at all."

The guys exchange a look, but nobody says a word.

"What?"

Another look, and finally, Adam squeezes my shoulder. "Hey, big guy. Is it possible you have a cru—"

"Don't," I mutter. "Don't say it. Don't you dare say it."

"Crush," Carter whispers. His eyes bounce between the others before coming back to me, and he nods eagerly. "Adam was gonna say *crush*."

"I don't have a crush on Lennon!" It comes out slightly louder than I mean it to, and the four of them share yet another look, brows high. "Don't look at each other like that! I don't have a crush on her! Sure, she's cool. She makes me laugh sometimes, and I don't hate having a roommate. But-but . . . it's because I'm having sex. Like, all the time. The *best* sex. And—you know what? Fuck you guys. I'm not talking about this with you."

"Aw, come on, man." Emmett nudges my elbow. "We're just teasing. You can talk to us."

"Nah, it's cool." I shrug, stirring my chocolate milk with my straw. It's one of those loopy ones, and this diner stocks them only because Carter once asked the waitress if they had them, then pouted up at her, and when she said no he told her how much he used to love them as a kid. Seventy-seven-year-old Ethel was no match for the Beckett pout, and the next week our chocolate milks arrived with these straws in them. "Nothing to talk about."

Carter smiles at Ethel when she drops off a second round of chocolate milks, and hands her a wad of cash. "Okay, well, if you wanna talk about it—"

"I don't."

"In the future—"

"I won't."

His eyes narrow. "Britney's Bitches are here to help," he rushes out before I can cut him off.

"I—" I frown. "Britney's Bitches? Who are Britney's Bitches?"

The four of them raise their hands. "We are."

"Uh . . . why?"

"You know."

"Trust me, I don't."

"It's Britney, bitch," Carter says simply, rolling his eyes when I only blink at him. He throws his arms out. "*We're* the bitches."

"Wanna hear our tagline?" Garrett asks.

"I really don't."

"'Oops, I did it again.'"

I clap my palm to my face, dragging it down in excruciatingly slow motion. "Can someone please explain to me what the fuck is going on?"

"It's where we talk about our girl troubles," Adam clarifies. "Carter insisted we needed a team name."

Carter grins proudly. "Team names build team spirit."

Who the fuck made this guy?

"Okay, let's pretend that's normal. You guys don't have girl troubles. Why do you need a group?"

Emmett snorts a laugh. "You think just 'cause I'm married I don't have girl troubles? First of all, Cara's scary as fuck, so I *always* have girl troubles. Second, we fuck up all the time."

Adam scratches the back of his neck. "*I* don't fuck up all the time."

"Carter fucks up the most," Garrett explains. "So we mostly gather to help him figure out how to get back on Ollie's good side. Like now, they're arguing about whether to have ponies at Ireland's birthday party next month."

Carter rolls his eyes. "One of us thinks our little princess deserves ponies at her first birthday, and the other one of us is unreasonable."

Garrett ignores him, which is almost always for the best. "We all need help sometimes, and it's nice to have people to talk to."

"You know, Jaxon." Carter sips his milk. "Britney could always use one more bitch."

"Thanks, but no thanks. I don't have girl problems."

Garrett winks. "Okay."

"I don't."

"Uh-huh," Emmett hums.

"You know why?"

"No, but we're sure you're about to tell us," Adam murmurs.

"Because *I* don't have a girl."

It's silent for a whole second before they explode with laughter, and I stand, grabbing my coat.

"I don't have a girlfriend, so I can't have girl problems!" I shove my things into my pockets. "I don't need you, and I don't need your stupid group!"

"It's okay if you want a valentine," Emmett calls after me. "Nothing to be ashamed of! Happens to the best of us!"

A valentine? *Ha!* I've never been more insulted in my life.

"I don't need a valentine!" I shout over my shoulder, ignoring the looks from the other diner-goers. "I have a cat!"

"Aha!" I clap my hands to my cock, rolling off my bed and onto the floor. "You're not getting me this morning, fucker!"

Mittens glares at me, ears back, bushy tail standing tall. He crouches, and when he pounces, I roll away and leap to my feet.

"Too fast for you! You're slowing down, buddy. All those treats Len's been feeding you."

Another crouch, this one extra low, tail whipping back and forth, and I follow his dilated gaze to my crotch, now unguarded. Mittens pounces, claws out. I screech, diving into the bathroom, slamming the door, and Lennon's cackle rings from the abyss.

"Get it, Mitts!"

"It's not a toy!" I shriek as his chunky body collides with the bathroom door. "It's a precious, vital limb, and you need to treat it with kindness!"

"For fuck's sake, Jaxon!" Lennon yells. "It's a goddamn dick!"

"Well, you sure worship it like it's a god!" I scream back.

I roll onto my back, listening as my bedroom door opens, as Lennon scoops up Mittens and tells him he's the *bestest boy ever.* When I'm finally safe, I empty my bladder, wash my hands, and brush my teeth. My cock's still hard by the time I'm done, which is a shame. It's Valentine's Day, so even though I *want* to hoist Lennon up on the kitchen counter and have her for breakfast, I can't.

When I leave the bathroom, my phone pings, and I smile down at the picture of Ireland wearing a headband with two hearts attached to springs. She's got her thumb shoved in her mouth, grinning at the camera, and is wearing a shirt with a heart on it that says *my uncles own my heart.*

Olivia: Happy Valentine's Day, Uncle Jax!

Me: Does Carter know she's wearing that?

Olivia: I took it yesterday while you guys
were at practice. Carter couldn't handle her
wearing it on *his* day.

She sends another picture, Ireland wearing the same headband and dimpled grin. But this time, her pink shirt has a heart with Carter's face on it, and says *my daddy is my valentine.*

Olivia: Speaking of, Carter's walking around
the house sighing loudly every ten seconds
because it's 8:30 and you haven't wished
him a happy birthday yet. I don't like asking
for favors, Jaxon, but for the love of God,
please put me out of my misery.

I huff a laugh, pulling up his contact.

Me: Happy bday bud. Hope it's a good one.

His response is instant.

Carter: thx!!!! luv u!!!

Carter: ???

Me: What?

Carter: i said i luv u

Me: I know. Thanks.

Carter: . . .

For fuck's sake. My fingers hover over the letters, but for some reason, I can't do it. Can't type a fucking four-letter word. So I send him the next-best thing.

Me: *heart emoji*

Carter: it'll do!

I roll my eyes, and the second I put my phone down, it pings again. It's Carter, but this time he's in our group chat.

Carter: jaxon said he loves me!!!

Me: I did fucking not!

Emmett: What's the context?

Carter: i said i luv u, and he sent me a heart back!

Me: Which is hardly an I love you.

Emmett: I've consulted with Cara. Can confirm: Jaxon loves Carter.

Garrett: What the fuck?? Where's my I love
you, Jaxon???

Garrett: Oh wait. Last week he clapped my
shoulder and said "Your haircut looks nice,
buddy." Was that an I love you??

Carter: That's definitely an I love you!!!

Adam: I think it's nice you're getting
comfortable displaying your emotions. We
love you, buddy.

Emmett: This calls for a group hug.
Tomorrow at 7, pre-plane?

I groan, and right before I can toss it on my bed and pretend
none of this happened, it pings again. This time, it's Lennon.

Tidbit: I think it's really sweet you dug deep
and conjured up an "I love you" for Carter's
birthday. You're not as tough as you like
people to think *hug emoji*

Tidbit: Also, please put on clothes before
you come out. I'm on a video call.

Me: What if they wanna meet
Magic Mike?

Tidbit: Trust me, he doesn't.

He?
Don't do it, don't do it, don't do it.

Me: He?

Damn it, I did it.

I don't wait around for her answer, and I only partly accommodate her, yanking a pair of underwear up my legs. If I have to scare off another man, the best way to do so is by letting him know I have a huge dick. Right?

Throwing open the door, I strut down the hall and into the kitchen. There's a fancy latte waiting for me on the counter, because Lennon loves the instruction manual I made her. Every time she's up first, I wake to a new creation.

I swipe the steaming mug off the counter, sipping it as I stroll into the living room. Her gaze comes to me over her shoulder from where she's curled up on the couch, and she rolls her eyes.

"What?" I glance at my bulging dick in my tight boxer briefs. "I put on underwear."

"That your roommate?" a deep voice asks from the laptop balanced on her knees, and my feet pick up their pace.

Lennon is mine in the morning. Her sleep-rumpled curls, piled on top of her head, spilling down her neck. Her lazy, quiet smile, and the bright sparkle in her brown eyes after an incredible sleep following the dicking of the century. The baggy cropped T-shirt hanging off her shoulder, the morning sun kissing her copper skin. The drop of coffee that clings to her plush lower lip when she pulls her mug back, and I have to stop myself from swooping in, catching her mouth with mine and stealing that droplet.

I'm not a jealous man, but . . . fuck it, I'm a little jealous.

That's why I strategically position myself right behind her, stretching obnoxiously. I hike my leg up on the back of the couch in some sort of weird lunge, essentially shoving my crotch in her face and the face of the man on the screen, and I sigh.

"Who we talking to?"

"Are you for fucking real right now?" She gestures at my sweet lunge. "What is this?"

"This?" I slide my palm over my quad, flexing. "Upped my leg day weights. Nice, huh? Yeah, these thighs are *pretty* powerful if you ask me."

"Yeah, I'm sure this is exactly what my brother wanted to see this morning."

I pause in my flexing. "Your brother?"

"My kind of Valentine's Day," the voice from the laptop says with a chuckle, and then, "Holy fuck, Len. Is that Jaxon Riley? You're rooming with Jaxon Riley?"

I lean over Lennon's shoulder, gripping her laptop screen. I can't be certain, but the man looks just like the third baseman for the Toronto Jays. "Devin Hayes?"

He grins, and there's no mistaking it. From the chestnut curls on top of his head, the brown copper skin, lips the exact same heart shape, pulling up into the exact same smile.

I look at Lennon. "*Devin Hayes* is your brother?"

Her slightly horrified eyes move between us. "Do you two know each other?"

"No, just a fan," Devin and I say at the same time, and then point at each other. "*Eeeh!*"

I set my coffee down and throw myself over the back of the couch, crushing Lennon into the arm of it. "Scooch over, tidbit."

"Tidbit?" Devin asks.

"Oh, yeah. She thought Timbits were called Tidbits. Can you believe that?"

"*Tidbits?* Len, come on! You were *born* in Canada! I live here!"

"I can't believe you didn't tell me who your brother was."

She crosses her arms. "Does it matter?"

"Well, number one," Devin says, "it immediately ups your cool factor, because—" He gestures at his body. "I mean, come on."

"He's not wrong. What are you benching these days? You smashed that ball out of the park back in September. Couldn't believe it."

"Oh! In Boston? So fucking close to breaking that record."

"This season," I tell him. "I know it."

Lennon huffs, and I turn to her, sipping my coffee. She's got her arms pinned across her perfect tits, and if it weren't Valentine's Day I'd end this call and offer to fuck that ferocious scowl right off her pretty face.

"What's with the pout, tidbit?"

She throws her arms in the air, nearly taking out my eye with her elbow. "That's *my* brother! And you're *my* roommate! You can't be friends! It messes everything up!"

I look to Devin, silence stretching between the three of us.

And then: "Jaxon, when you playing in Toronto next? I'll look at my schedule, see if I'm in town, and we can hook up."

"Oh my *God*." Christ, there go her arms again, and I get a face full of her ass when she shoves the laptop onto my lap and stands. She swipes my coffee mug. "You don't deserve this." She smiles at us, extra syrupy. "Enjoy your *date*."

"Okay, bye." I stretch out on the couch, scooping Mittens up off the floor when he tries to chase after Lennon. "Oh, hey, Len? Can you get me Mittens's catnip toy? It's—"

She snatches my cat up. "You don't deserve *this* either."

I gasp, but it's the words she mouths to me as she's walking away that really hurt.

No pussy for you.

"I didn't want it anyway!" I call after her disappearing ass, about both the cat and the pussy, and yes, I'm fucking lying. "Sorry," I mumble to Devin. "She's always yelling at me."

"Hey, I'm just happy she wasn't crying when she picked up the call. First Valentine's Day in . . ." He scratches his chin. "Way too long, that's all I know."

"What do you mean?"

"Valentine's is her favorite holiday. Used to decorate the shit out of our house, turn the whole thing red and pink."

I chuckle, gaze moving around my pink-and-red condo.

"Her first Valentine's Day with Ryne, she called me crying. He forgot, and instead of apologizing he told her Valentine's Day was just a day women invented to get men to spend money on them. For fuck's sake, man, she just wanted some pink tulips. How hard is it to get your girl her favorite flowers once a year?" He shakes his head. "He tossed a fifty-dollar bill at her and told her to go buy her own flowers."

Anger churns in my gut as I sit up. There's only one thing I know about Ryne, and it's that he's a massive, steaming pile of shit.

"Never did buy them for herself. Said it was the thought that counted, not the present. Didn't stop her from hoping each year, and inevitably calling me in tears."

I rub the back of my neck. "And she wasn't crying today?"

"Nah. She was all smiles this morning. You didn't get her tulips, did you?"

"No. I mean, I didn't know they were her favorite . . ."

"Ah, well. Maybe she's just happier now. Seems it, anyway."

Does it? I think back on the earliest version of Lennon, the one I met in Cabo. I got so much joy out of bugging her, trying to crack that grumpy façade and earn a smile. She still loves to hurl insults at me when I piss her off, and I still immensely enjoy pissing her off. But does she seem happier?

Footsteps pad down the hallway, and Lennon enters the living room with a breathtaking beam on her face, Mittens tucked under her arm and looking dapper as fuck wearing a red sequin bow tie, a basket full of pink and red in her other arm, her camera hanging from her neck. She holds up three pink-and-red crocheted vests with hearts on them, one of them tiny. "Look what just got delivered! Gran sent us matching Valentine's vests! We're gonna have a Valentine's photoshoot!"

Fuck my life.

Yeah, she's happier. So much fucking happier than when I found her in Cabo.

The scary part? I'm happier too.

So, like the mature adult I am, after a Valentine's-themed photoshoot that Gran cackles at over FaceTime, I spend the rest of the day avoiding her. Because my happiness definitely does *not* have anything to do with her.

And I am definitely *not* getting my roommate-with-benefits flowers on Valentine's Day.

And when she goes to the grocery store, I change the sheets on her bed to the new silk ones I bought her, but only because they just came in, and they're definitely *not* a gift.

And when she comes home from the store, I immediately leave for the gym, and when she asks me what time I'll be back, I tell her I don't know, but then pop my head back in and tell her I'll be home by five. But it's definitely not because I want her to know, and just because I'm not rude.

And when I'm driving aimlessly around the city, I definitely don't wind up in front of a random flower shop, and I definitely don't go inside and ask if they have pink tulips. And when the man behind the counter tells me they close in two minutes and he doesn't have time to make up a bouquet, I definitely don't hand him two hundred dollars and ask if he can make the time.

The thing about me is that the only woman I've ever bought flowers for is my gran. I tell myself that's why I'm standing outside my door at 4:55 p.m., staring at the pink tulips in the pretty, pink, heart-shaped glass vase, transferring them from one hand to the other so I can wipe my sweaty palms on my track pants.

It's definitely *not* because I'm nervous.

I crack the door, one slow inch at a time, pulse thundering in my ears as I peek inside. It smells like heaven in here, but it almost always does when Lennon's cooking, which is exactly what she seems to be doing, AirPods in, bent over a cutting board while she slices something. One of the stools from the island is beside her, Mittens sleeping on top, and he appears to be wearing some sort of T-shirt.

I slip inside, silently setting the vase on the counter, watching Lennon as she works. Her tight curls are pulled high on her head, secured with one of those big claw clips she likes so much. She's wearing next to nothing, a little red satin set with scalloped lace hems, and Magic Mike wants to know if I was being serious earlier when I said we weren't having sex on Valentine's Day.

"Holy tits," Lennon murmurs suddenly, breathless. "Both holes at once? His cock *and* the vibrator? Oooh, girl. I'm jealous." She snaps upright, pausing in her chopping. "Not the clit sucker too. Jesus fuck, Audrey, how are you gonna walk out of here?"

She spins around without warning, extremely large and sharp knife in hand, and shrieks when she sees me.

I should be the one shrieking.

"Jesus Christ, Jaxon." She places a hand over her heart. "You scared me. I didn't know you were home."

My arm rises in slow motion, my finger pointing as laughter bubbles in my chest. "What . . . what the fuck . . ."

Lennon's hand comes up to her face, touching the very thing I'm pointing at.

The swimming goggles she's wearing.

"What the fuck are you wearing?" Laughter explodes from my chest, and I keel over, clutching my stomach. *"Why are you wearing goggles?"*

She slices the knife through the air, pointing at the cutting board. "It's the onions! I don't want the fumes to get in my eyes!" She drops the knife on the counter, whips off the goggles, and shoves at my chest. "Shut *up*, Jaxon! It stings!"

I laugh harder, pointing at her face. "You-you-you—" I rake

my hands down my face, over my wet cheeks. "You have indents around your eyes from the goggles!"

"Oh my *God*. I *hate* y—" She doesn't finish her sentence, stopping when she spins toward the island. I wipe my tears away, swallowing the rest of my laughter as I turn away, busying myself in the fridge. "What are those?"

"Huh?" I glance over my shoulder. "Uh, flowers. You sure those fumes didn't get in your eyes?"

"They're tulips," she murmurs, slowly approaching them, tugging them closer, reaching for the petals but pulling back at the last second, like she's not sure they're real. "Pink tulips."

"They look more fuchsia to me. Magenta, maybe."

"These are my favorite flowers, Jaxon."

"Are they?" I pull out the first thing I can get my hands on, which happens to be a jar of solidified bacon grease.

"Did you get these for me?"

"What? Pfft. *No*. I get flowers every week."

"Jaxon, I've been living here for nearly a month, and never once have you bought flowers."

I spin around to remind her we're not dating, for her sake or mine, I don't know, but it's a huge mistake. She's looking at me with gigantic, watery brown eyes, and my stomach sinks. I wanted to be her first happy Valentine's memory, not another reason she cries.

"Please don't cry."

"It's the onion fumes," she lies on a whisper. "And the silk sheets that appeared on my bed while I was at the store?"

I shove my finger in her face as she approaches me. "That was *not* a Valentine gift. It's good for your hair."

"I have a silk hair wrap, Jaxon."

"Lennon, three days ago I couldn't find your wrap after I tucked you into bed, and the next morning you accused me of stealing it!"

"Your hair was exceptionally silky and frizz-free that morning!"

"Oh, well, fuck me for getting you silk sheets so you don't accuse me of theft again the next time you forget to wrap your hair!"

She stops in front of me. "Are the flowers for me?"

My heart hammers. "No."

"Jaxon."

"No."

"Jaxon."

"Yes!" I throw my hands in the air. "Yes, goddammit, they're for you! There! Are you happy now?"

Her chin trembles, and when those tears tip over her cheeks, she throws her arms around me. *"So happy!"* She pulls her sopping face from my sweater and yanks my face down, pressing a kiss to both cheeks. "You are such a sensitive boy, Jax. The girls are gonna have a field day over this."

"What? No, you can't—"

"Look what I got you!" She scoops up Mittens, showing me his T-shirt-covered belly. His shirt is identical to Ireland's *my daddy is my valentine* shirt, except instead of Carter's face in the heart, it's mine. Then she sets him down, shoves a sweater at my chest, and claps her hands excitedly. "Put it on!"

Slowly, I pull it over my head. It's one of those huge hoodies, super oversized, and when I look down, I find the giant front pocket that opens at the top. My jaw drops in slow motion. "Oh my God. Oh my God, Len, is this one of those—"

"Cat sweaters!" she shrieks, picking up Mittens again, shoving him in the pocket of my new favorite hoodie. "Now you can bring him everywhere!"

I do a spin, and Mittens doesn't even budge, safe and secure in my hoodie. "This is the best gift *ever*!"

"I know! I'm such a good gift giver." She fixes her goggles back over her face. "And I'm making Mimi's famous smothered

Salisbury steak with collard greens, macaroni and cheese, and fried cornbread."

"I fucking love Mimi," I murmur, following her to the stove to peek at what she's got going so far.

"Yeah, she's great." Lennon turns around, poking me in the chest, and it's so damn hard to take her seriously with her onion goggles on. "This isn't a date."

"Psssh. Obviously fucking not. I don't date."

"Don't think I don't know you were avoiding me today."

"Maybe I was sick of you."

"You're never sick of me," she says so confidently, and fuck me, she's right, goggles and all. "And listen, I enjoy having sex with you."

"Yeah, you do!"

"A solid six outta ten every night."

"Like fuck, goggles."

"But we should skip the sex tonight."

"Took the words right outta my mouth, tidbit. I don't want you to get—"

"—attached," she finishes for me. She circles a hand around my face. "You give clingy vibes."

I bark a laugh, clapping a hand to her ass as she turns back to the stove. "Yeah, I want you and your goggles all to myself." I tug on the strap of her top. "Why'd you wear this if you didn't wanna fuck?"

"To get you worked up. I love saying no to you and watching you get all whiny."

"You think I can't resist you in this?"

"I *know* you can't resist me in this, fuckboy."

"Wanna bet?"

She spins to me, pulling off her goggles. Mittens jumps out of my sack and struts down the hall, casting us a narrowed glance over his shoulder, like this entire interaction is making him uncomfortable. "Does losing make you hard or something?"

"I'm not gonna lose, honey. Not to you."

She smirks, and fuck, I love it when she does. She deserves every ounce of confidence she has. "Hey, can you pass me my AirPods?"

"Good book?"

"*So* good." She takes the buds from me and hoists herself onto one of the stools at the island, hiking one leg up, showing me the crotch of her red satin shorts.

And the wet spot in the center.

Lennon lifts her brows, the tip of her thumb between her teeth as she winks at me. "You have *no* idea how wet it was making me." Her head tilts. "Jaxon?" She follows my gaze. "Oh, shit. Silly me. Did I forget to wear panties again?"

I definitely don't have her naked and on the kitchen counter in thirty seconds flat.

And I definitely don't spend the rest of the night fucking my roommate on Valentine's Day.

And I most definitely *do not* come all over her pussy four times before the night is over.

I also come in her mouth, on her tits, and all over her perfect ass.

Oops.

Happy Valentine's Day.

16

WILL GET ON MY KNEES FOR HIS TEARS

Lennon

I'M NOT SURE OF MUCH in my life, but I am sure of this: in another life, Carter Beckett, superstar hockey captain, dad extraordinaire, obsessed husband, would've made an incredible, unstoppable, Academy Award–winning actor.

Adam and Emmett stroll toward me, looking dapper in their three-piece suits. They flash their signature grins to where I'm stationed on the floor of the hallway with my camera, snapping their photos for our Game Day Fits highlight on Instagram.

A throat clears to my right. Adam and Emmett roll their eyes when they spot their captain, one hand braced on the wall, the other tucked in his pants pocket as he gazes at me over his shoulder.

"You wanna get this shot, Len?" he asks as Adam and Emmett walk away, mumbling about how he's my problem now.

"I've already taken your picture," I remind him. Again. "About twenty-five times."

"Give the people what they want, am I right?" He swings his head all about, tossing his tame waves into perfect disarray, and pulls his hand from his pocket, circling it over his butt cheek. "What about now?"

I snap the picture, because he's unfortunately right: the fans go wild for any ridiculous content from their Vipers, and especially their captain. "Is this for Olivia?"

"That's a good idea, actually. I'll save it for next week, after Ireland's birthday party, 'cause she's gonna be so mad at me."

I drop my camera. "Why is she gonna be mad at you?"

"Huh?" He drops his hands, looking all over the floor for his words. "What did you—did I—did you see that?" He points at a speck on the floor.

"Carter. Why is Olivia gonna be mad at you?"

Scared green eyes come to mine. He swallows. "No reason."

I roll my eyes, waving him back to the wall. "For shit's sake, Carter, you're lucky I like you. Get back over there and give me your best one."

He scurries back to the wall, bracing his palm against it, and sinks into a squat. He rubs his butt cheek again—he really seems to like doing that—and pumps his brows before his eyelids hood. "I'm giving you a firsthand look at how I made Ollie fall in love." He tosses his hair again. "Guard your heart, Lennon. This bad boy's been known to break them."

"Beckett!" someone screams, and Carter scrambles off the wall.

"Yes, Coach! Coming, Coach!"

I snicker as he hauls ass down the hall, snapping pictures as more of the team filters into the arena, looking sharp and ready for the game.

Charlie McCarthy, Jaxon's defense partner, winks at me. "Hey, gorgeous. You goin' to the bar after the—"

"Fuck off, McCarthy," a grumpy voice mutters. I don't have to look up to know it's Jaxon. The man's made it his mission to thwart any and all flirting attempts from his teammates. Last week, one of the rookies sat beside me on the plane, wearing a giant grin, and Jaxon stood over him, arms pinned across his chest. He didn't say a single word, but he didn't have to. It took approximately five seconds for the look in his eyes to do the talking, and my entertainment for the flight—watching that vein in Jaxon's neck pulse while he watches me flirt—was over before it could begin.

I smile at Charlie. "You might find me there, handsome."

There's a snicker, and I know it's Garrett. He and Jaxon almost always ride in together, and he takes immense pleasure in watching me irritate his bestie.

I look up, and my heart trips over itself when I spy Jaxon. I left an hour before him, and he was walking around naked after his shower, swinging Magic Mike about. A beautiful sight, but Jesus, there's something so heart-stopping and fanny-fluttering about this man in a bespoke three-piece suit, a gorgeous, deep shade of burgundy, making the gold and green flecks in his hazel eyes sparkle. He hides all those tattoos and tames those mussed waves I love burying my fingers in, tugging to my favorite spot between my thighs. He pastes on that mask of indifference, pretending like he has zero fucks to give, but then his eyes coast to mine, the corner of his mouth quirks, and when he winks, butterflies take flight in my coochie.

Except right now, because I've just called his teammate handsome, his eyes are narrowed on me. Normally, I live for his irritation. Right now, though, I'm having trouble focusing on anything other than how he looks so put together in his suit and how badly I want to find an empty room, get on my knees, and ruin that perfect, composed image.

I swallow down the lust clogged in my throat, and Jaxon smirks, like my thoughts are written all over my face. So I shove my camera in front of my face, snapping a picture of him and Garrett as they stroll by. "Looking cute, boys."

Garrett stops, pivoting back to me. "Cute? No, Len, cute doesn't work. Goddammit." He looks around, then heads to the wall, getting into a position oddly reminiscent of Carter's just minutes ago. "What about now? Still cute?"

"It sure is something."

"No, not cute. Not even remotely. The correct answer is powerful. Rugged. Dare I even say"—he squats low, pumping his brows—"sexy."

"Dare you to try," I mutter, immediately transferring one of the photos to my phone, sending it to the girls, then uploading it to the Vipers' Instagram as a poll, asking people to vote whether their favorite right winger looks A) cute; B) rugged; or C) sexy.

"I don't even need to see the pictures." Garrett crouches, wrapping my head in a hug. "You're the best photographer in the whole world."

I almost feel bad that option C isn't going to be the poll winner.

"Go get ready for your game," I call after him, sorting through tonight's photos, binning the crappy ones. "And keep your buddy out of the penalty box!" I look up, and Jaxon startles when I catch him standing there, staring at me. "That's you. You're the buddy that needs to stay out of the penalty box."

"Yeah, well . . . I don't follow directions well."

"You're telling me." Back to my camera I go, and Jaxon doesn't move. After a minute, I look up, arching a brow. "Bye."

He jumps, gripping the back of his neck. "Bye."

I resume my duties as his footsteps fade, taking photos of the rest of the boys as they come through. Two minutes later, Jaxon walks by again, going the opposite way, pausing to look at me over his shoulder. Three minutes after that, he heads back this way. Then a minute later, the man comes sauntering down the hall at the literal pace of a snail, whistling, hands tucked in his pockets.

"Jaxon."

"Huh?" He whips around so fast, stumbling over his own feet. "Oh. Lennon. Didn't see you there."

"Really? Weird, 'cause I've been sitting here for forty-five minutes, and this is the fourth time you've walked by me."

"Well, it's just . . . I mean . . ." He scratches the back of his head. "Aren't you gonna take my picture?"

"I did." I show him the photo of him and Garrett.

"Yeah, but . . . you did individual pictures with everyone else." He sniffs. "Maybe you wanna put one on Instagram and see what people think of my suit tonight, like you did with Gare."

"Are you monitoring the Instagram page?"

He looks away. "I always look to see what you post. You're funny." Those last two words are a whisper that makes my brows jump.

"What was that?" I touch my ear. "Can you repeat it?"

Narrowed hazel eyes come to mine. "I said you're annoying."

"No, you said I'm funny." I point at his eyes. "And those? The twinkle in those says I'm your best friend, and you can't imagine your life without me."

His brows tug so far down, forehead crumpling, and I know I've done it. I've secured my hate-fuck later tonight. I blow him a kiss, and he rolls his eyes, stomping away.

"Jaxon." I look at him through my camera lens. "Keep your fists to yourself. Don't need you complaining all night about another split lip."

All that irritation fizzles. He grins, a beautiful, lopsided sight. "But your pussy is the perfect balm when you come all over my face." He winks, and I capture the moment forever.

When he walks away, I stare down at the photo for too long, the way that smile transforms every inch of his face. Without that smile, he's the broken, closed-off man who thinks he's not good enough to hang on to all the good that comes his way. With it, he's the boy in that frame on his bookshelf at home. Full of hope and light and laughter and mischief.

I transfer the photo to my phone and delete it from my camera. I don't want to share this smile with anyone else.

"I LITERALLY TOLD HIM NOT to fight. Right before the game I said, 'Keep your fists to yourself.'" I shake my head, angrily snapping photos of him as he grips the jersey of Montreal's centerman and hammers him in the face. "Why doesn't he listen?"

"But it's so hot," Cara argues, shoving a fistful of candy into her mouth before holding the bags out to me. I bypass the Skittles and go for the Milk Duds. I love Skittles, but the night I met Cara, she was eating mixed handfuls of them and M&M's. Two days later I went into anaphylactic shock. Ever since then, her M&M's, which may contain nuts, have been replaced with Milk Duds, which are, coincidentally, nut-free. So when she offers me Skittles and Milk Duds, I always choose the Milk Duds. I still wholeheartedly disagree with her mixing chocolate and candy. "I'm such a slut for displays of violence, and I don't even know why. And when Emmett comes home with a black eye or a split lip?" She whistles. "Bend me over, slap my ass, and fuck the feminist right out of me, you know?"

"And after the game, there's so much adrenaline running through them still." Olivia absently traces the shape of her lips with her fingertip. "My favorite is when Carter's so worked up he can barely talk. I pull his tie off for him, and . . ." She trails off, cheeks splotching with color as her gaze shifts to us. "Well, we use the tie."

"We all use the tie," Jennie murmurs, eyes following Garrett on the ice as he yanks the centerman off Jaxon.

"Oh, no, Adam," Rosie says, so fucking half-assed it's ridiculous, watching as Adam skates to the red line, mouth moving quickly before he bumps into the other goalie. She clasps her hands together, eyes alight as she inches closer to the plexiglass. "Please, no fighting . . ."

"Y'all are a bunch of puck bunnies." I laugh, as if my nipples aren't sharp enough to cut the very ice Jaxon's shoving this douche around on.

Four sets of eyes come to me.

"What?"

"Lennon, *you're* a puck bunny," Jennie says as if it's common knowledge.

"Me? A puck bunny? That's ridiculous. I didn't even watch hockey before—fucking *nail him*, Jaxon! *Yes!* Atta boy! Jesus, I wanna suck his c—" I clamp my mouth shut, slowly lowering my camera. "Holy tits. I'm a fucking puck bunny."

Cara kicks her feet up on the glass, sipping her wine cooler. "Welcome to the crew. We're lifers."

I laugh, but for the first time, something . . . hurts. It's a hollow, empty feeling, and I place my hand over the ache in my chest. They're lifers. They just said it. I'm . . . not.

I'm the photographer. The girl he fucked in Cabo, and now his roommate. But one day, I won't be. And one day, there will be someone else.

I'm temporary. And I don't think I've realized that until this moment.

I'm quiet as Jaxon takes his five-minute penalty, as the game carries on, tensions running high on the ice and off. I snap picture after picture of my favorite boys, and when Carter passes the puck back to Jaxon, when he fires up, slapping the puck across the ice and right above the goalie's shoulder, my chest fills with pride as the boys pile on top of him. He wears the brightest, proudest grin as he stops in front of me, knocking on the glass.

"Did you get that, Len?"

"No," I lie, unable to contain my grin as I snap a close-up of his smiling face.

"Don't worry." He dips his sweat-drenched face, playful smirk in place when he winks at me. "I'll fuck it into you later."

"Jesus Christ," Olivia murmurs.

Rosie fans her face. "Yup. Yup, I'm so glad Connor's at a sleepover tonight."

Jennie runs her fingers down her braid, toying with the crimson velvet ribbon tied in a bow. "I knew there was a reason I wore this tonight."

Yeah, I'm not even gonna lie: my panties are straight-up wet. It's just . . . too much. The ego, the arrogance, the violence, the goal, the pride, and the filthy fucking mouth. A girl can only handle so much, and my line in the sand was washed away a long time ago.

"This team is a bunch of dicks," I mutter, watching as they pull every shit-ass behavior imaginable every time the refs' backs are turned, jabbing, hooking, yanking their sticks through our players' legs, trying to knock them on their ass.

The play moves into Montreal's end, and Jaxon sets himself up along the boards, waiting at the blue line. The refs are focused on the puck, deep in the corner, when one of the wingers lifts his elbow, jamming it against Jaxon's helmet. With his stick, he shoves the player off him right as the puck soars by him. He takes off after it like his ass is on fire, the centerman he nailed in the face earlier hot on his heels. The second he cradles the puck on the blade of his stick, the centerman hooks his own stick around Jaxon's ankle, yanking.

The crowd gasps as Jaxon flies forward, and when his head collides with the boards, everyone jumps to their feet, screaming.

When he sprawls across the ice, totally motionless, the arena goes silent, save for the sound of my camera clattering to the ground.

"WOULD YOU STOP LOOKING AT me like that?"

"Like what? I'm not looking at you any way. How am I looking at you?" I grip the steering wheel tight in my hands. "I'm not looking at you any way."

Jaxon's eyes come to mine, tired and unimpressed beneath the glowing red traffic light. "You're looking at me like I almost died."

"Well, if the shoe fits."

"It doesn't."

"Whatever you say." I tap the steering wheel, waiting for the light to change. "You almost *died* tonight, Jaxon!"

He groans, scrubbing his hands down his face. "It's a concussion. A little one."

"Your second one this season, apparently."

He pins his arms over his chest. "You're not allowed in the locker room postgame anymore."

This was only my first time in there. I don't love the idea of invading their space when they're wandering around in any form of nakedness. But did I use my position as the head photographer as an excuse to charge in there and check on Jaxon? Yes, yes I did. The way his eyes shot to me when I walked into the back room, where they had him up on an exam table, told me he didn't want me there. Or, more accurately, he didn't want me to hear what the doctor had to say.

Which was to stop putting a target on his back, because his brain was struggling to keep up, to snap back after one too many blows this year, and the year before that, and the year before that.

"It comes with the territory, Lennon," he mutters into the darkness as we crawl closer to home. "I'm an enforcer. Fighting is what I do." He sighs. "It's all I'm good for."

"That's complete bullshit, Jaxon. You can defend your net and your team without risking your brain."

"My brain's fine."

"You thought the Spice Girls were on tour!"

"So I forgot what year it was for, like, two seconds. I knew who you were the second you walked into the room." He hops out of the car the second I squeeze into a parking space, and when I get out, he leans over the roof. "My annoying-ass roommate who I regrettably *enjoy* living with."

"I knew it." I slam the door, chasing after him. "You love me. I'm your best friend."

"I *tolerate* you. But Mimi's famous recipes and the way you soak my face when you come all over it? Yes, those things I love."

"A win is a win!" I whoop a fist through the air, making to follow him into the elevator. He bars his arm across the entrance, stopping me. "What are you doing?"

"What are *you* doing? The group is heading to the bar."

"Okay, but you're hurt."

"I'm fine."

"I'll stay home with you."

"You'll go out and have fun."

"No, but—"

"Lennon." He grips my shoulders. "I'm fine."

My eyes roam his face, from the bruise beneath his left eye to the crack in the corner of his mouth. He's tired and beaten up, and I don't feel right leaving him. My heart protests the distance I haven't even put between us yet. "You promise?"

"I promise." He turns me around, patting my ass. "Go have a frozen pink drink for me, and when you come home, I'll fuck you until you're the one who thinks the Spice Girls are still on tour."

I snicker, spinning back around, pressing my lips to his before I can think twice about it. "I won't be late," I tell him, dashing back to the car. "And I promise we won't have any fun at all without you and everyone's going to miss you so much and we're all just going to be talking about how incredible and brave and resilient you are." Pulling open my door, I pause to glance back at him. He's not listening.

No, he's standing there, eyes on the ground, fingers pressed to his parted lips.

For a moment, I think I've fucked up. I almost call out an apology, say I'm sorry if I overstepped, if I scared him.

But then, right before the elevator doors slide closed, he smiles.

And, fuck, it's a dangerous smile. It roots in my brain, growing like a weed, until it's all I can see, all I can think about. It's why I make it to the bar only to spend fifteen minutes in my car, staring down at my phone, watching in real time as Jaxon goes through my Instagram profile, liking every single one of my posts. There's only one photo of Ryne that somehow slipped through the cracks on my mass delete, four years deep, and when Jaxon gets there, he leaves a thumbs down emoji. Then he sends me a screenshot of the post, along with *Len, this guy's a fucking tool, delete this before I delete his face*, which doesn't even make sense, but I delete it anyway.

It doesn't get better when I drag myself into the bar. When the guys recount Jaxon's fight tonight, his goal, all the ways he's defended his team. When the girls talk about how much he's changed since he arrived a year and a half ago, and especially in the last two months.

But what kills me is when Carter posts a picture of the nine of us in our giant booth, and Jaxon comments ten seconds later, *looks fun.*

Period. Looks fun, *period.*

The tiny, inconsequential punctuation mark does me in, and I call it a night, kicking it home to Jaxon.

The scene at home, it's . . . it's a cry for help.

The six-foot-five tattooed enforcer with the busted lip and black eye is in nothing but his underwear, sprawled out on the couch in the dark, eating ice cream from the container while the cat sleeps next to him, a Disney movie playing on the TV.

I approach slowly and cautiously, as you would a scared, caged animal.

"Hey, big guy," I murmur. "Watching *Toy Story*?"

"*Three*," he whispers, sniffling.

"What?"

"I'm watching *Toy Story Three*," he snaps, voice cracking.

I pause, head tilting, then slowly sidestep around the couch so I can see him . . . and the tears sliding silently down his face. "Um . . ."

"Shut up!" He swipes frantically at his face. "It's emotional!" He gestures at the screen, where a teenage Andy is giving his childhood toys to a little girl. "He doesn't want to give up Woody, but he knows Woody deserves to be played with. And he's-he's-he's . . . he's saying all these really nice things about Woody, and Woody really needs to hear them."

My gaze slides back to the TV. When Andy and the little girl start playing with his toys, a choked sob cracks from my left.

Jaxon buries his face in his hands. "That's the last time Andy and Woody will ever play together!"

"Right. Um . . ." I scratch my nose. Seeing him like this is . . . painful. And also? Kind of hot. Don't ask me why. I'm all sorts of fucked up, and now I'm also, somehow, all sorts of turned on. "Would a blow job help you feel better?"

His crying ceases immediately. He lifts his head from his hands, red-rimmed eyes coming to mine. He sniffles, scrubbing his forearm across his eyes. "Yeah. Yeah, it would."

Jaxon stands, drops his boxers, fists his cock, and flicks his head to the spot at his feet.

"Come on, honey. I always feel better when you're on your knees."

17

IT'S IRELAND'S BIRTHDAY AND I'LL CRY IF I WANT TO

Jaxon

"I'M SCARED."

I look at Lennon, pretty as always, but especially banging this afternoon. Her spirals are fresh and glossy, extra bouncy and hanging past her shoulders. Her plush lips are painted a shiny, deep plum that I want to tattoo on my cock, and her long, toned legs are on display beneath that sweater dress she's wearing, the black lace beneath it that makes it a little longer, before those calves disappear in a pair of knee-high leather boots.

And did I choose my sweater because it's the same color as Lennon's?

No, but also, yes.

"You should be," I finally reply, staring at the front doors of the rec center Carter rented out for Ireland's first birthday.

If there's one thing you should know about Carter, it's that he doesn't half-ass anything. When he's in, he's all in. And when it comes to his daughter? I mean, Jesus, the man basically pays his twelve-year-old neighbor a full-time salary with all the custom shirts he has her making for him, 90 percent of them with his and Ireland's faces on them. Yeah, he's all fucking in when it comes to his daughter.

"He said Olivia was gonna be mad at him. Why is she gonna be mad at him, Jaxon?"

I swallow, because I'm 99.9999 percent sure of the reason. The guys and I took Olivia's side on the whole pony/birthday debacle, and Carter went silent about it. But last week, I caught him asking Google how many garbage bags he'd need to clean up after three ponies. His eyes met mine, he stood slowly, trying to make himself look bigger than me even though I've got an inch on him, and said, "You saw nothing, Riley."

For the sake of my balls, I nodded, hands up in surrender.

"Jaxon?" Lennon prods, and I swallow again.

"I don't . . . it's not . . ."

A shadow falls over us, and a tiny body attaches itself to my leg.

"*Unc'a Jax!*" Connor squeals, hugging my thigh.

"Hey, buddy!" I scoop him into my arms, tossing him onto my shoulders, enjoying the interruption.

Adam sighs as he and Rosie join us. "He got the fucking ponies, didn't he?"

Rosie gasps. "*No.*"

Lennon's eyes widen, and she cocks her head, looking at me like *I'm* the one who got the fucking ponies.

"Connor, doesn't Lennon look *so* pretty today?" It's a half-shout, because this morning she spent an hour doing her hair and makeup in my bathroom, and when I accidentally knocked her diffuser attachment off the blow dryer while Mittens and I were playing dangly toys, and subsequently her entire collection of hair products off the counter when I dove to save it, then watched everything clatter to the floor in slow motion, Lennon simply stared at me for a long moment before smiling sweetly, turning back to the mirror, and saying softly, "I'm gonna attach a jingle bell to a ribbon, then tie the ribbon to your dick while you're sleeping. Let's see how Mittens likes *that* dangly toy in the morning." So, yeah. I left the bathroom slowly and backward, and sue me for being a little afraid of getting on her bad side right now.

"Lenny pwetty," Connor says, bending over my head. "Conn'a kiss Lenny?"

"You know I'll never say no to that," Lennon croons, stepping in to get a smooch from the little man.

"Aw, come on, dude. Quit stealing my girl." The words are out of my mouth before I can stop them, and I freeze. Lennon, too, and Adam and Rosie. In an ideal world, I'd reach out and grab those words, shove them right the fuck back down my throat where they belong. Since I can't do that, I yell, *"Carter got the ponies!"*

"I fucking knew it!" Cara calls, racing up the walkway behind us. "When I was setting up earlier he asked me to leave a space big enough for every little girl's big dreams." She shoves Adam out of the way. "Move over, big boy! Mama needs to see Liv hand Carter his balls!"

Emmett sighs, hands in his pockets as he joins us. "She cleared space on her phone just in case there was a fight. She said we could dissect the playback later tonight."

"Carter!" Olivia's scream slips out the doors and onto the walkway. *"Is that pony poop?"*

We race inside, skidding to a halt next to Cara, Jennie, and Garrett, who's got the birthday girl clutched safely to his chest.

"What the—" Carter claps two shaky hands to his cheeks in the worst display of fake surprise I've ever seen in my life. "Oh my God. *Ponies?* What the—" He turns to us, hands still on his cheeks, mouth agape. "Did you guys do this? Ollie said *no* ponies. You knew this." He heaves a long, theatrical sigh, running a hand through his hair as he turns back to Olivia. "Well, I guess since they're already here, we have to keep them. Don't worry, pumpkin. I'll talk to them later about deliberately disobeying you."

Olivia's slanted eyes say she's not buying an ounce of this. She plants her fists on her hips. "No ponies. That was the *single* rule I gave you. I let you have everything else. *Everything.* All I asked for was *no. Damn. Ponies.*"

Carter raises his brows at us, crossing his arms over his chest, head bobbing. "Yup. She told you guys: no ponies. Look, we're not mad, just disappointed."

"Oh, for fuck's—" Olivia buries her groan in her hand, and I'm almost certain she's murmuring a reminder to herself that she loves him, *chose* him even. "You know damn well I'm talking to *you*, Carter Theodore Beckett."

His arms fall, right along with his jaw. We all gasp.

"Did she just full-name him?" Lennon whispers.

"She just fucking full-named him," Jennie murmurs.

"I've never seen anything like it," Rosie mumbles. "It's beautiful and scary at the same time."

"Got it," Cara mutters from behind her phone. "This is going in my year-end highlights reel."

Carter throws his arms in the air. "She only turns one once! She needs ponies!"

"She's not even going to remember this! She does not *need* ponies!"

Another gasp, and Carter rushes over to Garrett, clapping his ears over Ireland's ears. "Ireland, baby, don't listen to her. Every little princess needs ponies."

Ireland blinks, staring up at her dad, head tilted. Then she points at the pile of pony poop in the corner of the room. "Poooooh."

A third gasp, and Carter claps. "Pooh! Yes, baby! You're right! That *is* pooh!" He presses a loud smooch to her forehead. "Fuck, I love her." He lays a hand over his proud, puffed chest. "And I made her, therefore I also love myself."

Olivia lifts a brow. "*You* made her?"

"Well, I seasoned the . . ." He stops when Adam shakes his head, mouthing *no* at him. "What I mean is, if she were a meal, I prepped it, and you cooked it."

Olivia's brow, somehow, rises higher. She presses the heels of her palms to her eyes. "I can't even." Walking off, she leaves Carter fumbling for words.

"*Ollie!* I-I-I . . . I was merely your humble sous chef, but you were the master chef!"

She circles her hand around her crotch, and Carter gasps before she even opens her mouth.

"Don't say it," he murmurs. "Don't you say it."

"You can say goodbye—"

"No."

"—to *this*."

Another gasp, louder than I've ever heard, and when Olivia disappears, Carter screeches, "*Britney's Bitches! Assemble!*"

Emmett throws his arms over his head, rubs his torso. "Oh, man. I sure am tired. I should head out."

Adam points at Rosie. "You needed that, uh . . . you needed help with that thing, right?"

Garrett panics when Carter's gaze moves to him. "Oh—*oh*. I think—" He lifts Ireland's bum to his nose. "Oh shit, yeah. She pooped. I'll just go change her."

"Really?" Carter frowns. "Weird you can even smell it over the pony poop. Here, lemme see."

"No, it's o—"

Carter steals his daughter from Garrett's grasp, patting her bum before sniffing it. "Nah, no poop. We can do girl talk later, though. It's time to get changed. Ireland's guests will be here soon."

"Oh, good." My gaze drops to his T-shirt. *Father of the birthday girl*, it says in giant letters. "I'm glad you're changing."

"Yeah, gotta put my tux on."

"Your—" I choke on air, coughing into my hand. "Your *tux*?"

"Always dress my best for my girl." He grabs a garbage bag off the floor, digging around in it before he shoves an outfit at my chest, doing the same to everyone else. "Costume change! Everyone go get dressed!"

"What the—" I hold my costume up. "Is this Mr. Fucking Potato Head?"

"I believe he just goes by Mr. Potato Head."

"I'm not—"

"Ireland's favorite movie is *Toy Story*, and I promised her all her friends were coming." He jabs my shoulder. "So put on the damn costume and give me your best potato."

"I'm *Mrs.* Potato Head?" Garrett shrieks from beside me.

"Wait." I thumb at Garrett. "We're *married*?"

"Happily."

"But-but . . ." I scratch my head, looking at Jennie. She's currently pulling on a dinosaur costume. Why the fuck does she get to be Rex? And Lennon— "Aw, *man*. Lennon gets to be Buzz?"

Lennon meets my gaze, winking as she lifts her cool-ass communicator thingie on her arm to her mouth. "Star Command, can you hear me? It's Buzz Lightyear. Jaxon's throwing a hissy fit; we might need backup."

I ball my costume up, but I definitely don't stomp my foot. "This is bullshit. Why didn't you just partner Garrett and Jennie together?"

"Because this is funnier," Carter says simply. "Now go get dressed."

I throw my arms up. "What about Mitts? He hates being left out of anything. He has major FOMO. If Lennon and I go home with costumes for us and none for him—"

Carter pulls out a fuzzy pink hat with a pink button nose, and holy fuck, I can't wait to go home and turn him into the most adorable pig anyone's ever seen.

"*Hamm?* Mittens gets to be *Hamm* and I'm stuck with this—"

"This what?" Garrett demands, getting in my face. "If you want a divorce, Jaxon, *just say so!*"

"I didn't even wanna get married to you in the first place!"

"Oh, well, *sor-ry* I wasn't your first choice!"

A boom of laughter comes from behind me. I glance over my shoulder, finding Rosie and Adam attached, Rosie at the front, Adam at the back, the two of them dressed as Slinky Dog. Adam is curled over, howling with laughter, and Rosie is wiping tears from her eyes, her entire body shaking.

Connor tilts his head, looking past me. "Unc'a Emmett?"

"Yeah, buddy," Emmett whispers from behind me. "It's . . . it's me."

I spin around, stopping dead when I find him. Dressed in a pink-and-white gown, a matching pink bonnet tied around his head, and the crook he holds is, I think, to herd sheep, since that's what Dublin, Carter and Olivia's dog, is dressed as by his feet.

I step closer to Garrett, and him to me.

"Hi, hubby," he whispers.

I swallow. "Hi, wife."

And then Cara bursts through the doors in a barely there cowboy costume, arms out wide, jazz fingers on display. "Sexy Woody, baby!"

Connor shrieks, running over to Cara. "*Yeehaw!*"

"There's a dress-up center in the castle," Carter tells Adam and Rosie. "I didn't want any of the kids to feel left out if some had costumes but others didn't. Connor can pick one there."

"Hold the fuck up." I brace my hands out between us. "There's a *castle?*"

"Oh my God, *yes*, Jaxon, there's a castle. Ireland is a princess.

Keep up, please." Carter claps his hands. "Okay, Ireland and I need to get ready. You guys go wait in the party room and greet the guests as they come in." He looks at his watch. "Showtime is in twenty."

Lennon tucks herself into my side as we make our way to the party room. "Are you also nervous that he said *showtime*?"

"Terrified." I look at her, smile crawling up my face. She looks ridiculous in her costume, but when she takes me in in my potato costume and grins, I reach forward and slam the visor on her helmet closed.

She whips it back open and karate chops my wrist before gripping one of my Mr. Potato Head ears, yanking me into her. "Touch my helmet again and I'll rip off every single one of your facial features." She drags me closer. "One. By. *One*."

I smirk, grabbing the tip of her wing when she tries to walk away from me. Hauling her back against me, my mouth dips to her ear. "Thank fuck for my potato. You know I love when you catch an attitude problem. I'm hard as fuck right now, and you can't even tell."

She yanks her wing from my grasp, walking backward so she can look at me. "My Buzz Lightyear costume is making Jaxon hard, he just told me!"

Goddammit. I hate how much I don't hate her.

I busy myself with walking around the room as it begins to fill with people. The décor is stunning and elaborate, but then, Cara does run her own event-planning business, and she personally set everything up because she'd never forgive herself if there was even a single thing out of place at her niece's birthday party. *I'd simply have to leave the country*, she said earlier.

I stop in front of the castle. It's pink and purple and two stories high. Next to it, there's a wild bouncy house with a giant slide that empties into a ball pit. Whistling, I stroll closer to the warning label affixed near the bottom. *Recommended weight limit is 200 lbs per user.* Damn it.

Garrett sidles up beside me, drink in hand. He points lower on the label. "Twelve hundred pounds total weight limit."

"Hm. Interesting. You were checking it out before?"

He shrugs. At least I think he does. Hard to tell under all that potato. "Maybe I was, maybe I wasn't." He brings his drink to his mouth. "Bet you Carter is the first adult on it."

I'm about to tell him I'm not taking his shitty bet—obviously it'll be Carter—but the room erupts behind us with shrieks and giggles, flooding with the kids from Second Chance Home. Little Lily is the last one standing as they all run off, nervously twisting her long brown hair around her fingers, shifting on her feet.

And then Adam calls her name, and her entire face lights as she dashes across the room, not stopping until she crashes into his arms. She hugs his neck tight before demanding Rosie, and I watch as the three of them sink to the floor in a group hug, where Connor dashes over, throwing himself on top of them.

"They're cute," Garrett says.

"Yeah." I sniff. "I guess."

"Don't tell Carter, but I'm pretty sure Axel is flirting with his mom." He gestures across the room at our GM, who is definitely, 100 percent flirting with Holly Beckett. Holly looks like she's short-circuiting, unsure of what to do. She just keeps laughing, a little high-pitched and halfway to hysterical. "Jennie's already meddling. Invited Axel to her studio grand opening next month. Told him she'll be running a short dance class for couples, in case there was anyone there he wanted to dance with." Garrett snorts. "His eyes went right to Holly."

"Good luck to him." I hold my hand out, and Garrett deposits his drink in it. I sip it, unsurprised but still disappointed it's not alcohol. Jennie doesn't drink, so Garrett doesn't like to drink when she's around. I hand the drink back. "Carter will be on that like flies on shit."

"My God," Jennie murmurs, joining us. "Sharing drinks? You two really are an old married couple, aren't you?"

I leave them, but only after flicking Jennie in the shoulder, heading over to Rosie. She's sitting alone, eyes on Adam, Connor, and Lily as he helps them pick out costumes. She watches as Adam helps Lily into a princess costume, sweeping her hair over her shoulder so he can tie it at the back. Rosie sniffles, her smile as beautiful as it is heartbreaking.

"You really love her, huh?" I ask softly, nudging her side.

"I really, really do." She nibbles her lower lip. "Can I tell you something?"

"Always."

"We passed our PRIDE training yesterday. We're officially eligible to be foster parents." She swipes at a tear the moment it falls. "I can't wait to bring her home. I just hope we do right by her."

"That's amazing, Rosie." I sling an arm over her shoulder. "I'm so excited for you guys. And of course you're going to do right by her. You're going to do *amazing*. You're lucky to have each other."

She squeezes me softly. "Thank you, Jaxon."

I sit back, and when I hear a laugh a little higher than the rest, my gaze coasts the room, finding Lennon. She's got a crowd of kids gathered around her, enthralled with Buzz Lightyear, and she's really owning the part, putting on a show trying to defeat a cluster of stuffed space aliens.

Rosie nudges my shoulder with hers. "What about you?"

I smile as Lennon judo chops a stuffed space alien out of midair. "What about me?"

"You look like you're thinking about keeping her, that's all."

My pulse pounds, heat pooling in my cheeks. "The sex is great and Mimi's famous recipes are even better."

"Mhmm."

"What?"

"Nothing. It's just . . . don't be afraid to admit when you have feelings for someone."

"I don't have feelings for her!" It comes out a little louder than I mean it, and an older couple turns to look at us. I lower my voice. "I mean, sure, she's great. Fantastic. Honestly? She's the best. I really like having her around, and I hate it when she cries. So, yeah, I care about her. But I don't have romantic *feelings* for her. If there's one thing I don't catch, it's feelings. Colds? All the time. The flu? Had it bad in December. But feelings? Nah. Not me."

Rosie smiles, patting my arm. "Okay, Jaxon."

I'm about to tell her to shut it when a speaker crackles, and a gentle voice travels through the room.

"Excuse me." Hank, Carter's old friend, speaks into the microphone, smiling. He grips Olivia's hand. "Olivia here doesn't much care for public speaking—that's her husband's forte—so I offered to do it for her. I'm blind, after all, so I can't see you fine folk anyway. Hell, I'm telling myself there's only five of you here, even though I know there's no way Carter didn't put his whole ass—oops, butt— into his daughter's first birthday party."

Yeah, that's Hank. He's in his mid-eighties, blind, as mentioned, and the coolest old person I know, aside from my gran. But right now, I have an issue with him, and that issue is that instead of being forced into costume like the rest of us, he's wearing a T-shirt that says *great-grandfather of the birthday girl*, even though they aren't technically related.

Hank gestures to his left. "If everyone could kindly clear the doorway and gather over here—"

Olivia whispers in his ear.

"Ah, whoops." He swaps hands, gesturing to the right instead.

"Gather over *here*. The birthday girl is ready to make her grand entrance."

"Grand entrance?" I whisper in Olivia's ear when she scurries over. She's strung out, shaking like a leaf. "You gave Carter a grand entrance?"

"Jaxon, you don't even want to know what I've been dealing with for the last four months. We had a few people cancel last minute because of family plans, since Easter falls early this year, and this morning I caught Carter giving Ireland a pep talk in her bedroom about it. Wanna know what he said to her?" She leans closer, eyes wide. " 'It's your month, not Jesus's. Don't let anyone take that from you.' "

"Christ," I mutter. "He's unhinged."

Unhinged must be his cue, because suddenly, the lights go out. We're shrouded in darkness, murmurs rippling through the room, and then—*because why the fuck not*—a spotlight flicks on.

"I'm scared," Lennon murmurs, clutching my elbow.

"We all are, Len," Emmett mumbles, eyes glued on the doors. "We all are."

The doors burst open, and thick clouds of smoke billow into the room from the fog machine I caught Carter putting in his Amazon cart four days ago. "Isn't She Lovely" by Stevie Wonder spills through the speakers, and from the smoke emerges a sight I never thought I'd see in this lifetime: Carter in a black velvet tuxedo, leading his daughter into the room, fully decked out in a ball gown, tiara adorning her dark curls, and . . .

Riding a fucking pony.

Gasps fill the room—gasps of wonder or horror, nobody knows. Carter seems to think wonder, based on the extremely ~~delusional~~ proud smile he wears as he leads Ireland and her pony in a circle while waving at the guests, mouthing *thank you, thank you so much*, even blowing kisses at the crowd.

"I thought I knew what he was capable of," I mutter.

"I fought him on this," Olivia promises. "I said, 'Entrance songs are for weddings, Carter.' Do you know what he said?"

"I'm not sure I want to know," Adam murmurs.

"'Don't clip my wings, Olivia. You can't keep this free bird from soaring.'"

Garrett scrubs his hand over his mouth. "Jesus fucking Christ."

"Emmett," Carter calls, snapping his fingers at him before lifting Ireland off the pony.

Emmett dashes over, and Carter shoves the pony's reins into his unsuspecting hands. "What the fuck am I supposed to do with this?" he whisper-yells as he drags the pony over.

"Can we take it home?" Cara asks, pouting.

"Are you—" He shakes his head. "No."

"I'll suck your dick."

"Fine."

The music changes before I can ask if he's serious, if all it takes is the promise of a blow job to get him to do anything she wants. Every woman in the room *awws*, melting into a puddle as Carter holds Ireland to his chest, slowly spins her around the room while Tim McGraw sings "My Little Girl."

Olivia is the first to cry, which is no surprise. She hides a lot of emotion beneath her sass. Jennie and Rosie follow two seconds later, clinging to each other as Carter sings along, pressing the words to Ireland's temple. Garrett is next, and when Garrett starts, Cara and Lennon follow, choking on their sobs.

Adam drags his shirt up, using it to swipe at his eyes. "Fuck, man. What the hell?"

Emmett sniffles, then coughs, and when he blinks, two tears stream down his cheeks. He drags his forearm across his eyes and points at me. "Don't fucking act like you aren't seeing this, Riley!"

Oh, I'm seeing it all right. Seeing Carter smile down at his daughter, his own tears shining in his eyes. Seeing him smooth her curls back, press his lips to her forehead. Seeing him tuck her head beneath his chin, clutch her tight to his chest, whisper, "How did I get so lucky?"

My throat squeezes. My eyes burn. My nose scrunches, and a strange sensation touches my cheeks. I lift my fingers to them, sighing when they come away wet.

I look up, finding every set of teary eyes on me.

"Don't look at me!" I cry, swiping at my cheeks. "I'll cry if I want to!"

Olivia's the first to throw her arms around me, and everyone else follows. Suddenly, the nine of us are huddled together, sobbing at a first birthday party.

Nothing else could possibly go wrong.

18

ADD THAT TO MY LIST OF THINGS TO BE SCARED OF

Jaxon

"There. Right there."

Cara aims the remote at the TV, pausing the playback of the party. She pins her arms over her chest, slowly pacing back and forth in front of the couch in Carter and Olivia's living room, where Carter, Adam, Emmett, Garrett, and I are squished in shoulder to shoulder. She stops, opens her mouth, then snaps it shut. Shaking her head, she resumes her pacing. My skin crawls in the silence, awaiting our punishment. Her feet stop in front of me, and I tense.

"Why is it that when something happens it is *always* the five of you?"

She gestures at the TV, and I cringe at the paused scene.

Me, screaming, diving headfirst down the slide. Adam, trying to claw his way out the side to freedom. Garrett, halfway out, with Emmett's arm wrapped around his head, yanking him backward so he can save himself. And Carter, on his knees in the center of the quickly deflating bouncy house, a look of pure horror on his face, a plate of chocolate cake in one hand, a fork in the other, his mouth in the middle of saying *oops*.

Yep, that's us. I bet you're wondering how we got here.

"This is *your* fault," Adam grumbles beside me.

"*My* fault?" I shove his shoulder. "You were the last one to climb on."

Adam turns and shoves Garrett. "You were taking too long with your turn."

"I just got on!" Garrett shouts. "I was only on for, like, five minutes! Ten, tops!"

"Stop it!" Emmett yells. "It was Carter's fault! He's the one that brought the fork in!"

"Oh, well, *excuse me* for wanting to have fun *and* eat my cake!"

"You can't have your cake and eat it too!" Emmett screams at him.

"What does that even mean?" Carter shouts back, arms flailing. "I never understood that saying! And guess what? I had my cake, and I ate it too!"

"It means you can't jump in the bouncy house *and* eat your goddamn cake with your goddamn sharp pointy-ass fork!"

The five of us leap to our feet, screaming and shoving, until a roar cuts us off.

"Enough!"

I blink at Olivia. There's no way that just came out of someone so tiny. Her eyes narrow on me, daring me to say it out loud. I mash my lips together.

"I should've known. I should've known, that at a party for *children*, the biggest *children* would be the ones to cause an issue. I just didn't think that issue would be popping a bouncy house. I mean, for fuck's sake, it said right on there, the individual weight limit was two hundred pounds."

"But, Ollie!" Carter protests. "We did the math!"

"The total weight limit was twelve hundred," Emmett explains.

"We came in at eleven hundred and ninety-seven!" I show her the calculator on my phone, still displaying our combined weights.

Garrett nods excitedly. "Three pounds to spare!"

Adam shrugs. "If anything, it's the manufacturer's fault for—" He snaps his mouth shut, wide-eyed at Olivia's expression. "I heard it. As soon as it left my mouth, I heard how ridiculous it was." He hangs his head. "I'm so disappointed in myself."

Behind us, the rest of the girls snicker, quickly hiding behind coughs.

"Yes, well," Olivia starts, and do I detect a hint of Carter's typical theatrics? "I simply don't know if I'll recover. I just wanted it to be perfect, and—" She breaks off, sobbing into her hands, and the girls rush around her. "It's just, with Jennie's dance studio opening in a couple weeks, now I'm worried about a repeat incident like this, and—" Another sob, and the girls rub her back, shooting us glares. "God, you know, I could really use a three-night stay at the Sonora Château with the girls."

"Yes!" Carter claps his hands. "Excellent idea! We can totally make that happen, right, boys?"

The four of us nod our agreement, a chorus of *totally* and *absolutely* and *you ladies deserve it* ringing out.

"Thank you. That would be really nice." Olivia sniffles, wipes the theatrics from her eyes, and grins. "All right, I'm ready for a drink."

"I feel like I just got played," I grumble to the guys as we head to the kitchen to prepare drinks and snacks for the girls.

"Olivia just played us like a fiddle," Emmett mutters.

"Nooo." Carter looks at her across the room, tilting his head. "You think?"

"Dude, did you see that rebound?" I point to my eyes. "It took me longer to recover when you were dancing with Ireland."

"Well, shit." He pops his fists on his hips, grinning. "My acting skills must really be rubbing off on her."

My phone vibrates in my pocket, and I pull it out.

Tidbit: Can you make me a latte please?
Somebody needs to stay up all night and
teach you a lesson for being a bad boy.

I shove my phone away, yank the pantry open, and pull out all the fixings for a latte. Carter doesn't have all the fancy syrup flavors like me, only vanilla, so we'll have to make do.

"So Lennon's really moving out, huh?" Garrett asks, brewing a tea beside me for Jennie. "Gotta say, given that it's already been two months, I definitely thought you'd be past this *we're just fucking* stage by now."

Emmett snorts. "He needs more time than that."

"Give him a minute to get there," Adam says. "He's new at this."

"Huh?" I look between them. "What are you guys talking about?"

"Lennon," Carter whispers. "'Cause you have a crush."

"What? No, I—" I shake my head. "Back up. Moving out?"

Garrett lifts a brow, then tilts his head toward the living room, where the girls are snuggled up on the couch, Lennon in the middle, showing them something on her phone. "She's going to see a couple apartments next week. She's showing the girls now."

"What?" Before I can stop myself, my feet are carrying me across the room. I lean over the back of the couch, sweeping Lennon's curls over her shoulder so I can squeeze myself in. "What we lookin' at?"

She turns to me, and I'm thrown by the closeness. I see her like this nearly every night, but there's something about touching her in front of other people, being close enough to her mouth that I can nearly taste her on my tongue, letting everyone else see the way her eyes dance when she looks up at me, the same way mine do when I'm looking at her. There's something about it that feels real and raw and vulnerable. Scary. I lick my lips, hands shaking as I try to quell the urge to lean in that last inch, steal a kiss I've been thinking about since I last tasted her this morning while she was pressed up against my living room window.

"Len's showing us the apartments she's going to see next week," Jennie says.

"We're gonna go with her," Olivia adds, and Cara just smiles at me, cocking her head like she's studying me.

"Yeah? Lemme see."

Lennon sighs, showing me her screen, flipping quickly through a set of pictures.

"Hold up." I bat her hand away, flipping back two, and tsk. "Ah. Just as I thought. Formica countertops. Next."

She rolls her eyes but indulges me with prospect number two.

"Crack in the wall below the window."

She purses her lips, moving on to number three.

"Pretty sure those floors used to be white."

Number four, her favorite, apparently. And it's . . . perfect for her. Bright and spacious, with a far-off view of the mountains. A small den, a little balcony, a new kitchen, and in a safe little pocket.

But what's wrong with living with me?

"Len, are you kidding me? That's practically in another city. And you know what?" I squint at the screen. "Yeah, that's definitely the same place. I know someone who used to live there. They said the water pressure was *horrible*. Really fucked with their day-to-day."

"The water pressure was horrible," Rosie murmurs slowly, but I can't tear my gaze way from Lennon's narrowed one.

"What is going on with you?" Olivia asks.

Jennie tilts her head. "Yeah, these are all great, but you're finding an issue with all of them."

"Yes, Jaxon," Cara hums. "It's almost as if you . . . don't want Lennon to move out."

"Pssshhh. That's . . ." I swallow. Has my throat always been this itchy? "Not true."

"He always does this. Comes up with a reason why it's not a good choice. Last week, he didn't even give me a reason, just snapped my laptop shut as he walked by and said, 'Nope.'"

"Why don't you want Lennon to move out?" Cara asks.

My pulse races, and my heart pounds an uneven beat. Adrenaline buzzes through my veins, down into my legs, begging them to move, to run. "It was . . . it was . . . It was in a bad area."

"Why don't you want her to move out?" Cara asks again, but it's softer this time, curious, and I feel the weight of everyone's gaze. It's just as heavy as disappointment, the kind you feel in yourself, but not quite as heavy as grief. It's when you combine the two that everything gets really fucked up.

Blood thunders in my ears, an angry, violent sound that drowns everything out except the memory of a redheaded boy as he gasps for air, the cries of his twelve-year-old friend who was too late to save him.

Something in Lennon's gaze shifts, softening. An understanding, maybe. Empathy. "Jaxon," she whispers, and it sounds the same way it did back in January, when she was begging for her life in my arms, when she thought it was already slipping by her. She covers my hand with hers, a gentle touch I've never deserved, and I rip it away, forcing myself backward.

But it's the hurt in her eyes that seals the deal, brings words I never wanted to say pouring from my mouth, even if I trip over every one of them.

"If you move out . . . You can't, because . . . Because I-I-I . . . I can't save you if you're not here with me."

Jesus Christ, the words hurt. They rip through my lungs like a rusty knife, burn like acid, and I clutch at my chest, desperate to get rid of the pain, the memories.

Lennon's forehead crumples, and she stands from the couch, slowly moving toward me. "I'm right here, Jaxon. I'm okay."

I shake my head, fingers pressed against the memories playing out like a headache in my temples. "But you weren't. Your EpiPen was too far, and you were—you were . . ."

A hand lands on my shoulder, squeezing gently. "Hey," Garrett says softly, firmly. "We're here with you. What's going on?"

And that's all it takes. That surrounded feeling I've been chasing for too long. That feeling of family. Someone caring enough to ask.

"We were playing in the forest out back. It was only . . . it was only a two-minute walk. Bryce forgot his EpiPen, and . . . he was . . . I didn't even see the bee, it happened so fast."

"Oh, Jaxon." Lennon stops before me, but she's all blurry. I can't see her properly, and I hate it; I've never seen anything as pretty as her. Warm hands cup my cheeks, and when her thumbs brush below my eyes, I realize I'm crying.

"It was right there. *Right fucking there*, on the kitchen counter, right beside the back door. I ran as fast as I could but I . . ." My voice cracks, or maybe it's my chest, split right down the middle, every single heartache spilling out, the way my gran always said it would. "I wasn't fast enough."

Is this what it's supposed to feel like? Being part of a family built from the ground up, where people choose you day in and day out?

Because one moment I'm standing here, and the next I'm being held up by nine people who don't have to support me but are choosing to anyway.

And it's a staggering, powerful feeling I'm terrified to lose.

better than anything he ever gave me. That I'm not going to stand for anything less.

I want to enjoy the little moments along the way, small lines in the sand that mark the beginning of a new change, a new *after*. Jaxon making me see stars on my honeymoon. Jaxon making his home nut-safe when he didn't know I was watching. A handwritten guide on how to make my favorite coffees with the world's most complicated espresso machine, Timbit cereal because I can't eat real Timbits, my favorite flowers on Valentine's Day, extra shelf space in the shower, the heating turned up, and a step stool in the kitchen.

An intimate, broken confession, where one person's heartache became the heartache of an entire group.

Small moments, many of them inconsequential on their own, that slowly draw that line down the middle, giving you the after you've always dreamed of, the kind you deserve.

That's what I'm thinking about this morning as I stand at the kitchen island, staring at a bright and fresh bouquet of pink tulips.

I never see him do it. Throw out the old ones, put out the new ones. And Lord knows the man always acts like he has no idea how they got there. But every week they appear, as soon as the old ones show the first sign of wilting, and always in a brand-new vase. Today, it's a ceramic cat paw, painted in white and orange, like Mittens himself is gifting me my favorite flowers.

A few steps farther, until I stop in front of the espresso machine, looking down at the drink that waits for me, next to a bowl of Lucky Charms and a carton of milk, and a single, extra-large Sour Key half-dipped in chocolate beside my spoon.

And that line extends itself a little further.

I take my cereal to the living room, standing over a passed-out Jaxon on the couch, Mittens tucked into the crook of his arm. They're wearing the shirts I got them a couple days after Ireland's

19

HOPE, CRAMPS, AND—
HOLYFUCKITSYOURDRAGONDILDO

Lennon

DO YOU EVER HAVE THOSE moments where you realize that this is it? That this is where everything changes? Sometimes it's a day, a week, or a month. Sometimes it's one single moment, a blip in time when it feels like the world stops spinning and lets you take everything in exactly as it is in this moment, to remember it, because nothing will ever be the same again. This is that moment in time where you can draw the line right down the middle and definitively say, "That was life before, and this is life after."

I think I've been having those moments since I heard Ryne's voice over the speakers in the dinner hall as he told the waitress what a good girl she was. That was the first one, the line that would officially mark the *before*.

Some people want to forget the *befores*. Not me, though. I don't want to forget what it felt like to have my dreams belittled on a regular basis, to be talked down to when I disagreed with anything, pushed just a little on something I wanted. I don't want to forget the silent treatments, the rolling eyes, and the general way I was made to feel like I should be thankful someone was putting up with my attitude.

I want to remember the way Ryne treated me, and I want to remind myself, day in and day out, that I deserve so much *damn* birthday. Mittens's says *MY DAD IS A DILF* and Jaxon's simply says *DILF*. He's also sporting the ball cap I had made for him, *SUPPORT YOUR LOCAL CAT DADS* embroidered in pink. It's maybe my favorite sight, so I pull out my phone, snap a picture, and immediately upload it to Mittens's Instagram page. I'll save it for the next game day, too, post it on the Vipers' page next to his game-day suit and ask the fans to vote for their favorite fit.

I got everything to cheer him up. It's not so much that he's been sad, but that he's been quiet. We haven't had sex since he told us about Bryce a week ago, but he hasn't spent any less time with me. He still spreads out next to me on the couch at night, or hangs over my shoulder while I'm cooking. He watches me get ready in his bathroom, eyes hooked on me while I blab on and on about anything I think might make him smile. I usually earn a few, even if he looks away to try to hide them.

Hell, two nights ago in Florida, he even showed up at my hotel room after their game. He didn't feel up to going out with the guys, so he wanted to know if he could hang with me. Twenty minutes later, the rest of the boys showed up, pizzas and snacks in tow, saying they'd rather stay in with us. I got to attend my first Britney's Bitches meeting, and helped Carter untangle the great pony debacle and win back Olivia's affection. Jaxon was the last one out the door at midnight, and he hesitated so long I nearly asked if he wanted to spend the night in case he didn't want to be alone. But then he rubbed the back of his neck, glanced at me one last time, and whispered, *Thanks for tonight, honey.*

I know he's going through it. Jaxon's not someone who shares easily, and from the way he stumbled through a story about Bryce, giving us the bare minimum, just enough to know what he lost, the words fractured like pieces of a puzzle we need to put together, it's not hard to see it's a memory he's tried so hard to suppress. Now he's reliving it, dealing with the grief all over again, and I have to sit by and wait until he's ready to come to me with all of it. If he'll ever be.

Beyond that, I get the sense he's embarrassed of the emotions he showed when trying to tell us about Bryce, when the nine of us gathered around him, wrapped him in our arms, but he has nothing to be embarrassed by. Friends are supposed to support you. *Good* friends will take the weight off your shoulders and put it on theirs without needing to be asked, just to help you breathe. And that's the type of friends Jaxon has.

All of that is what I told myself to justify why I canceled my apartment viewings this week, but the truth is what I'm smiling down at right now. A man and his cat who took my broken heart and healed it without consciously doing it.

I nudge his thigh with my knee, shoveling my cereal back. When he doesn't move, I lift my foot, giving the lump in his sweatpants a quick tap.

His eyes fly open, and he shoots up to sitting, knocking Mittens to the ground. "I'm awake! Are we fucking?"

"You wish, fuckboy. Why you sleeping anyway? It's almost eleven."

He scrubs the sleep from his bleary eyes, flecks of green and gold dancing in the sunlight. "Uh, 'cause we landed at two this morning, and then I got up early to go get you your flow—" He mashes his lips together.

I lift my brows. "My what?"

"Nothing."

"Oh, 'kay, 'cause for a second there I thought you were gonna admit to being responsible for the bouquet of tulips on the counter every week."

Jaxon stands, adjusting his cock in his pants. "I dunno what you're talking about."

"Uh-huh. You never do. How convenient."

"Life is all about conveniences, tidbit. Like right now, you're wearing those teeny jammy shorts that you never wear panties with, and Magic Mike"—he gestures at the cock tenting his pants— "is dying to say hello. Convenient, wouldn't you say?"

"Mmm." I lift my bowl to my lips, draining the milk. When I'm done, I tug on the waistband of his sweats, peeking down at Magic Mike, happy as ever to see me. "Hi, baby," I coo, then snap the band back in place. "Can't. I'm on my period."

"What? Since when?"

"Since halfway through our flight last night." I'm as disappointed as his pout says he is. Period backing onto a sexless week? *The horror.* This will be the longest I've gone without sex since I moved in here. On top of that, my cramps are coming on strong, just like my migraine, so I anticipate spending the next two days curled up in bed whenever possible. I swipe my Sour Key off the counter on my way back to my room. "Chocolate-covered candy for breakfast was a great idea, Jaxon. Thank you."

"Where you going?" he calls after me. "Don't you wanna spend time with me?"

"I spend time with you every day!"

"Yeah, so why ruin the streak now?"

"Gonna go hibernate in bed and shop for birthday outfits!"

"Get something sexy!"

"Don't worry, I will!"

It's not me I'm shopping for, though; it's Mittens. Because if there's one day of the year I'm going to get away with having a photoshoot where I dress that cat in whatever I want, which may or may not include a mermaid bikini with a fin, it's my birthday.

So that's what I do. I spend the day alternating between express shipping the most endearing/ridiculous—depends who you ask—outfits imaginable for Mittens so they'll be here in time for my birthday, watching reruns of *Girlfriends*—Joan Clayton is unmatched; fight me—and napping.

When I venture out late in the afternoon, I find Jaxon in his room, headphones on, muttering along to whatever song he's listening to, and . . . dancing? He claps his hands above his head while shaking his hips, and my God, he's rigid as a fucking board. Leaning in the doorway, I watch as he stomps his right foot, then his left, then spins himself in a circle, rolling his hips as he goes.

It's . . . Christ, it's utterly horrifying. Mittens is crouched low to the ground, ears back, tail whipping back and forth, pupils dilated and fixed on what I can only assume from here is Jaxon's crotch.

I pull out my phone, recording him as he hops, slides to the left, then to the right, jumps, criss-crosses his feet, and finally, cha-chas real slow.

"Whaddaya think, Mitts?" Jaxon yells over the music in his ears. "Is Daddy's dancing magical, or what?"

Or fucking something.

I can't take it. Laughter rumbles deep in my belly, and I fold over as it barrels out of me. I clap my knees, losing my balance and catching myself on the wall. Jaxon whips around, eyes wide as he spots me.

"Lennon, what the fuck!" Mittens jumps at his ass, and Jaxon screams, clutching his butt cheek as he falls to the ground. "*Ah! Man down! Man down!*"

"The best part," I wheeze, swiping at my eyes with one hand, shaking my phone in the other, "is that I'm still recording."

"Out!" he shouts, scrambling to his bed. "Get out!" He scoops up a pillow, chucking it across the room. I deflect it, cackling as I dash down the hall and back to my room.

I collapse on my bed, catching my breath, grinning as I send the video to my group chat.

Two minutes later, Jaxon screams my name, and for the first time, my mind wanders to a future where I spend the rest of my days annoying him. My laughter slowly fades, until all I'm left with is the gentle, quick patter of a heart that should be too broken to feel anything again.

A heart that has no right hoping for a future with a man who once told me he'd planned to avoid living with a woman for the rest of his life.

I may be the exception to his roommate rule, but it would be silly of me to hope to be the woman the playboy settles down for.

Wouldn't it?

I lose myself in another episode until my thoughts are buried, until my cramps are bad enough to pull me out of bed. Wrapping myself in a blanket, I hobble into the hallway. Jaxon's bedroom door is cracked, and I poke my head inside again, because good things seem to happen when I do.

He's in his bathroom, leaning over the counter, the quiet hum of his beard trimmer working in time with the hum of his voice. I like watching him when he trims his beard. He's meticulous, always keeping it short and tame, just long enough to tickle the insides of my thighs when he buries his face there and lavishes me with attention.

I creep closer, smiling as a little more of him comes into view. Mittens is on the counter, rolling around on his back, using his dad's elbow as a chew toy, and Jaxon is singing what sounds a fuckload like Reba McEntire, except these are *not* the lyrics I remember my mom singing in the car on the way to Mimi's house on Sunday mornings.

"A single dad who works too hard, who loves his cat and never stops. With handsome hands even though he's a fiiighterrr. I'm a surviiiv—"

I clap a hand over my mouth, running from the room before he can finish that word. When I'm safe in the kitchen, I let the giggles free. Pulling the pantry open, I take out my stool, climb to the top step, and grab the first pill bottle I can get my hands on. Extra-strength Advil, which is not Motrin, what I usually take when I'm cramping this hard.

I turn the bottle in my hand, looking for the dosage. *"Jax!"*

"There's nobody here by that name!" he shouts back.

"I have cramps! Do I take one Advil or two?"

He sighs. "Regular strength? Just read the bottle, Len."

"Extra-strength! It says only one every six hours, but my cramps hurt real bad!"

He doesn't answer.

"I'm just gonna take two!"

Footsteps thud, and he slides into the room. "Lennon, you can't take two if it says only take one!" He rips the bottle away, glaring at me. "Gimme that."

I hide my smile behind a glass of water as he dumps a single pill into his hand, transfers it to mine, and pockets the bottle.

"Thanks." I chase the pill with my water, letting Jaxon take the glass. A shiver runs through me, and I pull the blanket tighter around my shoulders.

His eyes coast over me. "You cold?"

"A little." I shiver again, exaggerating maybe a touch. "I always feel colder on my period."

"Want me to turn the heat up?"

"It's okay. Then it'll be too hot for Mitts."

His head bobs as he nibbles his lip, looking at me, then away, back to me, then away again. "So, um . . . I guess you're not going to Adam and Rosie's, then. Since you're . . ." He points at my crotch, then circles his own.

My brows rise. "I'm not bedridden, Jaxon. I'm on my period. I can still live my life."

His eyes widen. "Oh. Yeah. Obviously. *Obviously* you can still live your life while you're on your period."

"Women have been doing it for years."

"I just thought . . . because . . ." He tugs at his shirt and looks away. "You're not feeling well. Both times I checked on you, you were sleeping. I wasn't sure if you were up for going out."

I force myself to ignore those four words.

Okay, no, I don't. I fixate on them like any normal, rational person would.

"You checked on me?" I wave the words away. "Yeah, I'm gonna stay in. I'll take a hot shower to help with the pain, then curl up on the couch for a movie with Mitts."

"Okay. Cool." He scratches his head, hazel eyes dancing with uncertainty. "Um, so, I guess . . . see you later, then."

"See ya."

He waves, but doesn't move.

"Bye, Jaxon."

"Oh. Yeah. Bye." Slowly, he backs out of the kitchen, making it halfway down the hall before he spins and books it the rest of the way, slamming his bedroom door behind him.

I do feel like shit, but the truth is I'm horny as fuck on my period. My experience with Ryne dictates that men don't want to go anywhere near women when we're menstruating, so I wait until I hear Jaxon leave a few minutes later before doing what I'm used to. I fill the bath with steaming water and grab my waterproof dual-stimulation vibrator, sighing as I insert it and fix the suction over my clit. Then I grab the remote control, climb into the bath, slip my AirPods in, turn on my audiobook, and crank that toy up to ten while definitely not thinking about Jaxon.

When I'm satiated, I hop in a quick shower to wash my hair, which is, as predicted, my worst mistake. I'm too tired and sore to go through my routine, so I wrap it in my microfiber towel and decide to make it Tomorrow Lennon's problem. Once I'm snug in one of Jaxon's Vipers T-shirts and a pair of sweats I stole straight from the dryer three weeks ago that he never asked for back, I make my way out to the living room to put on a movie.

Mittens is exactly where I expect him to be: sprawled out on the chaise lounge. It's everything else that's out of place, pulling my feet to a stop.

Netflix already on and waiting for me. Tiny, snack-size boxes of cereal on the coffee table. One bowl of Smarties, one of mini Sour Keys. A heating pad, and Jaxon Riley, NHL bad boy, walking toward me, a steaming mug in his hand.

He sinks to the couch, and I can't breathe.

"What are you doing here?"

"I live here."

"Jaxon." I step in front of him, blocking the TV. "What are you *doing* here?" I motion around us, all the thoughtful gestures that are just for me, even if he acts like they're not. "What is all this? Why aren't you at Adam and Rosie's?"

He tosses a handful of Corn Pops in his mouth. Tilts his head, peeking around me, scrolling through Netflix.

When I cross my arms and jut a hip, he sighs.

"You've got a case of FOMO worse than Mitts, so I'd just have to deal with you asking me five million questions about what happened when I got home."

I arch a brow, and he throws his hands in the air.

"I didn't want you to feel shitty at home all alone! I got halfway to Adam's, then suddenly I was at the store, picking up snacks for you. There, are you happy? Fuck." He grips my wrist, yanking me down beside him. "Sit your ass down." He gestures at the steaming mug. "I made you your stupid chai tea that you like at night."

"Chai," I murmur, smiling against the warm mug.

"Huh?"

"It's just chai, because chai means tea. Calling it chai tea is like calling it tea tea, the same way calling naan 'naan bread' is like calling it bread bread."

He blinks at me. "I fucking hate you."

I grin. "You fucking love me, bud."

He grabs the Sour Keys, glaring at me as he sucks one into his mouth. I reach for the bowl, and his scowl deepens as he tugs it out of reach.

"Give it! You can't keep candy from a woman on her period!"

He rolls his eyes, relenting, resting his hand on my thigh, bowl in his palm. He looks at my towel. "I thought you don't like to sleep with wet hair."

"I don't. I wasn't thinking when I washed it. But I'm too tired to do it tonight."

Jaxon nods, quiet as he resumes scrolling on Netflix.

"Oh!" I clap his thigh, pointing at the movie he just passed. "That one!"

"No. Fuck no."

"*Please*, Jaxon! It's one of the greatest romantic comedies of all time!"

His face twists in disgust. "*She's the Man*? *She's the Man* is one of the greatest romantic comedies of all time?"

"I said what I said."

Another roll of his eyes, but he presses play, huffing out the longest sigh anyone's ever sighed as he stands and storms off. His footsteps return two minutes later, and I pat the spot next to me, shoving a Sour Key between my lips.

"Oh, good. Just in time. You don't wanna miss Viola break up with Justin. He's such an egotistical ass. Typical male toxicity, threatened by talented women." I cock my head at his full arms. "Whatcha got there?"

He starts unloading, setting everything up on the coffee table.

My heartbeat trips, and when it restarts, it gallops like a horse. My leave-in conditioner and my comb. My curl butter and my favorite mousse. My hair dryer and my diffuser.

Jaxon sits on the edge of the couch, spreading his legs. He gestures to the space there and picks up my comb. "C'mon, tidbit."

"What . . . what are you . . ." I swallow, pleading away the sting of my nose, the burn of my eyes. "You're going to do my hair for me?"

"I'm gonna try my best. I think I've watched you enough." He takes my hand, guiding me to my feet, then down to my bum, settling on the rug in the space left for me. "Besides, you love correcting me when I'm wrong."

"Put it on my résumé," I whisper. "I'm so fucking good at it." My chin quivers, and I try so hard not to, but I sniffle.

Jaxon glides his hands up my arms, squeezing my shoulders. "Don't cry, honey. Please. The girls are starting to tease me every time I text for help." He unwinds the towel, letting my wet curls fall down my back. "It's just hair, Len. I'm happy to help."

It's not just hair, though. It's shelves full of products, hours spent washing and styling. It's not being able to just crawl into bed on my most tired nights without pausing to protect my hair, regretting it the mornings after I've forgotten. It's my mom's dedication to learning everything she could about caring for Black hair, swallowing her pride and asking the Black women in her life for help so she could send me off to school with the biggest smile on my face. It's countless dollars spent finding the right products, hours and hours spent watching video tutorials. It's a routine I've spent years fine-tuning, and it's not just hair. It's a part of me, and Jaxon . . . he's making it a part of him now too.

"I can stop," he says softly. "Say the word, Len."

Tears gather in my eyes, and I bat them away, pulling in one steadying breath after another.

When I stay seated, Jaxon asks, "Leave-in conditioner first, right? Then comb it through?"

I nod, and when he rakes the cream through my hair, I let my eyes close, leaning into his touch.

"Let me know if I'm hurting you," he murmurs, slowly gliding the comb through my hair. Fingertips dance over my shoulder, and I watch as he twirls a lock around his finger before letting it bounce free. He picks up my curl butter and mousse, looking between them before holding the purple tub of curl butter out to me for confirmation.

I smile, nodding, and butterflies take flight in my stomach as he carefully sifts his fingers through my hair.

"Tell me something."

The quiet words startle me, and I search for something to say, anything other than *uh-oh, I think I might be falling for you, but, like, don't freak out, because then I'll freak out, and then we'll both be freaking out.* I settle on, "Like what?"

"Why did your parents name you Lennon?"

"Why else does anyone call their kid Lennon? My mom was obsessed with John Lennon, and my dad was obsessed with her."

Jaxon chuckles. "That's it, eh? End of story?"

"Man obsessed with woman is always the end of the story."

"Mmm. Maybe." He sprays mousse in his palms before smoothing them over my hair. "Would you have been happy? If what happened hadn't, you got married in January, and Ryne had been the end of your story?"

I pull my lower lip between my teeth, hesitating. "No. But I think it would've taken me a while to admit to myself that I was miserable. I tried so hard to fixate on all the good stuff, like breakfast in bed on the weekends, pretty dresses in my size waiting for me when I got home from work, a note telling me to be ready at eight for a special dinner, the way my stomach flipped every time he told me I was the reason his life was as beautiful as it was." I lift a shoulder. "Classic case of seeing what we want to see and ignoring all the bullshit."

"I can't imagine you doing that. Ignoring the bullshit. You're pretty comfortable calling me out on my shit, and you have been since day one."

"Sure, but I wasn't trying to impress you when we met. I also met Ryne in high school. I was young and desperate to be in love. He was older and popular, coveted, and society dictated that women should be agreeable to be desirable. When you're young, it's easy to convince yourself that you're too much, that you should make yourself smaller to keep others happy. That's what I did, even though I spent years telling myself I wasn't."

Jaxon works my curls in silence.

"What are you thinking?"

"Nothing," he lies.

"Jaxon."

He sighs. "Just that Ryne is a piece of shit. An agreeable version of you who sits quietly by, blending in instead of standing out, isn't my Lennon."

My heart pounds at that simple two-letter word. "I thought you liked quiet."

"Before you, maybe."

"And now?"

"Now I like loud."

Goose bumps dot my arms, the tension in the air as palpable as the heat of his body against mine.

Jaxon's eyes meet mine as he scrunches my curls in his fist. "Am I doing this right?"

"You're doing great." I pull my phone out, aiming it at us and hitting the record button so I can watch him, thankful for the distraction. The blush that spreads across his cheekbones is the most fascinating shade of pink I've ever seen. He laughs, a soft, low sound that warms the exposed skin on my neck, rolling across the surface of my body like the summer sun. He glances away, and when his gaze comes back, it focuses on my lips. When I smile, he smiles too.

And then he does something that lights my insides on fire.

He slides his rough palm over the nape of my neck, squeezing tenderly, and angles my face over my shoulder. The sharp rise of his chest matches mine, and a moment later his lips are on mine. Tasting them softly, coaxing them open. His tongue sweeps inside, and he kisses me hungrily, like he's been craving nothing else.

He kisses me until I'm breathless, twisted between his legs, clinging to his shirt, and when he tears his mouth away, he whispers, "Been thinking 'bout that for a few days."

Well, okay, then. Caught that all on video, which is . . . nice. Yeah, nice. In case I need it later for . . . informational purposes. Or whatever.

As Jaxon starts diffusing my curls, I forward the video to Serena. It takes her ten seconds to start responding, and I hide my phone between my crossed legs so I can read it without Jaxon seeing.

Serena: Oh my fuck??? Is he doing ur hair???

Serena: OH MY FUCK??? THE WAY HE'S LOOKING AT YOU???

Serena: OH MY FUCKING FUCK, THAT KISS??????? MARRY HIM. MARRY HIM RIGHT NOW. MAN'S OBSESSED. ***OBSESSED***

Serena: What's he doing now???

Serena: Is the answer you? The answer is you, isn't it?

It's not, obviously, but I wish it was. Instead, I snap a picture of Jaxon diffusing my hair, a small crease between his brows as he focuses on the task.

Serena: Fucking swoon, what the hell???

Serena: You like him, don't you?

Serena: Len?

Serena: Oh, you're ignoring me now? We're playing that game. K. *music notes emoji* Lennon's got a cruuush, Lennon's got a cruuush *music notes emoji*

It's an interesting thought, but I'd rather not dwell on it further than I already have tonight, so I switch my phone off. Another problem for Tomorrow Lennon.

Instead, I close my eyes, letting myself relax as Jaxon dries my hair.

"*Voilà.*" He sets the hair dryer down and hands me his phone, camera open. I run my fingers over my curls, checking out his handiwork. Some of the corkscrews are misshapen and tangled, it's significantly frizzier than usual, and somehow the left side is hanging a good inch longer than the right.

My nose tingles, chin quivering. I swat at the single tear that works its way free. "It's perfect, Jaxon. Thank you."

"You're welcome, honey."

I stay on the rug between his legs, thoughts running rampant. I think about a little girl who dreamed of seeing her photography in nature magazines, of a man who crushed that dream. A man who didn't care enough about her interests, what made her smile and what made her feel special.

And I think about the man behind me, the one I've known just shy of three months, who has no obligation to but goes out of his way to do the complete opposite.

I wonder if he even knows he's doing it.

"Ryne got me cash for Christmas," I blurt before I can stop myself.

"What?"

"Cash. He opened his stocking on Christmas morning, the one I spent hours meticulously curating, and when he was done, he took out his wallet, counted out a thousand dollars, handed it to me, and told me to buy myself something special."

"Jesus, honey." Jaxon runs a hand over his mouth before offering it to me, helping me onto the couch beside him. "He didn't get you anything?"

I shake my head. "You know, that's not even the worst." I wring my hands, afraid to say the words out loud. I've never told anyone. Whenever anyone asked me what I'd asked for from Ryne for my birthday, I told them I'd asked for a nice dinner, because that's always what I got. It was easier than answering what their inevitable follow-up question would be, which is *Why didn't he get it for you?* "Do you remember me saying I'd wanted to go into astrophotography?"

"You said a perfect life would be one where you spent the rest of it stargazing." He grins, sheepish and boyish, my favorite. "You had your thighs wrapped around my head when you said it, and all I could think was that my perfect life would be one where I spent the rest of it with you riding my face."

I snicker, giving him a shove before pulling my knees to my chest, wrapping my arms around them. "I've always loved the stars. Anything that happens in the sky, really. It's just . . . surreal, you know? Ethereal. You see the sky every day, and most people, they just get used to it. It becomes part of the background. I never understood that. You'll never see the same sunrise twice. The sky looks different every night, even though it's the same constellations. It's just . . . magnificent. My parents bought me my first telescope when I was seven. I'd dog-eared the Christmas toy catalogue, and on Christmas morning, there it was, set up beside the tree. I ran that thing into the ground, and for my twelfth birthday, Mimi replaced it. And two months before I turned eighteen, when it was stolen from the trunk of our car, I asked Ryne for one." The memory squeezes my throat like a fist, impossible to swallow down. "He said it was a silly hobby. Took me for dinner at the clubhouse our grandparents were members at instead. And when he saw my college application for the astronomy program at the University of Georgia, he told me to be for real about my future, to pick a real job, because hobbies don't pay the bills. 'Stargazing is a fun activity when you're a kid, sweetheart, not a job,' he'd said. And when my parents asked me why I didn't apply, I lied. Told them I didn't love it the way I used to, because I was embarrassed."

I smile as Mittens wakes, stretching before hopping up to spread out between Jaxon and me. "For my birthday last year, I worked up the courage to ask Ryne to take me to see the Northern Lights. There's a place in Georgia, Brasstown Bald, that's supposed to have incredible views, and it was always on my bucket list. It was a little over three hours away, so I suggested a hotel, and Ryne agreed, said it was a good idea, and gave me a kiss." I swallow the lump in my throat. "He forgot my birthday. Got home at nine that night, looked at the flowers all over the kitchen counter, the birthday balloons, the bag I'd packed for us for the night, and groaned. 'Ah, shit, Lenny,' he said. 'It's been a shit week at work. Don't make me feel bad about it. Providing for our family is a little more important than going stargazing.' Kissed my forehead, reminded me he treated me like it was my birthday every day, and went for a shower."

Jaxon's hand moves over my back. "I'm sorry, honey."

I tuck my chin on my knee. "It's just . . . it's the thought that counts, you know? It doesn't need to be big or expensive or flashy. I just want to know that you've taken an interest in me. That you're listening. I want to feel heard, and I guess . . . I guess I wasn't. Not there. Not with him. I wish I would've admitted that to myself years ago."

"No more." Jaxon grips my chin, forcing my gaze to his. "No more quiet Lennon. That's not you. You're not gonna let people like that walk all over you, make you feel like you're selfish for asking for something you deserve."

"It's not that big a deal. The telescope—"

"I'm not talking about the telescope, Lennon. I'm talking about love. You asked to be loved, *deserved* it, and he failed to do it. He never deserved you, honey. Not an ounce of you. Not at seventeen, not at twenty-six, and not for the rest of your life or his." His eyes move between mine. "You deserve better. So much fucking better. Got it?"

I lick my bottom lip, sucking it into my mouth. Jaxon tugs it free, scraping the pad of his thumb across the soft flesh, his eyes tracking the movement.

"Tell me," he demands gently.

"Got it," I whisper, and he swallows the two words with his mouth. My chest heaves as his tongue sweeps mine, his palm gliding roughly over my hip, dipping beneath his T-shirt I wear, gripping my waist. He keeps me there, holding me beneath him as he explores my mouth, and every nerve ending in my body fizzles and pops.

I've never, ever been kissed the way Jaxon kisses me, like he'll die if he doesn't get just one more taste. I don't know how I'll ever be able to go without it again, now I know what it feels like.

He drags his mouth from mine, along my jaw and up to my ear, where he presses three whispered words that make my blood run hot. "Good girl, honey."

We watch the movie in silence for a few minutes, though I get the impression Jaxon is taking in about as much as I am: nothing at all. It's a tragedy, especially when I realize I've missed the infamous Gouda line.

All I can focus on is him. I'm hooked, fixated on every movement, the way he taps a single finger against the arm of the couch, mindlessly strokes Mittens's forehead. He scoops the cat into one arm and deposits him on the chaise lounge by the window, and when he sits back down beside me, he spreads his legs wide and lets his palm fall to my thigh. I watch as he runs it slowly up and down before letting the tip of his pointer finger take its place. He picks up the strings hanging between my thighs, and my vagina squeals at his proximity.

Calm the fuck down, bitch. We're bleeding, remember?

He twist the string around his finger. "Pants today?"

"I'm . . . cold?" *Lies.* I'm burning up, horny as hell, and why do gray sweatpants highlight dicks so fucking flawlessly? I can practically trace the entire shape of him with my eyes right now.

"Mmm. Don't know if I like you in your shorts more, or my pants. One screams easy access."

My throat dries. "And the other?"

Playful eyes coast to mine, a lazy, arrogant smile pulling up on one side. "The other screams mine."

Oh. Oh, *fuck.* No. Nope. Not today, Satan. Today of all days, with my uterus literally shedding, is not the day to be testing me.

I shove his hand away from my coochie, flinging my arms wide in a faux stretch, nearly hammering him in the face as I give him an Academy Award–winning yawn and leap to my feet. "Well, I'm beat. Off to bed I go."

"Not gonna finish the greatest romantic comedy of all time?"

"I know what happens, and you do too. Don't act like you haven't seen this at least five times. I caught you dancing to the 'Cha Cha Slide' today, Jaxon. The song you pretend not to know when the guys try to get you to dance at the games."

He watches me with an arched brow as I scoop up the treats, tucking everything away in the kitchen. Fold the blanket, fluff the cushions via karate chop, dust the bookshelf for no reason, rearrange my books, and finally, gather my hair products in my arms.

I pause, then place them back on the table. "Actually, these go in your bathroom, so I'll let you . . ." I fiddle with my curls, twining them around my fingers until they tangle and get stuck. "Bye. Thanks. Good night. Thanks again. For the hair."

My exit begins a walk, but the second I round the corner, it turns into a mad dash down the hall and into my bedroom, door slamming behind me. I don't have time to run myself another bath—I'm much too horny—so I crank the shower for a second time and hope Jaxon won't be upset with me for ruining his fresh 'do. I tug all my clothes off, clean out my period cup, grab my dragon dildo, and then scream bloody murder when the bathroom door swings open.

"Hey, Len, do you have my—*holyfuckitsyourdragondildo.*" Jaxon's eyes widen, glued to the ridged dildo gripped tightly in my fist. He covers his mouth with one shaky hand, the other rising to point at my toy. "Were you gonna . . . you were gonna . . . *holy fuck, it's your dragon dildo.*"

I shove it behind my back, hands shaking, embarrassment pooling in my cheeks. "Lots of women masturbate on their periods," I rush out, hating how the words tremble, ready to be torn down. "Hormone levels peak, there's an increase in blood flow to the pelvis, which makes us ultrasensitive, and it's totally, completely normal to have amplified sexual desire."

His hands fall to his sides. The wonder in his eyes clears as he tilts his head, looks me over. Something like disappointment creases his forehead, and my stomach sinks. "Jesus, Ryne really was a piece of absolute shit, wasn't he?"

I open my mouth to argue more about the science behind masturbating on your period, but then his words settle, and my thoughts jumble, especially as he slowly ambles toward me. "What?"

"You think I'm turned off by a little blood, honey?"

I point at him, and I hate that it's the dildo hand I do it with. "Don't do that. Not the honey. You know what it does to me."

"Turns you on. That's good. I'm always turned on by you." He wraps his hand around mine until my dildo is gripped tightly by both of us. "Period or no period, Lennon. I'm *always* fucking turned on by you."

I shiver, head tilting as the tip of his nose drags up my neck, replaced by his mouth as he showers my throat with hot, wet kisses. "I don't blame you. I'm really hot."

Jaxon sinks his fingers into the hair at the nape of my neck, pulling my head taut, leaving me at the mercy of his mouth as he drags it wherever he pleases, lavishing me with attention. "My mouthy girl. Always begging to be fucked when you talk like that, huh?"

Fingertips dance down my side, and I freeze when he slips his hand between my thighs.

"Jaxon, you don't have—" I swallow my words, fingernails digging into his broad shoulders as he slowly circles my clit. I pull his mouth to mine, burying my moan there, loving the way his chuckle tastes on my tongue.

"You were gonna fuck this while you thought of me."

The head of my dildo slips through my folds. I moan, rocking against it.

"Say it."

I shake my head, and the dildo disappears. Frantic, I grip Jaxon's wrist, bringing the cock back between my legs.

"Say it," he demands, gliding it over my soaked, throbbing pussy. "Tell me."

"I was gonna fuck my dildo while I thought of you."

The dildo disappears again, and my eyes snap open, zeroing in on the man I'm about to dismember. But every threat I want to hurl at him dries in my throat as he pulls his shirt over his head, shoves his pants and boxers down, his cock bouncing up to his belly button, and holy fuck, I want to swallow it.

He fists his cock, slapping my dildo down in the square sink before he stalks toward me. "Show me. Show me how you fuck yourself when you wish you were fucking me, honey."

"Jaxon, I . . ." I rub my thighs together, because the idea is tantalizing. Me, on the counter, spread wide in front of the mirror, watching my pussy swallow a thick cock while Jaxon strokes himself. I shake my head. "There'll be blood."

"I don't mind."

My chest heaves as my eyes bounce between Jaxon and the dildo waiting for me. I wring my hands, lick my lips, unsure where my voice has gone. Words stolen by Ryne even when he's not here. "I'm worried you'll be grossed out," I finally whisper.

The hard edges of Jaxon's gaze softens. "I already told you, honey, there's nothing about you that turns me off." He wraps his palm around my neck, lips meeting mine for a soft, slow kiss. "If you're uncomfortable, Lennon, I understand. I won't push. But I don't want you to feel ashamed for something that's natural. Make yourself feel good however you want to, and don't let words somebody never should've spoken take up space in your head. He's not worth it." He presses a kiss to my forehead and reaches for his pants.

"Wait!" My lower lip slides through my teeth, and I glance at the dildo bouncing around in the sink. "How do I get up there?"

Jaxon ditches his pants over his shoulder, racing back to me. "At your service, my short queen." He flips me up into his arms before I can protest the newest nickname, depositing me on the counter, legs spread wide, feet flat. He bows, tipping an invisible hat, and I can honestly not believe how hard his cock is. "Milady."

I snicker, and his eyes move over me in the mirror, the heat stacked behind them leaving a trail of fire as they go. He moves behind me, palms scraping up my calves, my thighs. He palms my breasts, and I marvel at the sight, sun-kissed skin covered in tattoos, corded forearms and perfect, broad fingers that tug at my nipples, rolling them while I squirm.

"Fuck, honey, look at you. So damn flawless, I couldn't have dreamed you up. Spread your legs wider. Lemme see that perfect cunt."

"Jaxon," I gasp, and he smiles against my neck. When my legs fall open, he sighs, a long, low sound that scrapes against my clit.

"Look at you, Lennon." He grips my chin, forcing my gaze to my reflection, where I take in the sight of my pussy, drenched and weeping just for him. Grasping my hips, he shifts me, and I gasp as my clit rubs against the ridges of the cock. "You're gonna enjoy this, honey. So am I. And when you're done watching yourself come all over this cock, then you can have mine." His mouth dips to my ear as his hands slide under my ass, lifting me, positioning me over the dildo. "You can come all over my cock as many times as you want."

I cry out as he drops me on the dildo, throwing my head over his shoulder as I adjust to the size, the ridges.

"Jesus, honey. Look at you. Look at your pretty pussy taking every inch." His hands run over my quivering arms. "You're trembling already. You're not gonna last."

I shake my head, whimpering as Jaxon dips his fingers to the cleft of my thighs. With torturously slow circles, he works my clit, his mouth moving over my neck as he rolls my nipple between his thumb and forefinger, until my hips start rolling, lifting. I ease myself up the length of the dildo before lowering myself, then do it again and again, hooked on the way I stretch around it.

"Is this what it looks like?" I manage on staggered breaths. "When I take your cock? God, it's . . . it's . . . it's fucking incredible."

He laughs, a low, husky sound, and when he coats his fingers in my wetness and brings them around to my backside, gently rubbing that tight hole, I moan. "Close, honey. So close. When it's my cock sinking inside your pussy . . . it's fucking euphoric. The most addicting sight I've ever witnessed."

He pushes a single finger inside, and my eyes flutter closed as I take it, *love it*. It used to be uncomfortable at first, take me a minute or two to adjust to the fullness. Now I chase it, crave it. A second finger brushes at my entrance.

"Two?" Jaxon asks quietly.

"Two," I breathe out, a shiver of pleasure rippling down my spine as I arch my back, taking the second finger. I barely recognize my reflection, and yet in this moment, I've never felt more me. I can't begin to explain how freeing it is. To be with someone who appreciates me, respects me. Hears my desires and feeds them all while shedding the shame I've carried too long. There's no hiding here. My slick, flushed face, quivering limbs, and bouncing tits say as much as I fuck the dildo on my bathroom counter, leaving streaks of blood on it every time I lift myself up, Jaxon fixated on me, unable to tear his gaze away.

"I'm a mess," I sputter, face falling forward as pressure coils low in my belly.

"You're a goddamn masterpiece."

The best part? *I feel like it.*

"Can't see you," Jaxon huffs, nose nudging at the curls curtaining my face.

I gather them in my fist, piling them on top of my head. "It's called volume, baby."

He huffs a laugh, and when a moan slips out of me, long and low, and I arch away from him, pausing my movements, he smirks. "Already, honey?"

"Oh, *God*, it's so g-g-gooood." I roll my hips as he works his fingers inside me, slow, deep thrusts, delicious twists that have my legs on the verge of giving out. "Don't stop, p-p-please."

My head falls over his shoulder, and he suctions his mouth over the spot where my neck meets my collarbone. When he pulls away, the skin is a dark shade of purple, and the sight alone makes me shiver. He twists his fingers inside me, and the sound I make is some sort of strangled mewl, desperate for more. Jaxon just smiles.

"You want my cock here one day, honey? That's the only future you have with two cocks at once. Never been a jealous man, but honey, you got me all kinds of possessive. This pussy is mine. This ass is mine. These perfect tits. This fucking mouth? Fucking *mine*, honey. And I'm not fucking sharing." He pulls his fingers from my clit, bracketing my jaw as he brings my gaze to his. "Got it?"

"Got it."

"Good girl." He steals the whimper right from my mouth. "Let go, honey. Now." He slaps my clit, and I cry out, shattering around a cock I wish was his, squeezing his fingers deeper inside me.

I'm barely done when he pulls me off the counter and pushes me into the shower. I don't have time to apologize for having it running this entire time, because he shoves me against the tiles, hooks my legs over his arms, and buries himself to the hilt in a single, punishing thrust that has me crying out his name.

He groans, resting his forehead against mine as the water soaks our faces, and he grins. "Honey, I'm home."

Five. That's how many times I come before I pass out. Once on the dildo, once on Jaxon's fingers, and three times on his cock. Three times in the shower, and twice on a towel in the bed.

He doesn't leave me until three in the morning, after cleaning the spot between my legs and when he thinks I'm fast asleep. He's back two minutes later, leaving water and Advil on my bedside table, cupping my face in his rough hands for a long moment before his lips brush softly against mine.

"Night, honey," he whispers, stroking his thumb over my cheekbone.

And then he's gone, and I'm flopping over in bed, mind blown, heart thrashing.

Because everything inside me screams that this isn't typical. That nothing about this, about us, is ordinary or mundane. There's something here, something real and different and new and . . . exciting. For the first time in so long, I'm excited about a future with a partner at my side. Even if Jaxon Riley doesn't do relationships.

So maybe it's silly of me to hope to be the exception to his rules, but . . . isn't that what hope is?

I'll tell you something, though. Hope is a funny, fickle thing. You hold on to it for so long, refusing to give it up, and one day you just loosen your grip, watching it sift through your fingers, so damn tired you don't even care as it disappears.

And then you wake up one sunny morning in April on your twenty-seventh birthday to a note on your pillow.

Happy birthday, honey.
Don't make a big deal of it.

And when you find the telescope you've been asking for waiting for you beneath your bedroom window, you don't even try to stop the tears from coming.

And all that lost hope? It comes rushing right back, and you stand there, open your arms, and soak it all in.

20

SEEING STARS

Lennon

ONE THING ABOUT ME: I'M always prepared for a face full of dick.

In this home, there's simply no other way to live.

That's why I'm not surprised when I fling open Jaxon's bedroom door at seven in the morning, right as he's stepping out of bed. Why I don't hesitate when I'm met with a face full of rock-hard dick as I bound across the bedroom, throw my arms around his neck, and tackle him to his bed.

"Jesus, honey," he grunts out as I straddle him.

"Thank you, thank you, *thank you*," I cry, face stuffed in the crook of his neck.

His hands scrape up my thighs, grasping my ass. "If this is you not making a big deal out of it, I'd hate to see when you're outwardly excited."

"It's the best gift ever in the history of gifts." I sit up, slapping at my happy tears, and Jaxon hisses as the head of his cock slips beneath the flimsy crotch of my shorts, meeting the warmth pooled there. "I wasn't expecting it."

"Uh-huh," he murmurs, nails digging into my thighs, hooded gaze fixed on where we're connected. He shifts me backward, just an inch, then slowly tugs me forward, grinning when I gasp at the feel of his hard, thick cock sliding inside me. "Birthday girls get spoiled around here."

"Have you ever spoiled a birthday girl?"

"Paid off Gran's mortgage for her sixty-third birthday when I signed my first contract. Still take her on our annual birthday date night too. She likes dinner at McDonald's, a dipped cone from Dairy Queen, a walk in the park, and we finish the beautiful evening with *Goodfellas*, 'cause Gran says there's little in life prettier than a young Ray Liotta."

I snicker, letting him guide my hips. "You gonna take me to McDonald's after the game tonight, Casanova?"

"Fuck yeah." With his hand on my ass, he flips us over, pinning me beneath the weight of his body. "Gonna spend all the time in between fucking you first, though." He pushes my knees wide, sinking so deep inside me, every thought in my head gets up and walks out. "Twenty-seven today?" Blows out a hard breath, grinding his pelvis against my clit, working me into a frenzy as he reaches behind him, fiddling with his bedside table. "Tough, but I think I can do it."

"You can't possibly—*ooohJesusfuckshit.*" I claw at the sheets as he holds a small wand vibrator to my clit.

"Hold that for me right there, honey. Yeah, just like that. Good girl." He pulls out, sinks back in at an achingly slow pace, and I'm shaking, begging. His mouth hooks up in a crooked grin. "Let's start with this one right here," he murmurs, pulls out, and slams back inside me as hard and deep as he can, making me see stars right here in the bedroom, in broad daylight, no telescope needed.

Three hours later, when he strolls through the door after morning skate, I'm about to go from spoiled birthday girl to run-and-hide birthday girl. Can't find it in me to care.

"Mitts!" Jaxon calls. "Daddy's home!"

"Oh, yes," I mutter, clicking away on my camera as Mittens stretches out on his back in the kiddie pool, beneath the golden rays of the sun. He looks utterly exquisite in his shiny green-and-purple mermaid suit, a teensy shell bikini top with a matching fin bottom. The water and fish I'll Photoshop in later will be the finishing touch. "Work it, baby."

Mittens rolls around—he's a natural, a star—ignoring Jaxon's *pss-pss-pss*. He's such a determined model, focused, and if I'm being honest, a bit of a slut for all the attention from his Instagram fans, of which there are now more than half a million.

"*Mittens!* Come see Daddy, my handsome little marshmallow! Come see Daddy! *Pss-pss-pss!*"

"Hey." I snap my fingers, bringing his green eyes back to mine. "Ignore him. It's just you, me, and the camera."

"*Meow!*"

Footsteps pad closer, and I frantically snap photos, knowing our time is about to be cut short. Rolling my eyes, I drop my face to the rug as Jaxon starts singing.

"Silly kitty, chunky kitty, I kiss your tiny nossse. Fluffy kitty, handsome kitty, I love your extra toesss." His footsteps stop behind me. "Oh, hey, there you guys—*ah! Mittens! What are you wearing?*" He rushes over, hands on his face as he examines the scene, eyes wide with horror. "*What has she done to you?*"

Mittens meows, rolling leisurely in his pool, rubbing his face on the catnip goldfish I lured him in there with.

"I told you the other week I was ordering birthday outfits!"

Jaxon tosses his arms wide. "I thought you meant sexy birthday outfits for you!"

I gesture at the pile of cat costumes on the floor. "Clearly I meant sexy birthday outfits for Mittens!"

Jaxon starts scooping up the outfits. "That's it. You're out of pocket, Lennon. This is over."

"No, but—" I ball my fists up, groaning. Leaping to my feet, I rip a red handkerchief, tiny cowboy booties with plastic spurs on them, and a cowboy hat out of Jaxon's hands. "We still have to do Buckaroo Mitts! He's the biggest, baddest cowboy in the Wild West!"

Jaxon blinks at the outfit. "Fuck, that's cute." He shakes his head. "But that's beside the point! *I'm* his dad; you need my permission before you dress him up! Plus"—he props his fists on his hips, looking properly outraged—"if I'd known you were doing a fashion show, I woulda got his tux steamed!"

"Mittens has a tux?"

He scoffs, a look of utter disgust on his face. "Every respectable cat dad has a tux for their son, Lennon. Please. You insult me."

"Okay, then," I mutter, finding my bag of accessories, pulling out a real cowboy hat. "I got you a matching one."

His eyes glitter, and he slaps the tiny hat on Mittens's head. "C'mon, cowboy." He smooshes their faces together, grinning at my camera. "Handsome boys only."

As expected, what started as a photoshoot of Mittens turns into a cat-and-dad session, swapping out one ridiculous accessory for another. When I'm tucking my camera away, Jaxon calls out for me to wait.

"We need one of all three of us." He keeps on his pink heart-shaped sunglasses but unwraps his pink feather boa, wrapping it around my neck. Mittens has both, looking like an absolute queen as Jaxon cradles him between us. He smiles at my camera for the first picture, kisses my warm cheek for the second, and my surprised lips for the third.

When I return from lunch with the girls later, he's fixing his hair in his bathroom, wearing a pair of dark blue slacks, brown leather shoes and a matching belt, crisp white button-down tucked into his pants, looking so fine I briefly consider the beautiful babies we'd make.

He glances at me as I flop down on my belly next to Mittens on his bed. "Good lunch?"

"Amazing. They spoiled me." I roll onto my back. "I offered to photograph Jennie's grand opening for her studio at the end of the month. She said she didn't want me to feel pressured. I said if there are grown men who pretend to be badasses but melt for all the little girls who are going to ask them to dance, there must be photographic evidence."

He huffs a laugh. "As long as there's no karaoke."

"Of course not, Jaxon. It's a dance studio opening." I check my nails. "The karaoke bar is the celebration later that night."

Something clatters to the sink. "Karaoke *bar*?"

"Jennie said her and Carter need a bigger stage."

"*Why?*" He drags his hands down his face then gestures wildly around the room. "The whole *world* is their stage. When will it be enough?"

"That's so funny. Olivia said the *exact* same thing."

Jaxon groans, stalking to his closet. He shrugs into a navy suit jacket, notching his *fuck me* factor sky high. Twenty out of ten, keep the suit on and put a baby in me. I'm ready.

"You riding with me?" His eyes twinkle as he watches me slither beneath his covers. "Guessing that's a no."

"I don't have to be there for another hour and a half." I scoop Mittens into my chest, inhaling the smell of Jaxon on the pillow. "Gonna take a thirty-minute catnap."

He chuckles, clapping a hand to my ass and kissing my temple before he heads for the door. "Oh, I almost forgot. I found something at the grocery store earlier that reminded me of you, so I picked them up for you. Bag's under the bed."

I launch myself over the bed, smacking around at the floor until my fingers find it. Despite the paper bag with the neighborhood grocery store stamp, I can tell this wasn't bought there.

I lift the hand-painted cheetah-print Crocs from the bag. "So weird. I didn't know Urban Fare sold Crocs. Hand-painted ones too."

"Yeah, me neither. I just saw the cheetah-print pattern, and they reminded me of your neck pillow when we fly."

"Hmm. And the charms? They sell all these there too?" I run my fingers over the little charms. A cat, a camera, a hockey stick, the number 69, mountains, stars, and—

"Your onion goggles." He gestures haphazardly at the swimming goggles charm, then at the yellow slice of pie. "Mimi's famous key lime pie."

Oh. My. *God.* This man is the most adorable human to *ever* walk this earth, I'm sure of it.

Jaxon clicks out a beat with his tongue, clapping his fist into his opposite hand. "Anyway, your old Crocs are falling apart, so."

"You hate my Crocs."

"They're ugly." He points at the pair in my hands. "Those ones, though? Those are dope as fuck. Can't believe I just found 'em at the grocery store."

"Oh, Jesus Christ, Jaxon. These are clearly a custom order. Would it kill you to admit that you're an extremely thoughtful human? You got me the telescope."

He holds up a finger. "There was no name on the card, so you can't prove it was me."

I roll my eyes, setting the Crocs on Jaxon's pillow, tucking their bottom half below the blankets, like they're sleeping next to me. "You are the *most* annoying person I have *ever* met!" I shout as he heads down the hall.

"Yeah, likewise, honey!"

"Don't come near me at the game!"

"I'm gonna get in *all* your shots!"

"I *hate* you!"

"I hated you first!"

I smile, snuggling into his bed. "Thank you for the Crocs, Jaxon!"

"Welcome, honey!"

"How many fights do you think you'll get into?"

"Like, career total, or just this season?" Jaxon looks over his shoulder before turning left. "'Cause I'm already at—"

"*No fighting.* Right before you stepped on that ice tonight, I said, 'Boy, wouldn't it be so cool if you didn't fight tonight since it's my birthday?' And you smiled like you agreed."

"I smiled because I thought you were joking! I literally said to the guys, 'Did you hear Lennon's joke?' We laughed about it on the ice! They said you were funny!"

"I am funny, but that's neither here nor there!" I cross my arms over my chest, huffing. Sure, Jaxon getting all pushy and mouthy with another player is hot as balls, but watching him trade shots with a player with at least twenty pounds on him had my stomach in knots tonight. His head swung around so hard on the single punch he took, I was certain he wouldn't remember my name after the game. Then he laid the other guy out, spat the blood from his mouth, and winked at me as he skated to the penalty box, because heaven forbid he finish the regular season without another penalty.

"You weren't scared, were you?"

"What?" I swat his hand away when he glides it over my thigh. "That's ridiculous."

"Really? 'Cause you looked you wanted to hop over the boards and play doctor." He grins, eyes twinkling beneath the moonlight. "You'd make a hot doctor. I can be your patient later if you want."

I roll my eyes. "You're ridiculous." Purse my lips. "Maybe." Twisting, I squint out at the dark night. Somewhere along the way after the game, Jaxon took a wrong turn, and now we're on the highway, crawling up the west coast, shrouded in darkness, surrounded by mountains and inky pines. "Where are we? I thought we were going to McDonald's."

"I lied."

"You lied?"

"Don't worry. Got takeout delivered to the arena. It's in the back."

"You ordered takeout? Why? Where are we going? Does this mean I'm not getting ice cream for dessert?"

"Oh my God." He tugs at his tie, pulling it free and tossing it at me. "Put this on."

"Pardon?"

"Put it on. Over your eyes."

"Uh, pass."

"Please, tidbit. Let me surprise you. And I got you a fucking ice cream cake, okay? Nut-free. It's at home in the freezer. The sooner you comply and put on your blindfold—"

"Oh, God, now it's a blindfold."

"—the sooner you can have your ice cream."

Sighing, I place the silk over my eyes, tying it at the back, below my hair clip. My heart races, blood pounding in my ears as I listen, the sound of the engine as it pulls off the highway, the crunch of tires on gravel as we slow, the silence that follows when we eventually stop, and Jaxon telling me to wait here, that he'll be right back. All of it is heightened, filling the night, making my nerves dance. I'm confused and a little bit scared, because nobody's ever planned a surprise anything for me. But I'm excited, too, and when Jaxon takes my hand, helping me from the car and leading the way, I can't shut up.

"What are we doing? Where are we? Did you bring me a pair of your sweats? It's cold, and they're cozy. I'm hungry, but I'm also nervous and excited, so I don't know what's what in my belly. Hey, do you—"

"Lennon?"

"Yeah?"

"Shut up."

"Okay."

Jaxon comes to a stop, and all I can hear is the beat of my heart, the quiet lap of water against shore. It feels like it's right here, right at my feet and all around me, the moisture in the air kissing my cheeks.

And then Jaxon moves behind me, unknots his tie, and squeezes my shoulders. "Happy birthday, honey."

Uncertainty clenches my fists, and I pull in a deep breath, releasing it slowly. And then I open my eyes.

I gasp, hands flying to my mouth, and tears build in my eyes without warning.

Towering pines and endless mountains paint the skyline, touching the inky water, the slightest breeze sending a gentle ripple through the otherwise still bay.

And there, above it all, dazzling ribbons of green, orange, pink, and purple dance through the deep blue sky, thousands upon thousands of stars singing as the Northern Lights illuminate my world.

"What do you think?" Jaxon asks quietly. "Porteau Cove is supposed to be the best place out here to see the Northern Lights and stargaze. We got lucky today; the Kp index—which measures the earth's geomagnetic energy, if you didn't know, but I assume you do—is seven tonight. So, um, when the Kp is higher, the Northern Lights get farther from the poles, and then . . ." He gestures at the vivid colors before us, a look of wonder on his face before he smiles down at me. "Maybe they're dancing just for you tonight. For your birthday."

Okay, well. Shit. Fuck. "I . . . I . . ." Tears explode from my eyes, pouring down my face. I launch myself at Jaxon, legs around his waist, clinging to him.

His hand moves over my back as he whispers, "Do you like it?"

A simple *yes* would probably suffice. Instead I take his face in my hands and tell him, "You're my line."

"What?"

"The line that marks my before and after. I met you during the worst time in my life, and everything that's come since you has been so much better. This, Jaxon?" I gesture at a sky I've been dreaming of seeing in person for as long as I can remember. That's when I notice the blanket laid out by the shore, the pillows, a bag of takeout, a pile of warm clothes, and my brand-new telescope, set up and pointing at the stars. I sniffle, tears dripping down my cheeks. "This is my favorite day, and it's because of you."

"I didn't . . . I mean, I just wanted to give you something that you . . . that you like. That you wanted. And I wanted you to know . . . it's never too late to chase the dreams you had when you were a kid." He grips my neck as I fuse my mouth to his. "Just to be sure, because I've been called a lot of things, but never a line . . . Being your line, it's a good thing, right?"

I bury my laugh in his neck. "Remember the first game I was at? When we went to the bar after, and right before I walked away from you, you asked me if I wanted to be friends?"

"You said, 'That's a fuck no, fuckboy.'" He frowns. "Also something about preferring getting your period in white pants, which, when I look back at it now, was pretty mean."

"I'm sorry. You really didn't make a good first impression." I shush him with my finger over his lips when he opens them to argue. "*You*, not Magic Mike. Magic Mike made an outstanding first impression."

"Outstanding, *lasting* impression," he mutters.

"I didn't want to be your friend, Jaxon. I didn't even want to see you again. Now I hate when the plane lands in whatever city you're playing in, because road trips are the quietest, loneliest parts of my week. I'd choose you annoying me over a quiet head every day, Jaxon." I press my lips to his once more. "I didn't want to be friends, but somewhere along the way, you've become one of my best ones."

He swallows, dropping his gaze, his cheeks warming beneath my palms. "Nah, not me. I've never been anyone's best."

I tilt my head as I plant my feet back on the ground. "You really underestimate yourself, you know?" Taking his hand in mine, I lead him to the blanket. "Carter, Garrett, Adam, Emmett . . . you're a part of their best, the same way they're a part of yours. The girls too. None of them would trade you in, Jaxon. Same way I wouldn't."

He doesn't say anything, but I feel his eyes on me as I strip down to my panties, pull on the sweats he packed me. They're cozy and oversized and smell like my favorite version of heaven. We're not the only ones here, but we're on a quiet, empty stretch of pebbled shore, the other stargazers teensy blips along the dark horizon that make this night feel private and intimate, something for only Jaxon and me to share.

We spread out on the blanket with our late dinner—burgers the size of my head, an entire paper bag filled with Cajun fries, and a chocolate banana milkshake to split—watching the lights as they move slowly through the sky. When we're done eating, I test out my new telescope, aiming it at the constellations way up high. The silence is peaceful, emptying my head of every thought, every worry as I take in the wonder of the sky, something so incredible and ethereal about the way those stars up there shine every damn night no matter what.

I'm so wrapped up in the night, I almost miss the quiet crunch of Jaxon's footsteps as he moves toward me, the warmth licking at my back when he stops there.

Almost, but not quite. Because Jaxon Riley is impossible to miss.

"Come." I reach behind me, waiting until he slips his hand into mine, and then I pull him forward, letting him peer into the telescope. "Look."

"Holy shit," he gasps, head snapping up to look at the sky without the telescope, then with it again. "Len, what the fuck? There's, like, a million stars when you look through the telescope!"

"They say with the naked eye, on a dark, clear night you can see around ten thousand stars. With that, you could see, hmmm . . . fifty million?"

"*Fifty million?*"

"It's a good telescope." Incredible, really. Jaxon spared no expense for my birthday. He steps aside, letting me back in. I find what I'm looking for, then point to the sky. "You see those three stars there, brighter and bigger than the rest?" When he nods, I pull him back to the telescope. "That's the middle one."

"Ho-ly *shit*. Is that—"

"Jupiter."

"Lennon. I'm looking at a fucking planet right now." He whips his head up, wide-eyed and slack-jawed. "I can see its stripes!"

"Those stripes are actually wind and clouds. And do you see that red spot in the lower half? It's a giant storm that's been going on for hundreds of years."

"*What?* Holy shit." He stares through the telescope, hands cradling the body of it like it's a precious baby. "This is the coolest thing ever."

"Guess how many Earths can fit in the red spot."

"Uh . . . trick question? None?"

"Three."

His eyes pop. "*Three?* No fucking way! Wow! We're so tiny!"

We stand there for ages while I blow Jaxon's mind with mini astronomy lessons, and when we finally lie back on the blankets and pillows, it's close to one in the morning. I listen to the quiet patter of Jaxon's heart as I lay my ear over it, the pad of his thumb stroking my neck, his hand over mine on his torso while we stare up at the sky.

"Where do you think people go when they die?"

The words are so soft, so cautious, I almost miss them.

"I don't really think they go anywhere," I answer after a moment. "I think they stay with us."

"My gran once told me that we become stars when we die. That the people we love and lose are set free in the sky, where no one can dull their light." He swallows. "And they shine bright so . . . so we know they're still with us. That they're looking over us."

I tangle my fingers with his, squeezing gently. "That's really beautiful, Jaxon."

His hand glides up my neck, stopping at the clip in my hair. "Can I take this out?"

When I nod, he removes it, sinking his fingers in my curls. He sighs, absently twining my locks, and we lie together quietly for so long, until he opens his mouth and whispers seven words.

"I met Bryce when I was four."

As desperately as I want to sit up, I don't dare move. I know Jaxon well enough to know that telling this story is easiest for him without the pressure of my gaze. So I stay tucked in his side and hope knowing he's not alone is enough.

"First day of Tyke. He was my goalie, quiet and nervous, but fearless in net, even at that age. He was the smallest kid on our team, and he was picked on a lot that day by someone nearly twice his size. Shoved him down to the ice, and he couldn't get back up on his own in all his equipment." He pauses, and I glance up, finding him smiling at the memory. "I helped him to his feet, and then I rocked that other kid into the boards. Gran didn't know whether to be proud or mortified." His gaze falls to mine, and he brushes a curl out of my eyes. "No one ever messed with Bryce again. I became his protector that day." His smile falls, throat working. "I was supposed to protect him."

Memories flit across his eyes, and the pain there wraps around my heart and squeezes. It's so palpable, so raw, I place my hand over the ache, willing it to leave.

"We were inseparable, even though he lived in the next town over. We played on the same team every year, had sleepovers every weekend when we were older, and we drove my gran up the wall every summer. She said she was too old to keep up with two of us, but she made Bryce his favorite homemade strawberry ice cream every week anyway.

"Gran left after breakfast for her shift at the grocery store. We played hockey in the driveway all morning. Both of us, we were good. We *knew* we were good. Bryce was gonna be a goalie in the NHL one day, and when we were just playing around like that, he'd spend the entire time shit-talking me, reminding me I could never get past him. He said it was the only thing he could beat me at, but I think he was better than me at everything."

He looks down at our twined hands, licking his lips. "He said if I could score on him three times before lunch, I got to choose what we were doing." He swallows, and his voice cracks on his next sentence. "Took me two hours, but I chose the forest out back."

I sit up, tugging him with me, because I can't bear it anymore. The weight is crushing, suffocating, and I don't want him to carry it on his own anymore. With my legs crossed, I face him, holding his hands in mine, sweeping my thumbs along his cracked, raw knuckles.

"It's my fault. I didn't check to make sure he had his EpiPen first. I should've reminded him, but I was out the door as soon as our dishes were in the sink, running toward the trees, yelling for him to follow." Tears fill his eyes, and he looks away, wiping them on the sleeve of his hoodie. "Five minutes. We were there five minutes when he screamed. He was clutching his neck, saying something bit him. I moved his hand to look, and it was just this . . . *angry* red splotch, a small bump in the middle. But there was something sticking out of it, something so tiny, this little black pin, and I pulled it out, and . . . and . . ." Tears drip from his eyes, streaming down his cheeks. He doesn't bother trying to swipe these ones away. Instead, he looks down and cries. "He had brown eyes, Len. Big and dark, and when I look into yours, sometimes all I see is his. And I'll never, ever forget the way those eyes looked at me when he saw the bee stinger in my hand.

"I ran so fast. So fucking fast, I ran back to the kitchen. My gran was coming in the door from her shift, and I shouted at her to call nine-one-one. She watched me pick up Bryce's EpiPen pouch, and five seconds later, when I was sprinting back across the yard, I heard her demanding an ambulance.

"Bryce was on the ground when I got back, lying in the dirt, a pile of vomit beside him. His face was all swollen, and he didn't . . . he didn't even look like him. But then I got on the ground beside him, promised him he was going to be okay, and he opened his eyes, and there he was. As long as I had his eyes, he was going to be okay."

Tears run down my face, and I clutch Jaxon's hands tightly in mine.

"I looked away just long enough to inject his EpiPen, and when I looked back, his eyes were gone. He'd passed out. I pulled him into my lap, hugged him tight as I listened to the ambulance pull up out front, Gran shouting at them, footsteps thundering toward us."

He drops his head, shoulders shaking as he cries. I fling my arms around him, clutching him to me as he tells me how the paramedics couldn't find a pulse. How they tried CPR over and over, but couldn't get a pulse to restart his heart. How he refused to let go of him when they said he was gone, and how his gran had to tear Jaxon off him. How she held him for hours on the forest floor while he sobbed.

How his tie was a mess at Bryce's funeral three days later, because he could never figure them out, and Bryce always did it for him.

How Bryce's parents couldn't bear to look at Jaxon.

And how, when the funeral was over and his gran pulled him to the car, that was the last time he ever saw them.

"I wasn't enough. Not patient enough to slow down and make sure he had his EpiPen in the first place. Not fast enough when I ran back to the house, or back to the forest. Not fast enough or smart enough to save his life."

"It's not your fault, Jaxon." I grab his face in my hands, pulling his broken gaze to mine. "Look at me. It's not your fault, do you hear me? It was a freak accident, and you were kids. You did absolutely everything you could do. Do you understand? Bryce knows that, Jaxon. His parents know that."

He shakes his head, closing his eyes to more tears. "They hate me. They blame me. They were like parents to me, and when he died, it was like they died too."

I stroke his cheek, swiping away his tears. "They don't hate you, honey. They lost their child, and they didn't know how to survive in a world where everything reminded them of him. I bet they think about you all the time." I smile, and Jaxon's eyes track a tear that drips down my face. "Bet they watch all your hockey games, too, just like Bryce. You know he's watching, right?"

"You think?"

"Definitely. He's on my side about the whole fighting thing." I spin to the south, holding my hand out to Jaxon when I find what I'm looking for. "Here. Look up there, to the right. Do you see those three bright stars in a straight line? That's Orion's belt. Follow it down, and just there, right above the horizon, do you see?"

"The big, bright star?"

"That's Sirius, the brightest star in the sky. When you're looking for Bryce in the stars, look there. He'll light even the darkest nights."

Jaxon is quiet for a few moments, staring up at the sky. When I shiver, he moves behind me, pulling me back against his chest. I'm not ready to leave, so I'm glad he doesn't ask. Instead, we sit together in silence while he holds me, the beat of my heart slowing to match his.

He sweeps my curls off my shoulder, pressing a kiss below my ear before resting his chin on my shoulder. "You were distracting at the game tonight."

"I was?"

"Yeah. I like your curls down, the way they frame your face. They move when you laugh, and it makes me smile. But then you pulled your hair up in the second period, and I like when you do that too. You've got perfect cheekbones. And your neck, I . . . whenever you show off your neck, I just . . . can't take my eyes off you. Want my hands all over you, my mouth."

"Then why'd you take my hair down earlier?"

"To stop myself from kissing you." He hesitates, and I turn in his lap. He looks away, then back to me. "You give me a lot of you, Lennon. I think I admire that about you. Shitty things have happened, and instead of holding them in and letting them eat you from the inside out, you talk about them. I think that gives you some sort of power of the situation, you know? Anyway, I just . . ." He shifts his beanie up, runs his fingers through his hair. "I wanted to give you some of me too. And that story . . . I haven't shared it with anyone but the therapist I saw back then. I've never wanted to share it with anyone. Until . . ."

The single word is left unsaid, hanging heavy in the air between us.

You. Until you.

He glances down, rubbing the back of his neck. With my fingers on his chin, I bring his gaze back up. His eyes move between mine, and the fear there, the uncertainty, it makes my heart ache. In losing his best friend, he's lived all these years feeling not good enough. Not good enough to save Bryce. Not good enough for his parents to stay, to remember an innocent boy who lost so much. And now he sits before me, waiting to see if I'm going to do the same thing. If I'm going to leave, and forget all about him.

Where would I go? If there's one thing I know for sure, it's that this man sees me. He hears me. He *knows* me.

He makes me feel happy. Safe. Valued. He makes me feel capable.

And that right there? That's a powerful, magnificent feeling.

So right here, beneath all the stars and the fading, dancing lights, I capture his mouth with mine. I kiss him until I can't breathe, and then I pull his hoodie over his head. I stand, shimmying out of my clothes while Jaxon watches me the same way he watched all those stars shine in the sky. And then, in the cold, early hours of an April morning, I lower myself to his lap and show him there's nowhere on earth I'd rather be right now than with him.

21

FORGET MY HAIR, I NEED TO BEDAZZLE MY LIFE

Jaxon

"She's really pretty, Jaxon. Are you sure she likes you?"

Sarah looks up from Carter's phone, where he's showing her a picture of Lennon and Mittens from my cat's Instagram page. She looks me over, and the preteen gives me a smile so forced it hurts. "I mean, no offense."

"I never said she likes me."

"Oh, so you like her, but she doesn't like you back? That makes more sense."

"I don't like her! Not like that!"

Sarah's nose scrunches. "I'm confused, 'cause you been talking about her since you got here."

I pin my arms over my chest. "Have not."

She gestures at my hair, where she's currently attaching a pink gem to a strand. "You said you bet she'd like to bedazzle her hair too!"

"She likes doing fun stuff to her hair!"

"He definitely likes her," Garrett pipes up. "Jaxon's got a *big* crush on Lennon."

"I do not!"

"I think she likes you too," Adam reassures me. "Rosie says she talks about you all the time."

"You should take her on a date," Emmett suggests.

I open my mouth to argue that, technically, we go on dates all the time, but Carter holds his finger up. It's covered in craft glue, tiny paper hearts, and glitter, because Garrett has us on decoration duty for Jennie's studio opening next week.

"You have to say that it's a date out loud, or it doesn't count." He leans forward on his elbows. "Yeah, I learned that the hard way. Apparently, you have to 'ask' them to be your girlfriend now too. You can't just assume it." He rolls his eyes. "So even though you guys are basically boyfriend and girlfriend, you have to actually ask her to be your girlfriend."

"We're not basically boyfriend and girlfriend!" I half-screech, and Sarah swats my shoulder as my head jerks, pulling her bedazzler free from my hair. "I don't want a girlfriend!"

"Okay, buddy," Adam mumbles. His dark curls are pulled back with sparkly orange butterfly clips, streaks of purple eye shadow painted around his eyes, and Barbie-pink powder highlighting his cheekbones. He looks thrilled about it, but then again, his grumpy face and crossed arms could be due to the fact that Lily isn't here. She moved in with Adam and Rosie a few weeks ago, but her social worker suggested she stay home for now when Adam visits Second Chance. He's got more time than ever with her, but all it's done is make him hate every moment he can't be at her side. "Keep telling yourself that."

"Why don't you want a girlfriend?" Emmett asks.

"Because I don't wanna be tied down," I say out of habit, only this is the first time it's felt like a lie, and I don't like the way it settles in my gut, heavy and foreign. I shift in my seat, like I can shift the uncomfortable feeling.

"Right, but how come?"

"Kids, cover your ears," Carter says, not looking up from his craft to make sure they do. "Do you wanna have a Britney's Bitches meeting?"

"What? Psssh. *No.* I don't wanna talk about this with you guys."

"We can call a meeting, Jaxon. It's no problem."

"I don't need a meeting. There's nothing to talk about."

"We've been waiting for you to join us. Even had you a T-shirt made."

"Well, don't hold your breath. I don't need your advice." I cross my arms, staring down at my knees as I wave them in and out while Sarah winds an elastic around a chunk of my hair. "You get a girlfriend, and then before you know it, you're staying in on Saturday nights, waking up early on Sunday mornings, having coffee and waffles together while you read your books or watch the sports updates. And then you're going grocery shopping together, getting her flowers to make her smile, and you get dragged to the craft store to decorate for every holiday or season change, or just because the vibes are feeling off in the apartment."

"Sounds like you wanna talk about it," Carter murmurs.

I throw my hands up. "Oh, *and*? You're only having s-e-x with one person for, like, ever."

Sarah cocks her head. "You know I can spell, right? What's wrong with having s-e-x with the same person forever?"

I sigh. "There's nothing wrong with it. Some people just don't want to."

"Oh. And you don't want to do that with Lennon? You want to be with other people?"

I'm not answering that. I mean, *other people*? Ew.

My eyes coast the table, landing on Garrett, watching me closely. "What do you want, you turkey?"

"You realize you do all that right now, right?"

"Yeah, and I—"

"Love it. You love it, Riley. You're happier than I've ever seen you. You *like* living with Lennon, and you *like* the mundane routine you two have created."

"I think that's the thing," Emmett offers. "When the mundane doesn't actually feel mundane. That's when you know."

"I have to admit, Jaxon," Sarah starts. "It sounds like you're boyfriend-girlfriend, even if she's out of your league."

"I think that's part of the problem," Carter murmurs, painting a giant sun. "Jaxon has trouble seeing his worth, so he thinks Lennon is out of his league. He probably doesn't wanna be here when she realizes it."

"Wow," Adam whispers.

"Oof," Emmett puffs out.

"Spot on," Garrett mumbles.

Carter holds a sticky hand up. "I know, I know. I surprise even myself sometimes with my incredible emotional intelligence. I read somewhere it's directly related to how hot you are, so, that makes sense, obviously." He looks up at me, something like a challenge in his eyes. "What do you say, buddy? Did I hit the nail on the head or what?"

Definitely not. He definitely did not hit the nail on the head, and I say as much. I tell everyone at the table three times that I don't have trouble seeing my worth, that I don't think Lennon is out of my league, and I tell myself that the entire drive home.

I repeat it in my head as I ride the elevator, and again when I find the fresh-baked cookies on my kitchen counter, the kind I mentioned I was craving last night.

I repeat it as I take in the photos of Mittens now lining my living room wall, all taken and hung by Lennon. Some of him alone, and some of me and him together, but none of the ones the three of us took together.

I repeat it, over and fucking *over* again as I stop in front of my bookcase, the framed picture Lennon handed me three days after her birthday, when I told her all about Bryce.

It's from the Hubble telescope, she'd told me. *It's a starburst in a little galaxy within the Andromeda constellation.* Then she'd pointed to the date on the bottom of the picture and smiled up at me. *It was taken on the day Bryce became a star.*

Christ, it still fucking hurts. The way she wrapped her arms around me and squeezed before pressing a kiss to my lips and giving me the privacy she knew I needed without me having to ask for it. The way she listens but never pushes. The way she cares so deeply, how effortlessly thoughtful she is.

And I struggle to believe I deserve even an ounce of that.

I wander down the hall, following the sound of music to my bedroom. My sheets are on the floor where I left them when I stripped my bed this morning, because today I finally planned on swapping them for the silk set I've been hiding in my closet since I got Lennon hers for the days she's too tired to wrap her hair before bed, or when she can't find her wrap.

I pause there, staring down at them, squeezing my fists as I listen to Lennon sing along to her music. Soft whispers about coffee at midnight, burnt toast on Sundays, letting go of your fears, and falling in love.

My gaze rises to my bathroom, where my cat is sprawled out on a blanket on the floor, his eyes on the woman who works at the counter, the same way she does every day. I step closer, until all of Lennon comes into view, bent over the counter, moisturizing her face. Her chestnut curls hang down her back, fresh and voluminous, and I follow the line of her spine down to the curve of her ass, where my sweatpants are rolled, hanging off her hips, and only a thin sports bra hugging her perfect tits. I fight the urge to walk over to her, pull her back against my chest, press my lips to her shoulder, and take in our reflection, the way her smile has amped up so much since she's been here, she's nearly unrecognizable from the woman I met in Cabo.

And me. I don't know who I am anymore either.

Someone who thinks about somebody else when making decisions now. Someone who's constantly reading the allergy alerts on labels. Someone who gets up at the ass-crack of dawn once a week so there's a fresh bouquet of pink tulips on the kitchen counter and the brightest smile on the face of the woman who sees them when she wakes up. Someone who takes that same woman stargazing, because feeding her happiness is one of the best feelings in the world. Someone who fucking *communicates*, talks about the hard shit, even when it wants to stay buried.

Lighter, somehow. A part of something, maybe, because I feel a lot less alone then I did when I rang in this new year.

And happier. I feel happier.

How long will it last?

Lennon's gaze shifts to mine in the mirror, and a megawatt smile explodes across her face, punching me in the gut with enough force to knock me to my knees. "Hey, you."

"Hey."

"How were the kids today?"

I gesture at my face and hair, and she snickers, turning back to the sink. She comes out a moment later, cleaning the makeup from my face with a warm, wet cloth, gently pulling the beads from my hair.

"There." She touches her lips to mine, then shimmies back to the bathroom. "To be fair, though, you're extra beautiful when you're bedazzled."

Mittens meows like he agrees, but then Lennon pulls out a tiny, fluffy brush and crouches.

"Yes, handsome, I know." She dusts his face, nose, and paws with her brush. "You like to be pampered too." She tosses the brush back in her bag. "I got him his own blush brush. He thinks he's getting his makeup done, but there's nothing on it."

I sink to the edge of the bed, looking at my clasped hands as

Lennon prattles on about ideas for team content ahead of our first playoff game next week, how nice it's been to not have to travel during the break between the regular season and the playoffs, and about a star she wants to show me with her telescope on the balcony tonight.

"Why didn't you hang any of the photos of me and Mitts that you're in?"

Lennon's gaze meets mine in the mirror. "What?"

"The pictures in the living room. We took some with all three of us. But you didn't hang any of the ones with you."

"Oh. I don't know. This isn't my home, I guess." She glances down, nibbling her lip a moment before meeting my gaze again. "I'm just passing through, right?"

Something thick catches in my throat as I look at her, drink her in. She's beautiful, every inch of her. I'm addicted to the way the sunshine streams through the window, her brown skin basking in its golden glow. Addicted to the way her hips move to the beat of the music while she does her hair, the way she hums along to every song as she coats her lashes in mascara, paints her lips my favorite shade of berry.

If there's only one thing in this apartment that makes it feel like home, it's Lennon.

But she's temporary, like everything else in my life. Even she just said it.

The best I can do is remember it.

I swallow, looking away. "Right."

Lennon finishes her makeup, no longer singing as she works, her focus flipping between my reflection and hers. I alternate between watching her and scrolling through Instagram, because I'm wound tight right now and it's fucking me up. She has all my attention, and nobody, not even myself, has ever had that.

It takes me seven seconds to navigate to her profile, because apparently if I can't be looking directly at her, I need to be looking at her picture. Jesus, I'm all kinds of fucked up.

I switch to Mittens's profile instead, which, as it turns out, is just as shit an idea. It's loaded with photos of Lennon, tons of all three of us. I scroll through them all, one by one, settling on the most recent one, posted this morning. It's of the three of us on a walk yesterday evening. We drove to a quiet part of North Vancouver, got milkshakes, walked along a trail with Mittens on his harness until we got up to Cypress Lookout, where we sat on the stone wall and watched the sunset over downtown Vancouver. Mittens is over my shoulder, wearing a sweater Gran crocheted for him and gnawing on my milkshake straw. Lennon is smiling at the camera, and I'm smiling at Lennon.

Jesus, smiling isn't the right word, is it? It's not enough. I'm looking at her like . . . I'm looking at her like she's the sunset, and I'm seeing it in color for the very first time. That's how I'm looking at her.

And the comments? They all notice.

Ok ok, Mittens & Jaxon are the real love story but is anyone else hoping Jaxon & Lennon get together?

OMG Jaxon is SO in love with Lennon!!! Look at the way he looks at her!!!

I'd simply die if anyone looked at me the way Jaxon looks at Lennon.

Watching these two fall in love in real time is the single greatest highlight of my year so far.

Came for the cat, stayed for the roommates to lovers storyline.

"Hey, did you know that if Nashville wins in the first and second round, and you guys win in the first and second round, you'd play them in the third?"

My head snaps up, and I scramble to tuck away my phone as Lennon leans in the doorway.

"My family has this big cookout every year in May, back in Augusta. Mimi goes all out, obviously, and the Jays are in Atlanta that week for a series, so even Devin will be there. I didn't think I'd be able to go this year, since I'm here and I figure you guys are going to do so well in the playoffs, but I'm thinking it might be possible after all. Nashville's only an hour from Atlanta by plane." She lifts a shoulder. "It's a long shot, really. I mean, what are chances, even if you do play them, that we'll be in Nashville the day before or after?"

I watch her, the way she fiddles with the clip in her hands, her eyes glued to it. The way she moves back to the sink, licks her lips and takes a deep breath, same as she always does when she's nervous.

But what does she have to be nervous about?

It hits me the moment she starts pulling her hair back, her eyes coming to mine once more in the mirror, the hope sparkling in them.

And I do what I do best: I fucking panic.

"So, um, I was thinking. And you can totally say no. Like, no pressure, at all. But, um, I was thinking—and this is all hypothetical, obviously—if you guys do play Nashville in the third round, and the dates line up, maybe, um . . . maybe you'd want to c—"

"Hey, can you do that somewhere else? Your own bathroom, maybe."

Her clip clatters to the sink, corkscrew curls tumbling down her back. "What?"

My pulse pounds in my ears, an angry, thundering sound. Who am I angry at? Her, maybe, for reminding me she's only here temporarily before inviting me to her fucking family reunion.

Or me. For . . . everything. The dashed hope in her eyes, the confusion etched in her creased forehead, the hurt carved in her frown. For not being able to keep my dick in my pants and keep things platonic. For letting things get this far. For blurring lines. For getting comfortable.

For getting attached to someone I can't keep.

"I'm tired" is all I manage. "I don't really want company right now."

"Oh. Okay." She looks down, and when she curls her fingers into her palms, I hate myself. "I'll give you some space." She picks up her clip, and I stop her before she can leave the bathroom.

"Lennon."

Brown eyes rise to mine, wide and hurt, but hanging on to that scrap of hope. I want to apologize. Tell her I never meant for this to happen, for us to get this close. That I never wanted to hurt her. But it's better this happens now. She thinks I'm her best friend, but all I know how to do with a best friend is let them down. I'll fuck it up, one way or another, the same way I always do. The kind of way that gets me traded from one team to another, uprooting my life and perpetually searching for a place in this world.

The kind of way that has me living a life with my best friend's death on my hands.

The kind of way where his parents haven't been able to look at me in fifteen years.

The kind of way where, one day, this can't be repaired. This friendship can't be salvaged, and I lose everything, because I lose all of her. Because if I only have so long in the same city with Lennon, I'd rather we be able to coexist in a place where I can see her smile, hear her laugh, even if it's not with me, rather than be the one responsible for breaking her heart down the road when I eventually fuck this up and she realizes she's better off without me.

"Can you take all your stuff to your bathroom, please? And if you're keeping Mitts in your room tonight, can you keep your door closed so he doesn't scratch at mine in the middle of the night?"

"Oh. I . . ." Her chin trembles, and she presses her lips together before she looks away. She sweeps her things off the counter and into her arms, and I reach for her brush when it clatters to the floor. "No. Please. I got it."

"Len, I can—"

"No, you've done enough." She snags the brush and walks by me, hair curtaining her face. She pauses at the door, and I nearly ask her to stay. "I hope you feel better, Jaxon."

Mittens dashes by me, his belly swinging back and forth. He pauses to hiss at me before following Lennon into her room, and when she closes her door, I close mine, softly banging my forehead off it.

In the closet, I stare at the sheets for way too long, the unused silk set on the left, the regular linen ones on the right. They're just fucking sheets, but they're doing my head in. This morning when I stripped my bed, I thought of us in it tonight. I thought of the way she always curls into my side, sweaty and breathless. The way she lays her cheek over my heart. How every night I keep her longer and longer, let her sleep where I can keep her safe.

And then, eventually, I pull her into my arms, carry her to her bed, tuck her hair into her wrap, and on the nights I can't find it, she says, *Don't worry, you got me silk sheets, remember?*

This morning when I stripped my bed, I wanted silk sheets too.

I pick up the linen sheets, pulling them over the mattress, tossing the pillowcases on, and when I stand back, I hate it.

But I fall into bed anyway, because the last thing I want to do is fall into love.

22

MY HEART IS IN VANCOUVER

Lennon

I'VE HATED SILENCE ALL MY life.

It's always been a reflection of something missing. When I was a kid, it meant my dad was on the road with the MLB, often for two weeks at a time. We missed the way he stomped through the house like a dinosaur while we hid, stifling our laughter, the roars that exploded when he found us, when we ran screaming and laughing until he scooped us up and pretended to devour us.

When I was sixteen, the silence was my brother moving to Florida to play for the Jays' minor league team after being drafted at eighteen. The bathroom door that no longer rattled when he pounded on it, begging for me to hurry up. His bedroom, where Mom spent two weeks missing him but trying to be happy for him.

When I was twenty-one, it was the church where we held Gramps's funeral. Our home, where my dad sat with his head in his hands for weeks on end.

When I was twenty-two, it was the house I moved into with Ryne. It was days spent alone while he was out of town for work. It was silence when he was angry with me, or disappointed with me, or when he had a bad day at work. It was him taking no interest in my hobbies and us running out of things to talk about it. It was sitting on the couch on Christmas morning, watching him open his stocking while I sat there with nothing, and me dressed up and waiting alone at the kitchen table because he forgot about our dinner date.

This week, silence is Jaxon putting distance between us because he's scared. It's the thoughts running rampant in his head, the negative self-talk winning.

It's coffee and cereal waiting for me on the counter every morning but no one to eat it with. It's fresh tulips, an umbrella hanging on the handle of my bedroom door because it's raining, a brand-new bowl of Sour Keys on the coffee table, and the oil change warning on my car's dashboard suddenly disappearing.

I'd trade it all to have his shoulder pressed against mine at the kitchen island while we sip our coffee side by side.

I don't understand how something so quiet can feel so fucking loud. It's earsplitting, and I hate every second of it.

"I think I'm going to move out," I tell Serena and Devin, tucking my knees under my chin. "I texted my landlord for an update on the repairs, and he said he had someone starting next week. Shouldn't be much longer. I can grab a hotel until then."

"Do you think that's the issue?" Serena asks through my laptop screen. "That he wants his space back?"

I think the issue is that he realized the same thing I did. That what's going on between us is more than just two friends who fuck most nights, spend their free time tangled together on the couch, or hand in hand under the stars. And maybe if I'd kept quiet a little longer, let the realization sink in, let him get comfortable with it, everything would be okay. Instead, I opened my mouth and tried to invite him to meet my entire family, and that? That sent him running for the hills.

"I don't know. Not really, but I hate that I feel like he can't be comfortable in his own home now that he's trying to put distance between us." I press my cheek to my knee, trying to center my racing thoughts. "I want to ask him to talk to me, but I don't want to pressure him."

Devin scratches a hand through his hair, sighing. "I think it's something you gotta let him work through on his own. Sounds like he's always come to you with stuff when he's ready to."

That's one thing about Jaxon. At first glance, he seems like a vault. And maybe he has been. It certainly seems like it's what he's convinced himself he needs to do. But the reality is the man is desperate for communication. Connection. Understanding. Validation.

And aren't we all?

He's someone who tests the water first. Who climbs in slowly, wades around in the shallow end for a while before slowly working up to the deep end. He's never going to be someone who dives right in, opens up and spills it all at once. He'll give you a little bit of him, piece by piece, when he feels safe enough to give it up. I'm grateful he's ever felt safe enough with me to give me anything.

"Is there something I could be doing better to help him feel comfortable talking with me about what's bothering him?"

Devin gives me a soft smile. "Think that right there says it all, Len. That you care enough to even ask that question."

"You're doing everything right," Serena assures me gently.

"I guess I just want him to know I'm here." I sniff, trailing my fingers back and forth over the soft fur of Mittens's belly. "I miss him, ya know?"

A soft knock on my door cuts through the quiet, and I lift my head off my knees as Jaxon peeks into the room, handsome as ever, freshly shaved, waves tamed, in a pair of fitted dark jeans and a camel-colored sweater that stretches across his broad chest, hugs his muscular biceps, the collar and hem of his white button-up peeking out from underneath.

"Hey," he whispers, hazel eyes shifting to my laptop. He waves at Serena and Devin. "Hey, guys. Sorry, didn't mean to interrupt." His gaze comes back to mine, and he nibbles his lip, gripping the door frame. "Um, you ready to go?"

"Yep." I blow a kiss to my cousin and brother, and right before I can shut my laptop, Mittens walks across it, ending the video call with his talented paws. "Add that to your résumé, handsome boy," I murmur, scooping him up for a kiss before I set him on my pillow. I slide off the bed, setting my laptop aside. When I turn around, Jaxon's eyes are hooked on me, coasting down my body, then back up.

He clears his throat. "You, um . . . You're beautiful, Lennon."

I was hoping he'd say that; I've missed hearing it. It's not the words themselves, but the way he speaks them, like it's a revelation every time, as if his first thought every time he sees me is just . . . *wow*. Like he needs a minute to soak it in.

And I bask in that moment, the quiet murmur, the reverence that dances in his fixated gaze.

I also put a little extra sway in my hips as I walk by him, because these vegan crimson leather pants were an absolute *bitch* to get over my ass, and I'll be damned if his eyes aren't glued to it every time he's behind me today.

He holds my hand as I step into my heels, and I fumble both of them on purpose to feel him a little longer. On the way down to the parking garage, the elevator stops to let a family on, and Jaxon steps into me to make room that's not needed, his hand on my lower back. He helps me into his car. Puts his hand on my seat, brushing my neck as he looks over his shoulder to back out. And when I see a spider in the car, I scream, curling myself over the center console, gripping his shirt and remembering how sturdy he feels beneath my hands.

Hm. It's fluff, not a spider. Oops.

When we arrive at Sunshine & Serendipity Dance Haven for Jennie's grand opening, I watch as Jaxon says a quiet hello to everyone, wraps Jennie in a hug and congratulates her, and then busies himself with Connor, Lily, and Ireland, who are all rolling around on a large mat together. Under normal circumstances, it'd make me swoon. Today, though, as he keeps his distance from us, it's a reminder that he doesn't feel like he belongs here. And the nine sets of eyes that follow him feel the weight of it.

Garrett presses a kiss to Jennie's cheek. "I'm gonna grab the cupcakes and put them out, then you can say your speech, 'kay, sunshine?" He heads toward the back, his eyes bouncing to Jaxon. He pauses at the door before dashing over, wrapping his friend in a hug. "I'm glad you're here," I hear him say, and Jaxon hesitates before sinking into that hug for just a moment. "Wanna help me set the food out? I could use you."

"Me? Oh. Um . . ." He crouches down to the kids. "Is it okay if I go help Uncle Gare?"

Connor stands, thumbing proudly at himself. "Conn'a help too." He tucks his hand into Jaxon's, and Jaxon stares at the connection, the corner of his mouth quirking.

Lily smiles. "I'll stay here with Ireland. She's safe with me."

Jaxon looks our way, and when Olivia gives him two thumbs up, he nods and follows Garrett.

"Wait!" Lily leaps to her feet, tugging at the skirt of her dress, wide brown eyes set on Jaxon as he pauses in the doorway. "Y-you're comin' back, right?"

He smiles at her, and it's big and real and so damn beautiful. "Always."

Lily watches him disappear into the back, and before she sits down with Ireland, she dashes over to us. She grips Rosie's hand, pulling her down to her level. "You're not gonna leave, right? While I'm playing with Ireland?" She tucks her thick brown hair behind her ear and leans closer to Rosie, dropping her voice. "I don't want you to leave without me. I get scared when you're not with me."

Rosie cups her face, sweeping her thumb along the freckles dotting Lily's cheekbone. "I'm not ever going to leave you, sweetheart." She presses a kiss to her forehead, and Lily flushes, nodding before making her way back to Ireland.

"How's she doing?" I ask Adam and Rosie as our friends disperse among the growing crowd.

"She's doing well." Rosie frowns at Adam. "I think. Right? Fuck, I don't know."

Adam wraps an arm around her, touching his lips to her temple. "She's happy, which is what matters most." His blue eyes dance with anguish. "I wish we could tell her we're in the process of adopting her. She thinks it's temporary."

"She won't unpack her bag." The way Rosie whispers the words tells me she blames herself, somehow. "She says it'll be easier if it's ready to go when we decide to send her back." A tear sneaks from her eye, and she swipes it away quickly. "I don't know if I'm doing something wrong. It's so hard. We love her so much, and we just want her to feel it."

"I think she does." I look at the sweet girl, the one whose gaze lifts to find her foster parents every few seconds, the beam that lights her face like sunshine when she sees them. "It's about stability and consistency now. Unpacking the hard years a little bit at a time as she's ready, and making new, happy memories together as a family." I squeeze Rosie's hand. "You're doing great. Don't doubt that you're loving her right."

"Thank you, Lennon." She wraps her arms around me, and I lean into the connection. "I'm so grateful for you. And I'm grateful Jaxon found you when he needed you most."

It's been a long time since I feel like someone was grateful to have me. Since I felt like my presence was wanted, appreciated, not just tolerated. Not a day has gone by at Jaxon's that I've felt like a burden, like someone taking up space, grating his last nerve, the way that often had me walking on eggshells with Ryne.

But is he grateful he found me? Did he need me?

The swing of a door catches my attention, and Jaxon emerges from the back, holding a tray of treats, Connor perched on his shoulders and eating a cupcake. His eyes scan the room, stopping on me and Rosie, taking in the way we're embraced.

"Mama hug Auntie Lenny," Connor says. "Conn'a lub Auntie Lenny."

"She's pretty special, huh?" Jaxon's gaze stays on me for a moment, until Garrett calls his name. As he walks away with Connor on his shoulders, I swear I hear him say, "Auntie Len is super smart. She's teaching me all about stars," and I couldn't tell you why that sends my heartbeat racing the way it does.

I amble around the airy, bright studio, snapping photos of the décor. It's a beautiful space, homey and warm, with big windows and lots of natural light. Black-and-white photos line one wall, a little girl in a tutu and ballet slippers in each one. The proud smile she wears warms me from the inside out, and as I take in those tell-tale dimples decorating every picture, I realize they're all of Jennie.

On the wall opposite the floor-to-ceiling mirror is a stunning mural of Jennie, the only artwork of her as an adult. I place my hand over the painting, running the tips of my fingers over her skirt, my mouth wide with wonder. Because where Jennie has been painted in black and white, her dress is a vibrant shade of yellow, paint splattered over the wall, splashing around her, as if she's basking in sunshine, exuding it, sharing it with everyone.

"Hi, everyone," the very woman speaks into the room as I snap her photo. She waves at her friends, her pink-stained cheeks the perfect home to those deep dimples her grin pulls in. "Thank you so much for being here with me today to celebrate the opening of Sunshine and Serendipity Dance Haven. Each and every one of you is so special to me and has played a vital role in my life, and I'm so thankful for the support and love along the way. This studio is a haven, not just for me, but for everyone who wants a place to connect with others, to chase their dreams and do the things they love without risking their mental or physical health, or losing pieces of themselves along the way. Dancing was all that and more for me, and then suddenly, it wasn't. One day it lost its spark, and this studio is proof that I've fought like hell to take it all back." She takes a deep breath, turning to Garrett, who watches her in total awe from the sidelines, letting her have her moment. "But why Sunshine and Serendipity?"

"'Cause you're my sunshine," Garrett blurts, cheeks pink when he mouths *oops.*

Jennie giggles. "And you're mine. And none of this, the studio, the renewed love of something that's always been so special to me, hell, even my own sense of worth . . . none of it would be possible without Garrett."

His brows jump, and he points at himself, mouthing, *Me?*

"Yes, you, you turkey." She holds her hand out to him, and he hauls ass over to her, wrapping her in his arms, pulling her into his chest. The way she gazes up at him, like she'd been resigned to a life of loneliness before he looked her way, has my heart seizing in my chest. "Finding my best friend and soulmate in him was serendipitous, and he's made me feel like sunshine every step of the way." She takes his face in her hands, pressing her quiet words to her lips. "I love you."

Someone sniffles next to me, and I watch Carter swipe at a tear. I swear, I've never met a man so in tune with his feelings and comfortable displaying them for all to see as Carter Beckett.

"I'm just so proud of her," he's telling me for the fourth time, twenty minutes later as we twirl around the studio, my hand in his. "She deserves everything good in this world." His green eyes soften as he watches Garrett spin Jennie out before pulling her back in, the two of them laughing. "So does Garrett. I'm glad they found each other."

"That's really sweet of you, Carter."

"Hey, Carter." Garrett flicks his chin up as him and Jennie twist by us. "Remember how I said I was looking for those Oreo cupcakes for you in the back ten minutes ago?"

"Yeah . . ."

"I lied. I was looking for your sister's G-spot with my tongue." He snickers. "Found it."

"You motherfucker!" Carter lunges for him, and Garrett and Jennie spin away, cackling and high-fiving, and this feels like the wrong time for this, but—

"I believe *sisterfucker* is the word you're looking for," I murmur.

Carter groans, long and loud, wrapping his arm loosely around my back as he continues parading me around the room. Suddenly, he gasps. "Oh, *come on*. Look! Look at this!"

He twirls me around, until I'm staring at his mom and the Vipers' older, very attractive, very wealthy general manager.

"Axel Larsen is dancing with your mom."

"Yes. Yes, he is." Carter narrows his eyes. "I don't trust him."

I snicker, because there's no other acceptable response. Axel Larsen is one of the kindest people I've ever encountered. Did I mention he's hot as balls and super rich? He's got that salt-and-pepper thing going on in his short beard and by his temples, like he just jumped off the set for a Touch of Grey commercial.

"Your dad passed away?" I ask softly.

He nods. "Ten years this fall." He pushes out a heavy breath. "Fuck. Ten years. How the hell did that happen?"

"It's wild how time keeps moving, isn't it?" I squeeze his hand.

"I hope the memories you made with your dad bring you peace, Carter."

He looks at me a moment, head tilted as he weighs the words. And then he smiles. "Yeah, they do. Thanks, Len."

"I take it your mom hasn't dated since?"

"Nah, never."

"And what do you think?" I look to Holly, his mom, and Axel. "Do you want her to date?"

"I . . ." He frowns, looking away for the answer. It takes him a moment, but he looks certain of it when his gaze comes back to me. "I want her to be happy. Whatever that happiness looks like." His eyes find her again, and when she laughs, the corner of his mouth pulls into a smile. "I don't know all the answers when it comes to life and love. In fact, statistically, my answers are almost always wrong. I've always gone with the flow, and in the end it brought me my two greatest blessings. But what I do know is that life is too short to spend it thinking you're better off alone."

His gaze moves from his mom to the same place mine's been going the last ten minutes: by the window, where Jaxon's been taking turns spinning around Olivia, Rosie, and Ireland. He twirls Ireland once more before kissing her cheek, passing her back to her mom, and then holds his hand out to Lily. She tries not to smile, mouth scrunching, and then launches herself into his arms. It's a precious, incredible sight, especially when Lily throws her head back, laughing at whatever he says. And Jaxon? Jaxon's smile is as beautiful as hers.

"My only hope for my family is that they don't let go of the people who make them feel like the whole world is suddenly at their feet. The people who come into their life and suddenly renew the one thing they'd lost, even if they never realized they'd lost it."

Carter's gaze coasts the room once more, pausing on each of his friends. They stop on Jaxon, lingering there for a moment when he looks at Carter and me.

"And what's that?" I ask.

Carter smiles. "Hope."

"Auntie Lenny!"

Carter lets me go as Lily comes running up to me, throwing her arms around my legs. "Did you see me dancin' with Uncle Jaxon?"

"I sure did, honey!" I hoist her into my arms, closing my eyes as she clutches me to her.

"You feel like Jaxon," she says on a sigh. "Like Adam, and Rosie, and Connor too."

"Yeah? How's that?"

"Warm and safe. Like sunshine in a hug."

Sunshine in a hug. Four simple words that describe every single person important to me in this room. They shroud the darkest parts of me in light, take my broken, tainted memories in their hands, and turn them into gold, showing me what it feels like to be a part of something real and beautiful and special. With them, I feel like I'm radiating from the inside out.

It's in this moment I realize that, instead of remaining a temporary refuge for my heartache, somewhere along the way, Vancouver has become my home.

23

FALL WITH ME

Jaxon

I MISS HIM.

Three words. Three words I wasn't meant to hear, whispered in confidence to her family.

Three words that knocked me on my ass.

Never in my life have I felt important enough to be missed. If I was, surely Bryce's parents wouldn't have walked away. At the very least, they would have reached out, checked in on me. Right?

If I was important enough to be missed, the teammates I left behind after each trade, the ones I'd considered family, would've kept in touch. Instead, when I reach out at Christmas, wish them a happy new year, ask them how the family's doing, their responses—if I get one—cut me to the bone.

Who's this?

The only person to say those three words, to tell me they miss me, is my gran.

Until today. Until Lennon.

"What do you think it means?"

Cara blinks at me. Her eyebrows rise, slow and unimpressed, which is her usual expression. Holding up a finger, she pulls her phone from her pocket. "Hold on, let me dial a friend." She presses at her phone screen, making beeping noises that have me rolling my eyes. "Hi, yes, I have a very important question. My friend's crush said she misses him. What does that mean?" She pretends to listen, nodding along. "Mhmm. Oh, yeah. Okay, thanks." She tucks her phone away. "It means she misses you, dipshit."

I cross my arms over my chest, turning my attention to the stage. Big mistake, but then there's nowhere else to look; staring at Lennon isn't an option. "You're a jerk," I mutter, watching as Carter and Jennie parade across the karaoke stage, using every single fucking inch of it like they called ahead and asked for its dimensions, and then choreographed a dance routine to fit it perfectly. They're currently putting on what feels like a live-action remake of *Aladdin*, based on their performance of "A Whole New World," and this is their third duet of the night, because it's Jennie's night, and she deserves to celebrate. Each of them has gone solo too.

We've only been here an hour.

"And I never said I have a crush on her," I shoot out.

"Oh, good. Then you won't mind if she has company over tonight, right?"

My pulse thunders. "What?"

Cara checks her nails. "You know, in case she feels like entertaining that guy who's talking to her right now."

My head whips so fast, my neck screams out in pain. Lennon is seated at the large table our group is occupying, and there's some twat-waffle with a stupid man bun hanging over her, flexing his stupid biceps as he talks, and the worst part of it all? She's fucking *smiling*.

My feet move before my brain can catch up, marching me straight across the bar.

Nobody takes my crush home but me.

Lennon's eyes flick to mine as I approach her and her new friend in a totally calm, levelheaded manner.

Cara's eyes shine with delight as she slides back into her spot, and she nudges Emmett, who then nudges Olivia, who nudges

Rosie, who nudges Adam, who nudges Garrett. Garrett goes to nudge Lennon, then stops himself, frowning at his elbow.

Man Bun looks up at me as I stop at the chair beside Lennon, the one he's got his hand braced on.

I grab the back of it, yanking it out, flopping down in it. I do the man spread, legs wide until my knee rests against the skin-tight red leather pants Lennon's destroying the entire world with tonight. I look up at Man Bun as he staggers to the right. "Sorry, was I interrupting something?"

"The pretty woman was telling me what she likes to do in her spare time. She said stargazing, and I was just about to ask if she'd like to get out of here and go see some stars right now."

"*Ha!*" I snort, and Lennon's brown eyes narrow, burning into me. I narrow mine right back, sending her a telepathic message.

You'll need your telescope to find me, honey, because I'll be in outer fucking space before you go stargazing with anyone who isn't me.

She must have Do Not Disturb turned on, because I don't think she's getting my message. She grins at me, one of those scary, evil kinds that turns extra sultry as she looks up at this turtle dick between us. "My telescope is at home. Do you mind taking me there to get it?"

As fucking if.

His mouth dips to her ear, as close to it as I am from making sure he can never reproduce. "You're not gonna need a telescope to see the stars I'm gonna put in your sky."

I gasp; everyone else snickers. They must not have heard properly.

"So poetic," Cara murmurs, head tilting. "Don't you think so, Jax?"

"Hey, guys." Carter swipes the sweat from his forehead as he and Jennie rejoin the table, chests heaving, hands on their hips.

"What's going on? We just finished rocking the stage, and none of you even clapped."

"We clapped the first four times," Olivia mutters.

"Lennon was about to answer—" Cara looks to Man Bun. "Sorry, what was your name?"

He winks. "Bart."

Bart? I send Lennon another message with my eyes. *It rhymes with fart, honey. Are you sure about this?*

"Bart, yes, right. Such a strong, handsome name. Anyway, Bart asked Lennon out, and she was about to give him an answer." She threads her fingers together, resting her chin there, eyes on me. "We're on the edge of our seats to see what she'll say."

"But—*oh!* Oh!" Garrett claps, pointing to Lennon. "Didn't you say you really wanted to see Jaxon on stage tonight? You'd hate to miss that." He holds his hand up between himself and Lennon, winking at me. *I got you, bud,* he mouths.

"That's never gonna hap—" Carter pauses, squinting as he clues into Garrett's plan. "Oh. *Oh, yeeeah.*" He winks at me, forgoing the hand shield. "Yeah, and you were so excited to bust out your moves." He starts back toward the stage, gesturing for me to follow. "C'mon, Jaxon."

Emmett stands, and Garrett and Adam follow suit. "Yeah, c'mon. We'll do it together."

I pin my arms across my chest. "Like hell. I don't sing, *or* dance."

Lennon snorts a laugh, but before I can appreciate it, she sighs. "Well, I guess if I'm not going to see the only thing I wanted to tonight . . ." She stands, slinging her purse over her shoulder, and I rocket to my feet, tripping over them as I scramble after the guys.

"I'm coming!"

Five minutes later, I'm standing in line on stage, beneath the glare of the spotlight, which seems to be centered entirely on me, a microphone wrapped tightly in my trembling fist, while, like, a hundred people aim their phones at us. But Bart is gone, and despite the irritation etched in the arch of her brow, the flick of her wrist as she stirs her drink, Lennon's smiling.

At me.

Lennon is smiling at me, and there's no way in hell I'm going to regret this decision.

"Okay, Britney's Bitches, we're up." Carter paces before us before stopping in front of me. "This is serious." He points at his bugged eyes. "Do you see this? That's how serious this is. Jaxon's romantic life depends entirely on this performance, so that means—"

"Um, I wouldn't say—"

"I need everyone to give a hundred and ten percent. Got it? A hundred and ten." He claps my shoulder. "Jaxon, I chose this song for you. It's powerful, passionate, and moving, and I want to *feel* that energy emanating from every pore on your body."

"Okay, well, Bart's already gone, so—"

He grips the back of my shirt, hauling me back in line the moment I step out of it. "*Emanating.*"

I gulp. Nod. "Emanating."

He squeezes in beside me, closing his eyes, breathing deeply. "Showtime, Bitches."

Hey, remember a minute ago when I said there was no way in hell I'd regret this decision?

Yeah, that was before the screen before us lights up, and the lyrics to "Unwritten" by Natasha Bedingfield start rolling up it.

I GOT A STANDING OVATION.

"Hey, Len, did you see my standing ovation?" I reach over the center console, poking her thigh as we race through the dark night to home. "When everyone screamed and clapped for me? Did you see?"

She flicks my hand away. "Mhmm."

"Okay, 'cause you don't seem impressed."

"People scream and clap for you every day of your life, Jaxon."

"I—" frown. "Oh, yeah. You're right. But *you* weren't screaming and clapping."

"Hmm." She checks her nails. "Must've missed it."

Bullshit. *Bullshit, bullshit, bullshit.* Her eyes were glued to me, and that incredible smile was stuck on her face. I know, because mine were glued to her too.

Well, after the first thirty seconds. The first thirty seconds I almost vomited my dinner all over the stage. Then I watched Garrett shake his ass and knew with certainty there was no way in hell I could be worse than him.

But as we finish the drive home in silence, ride the elevator in silence, and enter the apartment in silence, one thing is clear: Lennon's not going to make this easy for me, and that's okay. She deserves better.

She deserves to know that nothing about this past week was a reflection of her, and only a reflection of me and my fucked-up sense of self-worth, which has prevented me from ever attempting to form some sort of meaningful connection with a woman.

And I'm scared. Terrified, really. Nothing is more obvious than that as I stand in my kitchen and watch Lennon walk away from me without a word.

I didn't know what I was missing before her. Not really. It'd been so long since I felt like I really belonged anywhere. Since I'd really, truly allowed myself to be happy. There was no choice when she came along. All that happiness? It just . . . *was*. It existed, and I lived in it.

The problem with feeling that kind of happiness is that when it's gone, the absence of it is staggering. The silence is earsplitting. And I can't go another day without Lennon and everything I made her take with her when I pushed her away.

That's why I'm in the middle of typing out a plea for help to the girls while Mittens eats his midnight snack at my feet when her bedroom door opens. I look up, watching as Lennon struts down the hall in nothing but those booty shorts I love/hate, one of my Vipers T-shirts that she's cropped to sit right below her tits, and *oh Jesus fuck she's not wearing a bra.* I stand here like a jackass, fixated as she gathers her spirals and secures them on top of her head, several slipping free, tumbling down her slender neck. It's when she uncorks a bottle of red wine—specifically, an eight-hundred-dollar vintage that she dumps into a glass while looking me dead in the eye—that I find my balls.

Without a second thought, I navigate to my music app, heading to Recently Played. It's a bunch of love songs, all Lennon's, because she uses my account. I choose my favorite one, the one with her nickname in the title, and watch as her eyes flicker when the song seeps from my speakers, drowning us in the soft acoustics. When I turn on the small light projector I picked up the other day and constellations fill the room, splashing across the walls and ceiling, her lips part with wonder.

"What is this?" Flecks of gold shine with uncertainty in her brown eyes as I slowly move toward her, take her wine from her. "What are you doing?"

I twine my fingers through hers, hauling her into me. "Dance with me, honey."

"W-why?"

"Because everyone else got a chance to spin you around today. Because I wanted to, but until right now, I didn't have the courage to ask. Because I missed having you in my arms." I loop her arms around my neck, my hands gliding down her sides, finding the soft dip of her waist. "Because I missed *you.*"

Her breath fans across my neck. "And the lights? The stars?"

"You deserve to have the things you love most at the tips of your fingers, honey." My gaze follows hers, watching the stars dance around us. "This is for the cloudy days. The rainy days and the cold days. The lazy days better spent in bed, and the days I keep you there, if you'll let me."

I've never thought of Lennon as small or meek. She's been a force to be reckoned with since the day I found her in Cabo. That she spent years feeling like she had to make herself smaller to be the person Ryne was comfortable with her being is devastating.

So when she looks up at me, gaze drowning in apprehension, when she swipes her wine off the counter and tips a third of it back because she doesn't know what to say, what she's *supposed* to say, I blurt out the first thing that comes to mind.

"Never have I ever worn swimming goggles to keep onion fumes out of my eyes."

Her brows jump, and she rolls her eyes, burying her snort in the sip of wine she takes. The glass dangles from her fingers as she wraps her arms back around my neck, softening against me. "Never have I ever sung 'Unwritten' by Natasha Bedingfield in front of a hundred people, while also gyrating."

"Cheap shot, Len. Just say you're jealous of my moves." I take a sip of her wine as she brings it to my lips. "All right, let's see . . . Oh, I know. Never have I ever felt bad about ruining someone's chances with a man named Bart."

Another snort. Fuck, I love it. This one says she knows I didn't give a fuck.

"You have to drink if you're sad you missed your chance with him."

She gives me a look, and I give her one right back until she relents. "His name rhymed with fart, Jaxon."

"That's what I said!"

She also doesn't drink, and my chest swells with pride.

"Never have I ever bought a bouquet of pink tulips every week because I know they're my roommate's favorite flowers only to pretend it wasn't me."

"Damn it," I mutter, stopping to take a drink.

"And never have I ever put so much thought into making an instruction guide for a coffee machine, even including a recipe guide and cereal pairings."

"Hey, it's my turn. You can't just—"

"Drink." She forces the glass to my lips. "And never have I ever secretly thrown out all my nut and tree nut products and disinfected my kitchen for a girl I didn't even like and who was only supposed to stay one night." Another slosh of wine she tips down my throat. "And never have I ever got a girl the one thing she wanted more than anything in the world, something someone else made her feel silly for wanting, and thought it was no big deal, even though that girl cried herself to sleep that night because it was, in fact, a huge fucking deal."

I grip her wrist, stopping her from lifting the wine to my lips. "You cried yourself to sleep?"

Lennon stares up at me, nostrils flaring, the slightest tremor in her chin.

The song has ended, leaving me with only the sound of my heart thrashing against my chest, begging to get out, to offer itself up to this woman before me.

"Never have I ever been afraid to tell someone how I feel about them," I whisper, a quiver in my hand as I slide my fingers over hers, gripping the wineglass, bringing it to my lips.

The crease in her forehead smooths out, lips parting with surprise. Surprise that I have feelings for her. Surprise that I'm telling her. Or surprise that I'm admitting I've been afraid. Fuck, I've been so afraid. To let go, let someone in, give them that kind of power over me. The kind of power where you walk knowingly to the edge of the cliff, stare down at all the possibilities waiting below, a chance at a future, a home, or another person who changes their mind. Both scary, and yet you look over the edge, and something tells you to do it, to give it a chance, so you do. You take a deep breath, let go, and fall.

But I don't want to fall alone. I want her to fall with me.

And if I hit the ground at full speed, splitting apart at the seams, I want to trust that she's going to be there, tucking her hand in mine, helping me to my feet. I'm tired of getting up all on my own.

I set the wineglass on the counter. Running my hand down her side, I find her waist, squeezing softly, feeling that she's here with me. I press my forehead to hers, sweeping my thumb along that trembling lower lip.

And I let go.

"I'm sorry, honey. I'm sorry that when I got in my own head, I asked you to leave my room instead of asking you to talk. I'm sorry I haven't been around the way I've always been. I don't . . . I don't know how to communicate. Not about this kind of stuff."

"What kind of stuff is this?"

"You. Me." I swallow. "Us."

"And do you wanna do that now? Communicate?"

I nod. Lick my lips. "I got scared. I *am* scared."

"It's okay to be scared, Jaxon. Can you tell me why, though?"

"Because you're . . . you're everywhere. My kitchen, my couch, my bed. My head. Fuck, honey, you're running around up there all damn day, and I can't think straight."

The corner of her mouth quirks, and she bites her bottom lip to keep that smile from shining. "And that's a bad thing?"

"I thought so. Getting attached to anything has never ended well for me. The last thing I ever wanted to do was get attached to a person."

"And now?"

"Now? Now I like having you everywhere. I like your hair products spread out on my bathroom counter. I like your books on my shelf, your telescope on my balcony. I like every piece of you that you've added to this house, and I like that my bedsheets smell like you. And, honey? I like me a whole lot better with you here too."

The rest of her hesitation dissipates, melting the edges of her gaze. Her hand brushes my jaw, cupping my cheek, and I sink into the warmth.

"I don't know if I liked being alone before you, but it was comfortable. I got used to the quiet. Felt like I belonged in it. But now, without you . . . I fucking hate the silence, Lennon."

Her fingers slide into my hair, gently twirling my waves. Slowly, she tilts her face, touching her lips to mine, a feather-soft kiss I haven't been able to stop thinking about all week. "I'm scared, too, you know? I came here to escape a ruined relationship, and to find myself. Instead, I found you. I thought you'd just be my rebound. That we'd have amazing sex while I was here, I'd ride your cock and your face into oblivion, and then we'd both go our own way when I moved out."

I chuckle, but the thought of us parting ways, of never feeling her skin slide against mine again, the scrape of her nails raking down my shoulders, never hearing her singing in the shower, makes me feel sick to my stomach. "I don't think you need to find yourself. I think you know exactly who you are, and you're confident being that person."

"You're right. I do know who I am, and I am confident being myself. But a big part of that is you, Jaxon. I can be myself here because you make me comfortable enough to do so. I'm not worried about censoring myself, or asking for the things I want, because I know you're going to accept me no matter what. You're not judging me."

"Just your onion goggles," I whisper against her lips, capturing her laugh with a kiss.

"So you have feelings for me?" She fiddles with the collar of my shirt, peering up at me with a smile, half shy, half smug. "What kind of feelings?"

I mean to be vague. To say something like *a lot of feelings* or *big feelings*, because I've never been good at giving my thoughts a voice, and especially my fears. Instead, I look in her eyes, warm and smooth like whiskey on a summer patio, sunshine streaking through the crystal glass, lighting it with breathtaking shards of amber. And I blurt out, "Looking at you, knowing you exist in my world, that you could be mine one day and gone the next, is the most overwhelming thing I've ever felt."

I know what loss feels like. I know what it feels like when your world is so intertwined with someone else's that you become two halves of a whole.

And I know what it feels like to lose it.

"Since Bryce died, it's felt easier to not try at all than to try and lose it all in the end anyway."

Lennon brushes her thumb over my cheekbone. "That's a sad way to live, Jaxon. Anticipating the worst. Bryce wouldn't want that for you."

Gran's always said the same, but I can't help it. Logic rarely ever wins when shattered hearts are involved.

"I'm happy with you, Jaxon."

"Even though I annoy you?"

"This relationship is built on annoyance."

Relationship. Fuck. Never been in one of those before.

"So . . . I'm not your rebound? You . . . you feel the same?"

"Why else would I come out here without a bra or panties and in your favorite booty shorts if I wasn't hoping to lure you into telling me you have feelings for me?"

"Mmm. Sneaky girl." I drag the tip of my nose along her jaw, up to her ear, and then freeze there, eyes wide. "You're not wearing any panties?"

She takes my hand, sliding it down her torso. "Why don't you stick your hand down here and find out?"

With my hand on her stomach, I ease her backward, until her elbows rest on the countertop as my hand slips beneath her shorts. I drag my middle finger through her slit, humming my approval when I find her soaked. I drag that wetness up to her clit, watching as her head falls over her shoulders while she moans, hips lifting, chasing my touch.

Bending over her, I drag my mouth up her throat, licking my way to her ear. "You're wet, honey. We're having a serious discussion, and you're over here, soaked and ready for my cock?" I push three fingers inside without warning, proof that she's ready, as desperate for me as I am for her.

"I can't help it." She moans, grinding against my palm as I finger her tight pussy. "Jaxon Riley, tattooed grump who thinks he's only good for fighting, talking about *feelings*, pouring his heart out to me . . ." She shudders, a wicked gleam in her eyes as she takes her lower lip between her teeth. "Turns me on."

"Hmm." I drag my thumb over that lush lip, tugging it free. "Such a pretty mouth. Wanna know my favorite thing about it, honey?" I press the whispered words against her ear. "The only way to shut it up is with my cock."

She grins up at me. "They say big mouths need big cocks to keep them satisfied." Slowly, she sucks my thumb into her mouth, and when my breath hitches, she pushes me backward, walking past me and down the hall. "You're not gonna fuck me like that tonight, though." Pausing at my bedroom door, she pulls her T-shirt over her head. Drops those booty shorts to her feet. Bats those thick lashes. "You're gonna fuck me like you've missed me for a week because you were too scared to talk to me. Groveling will bode well for you, *honey.*"

I don't know how it happens. Superhuman speed or something. 'Cause one moment I'm standing in my kitchen with my balls in my hand, and the next thing I know I'm through my bedroom door, winding an arm around her waist, flipping her around, pinning her to the wall.

We've been in this position before. Her wrists on either side of her head while I held her to the wall in my bedroom, my cock begging to be inside her. Then, I'd told her not to let Ryne have any type of power over her, the kind that has him second-guessing her worth. And she didn't. She's been in control this whole time, put one foot in front of the other without looking back. And I admire her for that. It's the one thing I've never figured out how to do.

Something changes as we stand here, pressed against each other, chests heaving. My hand trembles as I glide it along her jaw, gripping the nape of her neck. The clip in her hair dislodges, and all those incredible spirals tumble down around her shoulders, scattered across her glowing copper skin, kissing her dusky nipples, leaving me feeling the way I always do when I look at her: *utterly fucking overwhelmed.*

"Fuck, honey." I press my forehead to hers as we fight to breathe. "Who made you so beautiful?"

"I wonder the same thing about you. When you carry me to bed each night, tuck me in, and kiss my forehead because you think I'm asleep."

Fuck. Yeah. That'll do it. I grip her knees, yanking her legs up and around my waist, and then my mouth collides with hers. It's hot and wet, hungry and new, exploring a new side of me while I explore her. Her tongue glides against mine, and when she rocks herself against my cock, she swallows my groan.

I carry her to the bed, laying her down way gentler than I ever have. Her eyes track my movements as I strip my shirt off, let my pants fall to the floor, and the hunger in her eyes is different. Reverent, somehow. Like she feels as lucky to be here with me as I do with her.

When I sink to my knees, she stops me.

"I changed my mind," she murmurs, and my heart stops.

I bury my hand in my hair, gaze bouncing around the room. "Okay. Yeah. I get it."

"No, Jaxon. Not like that." Her hand slips down to mine, twining our fingers, and she guides me up on the bed beside her. "I don't need you to grovel. I just need you to be with me."

She lies back, tugging me toward her, until I'm looming above her, unable to comprehend why I was ever afraid of this. Of *us*.

I hike her leg up, scrubbing my hand over my mouth, because fucking Christ, she's perfection, her rich brown skin a stunning contrast to the cream silk sheets I finally put on my bed this morning, beautiful pussy swollen and weeping for me. She doesn't want groveling, but I still need a taste, and the only thing I want to accomplish by the end of this night is her knowing, without a doubt, that she has a place in my life for as long as she wants it. I'll spend all of that time worshiping this body.

I press my lips to her ankle, working my way up her lean legs, trading kisses for nips, until I'm lapping at the dampness at the juncture of her thighs. That clit is begging for attention, so I flick the tip of my tongue over it, enjoying the way she moans, buries her hands in my hair. Then I press my tongue flat to her center, drag it up achingly slow, and suck that clit into my mouth.

"God, Jaxon. Mouth. Love. Tongue. *Oooh fuuuck.*"

I love when she does this, makes no fucking sense. It's like hearing my thoughts when they're all about her.

I keep up my path, painting her hips with marks from my mouth, dragging kisses up her torso, twirling my tongue around her nipples while she whimpers and squirms. Sinking my fingers in her hair, I pull her head taut, showering her throat with attention while I hook one leg over my forearm, spreading her wide. My cock slides against her, nudging at her entrance, and she pulls my lips to hers. I squeeze my eyes shut as our mouths move together, unhurried, appreciating the slowness. And then, when Lennon lifts her hips, I push inside her, inch by aching inch, swallowing her sigh.

"You fill me so good," she murmurs, breathy and hushed as her hips roll against mine. "Like you were made just for me."

"Been thinkin' that for a while," I admit, pulling out, sinking back inside until my balls slap against her ass. I do it over and over, addicted to the way she reacts when I move faster, slower, deeper, when I roll my pelvis against her clit.

She's a beautiful, breathless mess, cheeks stained a deep crimson, lips swollen and glistening, begging for my mouth again. I give it to her, kissing her deeply, pulling away with a gasp as I pick up speed. With my forehead pressed to hers, she takes every inch of me, welcomes me deeper, squeezes me tighter as she whimpers my name.

I reach between us, stroking her clit as she trembles, rakes her fingernails down my shoulders. She's ready, right on the edge, and so am I. On instinct, I start planning where I want to come. I'm not picky; me on any part of her is a masterpiece, and Lennon particularly loves when I finish in her mouth. Says she loves the taste of her pussy on my cock, which usually has me immediately ready for round two.

But as we race up to that peak together, as we teeter on the edge, her wide eyes staring into mine, I'm struggling. Because the thought of my cum dripping from her freshly fucked pussy? Jesus Christ, that's a sight I'm feral to see. And the look in her eyes? The look in her eyes says she fucking knows it.

"Ask nicely," she barely manages, licking her lips as her eyes fall shut, her walls clenching around me. "Ask nicely, Jaxon, and I might let you come in my pussy."

A smirk tugs at my mouth. "Please, honey. Your pussy is the only place I wanna come." I dip my mouth to her ear. "Wanna watch it drip out of you, then push it back inside, so you're always full of me. And then I'll lick you clean, and when I'm done and you ask to taste yourself on my tongue, I'll say yes, because *no* is the last thing I'd ever say to you. So please, honey. Let me come in your pussy."

Her eyes come to mine, playful and beautiful. "No need to beg, Jaxon. A simple *please* would've sufficed."

I huff a laugh, but it quickly dies as our gazes collide. Her lips part as she struggles to breathe, her whole body trembling in my grasp. Mine is too. I grip her throat in my shaky hand, pressing my lips to hers, and when she lets go, shattering around me, crying out my name, I bury mine in her hair, filling her with my cum.

And I do exactly as I promised: watch it drip from her pussy, push it back inside with two fingers. Lick her clean, give her a taste, and then start all over again.

It's nearly three in the morning when we finally collapse, breathless and sated.

Lennon curls into my side, tucking herself around me. "Jaxon?"

"Mmm?"

"I missed you, too, you know."

I smile down at her, moonlight sliding against her flawless skin. "Yeah?"

"Yeah." Fingertips dance along my jaw. She pulls my mouth to hers, a tender kiss that settles my racing pulse. "You are worth every heartache."

Funny thing is, for the first time ever, with her in my arms, I believe it.

Pulling the sheets over us, I hug her against me.

"Jaxon? One more thing."

I chuckle. "Yeah, honey."

"Did you put these silk sheets on your bed for me?"

I press my lips below her ear. "Nah, honey. Put 'em on for Magic Mike. They treat him so gentle."

"Oh my God," she mutters, reaching back to pinch me. I catch her hand, gripping it in my fist as I fold her into my arms, burying my laugh in her neck.

Truthfully?

"I put these sheets on for me. Because now you have no reason to get out of this bed, and I get to spend the whole night with you right here." I press my hand over her heart, feeling the way it dances and patters, just like mine. "The best thing I've ever gifted to myself is, by far, the way I feel with you in my arms."

24

I GUESS YOU COULD SAY
WE'RE REALLY . . . NSYNC TONIGHT

Jaxon

"I FUCKING HATE THEM."

"The literal *only* way this could be worse is if Jennie were here too."

"Oh, fuck. Don't say that. She might hear you and come running."

"Well, hey." Adam shrugs, scratching the back of his neck. "I guess that's the positive, right? It could be worse?"

Emmett, Garrett, and I keep our eyes on Carter and Lennon a moment longer, the two of them shaking their hips, doing a spin, making up moves to some ridiculous song, before we twist our necks, in slow fucking motion, to glare at Adam.

"For fuck's sake, Adam," Emmett groans.

Garrett throws up his arms. "Can you not?"

I skate by him, shouldering him on the way. "For once in your life could you *not* look for the positive? Sometimes there *is* no posi—*oof!*" He silences me, sandwiching me between him and the boards.

"There's always a positive." He releases me, tugging me back with a fistful of my practice jersey. "Like right now, you're complaining that your girlfriend and one of your best friends are currently choreographing a dance that you have to partake in, and sure, that's shit. But you're overlooking the positive. Wanna know what the positive is?"

"No," I grumble, mindlessly waving my stick back and forth on the ice.

Adam pulls his mask back on, winking. "The positive is you get to work with your girlfriend and best friends every day."

Okay, well, technically, Lennon hasn't ever said girlfriend/ boyfriend, and Carter once told me that's a conversation you have to explicitly have, or whatever. Plus, like, I'm not trying to scare her with labels, so I'll just wait until she's comfortable enough to bring it up.

Because Lennon is totally scared.

Of labels.

And committed relationships.

Yes . . . Lennon . . .

"All right, boys." Carter claps his hands. "We're ready for you."

The sharp zip of skates sliding along the ice sounds behind me as I shift a stray puck back and forth on the blade of my stick, head down.

"Jaxon."

I glide aimlessly around one red circle, then head around the net backward, popping the puck in from behind.

"*Jaxon Eugene Riley*, Lennon said no more sex if you don't get over here. *Right. Now!*"

"I did *not* say that. I'm having the best sex of my life. Don't take that from me, Beckett."

"Awww," Garrett coos. "Did you hear that? Best sex of her life. Your girlfriend loooves you."

Lennon rolls her eyes, planting her foot against Garrett's ass, shoving him away. "Jaxon, for the love of God, get over here so we can teach you the dance before I off half your hockey team and you have to forfeit game six tonight by default."

Well, I can't have that. We swept San Jose in four games in the first round of the playoffs, and now we're up three-to-two heading into game six against Edmonton in the second round. Plus, today is really special for Adam and Rosie, since they're adopt-ready and asked Lily to officially be a part of their family forever. So, like, I guess I'll do the stupid dance, or whatever.

With a groan, I slouch over, skating toward the rest of the crew. When I stop next to Lennon, I tilt my cheek toward her, but keep my grump face on for appearances. She snickers, pressing a kiss to my cheek, and only then do I line up with the rest of the guys.

"Morning skate is done, you know," Emmett mutters, toeing at the ice. "Could be at home, fucking my wife on the kitchen counter." He sighs, looking up at the ceiling. "Or in my back seat, parked somewhere off the road, 'cause she loves the thrill of possibly getting caught."

"Oh my *God*! Can everyone just *shut up* and do the damn dance for once in their life?"

All of us turn, absolutely slack-jawed, to look at the person who's shouting at us. Because it's not Carter.

It's sweet, angel Adam.

"There's a little girl at my house right now who said 'I love you, Daddy' when I left to come here, only two hours after Rosie and Connor and I asked her to officially join our family." He tosses his stick and gloves to the ice, and his mask follows quickly. "So let's nail the damn dance so I can go home and be with my family before we come back here tonight, win game six, and seal our spot in round three against Nashville."

"Adam." Lennon presses the tips of her fingers to her mouth in a kiss. "Chef's kiss. Can always count on you to get everyone in line, and I promise, Lily is going to *love* this little performance on ice tonight."

"Wait. Wait, wait, wait, wait." I hold up my hand. "*On ice?*

Tonight? Are we not just, like . . . videotaping it? For the socials, or whatever?"

Carter scoffs. "What kind of intimidation tactic is that? This is just rehearsal for the pregame performance tonight."

"Intimidation tactic?" Garrett looks between them. "Why do we need an intimidation tactic?"

Adam sighs. "Great, now I'm skeptical. After my big speech and everything."

Emmett crosses his arms, mimicking Adam from a moment ago as he mutters, "Can everyone just shut up and do the damn dance?"

Adam shoves him into the boards, then promptly deflects what appears to be Emmett's attempt at a game of slapsies.

"Okay, boys, that's enough. When I took this job, I was told I'd be working with professional athletes, not children." Lennon snaps her fingers at the portable speaker sitting on the ledge by our bench. "Carter, will you let the team know what song they'll be dancing to today?"

He scrambles toward the speaker, picking up the phone plugged into it. "The honor is all mine," he breathes out, and as an unforgettable keyboard riff pours from the speaker, he grins at us. "What better way to say . . . 'Bye Bye Bye' . . . to the Oilers tonight than with a little . . . NSYNC?"

So, hey, is it too late to choose Option B, where Lennon offs half my team and we have to forfeit by default? Because I'm definitely not dancing to "Bye Bye Bye" by NSYNC in front of twenty thousand people.

I danced to "Bye Bye Bye" by NSYNC in front of twenty thousand people.

Honestly, I don't want to talk about it.

"Lennon said he was practicing at home all day."

"*I didn't wanna be bad in front of so many people!*" I screech, waving my arms—and stick—in the air. I turn to my . . . Lennon. "*Lennon!* That was supposed to be our little secret!"

She winks, wiggling her fingers at me before heading down the players' tunnel. "Uploading to Instagram as we speak! I'll be tallying votes for the fans' favorite dancer!"

"Okay, well, we all know who that'll be." Carter leans on the board ledge, pumping his brows as he squirts water into his mouth.

I swipe the bottle from him, quenching my humiliation. "Yeah. Me."

He scoffs. "Yeah, right."

"Only one of us was practicing all day, and it shows."

"I'm not sure we intimidated the other team," Garrett murmurs, eying the players in blue and orange warming up—and still laughing at us—on the visitor's side.

"Yeah, pretty sure they think we're jokes now," Emmett says.

"That's the whole point," Carter insists. "They think they've got this in the bag, 'cause all we're good for is dancing."

Emmett grimaces. "I'm not sure I'd say we're *good* at dancing."

"Speak for yourself." Garrett spins, jutting his hip. "Did you see me shaking my ass out there? Jennie saw, I'll tell you that much." He leans over the boards, wagging his brows at her. "And something tells me she likes what she saw."

"Lily loved it, huh?" Adam spreads his legs, slowly sinking down to the splits on the ice, leaning into the stretch.

I join him, bouncing into my lunge as Lennon emerges by the girls with her camera. She snaps pictures of the team as they warm up, but her camera never pauses on me. "Do you think she sees me?"

"Who?"

"Lennon. She's taking pictures of everyone but me. Maybe she hasn't spotted me." I look at Adam when he doesn't respond. He's busy winking at Rosie. "*Adam.* Give me attention."

"Huh?" His gaze snaps to me, and he grins, climbing to his feet. "Sorry. My attention's reserved for the pretty lady with pink hair." He grabs his mask—a brand-new one he had custom made for tonight, featuring a drawing Lily made of their family—and slips it over his face as he skates toward them. When he places his hand against the plexiglass and Lily and Connor touch theirs to the opposite side, the girls lose their shit, Carter whines because Olivia says something about Adam being a bigger DILF than him, and Lennon takes a picture.

I skate over, watching as she flaps at her eyes.

"That's it. That's the sweetest picture I've ever taken. The girlies are gonna go feral over this."

I knock on the glass. "What about me? Did you get my picture?"

Huh. That's weird. 'Cause I knocked on the glass to get her attention, but she's not giving it to me. Instead, she's taking a picture of Ireland and Carter, murmuring about perfection.

"Lennon? Did you get my picture? Look at this." I shimmy backward, drop to my knees, and spread them as wide as I can, bouncing into the stretch, kinda like I'm humping the ice. "Look how low I can get."

She flips through her pictures.

"Len?" I scramble to my feet, skating toward her, tapping the glass again. "Did you see me? Want me to do it again?"

"*Yes*, Jaxon," she finally answers on a sigh, her gaze swinging up to mine. "I saw you. We're all *so* impressed."

I grin, lifting a shoulder, leaning on my stick. "No big deal or anything. Just been told I'm a *pretty* impressive guy, so, thought you might wanna see."

She lifts a brow, and there it is. Right there in the corner of her perfect mouth, the curve that leads to the full, mind-blowing explosion across her face, the smile that lives in my head rent-free. And when she raises her camera, points it at me, I wink.

"Hey, honey?" she calls after me as I skate away. I stop, spinning back to her. "No fighting."

I can't make that promise, but I wish I could. I try, though, as hard as I can. I keep my body between Edmonton's offensive players and Adam, protecting my goalie the way I'm supposed to. I pin them to the boards, steal the puck, pass it up the wing and watch my guys fly into their zone, dominate, put three pucks in their net. Hell, I even assist for two out of three.

I keep my hands to myself as much as I can, and it starts off easy enough, until Edmonton's left winger starts chirping at Adam.

"Jesus, another one that's not yours?" Number 12 makes a show of looking over Rosie and the kids. "Your girl just have sex with everyone but you, or what?"

Adam's eyes flicker, but he keeps his eyes on the puck in the ref's hand as we line up for a faceoff in our end.

I press my shoulder against 12's as I crouch beside him. "Fuck off, Marshall."

He turns his grin on me. "Funny you're so defensive for guys who are gonna forget about you one day soon when you're traded. Isn't that what they all do?"

"Fuck *off*, Marshall," Adam spits, and when the puck drops to the ice and the play explodes, he glides from one side of the net to the other. Never taking his eyes off the puck, he tells me, "Not worth it, Riley."

"Your girlfriend doesn't think so either," Marshall says to Adam, chopping at my stick. "If she thought your dick was worth it, she'd probably ride it and make one of those kids yours."

I shove him away from the crease with my shoulder, trying to ignore the urge to crack him in the face. He's just mad because we're halfway through the third period, and we're up by one. If he's about to wave goodbye to his chance at the cup, he doesn't wanna leave without a fight.

But picking on the nicest guy in the league? For opening his home, his family, to kids who aren't biologically his? What the fuck's the point? How miserable do you have to be?

He nabs a pass from one of his defense, and I sandwich him against the boards the moment he winds up.

"Quit running your mouth," I spit out as he climbs to his feet and the puck gets tangled up at the blue line.

"But I'm so good at it." He slaps his stick against the ice, calling for a pass from his linesman. "Guess it's better to be a stepdaddy, though, huh, Lockwood? That way, when your girl eventually cheats, you have no ties to the kids. Right?" He smirks, glancing at Adam as the puck glides across the ice. "Wonder if this one will fuck her way through the roster the same way your ex did."

Adam blinks, and in the same moment, the puck hits Marshall's stick, ricocheting off it. Adam's catcher comes up a split second too late. The puck smacks the crossbar and sinks down into the net, tying the game at three goals apiece.

At the expense of Adam.

And it's my job to protect my goalie, and my friends.

I drop my gloves and stick to the ice, grab Marshall by the neck of his jersey, and throw my fist in his face, just once, 'cause Lennon's watching and she asked me not to fight. He swings at me, grabs for anything within reach, yanking my helmet off before the officials separate us. I grab my gloves and stick off the ice, sweat-drenched hair stuck to my forehead. "You need to verbally abuse the goalie to score? Disgusting."

I turn back to the net, where Adam waits with my helmet. I press my forehead to his mask, clapping him on the back. "You're an amazing dad, an incredible partner, and one hell of a goalie."

He wraps his arm around me. "Thanks for having my back."

I turn toward the penalty box, ready to serve my time.

"Hey, Riley?"

I glance over my shoulder, just in time to see Marshall hook his stick around my ankle and yank.

My feet go flying out from beneath me, and my ass hits the ice first.

The back of my head hits second.

Then my vision goes black.

YOU'D THINK HITTING MY HEAD and waking up as I'm being lifted off the ice on a stretcher was the worst of it. Or the verbal beatdown Coach delivered after he stormed in here when the period ended—we're going into overtime, by the way—and after he found out I'd be okay.

But no, the worst of it is the terrified voice shouting my name.

"Jaxon? *Jaxon!* Where is he? Is he okay?"

I look up at our team doctor with pleading eyes. "Please don't let her in here."

She holds my gaze as she opens the door and calls, "Over here, Len!"

Coach crosses his arms over his chest as Lennon rushes into the room, deflating when she sees me alive and conscious, lying up on the treatment table, naked from the waist up.

She lifts her phone to her ear. "Gran?" *Damn it.* "I found him. He's alive. I'll have him call you later." She says goodbye, tucking her phone away, and I'm in so much trouble.

"Ah, Miss Hayes," Coach drawls, and is his eye twitching? It's definitely twitching. "You're just in time. I was about to tell Jaxon that he needs to a) stay out of the penalty box, b) keep his fists to himself, and c) stay off my injured list, because this team needs him on the ice. He's no good to them anywhere else." The longer his sharp gaze stays on me, the more desperate I am to hide. "Is that clear, Riley? Cut the fights, unless absolutely necessary. You can't be our number one enforcer if you're not on the ice to enforce."

"Yes, sir."

Lennon wrings her hands, like she wants to touch me, but isn't sure she's allowed. I know it's not Coach she's worried about; it's me.

"C'mere," I murmur, hooking my finger toward her. Relief floods her face, and she dashes over, grasping my arm.

Coach looks between us, sighing. "All right, we've got an overtime to win. Riley, if you're dating our photographer, I need a love contract signed and in my hands before you step on the ice for your next game."

My heart stops at that four-letter word, attached to something as binding as *contract*. "A-a . . . a what?"

"Love contract." He waves a hand through the air. "Consensual relationship agreement, whatever you wanna call it. Just a contract signed by the two of you stating you're in a consenting, romantic relationship."

"Oh." That feels . . . big. Official. Scary.

But then Lennon twines our fingers, and I look at the way her hand fits in mine, so perfectly, like mine was always made to hold hers. And it doesn't feel so scary.

Coach leaves, and Lennon looks to the doctor. "What's the prognosis?"

"Just a minor concussion," I half-lie, trying to get up. It just so happens that Adam, Garrett, Carter, and Emmett choose this moment to clomp through the door on their skates.

Carter takes one look at me trying to get up, points his glove at me, growls *"Sit,"* and I lie right back down.

"Jaxon thought he played for Nashville," the doctor tells everyone.

I roll my eyes, scrubbing my hands down my face. "You misheard

me! I said I *used* to play for Nashville. Plus, we'll be playing them
next round if we win tonight."

The doctor blinks at me, and I keep my gaze on hers, because
it's easier than looking at the five people surrounding me right
now, the ones wasting their energy being scared for me.

"It's called post-traumatic amnesia," she tells them, because
she certainly already told me this in front of my coach, assistance
coaches, Adam's goaltending coach, and our fucking GM. "It's
temporary memory loss that happens due to an injury to the brain.
It can last anywhere from a few minutes to a few months. Luckily,
Jaxon was the former."

She looks back to me, and I feel the weight of everyone's gaze
burning into me.

"He's had too many whacks to the head in a short amount of
time without a break. Next time, he may not be so lucky. Next
time, the memory loss might not be temporary."

I WANTED TO SURPRISE HER, but as it turns out, it's incredibly hard
to surprise someone who's been hovering over you for four days
straight. Apparently, my last surprise to her, ever, will be those custom Crocs I gifted her.

At least she's wearing them tonight.

"Your Crocs look nice."

"They're ugly as fuck," I huff, staring down at my blue Crocs in
the passenger seat of my car while Lennon drives. Oh, did I forget
to mention I, too, now own a pair of Crocs?

"But . . ."

I roll my eyes. "But they're comfy as fuck."

"Ha! I told you! I converted you! I knew I would!"

She could probably convince me to convert to temporary
celibacy if she gave me those eyes, pushed out that lower lip, and

murmured a *please*, but I'm not gonna tell her that. I wouldn't put it past her to try, just for bragging rights.

Lennon glances at me, chin on my fist, elbow propped in the open window as we whizz along the highway, up the coast toward the spot we've been going to once a week since her birthday. "What's the matter, grumpy boy?"

I huff.

"Aw, c'mon now." She reaches over, tickles my chin. "What's wrong, handsome boy?"

"It was supposed to be a surprise, but you didn't even ask me for directions, you just started driving exactly where I wanted to take you, like you knew!"

She bites her smile back. "I'm sure I have no idea what you have planned, even though when I suggested going to bed so I could spend the night with Magic Mike inside me before I leave tomorrow for Nashville and Georgia, you freaked out and suggested a drive. At midnight."

I cross my arms over my chest. "I like midnight drives." I like anything if I'm doing it with Lennon, but Bill Cooke from NASA's Meteoroid Environments Office says the best time to start watching a meteor shower is at two a.m., and that it'll just get better and better until dawn. I wanted to get there with plenty of time to get set up and comfy so Lennon doesn't have to miss a minute of it. "I hate not being able to drive."

Lennon gives me a beautiful smile. "You're almost there, Jaxon."

Yeah, I am. I've got a checkup tomorrow after the team leaves for game one of the third round in Nashville, and the doctor feels confident in my recovery so far. If I'm cleared, I'll be allowed to drive, and to fly out to Nashville to play in game two.

Or Georgia, for Lennon's family cookout, which just so happens to be sandwiched between game one and game two. She hasn't tried to ask me to come again, but I know she wants me to; she's just afraid of what my answer will be. Kind of like how she hasn't come right out and asked me—in all seriousness—to stop fighting, but I know just as well that she wants me to. Is desperate for it, even, if the way she's been watching me at nighttime while she thinks I'm asleep as any indication, like she thinks she's at risk of losing me at any moment.

And I get it. I know well enough how hard it is to watch someone you care about get hurt. It's one of the reasons Gran had to cut back on coming to my games once I was sixteen. Too many fights that led to injuries, and when she'd drive me home from the hospital later that night, she'd swear she nearly wound up in the bed next to me from a heart attack.

I don't want to be responsible for someone's pain, not in that way. So for my gran, for Lennon, I'm going to make a conscious effort to try. It doesn't mean I'll never fight again. It means I'll try to keep my emotions in check enough so that I only fight when it's truly necessary. After all, I'm a defender. My job is to protect my goalie, my team. It's what I'm good at.

So I can do that. But I don't know if Georgia is a step I'm ready to take.

Lennon pulls off the highway and into the parking lot at Porteau Cove. It's far from empty, but our usual spot, tucked down on the pebbled shore, is as quiet as it always is. I help Lennon unpack her telescope, then watch as she gets lost in setting it up, the same way she always does.

"Just a quick peek," she murmurs, peering up at the sky through it as I spread out the blanket. *Wow,* her lips mouth, and then she takes two steps toward me before pausing and dashing right back. "One more peek."

That happens three times, and when she finally finds me, I'm lying on the blanket, watching her instead of the sky.

"Sorry," she whispers, crawling toward me.

"No, you're not." I snake an arm around her waist, pulling her into my side, my hand behind my head as my gaze coasts the sky, looking for Sirius. When I find it, the same thing happens that has ever since Lennon told me to look for Bryce there: a warmth starts in my toes, climbing up my legs like a vine, wrapping me in a feeling so secure, so comforting, like a hug I've been needing for fifteen years. It creeps up my face in the form of a smile, small and a little sad, but in this moment, I see him here, smiling back at me, and there's a strange sense of relief in that.

Lennon slides her palm across my chest, laying it over my heart as she sighs softly. "Hi, Bryce. Shining bright as ever, my guy."

Christ, this girl. I blink at the tears gathering in the corners of my eyes, letting them get lost against her hair when I press my lips there.

I'm not someone who wonders what life would have looked like for the people we loved and lost. It's too painful. Too fucking painful to think about Bryce filling out, eventually growing into his lanky form. To being the top goalie pick the year he should've been drafted. The trouble we would've gotten into in high school, the hearts he would've broken.

The voice who would've always been on the other end, only a call away.

I might refuse to torture myself with what could've been, but as I lie here beneath thousands of stars on a warm night in the middle of May, listening to Lennon tell the brightest star in the sky about all the trouble I've been getting myself into on the ice, I know with certainty that Bryce would love this woman.

And as the first meteor falls, then the second, and the third, as Lennon tells me all about the Eta Aquarids—like that they're debris from Halley's comet, or that they can travel as fast as forty-two miles in a single second—as she falls silent, staring with wide-eyed wonder out at the sky, her hand clutching tightly at mine, I can't take my eyes off the stunning woman at my side.

How lucky am I that of all the fingers she could have her own twined so tenderly through, she's chosen mine?

I watch with awe as a tear sneaks out of her eye, the starlight kissing the track it takes across her cheek. Her chin quivers, and she pulls her lower lip into her mouth.

"It's beautiful," she whispers.

I catch her tear on my thumb. "Stunning."

"Do you love it?"

My gaze traces the shape of her heart-shaped mouth, my favorite good-morning kiss. Follows the delicate slope of her jaw up to her high cheekbones, where the sunrise always paints her first. Takes in the spirals scattered softly across her forehead, the ones I love to twirl around my fingers when she's lying against my chest at night. I settle on those deep brown eyes, as endless as the sky above us, dancing with the same dazzling stars, and I smile.

"I do."

25

WELCOME TO THE DARK SIDE: THE COOCHIE GANG

Jaxon

"YOU'RE GONNA HURT YOURSELF, SWEETHEART."

"I'm not gonna hurt myself."

"It'll be the ladder or the hammer, one of the two."

"You have no faith in me. You never have."

"I've had nothing but faith in you your whole life, sweetheart, but your strength is on skates, not wielding a hammer. If that doesn't get ya, it'll be that damn cat at your ankles."

"Damn it, Mittens! Daddy's working!" I shake my leg, trying to free myself of his talons. He leaps into the air, batting at my foot, and the second he hits the ground, he's at it again. "Did Lennon give you catnip again this morning?"

Gran chuckles from my phone, where I have it propped up against a mafia romance so she can supervise me hanging these pictures. "Oh, Jaxon. That one is just stunning."

"Right? She's incredible with her camera." I hang the framed forty-by-sixty shot Lennon took a couple weeks back over the couch. It's my favorite of her shots, the Milky Way splashing across the navy sky at Porteau Cove, streaks of magenta and lavender blending flawlessly into the amber glow of the setting sun, right before it dips below the horizon. "I submitted it to *National Geographic*. Apparently they don't take unsolicited submissions, but—"

"You're a rulebreaker?"

I smile, running a palm down my proud chest. "Yeah."

Gran snickers, and I take in the artwork scattered across the walls: dancing stars, falling meteors, brilliant sunrises, lush mountains. *Lennon.* Lennon lives in every single piece, etched into the details, the sense of wonder, the same way she lives in my thoughts, running around all day, even when she's not here.

I hate it when she's not here.

"She's good for you."

My gaze snaps to Gran and her watchful smile. "Huh?"

"Lennon. It's been a long time since I've seen you smile like that."

I rub the back of my neck. "I'm just happy 'cause the doc cleared me this morning. I can play in Nashville on Sunday."

Her smile only deepens, blue eyes staying on mine as she works on her crochet piece. "Yes, you always look like you tripped over your own two feet and face-planted into love when you're thinking about hockey."

"Love? *Love?* Psssh. Gran, *please.* I mean, what does that word even mean anyway?" I scoop up Mittens, smooshing my face into his soft, floofy belly. "I *love* my handsome, squishy marshmallow. Yes I do, 'cause he's so fuckin' cute. Oh, hey, Gran, can you make Mitts a—"

She holds up a teensy blue-and-green vest, just right for a kitty. There's a pair of mittens stitched on one side, and a hockey stick on the other. "I still have to do the back."

"I want it to say *Daddy.*"

She rolls her eyes, muttering to herself about cats, grandkids, and great-grandkids.

"I didn't catch that, Gran, but—oh, what's that, boy?" I squish my ear against Mittens's face. "Mittens says you're the *meowy* best great-gran."

"For God's sake, Jaxon. Get out of the house. Go for a walk. Find your mind, 'cause I think you've damn well lost it."

"'Kay. C'mon, Mitts, let's get your harness."

"Leave the cat at home!"

I gasp, covering his tiny, adorable ears. "She didn't mean that."

Gran shakes her head, sighing. "Bless Lennon's sweet, selfless heart, she has to deal with this on a daily basis. Cat walks, custom sweaters, photoshoots—"

"I told you, the photoshoot was her idea!"

"Then you two really are made for each other."

I lift my shoulder, shrugging her words off. I have a hard time believing I was made for anyone, let alone Lennon. Nobody gets that lucky.

Gran's smile slowly fades, heartache working its way into her eyes. "One of these days, Jaxon Riley, you're going to realize you're worth it."

Will I? I've already been chasing it my whole life. The older I get, the further away it seems to be, and the more ingrained in me it becomes that I'll forever be trying to stack up to someone else's standards. I hate the feeling, the way it has the power to wind around my limbs and squeeze until I feel like I can't breathe. It renders me useless, another jab at the brain that hasn't figured out how to fight the negative thoughts even after all these years, the ones that convince me if I can't be better, I'll be alone.

But I don't want to be alone anymore.

Maybe that's why I wind up out front of Second Chance Home an hour later, my first time alone, asking Sarah's social worker if I'm allowed to take her for ice cream and a walk.

Sarah's bent over a magazine when her social worker tells her, and the way her face lights up makes me feel nice. Important, almost. Her head whips up, eyes finding me. She waves excitedly, leaping from her seat on the floor and running up the stairs, screeching about getting ready "like, so super fast, I promise." When she joins me out front ten minutes later, she's breathless and wearing a Vancouver Vipers hoodie with my name on the arm.

"Where'd you get that?"

"Isn't it cool?" She grips the hem, popping her hip left, then right, showing it off. "My social worker got it for me for my birthday."

"That's what you wanted?"

"Well, I wished for a family when I blew out my candles, but I had to ask for something that was actually possible for my real gift." She says it so easily, giggling while I roll my shoulders back, trying to dissolve the sudden bite of pain in my chest. "I said I wanted my favorite player's jersey, but she said I'm not allowed to wear your number 'cause it's a bad number, so she got me this instead. Isn't it great? It's *so* cozy."

I blink at her. "I'm your favorite player?"

She rolls her eyes. "Duh, Jaxon."

"I thought you barely liked me."

"Well, that's silly. Why do you think I'm always doing your hair and makeup? 'Cause I like you best."

Damn it, the pain isn't leaving. "Why do you like me best?"

"'Cause everyone else is always so happy and perfect, but sometimes you're grumpy and sad, and it makes me feel like it's okay to be grumpy and sad. I'm tired of pretending I'm always happy like everyone else." She throws her arms in the air. "Now can we go get ice cream already? I'm *starving!*"

We walk to Baskin-Robbins, and Sarah takes ten minutes to decide which two flavors she wants, and another five to decide if she wants it in a cone or a cup. She chooses a cone, fucking finally, but proves it's the wrong choice when she bumps into a table and drops the whole thing. When I order her another one, she stops the worker with a screech to *wait!* because maybe the cone falling was a sign that she chose the wrong flavors. I almost cry, and I do bang my head off the ice cream display window. A kind old woman pats my back and promises me it gets better, but not until age twenty-three or so.

"Holy smokes," Sarah says as we walk along Barbour Park Trail, eating our ice cream. "You're inhaling that!"

"Mmm, mhmm." I lick the edge of the cone where my chocolate peanut butter ice cream is dripping. "This is my favorite flavor. I haven't had it in forever."

"How come?"

"Lennon's allergic to nuts."

"So you don't eat them? What if you go out for lunch without her?"

"I'd rather avoid them altogether if I'm going to be seeing her. I don't want to risk her getting sick."

"You'll be happy when she moves out then, huh? Then you can have your favorite ice cream whenever you want."

I swallow, the ice cream souring in my stomach as I look at my half-eaten cone. "I can get a new favorite flavor."

Sarah licks her bubblegum cone. "Why? Is she gonna live with you forever?"

"I dunno. No. Maybe. I dunno."

She snorts a laugh. "Maybe I should ask her instead. I bet she knows."

I bet she does. I also know she's not going to answer, the same way she wouldn't answer me when I asked her what she wanted me to do with that love contract Coach said we have to sign if we're a real, super official couple. She says it's not about what I want *her* to do, but what *I* want to do. Now the damn contract is burning a hole in my underwear drawer, because I'm too scared to come right out and ask Lennon what I want to know, which is whether she's my girlfriend, all mine, for no one else but her and me.

"Hey, lemme ask you a question." I take one last look at my cone, mentally thanking chocolate peanut butter for the time we've had together over the years before I toss it in the trash and take a seat on the park bench. "If a girl spends, like, all her free time with you, and the first thing she does every day is kiss you good morning—"

"Does she brush her teeth first?"

"No."

"Yuck." She shudders. "'Kay. Go on."

"And if she laughs at all your jokes, and holds your hand in public, and asks you to hold her purse—"

"She asks you to hold her purse? That's big."

"Right? It doesn't feel like something you'd just task to anyone."

"I wouldn't." She looks me over. "And not to you. No offense, I just don't know if I'd trust you with a job that important."

"That's ridiculous. What am I gonna do with it? Run off and—" I close my eyes and breathe, hands braced in front of me. "Okay, whatever. If she does all that, *and* wants to introduce you to her family, does that mean she's your girlfriend?"

"Hmmm." Sarah squints, licking at her ice cream. "Does she kiss anyone else?"

"No."

"Are you *sure*?"

"Pretty sure."

"Her purse. Does she keep stuff in there for you?"

"She lets me use her chapstick, and she packs snacks when we're gonna be gone for a while, 'cause she says food makes me nicer if I'm acting grumpy."

"Interesting." Sarah crunches her cone, licks her fingers clean, dabs at her mouth with her napkin. "I would say yes, she's your girlfriend."

"*Yes!*" Jumping to my feet, I jerk my fist into my side. "*Fuck yeah!*"

"But you'll have to ask her yourself."

"What? *Nooo. Sarah!*"

"And see, that's why I wouldn't let you hold my purse. You're afraid to ask a girl to be your girlfriend, so if someone tried to steal my bag, you'd be too afraid to fight them off."

"Sarah, please. Have you seen me play hockey? I'd knock 'em out."

Sarah snickers, and as we walk back to the home, she asks me about Lily, how she's doing, if she's happy, asks me to give her a hug for her. When we reach the front steps, she grows quiet, looking up at the house.

"Jaxon? Why do you think I haven't been adopted?"

The question surprises me, and I'm disappointed in myself for forgetting. Forgetting that despite how happy these kids are, they're sitting here, waiting day in and day out. To be reunited with their family, to find another one. To be chosen.

"I've been here longer than Lily, you know. I mean, I'm really happy for her. I'm just kinda confused, I guess, 'cause I've been here since I was seven, and I'm gonna be thirteen after Halloween." She sniffs, shrugging. "Maybe I'm just not what people want. I'm a lot of work."

"Why do you say that?"

"Well, for starters, I take a long time in the bathroom 'cause I like to do my hair pretty every day. And I always make a mess practicing my makeup. I get it all over the place, then I gotta clean it all up. This boy at school says I never shut up, that I talk too loud and too much. I'm not good at math, no matter how much I try, and I came in last place at the cross-country meet because I got a cramp in my stomach." She frowns. "I guess that makes sense though. 'Cause after my mom died, her boyfriend said I was too slow and made us late for everything, and that's why he couldn't keep me." Her eyes water. "Is that it? Do I need to be faster? I can practice. I can be better."

Fuck. I crouch at her feet, gripping her hands, bringing her eyes to mine. "Hey. Look at me. You don't change a thing about yourself, okay? Don't change a damn thing. You are perfect exactly the way you are, and you know something? The people who think you aren't, are the people who don't matter. We don't give a fuck about those people, Sarah. We're better off without them. The only people we have room for in our lives are the kind who don't ask us to be anything or anyone we're not. Wait for those people, Sarah. That's the family you deserve."

She sniffles, swiping at a tear that rolls down her cheek. Then, she slips her arms around my neck, hugging me close. "You should stop being afraid to ask Lennon to be your girlfriend."

"How do I just stop being afraid?"

"Maybe you don't. Maybe you just give her your heart and trust that she's going to protect it. The same way she trusts you to hold her purse, even though you could lose it."

Sarah gives me one more squeeze, thanks me for the ice cream, then starts up the steps. She pauses at the door. "Do you like me the way I am? Slow and messy and talking too much?"

I smile. "I like you lots, just the way you are."

She grins, a beautiful sight. "My mom did too. She wrote it in a letter for me before her cancer got too bad. She said on the days where I felt unlovable, she hoped someone would remind me that I was. Thanks for making me feel lovable today, Jaxon. I hope your family helps you feel lovable on your hard days too."

Maybe I'm chasing that feeling today. Missing it with Lennon and the guys gone. Or maybe I'm riding the high of having that impact on Sarah's day. Maybe it gives me a sense of purpose, knowing that a gesture as simple as an ice cream cone and a few words of affirmation helped put a smile on her face, helped her stand a little taller. Maybe I want more of that, to help make some-one's day easier, memorable.

Maybe that's why when I check in on Rosie and she's on the verge of a meltdown, trying to juggle everything at home with Adam out of town, I offer to help.

"Connor's having a sleep regression, so he refused his nap today and won't go to bed. Lily misses Adam and wants him to read her bedtime story over FaceTime, but they haven't landed yet. Neither of them wanted dinner, the dogs need to be walked, and the cat got bit by a bug in the backyard. He's fine, but he's being an asshole because one eye is swollen shut and I keep laughing at him." She sighs, deflating as she lets me into the house. "If I don't laugh, I'll cry." Then she takes Mittens from my arms, kisses his nose, ushers him down the hall toward the sound of chaos, and pulls me into her arms. "Hi. Thank you for coming. You didn't have to, but I'm glad you did."

"Uncle Jax?" Two brown eyes peek around the corner.

"Hey, Lil." Crouching, I open my arms. "Feel like a hug?"

She sniffles, inching toward me in her Princess Ariel night-gown, long brown hair tied up in buns on either side of her head. When I lift her into my arms, she lays her head on my shoulder and cries. "I want Daddy to read me a bedtime story but he's still on the airplane."

"Can I read you a bedtime story tonight? I've never done it before, but maybe you could teach me."

"Daddy does the funny voices."

"What? You mean like this, little darlin'?" I ask in my best Southern drawl. "Or does he sound a wee bit more like this?" I switch to my best British, which is hot trash, but she's only five so she laughs anyway.

She scrubs her eyes with her tiny fists. "Can you do a teapot?"

"A teapot?"

"The teapot talks, and Daddy does her voice."

"How about I do my own voices, and that way whenever I read this book to you, we'll have voices that are special to us, and when Daddy reads it to you, you two will have voices that are special to you and him. How does that sound?"

She sniffs, nodding. "That sounds good."

More footsteps pad, and Connor comes running down the hall in Buzz Lightyear pajamas, Mittens clutched to his chest. "Unc'a Jax! Conn'a gots Mitts! *Meow!*" He scrubs his eyes, looking up at me with a sleep-drunk smile.

"You sleepy, buddy?"

"No." He shakes his head. "Conn'a not sweepy."

"Well, I was gonna go read Lily a bedtime story."

He tosses poor Mitts to the floor, scampering over, reaching up. "Conn'a wead stowy."

Setting Lily on her feet, I tell them, "Say good night to Mama."

Rosie embraces them, kissing their cheeks. "Good night, babies. I love you."

"I love you, Mommy," Lily murmurs, squeezing her again. "Thank you for loving me back."

"Lub you, Mama," Connor calls, waving at her over his shoulder as he races up the stairs. "Come, Unc'a Jax! Be'time!"

Upstairs, Lily shows me her room and tells me how she's been doing really good at sleeping in her own bed, but that she still likes to sleep with Connor some nights because they make each other feel brave. She's having trouble feeling brave tonight, so the three of us lie in Connor's bed while I read a story about an unlikely duo: a teapot and the silly bear who breaks it and then puts it back together again. Lily laughs at all my voices, and Connor passes out on page three. When I climb out of bed, she scooches closer to Connor, snuggling up as I tuck her in.

"That was fun," she whispers, yawning. "You can come back and do it again."

"I'd like that, Lily." I press a kiss to her forehead. "Good night, sweetheart."

"Uncle Jax?" she calls as I reach the door, the glow-in-the-dark stars stuck to the ceiling lighting her bleary-eyed smile. "I love you."

My heart swells and thumps. "I love you, too, Lil."

Rosie's coming in the front door with the dogs as I come down the stairs. "Everything okay? You look like you just saw a ghost. Were the kids difficult to get down?"

"Your daughter just told me she loves me. And I . . ." My throat constricts. "I don't know what I did to deserve it, so normally I'd convince myself it's not real. But . . ."

"It feels real."

"I . . . believe her."

"Yeah, I know what you mean. I spent my life feeling like I had to be someone else, earn the love I wanted. Then people like Adam and Lily, like you guys, you came around and gave it to me freely." She shakes her head. "Sometimes I wake up in the middle of the night, and for a moment, I think it was all a dream." Her fingertips flutter across her cheekbones, swiping at her tears. "Sorry, I'm so emotional lately. And tired. I fall apart so much easier when I'm tired. I'm so excited for you guys, how far you're getting in the playoffs. But I won't lie, I'm looking forward to having Adam home for a couple months when this is all done. Two dogs, a cat who lives up to his Dinosaur name, two kids and another on the—" She snaps her mouth shut, eyes wide.

"Another what?"

"Honestly, I forget what I was saying." She moves past me, heading for the kitchen. "Hey, wanna order some pizza? I'm starving. I'll see if the girls wanna come over."

"A girls' night?" I dash across the kitchen to the living room, jumping over the back of the couch, sprawling out on top of it with my hands behind my head. "I'm in. Oh! Can we wear robes? Does Adam have a robe I can wear? Imagine you send him a picture of me lounging in his robe? He'll be so mad." I rub my hands together, laughing under my breath.

Rosie's watching me, brows raised, menu in her hands.

"Can we get cheesy garlic sticks too?"

"Oooh, fuck yeah," she mutters, bringing her phone to her ear as she looks at the menu. I jog over, looking through it as she orders pizza and cheesy sticks.

"And wings," I mouth, pointing at the picture. "*Hot.*" I unravel the menu, checking out the rest of the options. "Oh, fuck. Jalapeño poppers. Oh my God, can we get onion rings?" I dip my mouth toward her phone. "Can we get an order of—"

"Jaxon, for fuck's sake." She bats me away. "Yes, I'll get you your damn poppers and onion rings."

"And my hot wings."

Her eyes narrow somewhat dangerously, and I smile, slowly backing away. There's a beautifully stocked wine rack on the wall in the dining room, so I point at it.

"Wine? You want some wine? You deserve it."

She rolls her eyes but laughs, turning away as she finishes up with our order. When she's done, I hand her a glass of red, and her face pales.

"Oh. Thank you." She swirls it around, staring at it.

I lift my glass. "Cheers."

She swallows, clinking her glass to mine. "Cheers."

I keep my eyes on her as I taste the vintage Syrah, and she keeps her eyes on the wine that she doesn't drink.

"Hey, remember earlier in the hallway when you said '*two kids and another on the—*' and then stopped talking?"

Her knuckles blanch as she grips the stem harder. "Uh-huh."

"Go ahead and finish that sentence for me."

Another swallow. She licks her lips. Clears her throat, but whispers that final word anyway. "Way."

"You're pregnant."

I expect a grin. Bubbling, giddy laughter, maybe. Rosie and Adam want a big family. A year ago, they didn't even have each other. Now they have all this. So when she bursts into tears, buries her face in her hands and sobs, I'm a little confused. I didn't know Rosie when she was pregnant with Connor, but Olivia was super emotional when she was pregnant with Ireland, and she always blamed the hormones. So maybe it's that.

"Hey," I murmur, running a hand over her back. "I'm sure it's a lot. You've got a busy household. But you guys are gonna be amazing."

"I'm the worst friend ever," she sobs.

The worst . . . "What?"

"Cara and Emmett have been trying for two years and I-I-I . . ." She shakes her head, shoulders quivering, and I pull her into my arms. "We weren't even trying yet. It just happened. Twice now, it's just happened for me, and they've been trying for so long."

"So you're afraid she's going to be mad at you?"

"She won't be mad. She's just . . . she's going to feel so sad for her and Emmett, you know? Imagine trying so hard for something over and over and never getting it, but someone else who doesn't even try gets it."

I know they've been trying, but Emmett doesn't talk about it much. And Cara? Well, Cara's one of those people who seems unshakable every minute of every day. And I made the mistake of assuming that meant she was doing okay.

"We'll be there for them, though," I remind Rosie. "All of us. I know it's not the answer, and it doesn't make everything okay, but they won't be alone." I squeeze her a little tighter. "I'm happy for you and Adam. For your family."

The front door flies open, Cara, Olivia, and Jennie's voices carrying down the hall. Rosie wipes her eyes, mouthing a *thank you* at me before the girls appear, all three of them in fluffy white robes, hair pulled up in messy knots.

Cara heaves two giant pink bags up on the counter and grins at me. "Welcome to the dark side, Jaxon. After tonight, you'll be a member of the Coochie Gang for life."

The words should scare me. On a regular night, they would. When I'm lying in bed later tonight, maybe I'll realize how reckless I was being, how lucky I am to have made it out alive.

Instead, two hours later, I find myself sprawled out on a couch in Adam's robe, four mojitos deep, a goopy pink mask globbed over my face, pizza box on my chest, and some sort of sugar scrub on my lips that tastes like bubble gum. I run my tongue over my lower lip, humming as I lick off the sugary goodness.

"Jaxon!"

I startle, throwing the pizza box to the floor when I sit up. My cucumber eyes slowly slide down my face, landing on my lap. "What? What happened?"

"Stop licking your lip scrub off!" Cara storms over, smearing more on. "Do you want your lips to be soft, supple, and kissable for Lennon or not?"

"Maybe Len likes him rough," Jennie says. "That's how I like Garrett."

"I like Carter rough," Olivia murmurs, licking at the icing on an Oreo.

"There's something about Adam when he's really rough," Rosie says, my cat, her cat, and both dogs curled up on or around her lap. "Like, he's such a gentle giant, but then the kids go to sleep, and he locks the bedroom door, and—"

"Is this all you guys do? Talk about sex?" I swipe a Sour Key from the bowl on the coffee table, carefully placing the entire thing on my tongue, bypassing my lip scrub. "Typical."

Cara checks her nails. "Sometimes we talk about Lennon's dragon dildo and how she likes to attach it to the bathroom sink and ride it."

I choke on my candy. "She told you about that?"

"The Coochie Gang is a Chamber of Secrets."

"What the fuck does that mean? Is that some sort of Harry Potter porn fan fiction?"

"It means this is a safe space to share. So you can share with us, Jaxon, if you want to."

"'Bout what?"

Cara lifts her brows. Shares a look with the girls. When I lick my sugar scrub off again, she rolls her eyes. "About your *feelings.*"

"These are Lennon's favorite," I murmur, poking the tips of my fingers through the holes on four Sour Keys, until I have one on each finger. "Sometimes I get her the chocolate-dipped ones." I chuckle. "I say it's 'cause she's sour *and* sweet."

Olivia snickers. Rosie drags her hand down her face, and now it's goopy. Jennie just grins, swirling a Dunkaroo in frosting.

Suddenly, all of our phones ping and light up on the coffee table. Olivia's the first to grab hers.

"Oh no. It's happening." She looks at us, eyes wide with fear. "One giant group chat."

I groan when I see the new thread.

Carter added you to a group chat.

Carter changed the group chat name to Real Hot Girl Shit.

Olivia changed the group chat name to Friendchips.

"Get it? Like friendships, but chips, because"—Olivia holds up a bag of Doritos—"I like chips."

Carter changed the group chat name to No Condom, No Problem.

Olivia changed the group chat name to Let's Taco Bout It.

Carter changed the group chat name to Caution:
The Tea Is Hot But Carter Is Scalding.

Olivia changed the group chat name to Ketchup With The Crew.

Cara levels Olivia with the dirtiest look I've ever seen. "Be so fucking for real, Olivia."

Adam: Help???

Lennon: Mommy I'm scared.

Garrett: She needs to be stopped.

Emmett: She's worse than Carter. How is it possible?

Carter: she's out of control.

Lennon changed the group chat name to
The Real Housewives of Vancouver.

Emmett: Hmmm . . .

Adam: I can live with that.

Carter: it's not horrible, i guess.

Carter: better than fucking ketchup crew

Carter: no offence princess i luv u *kiss emoji* *heart eyes emoji* *eggplant emoji*

Carter: send pics

Garrett: Send a pic of everyone, for clarity,
not just Olivia.

Well, that's easy. We already took about twenty earlier tonight. Cara sends them all and asks for some in return. Their night looks remarkably similar, food spread out on a table in a hotel room, the five of them sprawled over the two queen-size beds.

Carter: aw man! we forgot robes!

Adam: Jaxon, is that my robe?

Me: No.

Rosie: He dropped his goopy cucumber
eyes on it.

"Rosie, what the fuck!"

"Sorry," she says, but she doesn't sound *or* look sorry. In fact, she looks me dead in the eyes, stroking my cat's head while he purrs in her lap.

Emmett: Something's wrong with Carter.

Garrett: We're watching Shrek.

Jennie: But Shrek's not Disney???

Lennon: Carter said he missed Jaxon, and
then his next sentence was let's watch
Shrek. He's been going on and on about
how Shrek reminds him of Jaxon, because
of all his layers, and now he keeps referring
to Jaxon as onion boy.

Carter: becuz ur so wrapped up in layers
heart emoji

Garrett: *laughing emoji* it's so true!

Adam: I kind of love it.

Cara: Petition to change Jaxon's name to Onion Boy.

                                                Me: Fuck u guys.

I click on Lennon's name, sending her a separate message.

                                        Me: Honey, they're making fun of me.

                           Me: Also I did a sugar lip scrub so my lips will be really soft when you sit on my face next time I see you.

Adam: Uh, hey, buddy . . .

Emmett: Wrong chat *crying laughing emoji*

Carter: ollie did u do a sugar lip scrub?????

The girls bust with laughter as I toss my phone, groaning. I grab a slice of pizza, collapse back on the couch, and munch it while I think about how much I wish Lennon was here.

"Do you think Lennon's my line?" I blurt.

"Your what?"

"My line. The one that marks the before and after, where everything gets better." I stuff another slice of pizza in my mouth. "Should I go to Lennon's family thing in Georgia on Saturday? If I go, then that makes this super real, but then there's that love contract, too, that Coach wants us to sign. So I guess if I go, then I'd ask Lennon to sign that. But if I don't go, then what? Does that mean we aren't a real couple? I've never been in a relationship before. What if I fuck it all up?"

The room falls quiet, except for the sound of me chewing my pizza.

"He's asking us for advice," someone whispers. *"Us."*

"Well, obviously he can't trust the guys."

"It only makes sense that he'd ask us."

"Right? We're four extremely emotionally mature individuals with great heads on our shoulders."

"Know what else I'm scared of?" I whisper before I can stop myself. "What if I go and her family doesn't like me?"

Jennie watches me, head tilted. "If you go, I'm certain they'll like you. But it doesn't really matter what they think of you, does it?"

"I want them to think I'm good enough for Lennon."

"What about for you?"

"What do you mean?"

"You're the only person whose opinion of yourself matters, Jaxon. Stop worrying about being enough for other people. Be enough for yourself."

Oh. Well, that hurts more than it has any right to.

Fuck.

26

ICE, ICE, BABY

Lennon

THERE ARE SOME LETTERS OF the alphabet that should never go together. They just don't work, and the more someone tries to force them together, the more painful they sound, like rusty, disease-laden nails on a dusty-ass chalkboard. Like—and this is a totally random assortment of letters, and my opinion is totally unbiased—*R, Y, N,* and *E.*

"You two were such a gorgeous couple, Lennon, honey. He's so torn up about the breakup. Don't you feel like you owe sweet Ryne a second chance?"

I *feel* like I owe him a swift kick in the nuts. Sometimes I dream about gouging his eyes right from their sockets. And hey, wouldn't it be cool to punch him so hard in the throat it permanently damaged his voice box and no one would ever have to hear him say *good girl* again?

"Auntie Alma, respectfully, Ryne's a piece of shit." Serena holds her hand up, stopping Alma when she opens her mouth to protest Ryne's shittiness, or Serena's language. "Respectfully. Len doesn't owe him shit."

Auntie Alma isn't my real aunt, in case it wasn't obvious. Ain't no way a blood relative of mine is seriously suggesting a second chance with Ryne.

> **Me:** Quick, send me a voice note of
> you calling me honey.
> Mimi's BFF just called me it and it
> ruined everything for me.

> **Jaxon:** WTF? Do I have to fight her? Ur my
> honey, not hers.

A voice note appears ten seconds later, along with a message to listen to it alone. I slip around the side of the house and press the phone to my ear, Jaxon's rough, low voice sending shivers down my spine.

"I can't wait to see you again so I can eat your sweet cunt, then make you taste your own honey from my lips."

Sweet baby Jesus, my soul has left my body.

Another comes in, this one much tamer, but it makes my knees wobble all the same.

"I miss you, honey."

I press my phone to my chest, looking out at the yard. Okay, it's more like a park. Mimi's backyard is *just* shy of an NFL football field. She lies and tells all her friends it's two feet longer, but I've heard Auntie Alma gossiping with the rest of the girls: none of them believe it.

Despite the sheer size of it, she manages to fill it every year. Tables upon tables filled with food. A grilling corner and refreshment gazebo. Picnic tables for the kids, and linen-covered tables for the adults. A bouncy castle that would put Ireland's destroyed birthday inflatable to shame, an Olympic-size swimming pool filled with Tiffany-blue floaties, and an acrylic dance floor set by the small stage where the band will play once dinner is cleared away. Oh, and at least a hundred people.

This isn't a normal cookout. This is Mimi's Annual Pre-Summer

Social, and the only purpose it serves—other than bringing family together—is to display to her friends and frenemies how rich she is. Honestly, I approve. I eat the best I eat all year, I dance my ass off, and I go home wasted.

"Hiding already, darling?"

I glance over my shoulder as Mimi puts a cigarette out against the brick, waving her hand through the smoke before ditching the butt in a dish that she hides above the windowsill. I lift a brow, watching as she pops a mint in her mouth before producing a tiny bottle of Amorem Rose, her favorite perfume, spritzing it on her wrists, dabbing it behind her ears.

"I could ask you the same thing," I say as she straightens her dress, a butter-yellow square-neck floral midi that complements her rich brown skin and long legs. She hooks her arm through mine, and we stroll back to the party. "You're not supposed to be smoking."

"It was either a cigarette or telling Alma to shove it where the sun don't shine." The corner of her mouth hooks when I snort a laugh. "Always running her mouth, acting like she knows everything about everything. Drives me up the wall some days."

"She said I should give Ryne a second chance."

"I think the fuck not, darling."

The best part about my family is that we almost all run on the exact same wavelength. That's why it's not just Mimi who says those five words, but also my dad, my mom, and my brother—minus the darling—as we join them beneath a shady weeping willow.

I pout, batting my lashes. "But why ever not? We were such a sweet couple. Plus, we were high school sweethearts. Surely he deserves a second chance."

My family levels me with the same disgusted, unimpressed expression, and when Serena makes a move for my face, Devin wraps an arm around her head, holding her back.

"Thought you might need some sense knocked into you for a minute there." She tosses her long dark braids over her shoulder. "Was about to volunteer, only 'cause I don't see your boyfriend, who apparently lives to fight."

He's not my boyfriend. I almost mutter it, not because I believe it, but because I'm trying to convince myself that, since we never officially had that talk, it'll hurt a little bit less when I climb into bed tonight and accept that he didn't come.

"Yeah, Len, Jaxon really likes to go at it, doesn't he?" My dad tucks his hands in his short's pockets. "Never been much of a hockey guy, but watching him fight is good entertainment when Dev's losing on the field."

"You're watching Jaxon?"

"Like I said, it's good entertainment. Real fast paced too."

Mom rolls her eyes. "Every time the puck passes the bench, he screams, 'There's Len! There she is!'"

"I hoped your friend would come, darling. Since you seem so set on staying up there in"—Mimi shudders—"*Canada*, he must be something special."

"Canada is lovely," I tell her. "Vancouver is stunning. The mountains, the stars, I just love it there."

"Yes, darling, I know. But it's cold." She pats Mom's shoulder. "Your mother moved to Georgia from Canada. Maybe you can convince Jaxon."

"Last I checked, Georgia doesn't have a hockey team. Plus, we're still new. I'm not entirely sure, you know, how serious we are. Like, are we official? I know we're exclusive, but—"

"Because he didn't want to come meet us today?"

"No. Yes." I shake my head, eyes squeezed shut. "I don't know. I was afraid to ask, because if that was his answer, I guess I don't know what that means for us. But anyway, he's been recovering from his concussion. He just got cleared, so I didn't want to ask him to travel any more than he already needed to, or put more stress on him." I'm still trying to figure out how to have a serious discussion about cutting back on the fighting because I'm afraid he's going to forget me, or worse, do permanent damage to that beautiful brain of his. I'm just not sure if it's my place.

Mimi tilts her head, eyes moving over my shoulder. "And if he did come? What would that mean?"

I shrug, winding a curl around my fingers until it gets tangled.

"I see. Well, you better figure it out quick."

"Huh? Why?"

Mimi ignores me, stepping by me. "Well, hello there. Welcome to my home. Thank you so much for coming."

Dad's eyes widen, and Devin grins. Mom and Serena do that high-pitched squeal thing, bouncing on the spot and slapping each other's hands.

Slowly, I turn around.

My gaze finds a pair of wide hazel eyes, bouncing nervously around my family. When they land on me, a heartbreaking smile blooms, spreading like wildfire across the most handsome face I've ever held between these two hands.

"Hi, honey," Jaxon murmurs, usually mussed waves tamed, a crisp linen button-up rolled up to his elbows, showing off his tattoos. With shaky hands, he holds up the bags gripped tight in his white-knuckle hold and swallows. "I brought ice."

27

SO, UM . . . DOYOUWANNABEMYGIRLFRIEND?

Jaxon

"It's really wonderful ice, Jaxon."

"Oh, the best." Angela, Lennon's mom, nudges Devin. "Isn't the ice Jaxon brought so good?"

Devin looks down at the ice floating in his drink. He glances at Serena, cocking his head with a *what the fuck* expression, and she stifles her laugh. "It's just fucking ice?"

Mimi—can I call her Mimi? Grandma Hayes? Mrs. Hayes?—pats my forearm. "Wonderful ice. So thoughtful of you."

I rub the nape of my neck. "I didn't think anything I could pick up at a store would come close to comparing to your recipes."

"Bless your heart, darling." She smiles, broad and dimpled. "It really wouldn't."

"You just became Mimi's favorite," Serena tells me. "Every time someone compliments her cooking, another year is added to her life. We're afraid she's never going to kick the bucket at this point."

"You'll all be so lucky if I'm eternal." Mimi loops her arm through mine. "Come, Jaxon. Let's walk for a moment."

"Mimi!" Lennon gapes after us, stomping a foot. "Don't embarrass me!"

"Such a flair for the dramatics," she murmurs. "I've always loved her spirit."

"Yeah," I chuckle. "It's a great . . . spirit."

She takes a seat on a cast-iron bench beneath one of the many weeping willows scattered around the property, patting the spot beside her. I sit in silence as she grazes her fingertips over her coils, cropped short, more silver than brown. She spins the gold bangles on her wrist and lifts her cocktail to her crimson-painted lips.

"It's a . . . the weather is . . . blue sky . . . sunny sunshine . . ." I swallow. "You have a beautiful home."

"I know. My husband purchased it for me as a wedding gift." She squints up at the enormous home. "Used to be full of laughter, bickering kids, pattering feet. I remember dreaming about the day it would be quiet again." She sips her drink. "Never dreamed I'd hate it the way I do. There's something so inherently heartbreaking about silence, especially when you thought you wanted it and discover the hard way that you don't."

"Silence isn't all it's cracked up to be." I don't mean to say the words out loud, but they slip out anyway, maybe because her pain is palpable, and I've felt it. I used to love being alone, the peace and quiet that came with it. But did I really? Or was I just used to it?

The summer Bryce died started loud. Shrieks of laughter, staying up too late, pucks against the old garage door, and Gran shouting at us to turn the music down. It finished in silence. Silence I hated, because it reminded me of everything I'd lost, and at the forefront was a friendship I'd never be able to replace, but I didn't want to anyway. And somewhere along the way, I got used to the silence. Forgot there was any other way to live life.

And then Lennon walked into it, and life has never been quiet again.

"I'd do anything to have my granddaughter back in Augusta, Jaxon. I hate that she's so far away, and when she hauled herself over there, I worried I'd never get her back. But today?" She watches Lennon from across the yard. When she smiles, I see so much of my favorite person. And in her deep brown eyes shines the same warmth, the same love that tells me family is everything. "Today, I have her back. Not because she's here, but because somewhere along the way over the last ten years, we lost her. She lost herself. Lost her voice, her dreams, gave it all to a pigheaded dipshit—excuse the language—who molded her into his idea of the perfect housewife. I don't think I realized how much guilt I was holding on to, being the one who set them up." She sniffs, and when Lennon chucks a foam football at Devin's head and then runs across the yard, shrieking at the top of her lungs while he chases her, Mimi smiles. "Today she's my little girl again. Happy, laughing, and causing a ruckus. Thank you for that."

"With all due respect, I didn't do that. Lennon walked into my life knowing her worth and demanding I give it to her. I think that says more about the way she was raised than who she's been spending time with."

"Maybe, but don't sell yourself short. She's so comfortable demanding it with you because you give it to her without question. With you, she continues to elevate. That's the way it should be when you find the right person."

I open my mouth to argue some more, to insist that's all Lennon. I've never had that kind of effect of anyone.

"I see that mouth opening, Mr. Riley, and it best be to agree with me."

I press my lips together. "Yes, ma'am."

"Call me Mimi."

"Yes, Mimi."

Her playful gaze sparks. "You care about my granddaughter."

"I've never cared about anyone the way I care about her," I admit. "It's . . . scary."

"The best things in life are scary. That's why we close our eyes when we jump. But we still jump, don't we?"

I've never jumped. Come to think of it, I've never even closed my eyes. I walk into everything with my eyes wide open, prepared for anything and everything that can go wrong. I wish I didn't, but that's just how you operate when everything has had the same result, year after year.

I want this to be different, though. This thing with me and Lennon. I want a name for it. I want to hold on to it, do things differently, because how can I keep hoping for a different outcome without changing the formula? That's why I got on the plane one day early, flew to Georgia instead of Nashville. It's why I texted Devin for Mimi's address, and showed up here without telling Lennon. I wanted to see the look on her face when someone put her first. I wanted to be the one to do it. I wanted her to know that her family is important to me, because she's important to me.

And as the day turns into evening, and the sunset paints the Georgia sky in stunning hues of orange and pink, with Lennon tucked into my side and her family surrounding us, I know I've taken a step in the right direction.

"Everyone wants to leave me," Mimi complains after Serena's through detailing her plans to backpack in South America this winter. "It all started when Angela stole my baby from me all those years ago."

Angela rolls her eyes, exactly as dramatic as Lennon. "I did *not* steal him." She looks to me. "He was the assistant hitting coach for the Braves in Atlanta, and I was living in a small town just outside Toronto. He was in the city for a series against the Jays, and I was in the city for a friend's twenty-first birthday. We met at a bar after the first game, and—"

"He was in love with her by the end of the week," Mimi finishes for her with a soft smile, pressing a kiss to the back of her hand. "Hated the distance more than anything in his life. I'd never seen him so miserable."

"Took a job in Toronto the next season, and we were married in the autumn," Trevor, Lennon's dad, says.

Angela smiles wistfully at the memory, and Trevor kisses the smile right off her face. "We moved back here when the kids were young. We wanted them to grow up surrounded by family, and not a day has passed that I regret it. And now both our kids are living in Canada. Maybe we should—"

"Absolutely *not*." Mimi waves off her words, swiping her cocktail. "You've had enough of this, young lady." She drains the drink herself, and everyone laughs.

The party carries on around us, filled with introductions, talk of hockey and baseball and life in Canada. I get dragged onto the dance floor by no fewer than five women I don't know, plus Mimi, Angela, and Lennon. Serena refuses to dance with me because I, apparently, dance like a white boy, which is a nice way to say I have zero fucking rhythm. Lennon thinks I'm cute, though, and every once in a while when no one's looking, she backs her ass up against my cock and makes my brain short-circuit. When all three of her uncles catch us, lifting their brows, I panic, dragging Lennon off the dance floor and back to our seats. There, I look up to the sky, spotting Sirius, bright as always.

"Do you have stars like this in Vancouver?" Trevor asks me.

"It can be a bit hard to see the stars downtown, but Len and I get out to this little shore up the coast to watch them at least once a week. We've caught the Northern Lights a couple times, and a meteor shower last week. I can't believe how much you can see on her telescope, and the shots she gets on her camera are just . . . *wow*."

The murmured conversation around us comes to an abrupt halt.

Trevor's gaze snaps to Lennon. "You doing your astrophotography again? And your telescope? What telescope?"

Her cheek warms against my shoulder. "Jaxon got it for me for my birthday. He took me to see the Northern Lights."

Angela blinks at me, blue eyes glossing under the lights strung around the towering tree trunks. "You weren't dating during Lennon's birthday, were you?"

"They were certainly fucking," Serena mutters under her breath, and Lennon jams her elbow into her side.

"No, ma'am, we weren't dating."

"Angela," Angela cries, then promptly throws her arms around my neck. "Don't call me ma'am, you sweet, thoughtful boy."

"Oh, Christ." Lennon buries her face in her hand before prying her mom off me, tugging me to my feet. "'Kay, well, Jaxon's on a curfew tonight since he's playing tomorrow. We gotta get going."

I'm about to argue that I still have an hour, but at the mention of us leaving, the remaining fifty-plus people in the yard gather around to say goodbye. By the time we're climbing into an Uber, Mimi and Angela are still crying about the telescope, and I've only got fifteen minutes to curfew.

I relay the name of the hotel to the driver, looking at the tiny clutch in Lennon's lap, all she has with her. "I brought an extra toothbrush, and I requested silk pillowcases before I left."

"And pajamas? What will I do about those?"

Wrapping my palm around the nape of her neck, I work soft, wet kisses up her throat, feeling the rumble of her moan beneath my lips. "Honey, the only thing you'll be wearing tonight is my cum."

"Mmm . . ." She captures my mouth with hers, her hand sliding over my thigh until she's palming my cock beneath my shorts. "And they say romance is dead."

I carry her clutch into the hotel.

I carry her clutch to hide the massive erection I'm sporting, because she kept her goddamn hand on my goddamn cock the entire ride home, whispering in my ear about how good boys deserve to be rewarded. And when a family of four hollers for us to hold the elevator, I pray for forgiveness as I hammer the *close door* button.

"Jaxon," Lennon breathes, cornering me against the wall. She lowers my zipper, slipping her hand inside, squeezing me gently. "That wasn't very nice of you."

My gaze flicks to the camera in the corner of the elevator. "Honey, if you don't get your hand out of my pants, we're about to give someone a show."

"They can't see."

"Not from this angle, but it'll be hard to miss when I flip that skirt up and bend you over in thirty seconds."

"You're right." She sighs. "I'll keep my hands out of your pants." She withdraws her hand, and I'm both relieved and distraught. Then she takes my hand, guides it between her legs, dips my fingers into her sopping warmth. "But I'm not wearing pants."

"Jesus, honey. You trying to kill me?" I mean to pull my hand back. I swear to God, I mean to. But she's fucking drenched, and two of my fingers accidentally push their way inside, and the pad of my thumb accidentally finds her clit, teasing it slowly. "Where are your panties?"

"In my purse," she moans, rocking into my palm. "Took them off before we left."

The elevator climbs closer to our floor, and I pull my fingers out. Lennon's gaze hooks on them, and she licks her lips. I suck them into my mouth, smiling when she frowns. When the doors open, I step into her.

"Move it, before the security guard watching that camera has a chance to see how well you take my cock."

I clap a hand to her ass, and she yelps, dashing into the hall. She pulls off her top the moment we step into the room, and her bra next, letting her perfect tits bounce free. When I'm stripped, she lays me down with her hand on my chest, then climbs aboard, her little miniskirt the only thing she has on as she sits that lush ass on my chest. I scrape my palms up her thighs, spreading her wide as she shows me that glistening brown pussy.

"What was it you said you wanted to do next time you saw me?"

"Eat this pretty cunt." I dip a single finger, then smear it over her lips. "Make you taste your own honey."

She shudders, tongue dragging over her lower lip. "God, that's such a filthy word. I love it." Pressing up on her knees, she straddles my face, pussy hovering above my mouth. "Ask nicely, Jaxon."

"Please, honey." I flick my tongue over her clit. "Gimme this delicious cunt."

"Gimme gimme never g—*oooh fuuuck.*" Her head drops back as I jerk her down, latching my mouth over her clit. She buries her fingers in my hair, grinding her pussy against my face. "Fuck, fuck, fuck."

Christ, I'd die for her camera. Die to capture her like this, desperate and whimpering, tugging at her nipples while I devour her sweet, wet pussy. She's so beautiful, I'm not sure a photo would do her justice. So I just watch her, don't dare close my eyes as she rides my face, chasing my tongue and her orgasm. She rides through her first one, then without missing a beat, she turns herself over, lowers her pussy back to my face, and takes my cock in her mouth. I dip my thumb, thrusting it in and out, soaking it, and then I push it inside her ass, smiling against her pussy at the way she chokes out a garbled cry around my cock. She finishes twice more before I chase my first, coming down her throat before I come inside her pussy.

It's nearly one a.m. when we step out of the shower, her hair wrapped in my T-shirt to keep dry. She strips it away, following me into bed, curling into my side. As I smooth my hand over her thick curls, feel the warmth of her cheek pressed to my chest, everything feels right and good in my world.

"Thank you for coming today, Jaxon. It means a lot to me."

"Thank you for giving me a minute to get there on my own."

"I didn't want to pressure you. What good is a decision if it's not yours?"

I stare at the ceiling as she trails her fingertip over my chest, my arms, tracing the pictures inked into my skin, *I love you* in my parents' handwriting, *Proud of you* in my gran's, and *13*, the number Bryce wore.

My mouth dries as it tries to form the words I'm looking for, give the thoughts in my head a voice. I'm struggling, which is no surprise. She wanted me here. I saw the way her face lit up, felt the way she wrapped herself around my body and clung to me. And yet I'm still nervous her answer is going to be no.

"Um, so . . . you know how Coach said he wanted us to sign that, like, love contract or whatever, if we were gonna keep dating?"

"Uh-huh."

"I was, um, wondering . . . *doyouwannakeepdating?*"

She props her chin on my chest. "You want me to sign the contract?"

"If that's okay with you. Like, if you want to. No big deal if you don't."

"Where is it?"

I scramble off the bed, tripping over my feet when they tangle in the blankets. I don't even care when I face-plant, and Lennon's snicker chases me to the closet, where I tucked my weekender bag. With a shaky hand, I hold out the contract and a pen.

She flips through it, pausing on the last page. "You already signed it?"

I scratch my head. "Few days ago. But, um, like I said. No pressure. We can hold off. I can tell Coach we're cooling things off for a minute, and then maybe, before the next season, if you wanna sign—" I snap my mouth shut as she scrawls her name right next to mine.

Something happens to me. Something wild and unfamiliar, like butterflies taking flight in my stomach. My pulse races, and my heart slams against my chest. I squeeze my fists, licking my lips, and try to contain my excitement. "Oh. Okay. You signed it. Cool."

She sets the contract down and pulls me back to bed, settling into my side again. My heart won't stop, galloping so loud, so hard, there's no way Lennon can't hear it. As she flattens her palm over it, I'm certain of it.

"So, like, does this mean you're officially my, like . . ." I cough, burying the whispered word in my hand. "Girlfriend."

She tilts her head, leaning her ear toward my mouth. "What was that?"

Another whisper-cough. "Girlfriend."

She touches the shell of her ear. "Sorry, honey, you're gonna have to speak up. I can't hear you."

My eyes roll to the ceiling with my groan, and I kick the blankets off my feet. *Does this mean we're boyfriend-girlfriend?* Somebody in here sounds remarkably like a whining child, but it couldn't be me. "God, you're so annoying!"

Lennon grins, taking my face between her hands. "Annoying must be your type," she whispers, right before her lips meet mine.

She kisses me soft and slow, her mouth moving with precision, wet and warm, her tongue gliding fluidly against mine. I cup the side of her neck, my other hand pushing her hair back from her face as I haul her closer. I'll never get tired of this. Never get tired of tasting her excitement, her happiness. Never get tired of the warmth that rushes through me when she kisses me like

I'm the air she needs to breathe. Never get tired of the feeling in my chest, the way it pulls taut, like there isn't an ounce of space left inside me, because when she's in my arms, I feel full. I have everything I've ever wanted, even if I've pretended I didn't, and for once in my life, I feel like *I'm* everything someone else has ever wanted.

"Just for clarification," I murmur. "That was a yes, right? You're my annoying girlfriend?"

"I'm your incredible, exceptional, magnificent girlfriend. And you're my annoying boyfriend."

I punch a fist through the air, whooping. "A win is a win, baby!"

Lennon laughs softly, tracing the outline of the guitar tattooed on the inside of my right bicep, the cowboy hat that hangs off the headstock, the words below it. "The Stage . . . This is a bar in Nashville, isn't it?"

"Yeah."

"You played there?"

"They traded me to Vancouver."

She traces the black stripes on the Cape Hatteras Lighthouse inked on my forearm. "North Carolina? Did you play here?"

"Traded me to Nashville."

I close my eyes as she moves to the outside of my bicep, heart hammering as her fingertip glides over the LAX sign, the palm trees, the Hollywood sign in the mountains. Before she can ask me, I tell her, "Los Angeles signed me in the draft. They traded me to Carolina two years later."

"And these mountains?" She touches my thigh. "Are these for Vancouver?"

I shake my head. "West Virginia. Home. My first tattoo when I was eighteen."

"Do you have a tattoo for Vancouver?"

"Nah."

Her eyes rise to mine, a crease pulling her brows together in question.

Why not? If I have a tattoo for every place I've called home at one point in my life, why don't I have one for Vancouver?

It's a loaded question, one I don't feel like delving into right now. She'll give me sympathy, and I don't want it. I just want to lie here tonight with her in my arms and memorize the way she feels pressed against me, in case one day I don't get to hold her anymore.

Her gaze searches mine, and instead of sympathy, she gives me understanding. Patience. She cups my cheek and touches her lips to mine. Then she turns over, pulls my arm around her, and I fall asleep with my face buried in her neck.

I wake up with her mouth on my cock, a good-luck gift, she says, and when we walk into the arena later after flying into Nashville together, it's with her hand in mine.

The boys hoot and holler when she kisses me goodbye at the door to the locker room, and Coach can't wipe the grin off his face when I hand him the signed contract.

Maybe this really is it. Maybe this is my line, where everything is better than it was before. Maybe this really can be where I make my home. Maybe I can finally let myself be happy.

The doctor checks me over once more and gives me the green light. I fly through warm-ups with ease, adrenaline racing through me as my body loosens up, as I pop a puck over Adam's shoulder, as Lennon smiles at me behind her camera. I don't even care when my old coach looks away when we make eye contact, or that my old linemate, the one whose son I held when he was only twenty-four hours old, doesn't give me anything more than a nod of acknowledgment when I smile at him.

Okay, I kind of care. Only because that little boy is here, and now he's a toddler, and I didn't see him get there.

"You okay?" Adam asks me as we line up for the anthems.

"I don't wanna miss them growing up," I blurt.

"Who?"

"Connor. Lily. Ireland." I swallow. "I don't want to miss them."

Adam's brows pull together, and he follows my gaze to the little boy behind the glass, waving at my old partner. He claps his glove down on my helmet. "You're not gonna miss a thing."

That's easy for him to say now, when we're together more than we're not. But what happens if one day we're no longer all stuck together? What happens when this relationship is no longer convenient? Everything in me tells me this group of guys is different. That distance won't change a thing in our relationship, except how much face time we get.

But that's never been my experience with distance. Distance makes it hard for people to remember. Or maybe it just highlights your priorities. And the team I played with a year and a half ago? The one before it, and the one before that one too? Well, I guess I was no longer a priority once I was traded.

No, I wasn't a priority. I was a memory.

I tuck the worries away, and I keep the emotion out of my game when the puck drops. I have a phenomenal first period, stay out of the penalty box, and manage to stay clear of any altercations, physical and verbal. When we're heading out for the second, up by one, I'm alive with excitement. When Lennon grips my jersey, stopping me in the players' tunnel, crushing her mouth to mine, I'm downright giddy.

Nashville shows up hard for the second period, trying to even the score. They're shady and dirty, pulling sneaky shit every time the refs aren't looking, slashing anyone within reach, cross-checking Adam, grabbing the backs of our jerseys. They're grating my nerves, and everyone else's, if Garrett reacting and taking a penalty is any indication.

They're all over us during the penalty kill, running their mouths, trying to draw more reactions from us as they tire us out in our own end.

"Hey, Jason," Huber, one of my old teammates, says as he lines up next to me for a faceoff.

My jaw flexes as I force myself to ignore him. He's always been an asshole, and when I took a penalty in game seven of the third round two years ago, he made sure I knew I was the reason we were eliminated from the playoffs. My penalty cost us a goal, the game, and our chance at the cup. Two months into the start of the next season, I was traded to Vancouver, and Huber smiled for the first time I'd ever seen.

"How's Vancouver treating you?"

The puck drops, and Carter wins the face-off, passing back to me. I circle around the net, then fire the puck up the ice as hard as I can, my teammates racing to the bench to change lines, desperate for a break. I'm heading there when Nashville's goalie skates out of his net, intercepting the puck and firing it right back toward our end, where Adam is momentarily unprotected.

"*Fuck*." Spinning around, I race toward the puck, cradling it on my stick behind the net as I wait for my team to join me.

"How long you been there now?" Huber wears a smug grin as he follows me left, then right, trying to scare me into giving up the puck before I'm ready. "Nearly two seasons, yeah? *Oof.* It's about that time, huh?"

Adam shoves him out of the way. "Don't listen to him, Riley."

"Nobody ever keeps you longer than that."

I grit my teeth, passing the puck to my left, where Charlie, my partner, fires it up to our left winger.

"You got a fucking cat now, huh?" Huber laughs, a patronizing sound that works its way under my skin. "Hey, when you need love, you need love."

"Fuck *off*, Huber," Adam growls, gliding to the right to follow the play. "Jaxon doesn't need shit. He's got us."

"For now." He pumps his brows. "Hey, what about your photographer? You fucking her? What's the plan when you're traded? Try long distance and wait for her to forget about you? Bet she finds her way into the bed of your replacement within the month."

Before I know what I'm doing, I have him pinned to the boards, my stick across his chest as mine heaves.

His eyes sparkle. "Hit me. I dare you. Remind everyone that fighting is all you're good for. Be the reason your team loses today. They probably already have your trade papers ready to go."

"*Jaxon*," Adam barks as the whistle is blown, the play stopped. "Don't fall for his bullshit."

My gaze drops, roams as my fists clench and the officials shout at me to either let him go or get on with the fight. I see Lennon's face behind the glass, camera clutched to her chest, panicked eyes set on me. I don't want to be the reason for her fear. I want her to be proud of me.

My eyes come back to Huber, and I loosen my grip. Drop my stick and turn my back on his disappointed face.

"Not even good for that anymore, eh? What good are you, then?"

I skate toward the box, ready to serve my penalty for interference. It's a reckless, useless penalty, but the soft smile Lennon hits me with tells me she's glad I chose to keep myself safe.

It feels good, not letting her down. So when I step onto the ice two minutes later, I resolve to make up for letting my team down. I haul ass, hustle hard in our end, force the puck out, and use my body the way it was meant to be used, blocking shots and protecting my goalie.

Carter goes down on a missed tripping call, and the puck is turned over at our blue line, hurled toward Huber, who waits in front of our net.

Lunging forward, I intercept the pass before it can hit his stick.

"Me, me, me," Emmett hollers, tapping his stick on the ice, waiting just past the blue line.

I pull my stick back, and the moment I let the puck fly, a body connects with mine from behind.

I soar forward, stomach hitting the ice as my body glides across it, and the last thing I hear is the sickening crunch of my neck as the top of my head connects with the boards.

WHEN I COME TO, I'M laid out on an examination bed, surrounded by people poking and prodding me. There's a pretty girl hovering in the doorway, stunning chestnut spirals spilling from the top of her head, a deep crease set between her dark brows. She's got a big camera tucked beneath her arm, and she looks like she's on the verge of tears as she wrings her hands at her stomach.

My head pounds as she gasps, big brown eyes landing on mine.

"Jaxon," she whispers, dashing toward me.

I blink up at her as she takes my hand in hers. "Who are you?"

28

ONCE-IN-A-LIFETIME FEELING

Jaxon

WHEN I WAS TWELVE, I burned two images into my head. Two images I've been unable to forget, no matter how hard I've tried. Two images I'll forever be able to describe in detail.

Bryce's face when he realized he'd been stung by a bee and he didn't have his EpiPen. The terror drowning his wide brown eyes, the grief that twisted his face a moment later, like he'd already accepted his fate.

And his parents' backs as they walked away from me for the last time. Draped in black, the same way the rest of my days would feel without my best friend, tinged in darkness.

Six days ago, I added a third image.

I never could've imagined that I'd be desperate to forget a single second in time with Lennon. Fucking Christ, I was wrong. What I wouldn't give to wipe the memory of her face from my mind when she told me she was my girlfriend, and I told her I didn't date. In that moment, I didn't know her, but I felt her pain, felt the way she shattered when she pulled her hand back, forced herself away from me.

And then thirty minutes later, when my head cleared and my eyes met hers, it all came rushing back. She threw herself into my arms and sobbed into my neck, and I hated myself more than I ever have.

Still do.

"You're all clear, but I'm going to recommend that you sit out for the rest of this round."

"What? No. No fucking way." I shake my head, moving to stand, and Coach puts his hand on my shoulder, shoving my ass back to the examination bed, where I've been every other day since my concussion in Nashville. I look between him and the doctor who basically just signed my trade documents. "I need to be on the ice. I-I-I . . . I need to do something. Be useful." My gaze bounces back to Coach, and I'm ready to drop to my knees, beg. "Please. I promise I'll be useful."

He sighs, rubbing his forehead as he turns to the rest of the coaching staff. "Down our best fucking defenseman in the third round."

"I'm sorry," I sputter, getting to my feet. "I'm sorry. I didn't mean to—I tried to—I didn't hit him. Please let me play."

"You let him get under your skin, Jaxon. Yes, you came to your senses before you could hit him, but you let him draw a penalty out of you first. He used your interference as justification for his retaliation, and you landed yourself right back on my injured list. Now we're four games into the third round and they're leading the series by three."

It's my fault. That's all I hear. I let him get under my skin. I let him draw a penalty out of me. I'm injured, a-fucking-gain, because I couldn't keep my cool when it mattered, and my team is down a defenseman in the third round of the playoffs.

I've let my team down. My friends. My family. My girlfriend.

Again.

"Doc said I'm all clear," I argue quietly, because if I can't be on the ice to prove my worth, what good am I?

"She also said she recommended you stay off the ice for the remainder of the round."

"It's a risk we aren't willing to take," my assistant coach adds. "Shouldn't have let you play at all. All it did is exacerbate your injuries." He sighs, scrubbing his eyes. "You'll be no good to us in the final round—if we even manage to win the next three games to get there—if you go down again."

There it is. I'm a risk. A burden.

I've heard that before, and I know how it ends.

Me, saying a goodbye I'm not ready for, getting on a plane I don't want to get on.

Coach claps my shoulder. "We expect you to be at morning skates, keep yourself fresh, but take it easy. And if we manage to win this round without you, we'll talk about the finals. Now go home, Jaxon. Get some rest."

I stand there, fists clenched at my sides as they turn their backs on me, forget about me, talk about the replacement they pulled up from the farm team while I'm right there, how he's stepped up in my absence. I stand there as memories run rampant in my head.

The click of heels against pavement as Bryce's parents turned their back on me. The choked sobs that grew quieter and quieter, until they eventually disappeared right along with them as they climbed into their car and drove away.

The cold, blunt words LA used when they told me I was getting on a plane to Carolina the next morning. The same ones Carolina used two years later when they sent me to Nashville, and Nashville to Vancouver two years after that.

The unanswered texts that stared back at me every time I reached out, checked in on my former teammates. People I thought were family.

Me, two Christmases ago, sitting on my couch by myself all day, because Gran was sick, and I was too new in Vancouver, too nervous to ask my teammates for a spot at their table. The painful, hollow feeling in my stomach when I realized how alone I was.

How alone I'd always be.

"Hey, bud," Carter calls as I walk down the hall, hands tucked in my pockets. "Glad to see you back this week. Haven't heard from you much. What's the verdict?"

His footsteps follow quickly behind me, and I close my eyes to his tenacity, forcing myself to the exit.

"Jaxon? You okay? Need a ride home? Need to talk?"

"I don't need anything from you," I snap before I can bite my tongue. "I don't need anything from anyone." My shoulders curl, and I pause at the exit, feeling the weight of my words as they hang around me, settle over Carter. Blood thunders in my ears as I fight with myself to apologize. For my words, for being a disappointment that only makes mistakes, that forces my team to have to push harder, leaves them hanging without my help when they need it most.

Instead, I push the door open, because if I'm going to say goodbye to Vancouver one day soon, if I'm going to lose my friends and my family all over again, I might as well put the distance between us now. If I control the narrative, maybe it'll hurt less this time.

"Jaxon?" Carter's quiet voice pauses me in the doorway. "We love you, buddy. We're here when you're ready to talk."

I try to shake the words off as I walk through downtown Vancouver. They latch on to my thoughts, that four-letter L-word planting seeds in my head, sprouting roots when all I want it to do is die.

I don't know what love is. It's supposed to be eternal, isn't it? But then how come it always leaves? How come I've watched it walk out of my life over and over, let it drown my peace and shatter my hopes?

If I had to guess what love was, it'd be fear. Sheer, dizzying, debilitating dread that everything good in your life will be gone in the blink of any eye. Ripped from your unwilling grasp, leaving you to sink to your knees, alone, desperate for the pain in your chest to dissipate, for the thoughts in your head to make sense.

And when I walk into my apartment to find Lennon cooking at my stove while my cat sleeps at her feet, it's all I feel.

She smiles up at me, so bright and beautiful it hurts to look at her. It hurts even more when I look away. "Hey, you. How'd it go?"

"I'm out," I mutter, busying myself in the fridge.

"What's that?"

"I'm out for the rest of the round. As a precaution."

"Oh. I'm sorry, Jaxon. That's probably for the best, though, right?"

I shut the fridge. "For the best?"

"Gives you a chance to recuperate."

"I'm recuperated. I've been recuperating for five days. The doctor cleared me."

She looks up from the bowl she's stirring. "But suggested you sit out the rest of the round? They're worried about you getting injured again so soon. You were only back for twenty-five minutes when you hit your head again, and it was worse this time because of the prior injury. They're just being careful, Jaxon. You're valuable to them."

"I'm nothing but replaceable to them."

Lennon stops, placing the bowl down. She wipes her hands on the baggy T-shirt she's wearing, the one with my name and number on the back. "That's not true, honey," she tells me in that soft, patient voice she uses when she's trying to fight with the voices in my head. But right now, I just want her to agree with me.

I want her to tell me they're wrong, that I should be playing. I want her to tell me there's a good chance they'll trade me, because yes, I've disappointed them so many times this year, maybe too many, and there are piles of defensemen waiting for the shot I keep blowing, ones that could do it better.

Instead, she takes my face in her hands, thumbs sweeping over my cheekbones. "Your health is important. Your brain is important, and it's fragile, especially right now. They want to give you the time you need to make sure you're okay—"

"I'm okay! I'm fine!" I spin away from her, tugging at my hair. "Why does nobody believe me?"

"You're not fine, Jaxon."

"The doctor—"

"The doctor said you need to rest for the rest of the round." She steps in front of me, forcing my eyes to hers. "Another week. One more week to protect your brain."

I open my mouth to argue, and she shoves her finger in my chest, fire sparking in her gaze.

"Don't you dare tell me you're fine. You're okay, yes. I get it. You are physically capable of playing hockey, and you feel better. But you took one blow after another to your head when you were barely healed, and they told you. They warned you, Jaxon. They warned you that it could be worse, and it was."

"Barely. It was *barely* worse, and it was just bad lu—"

"*You forgot my name, Jaxon!*" Her fists shake as she clenches them at her sides, tears brewing in her eyes. "You forgot my damn name, and when I said I was your girlfriend you laid there and told me without a care in the world that you didn't date. The time before that, you forgot what team you played for. So don't you dare tell me it was bad luck, that it was barely worse, because I can't take another one of those. I can't watch you get knocked down time and time again and wonder when will be the time that you forget me altogether, that you forget about us and never remember."

"Nobody's forcing you to be here!" My chest heaves, my heart seizing at the shock on Lennon's face, the way she steps back, just slightly, like the words came up between us like a wall. My thoughts race, spiraling, and everything feels tight. I squeeze my

fists to keep from clutching at my chest, right where everything
hurts, where I'm struggling to get air.

"Nobody's forcing you to be here," I say again, quiet this time.
"If you're waiting for me to change, to be better, be good enough,
you might as well stop wasting your time. I can't change, clearly. If
I could, I wouldn't have pinned Huber against the boards, right?
Wouldn't have brought on his hit. I wouldn't have ever forgotten
your name, and then maybe I wouldn't hate myself, because—" My
throat squeezes, seizing my words. Lennon looks down, down at
my trembling hands, and when she moves to take them in hers, I
step out of reach. I don't deserve her. "Because how could I forget
your name? How could I forget you?"

Tears slide down her cheeks, and my fingernails dig into my
palms to stop me from reaching out, taking her face in my hands,
wiping her tears away.

"I'm not asking you to change," she whispers. "That's the last
thing I want. I feel really sad for you that you think so little of
yourself. That all these years, you've missed out on the incredible
person you are, the person we all know and love. The only thing
I'm waiting for, Jaxon, is for you to realize what we all already
know, which is that you're enough. Kind, passionate, loyal, patient,
funny, sarcastic, and so damn thoughtful." She sniffles, swiping
at the tears streaming down her face, even though they just keep
falling. "You're enough, Jaxon, exactly as you stand here today.
That's what I'm waiting for you to realize."

"You're going to be waiting a long time." The words are hoarse
and fractured, hopeless. If I could do it, I would. Would've done it
a hundred times over. "I'd do it for you if I could."

Lennon shakes her head, her gaze swimming with tears. "I
don't want you to do it for me. I want you to do it for you. I want
you to love yourself the way everyone else loves you. I want you to
realize you're worth it *for you*, Jaxon. Not for anyone else."

I don't know what to say. Telling her I've been loving myself exactly the way the people around me have loved me over the years doesn't feel like the right answer. Neither does telling her that I feel exactly as worthy as those same people have made me feel. And I wish they didn't matter, know they shouldn't, but how do I convince myself that's true? I don't know how, and I'm so fucking tired of trying and failing over and over again.

"Do you want me to leave, Jaxon?"

My head snaps up at her whispered words. The heartache in her gaze is as heavy as mine, and I want nothing more than to take it away. But I don't know how to carry both of ours when I can barely carry mine anymore.

"Because if you want me gone, you're going to have to tell me. Open your mouth and communicate it to me. Tell me you want me to leave, and ask me to go. Because I'm not leaving otherwise."

My head shakes frantically, my hands reaching out for her. I stop myself at the last second, pulling them back in, squeezing them into fists. The face of every person who's walked out of my life and never looked back flashes in my mind, and my thoughts race, a dizzying mess of insecurities bubbling just beneath the surface.

And yet my heart roars the loudest, protesting the idea of her walking out this door. Of not rolling over in the middle of the night, pulling her into my warmth. Not having my hand on her thigh in the car. Not coming home to her in the kitchen, wearing her goggles and chopping onions. Not seeing the wonder and utter adoration that dances in her eyes when she's gazing at the stars. Not feeling that same way when I'm gazing at her every moment of every damn day.

Because, Christ, I do.

Lennon is mine. My best friend, the hand in mine, the weight lifted off my chest. She's the sunrise when I spent too many years in the dark, and breathing easier for the first time since I was a kid.

And I am *terrified* to lose her.

I don't know how to ask her to stay, to wait for me. To help me. But, fuck, I want to.

Lennon's eyes move between mine. She swipes away her tears and nods, like my silence is the answer she was looking for. "Then I'm not leaving," she says with absolute certainty, no matter how quiet the words are.

She moves back to her bowl, wrapping it up while I stand here, watching her. She tucks it in the fridge, then lifts Mittens into her arms, kissing his forehead when he wakes with a yawn, then passes him to me. He licks my nose, nuzzles my cheek with his head, and then curls up under my chin.

Lennon pauses at the edge of the hallway, bloodshot eyes coming to mine over her shoulder.

"I'll wait, Jaxon. I don't care how long. Because this? This is a once-in-a-lifetime feeling. You're a once-in-a-lifetime find. I'm not walking away."

29

GET OFF YOUR KNEES: WORDS
I NEVER THOUGHT I'D SAY

Lennon

NO THANK YOU.

Three words I've heard on repeat this week. Three words that say everything I already know.

Do you want to go for a walk?

Do you want to go to Carter and Ollie's?

Do you want to watch a movie?

Do you want to go for a coffee?

Do you want to talk about it?

No thank you. Three words I hate more than anything.

Except the reason they're whispered.

Because honestly, I thought I knew heartbreak. I thought it couldn't possibly get much worse than hearing my fiancé's words to another woman. I thought there was no way anything could hurt more than the knife Ryne lodged through my chest when he cheated on me the night before our wedding, in front of our friends and family.

But this? Jaxon being so certain of his lack of worth, believing he's so utterly unlovable, that he's easy to walk away from, and even easier to forget? Jesus, this hurts *so* much worse.

It's eye-opening, too, in a way I wasn't expecting. I know how I feel about Jaxon. My eyes have been wide open since the day I woke up and found that coffee guide waiting for me on the kitchen counter, next to a bowl of cereal. I walked right into this, knowing full well where each slow, calculated step would eventually lead me. There is no part of me that's surprised by the love that swells in my chest when I look at this man.

But I didn't realize how earth-shattering love could be.

I didn't realize that what I felt for Ryne, the man I was supposed to marry, would be blown out of the water by a man I was never supposed to know, a man I couldn't stand at one point. I didn't realize that the next time I fell in love, it would make me question everything I'd thought I knew about it. That I'd wonder if I'd even ever really loved Ryne at all.

That the thought I might have married him, might have never met Jaxon, might have had to live my entire life without ever knowing what real, selfless love felt like would be gutting enough to bring me to my knees every day this week in the shower, where I would drown my cries beneath the patter of rain. The last thing I want to do, in the midst of Jaxon's inner turmoil, is give him more fuel for his fire, and that's exactly what my pain will do to him.

So instead, I'll do what I've been doing every day.

I'll stay.

I'll be here, right here where he needs me, even if he's trying to convince himself he doesn't.

Because that's what this is. This is him putting distance between us before it's put there by someone or something else. It's him trying to control the situation, because he thinks if it's his decision, maybe it'll hurt less. He's pulling away, because people have failed him time after time, abandoned him when he needed them most, and instead of realizing it only speaks to who they are, he's convinced himself it's who he is.

Or who he isn't.

Jaxon Riley, the man who's watched the people he's cared about walk away from him over and over, thinks he's not good enough for someone to stay.

Jaxon Riley, the man who's been displaced from one home after another, thinks he isn't good enough to be loved.

Jaxon Riley, the man who's spent the last five months loving me exactly the way I needed to be loved, is wrong.

And I'm going to be right here when he realizes it.

A door creaks behind me, and tiny footprints prance down the hall and into the kitchen. Mittens meows at my feet before winding himself through my legs.

"Well, good morning, my sweet, handsome marshmallow." I scoop him up, nuzzling my face against his, his loud engine purr making me smile. "I miss you, too," I whisper into his soft fur. "Yes, I do, Mr. Chunk."

Mittens has three favorite spots to sleep at night. The first is on Jaxon's pillow, wrapped around his head. The second is nestled up against my boobs. But his favorite above all favorites? Snuggled between his dad and me, purring while we take turns showering him in kisses and pets.

I'm not just missing Jaxon these past few days, but Mittens, too, because one of us needs the comfort more than the other.

Footsteps tiptoe down the hall, and Jaxon's voice graces my ears.

"*Mittens,*" he whisper-yells. "*Pss-pss-pss!* Come here, handsome chunk." I hear the unmistakable pat of his hands against his thighs. "*Pss-pss-pss!* Come on. I'll let you into Mommy's room. Go give her some snug—" Jaxon stops at the edge of the kitchen, his face paling as he stares at me. I'm certainly staring back, heart pattering and mouth agape, because did he just call me Mittens's mommy? "Oh. Hey." He rubs the back of his neck, and it's nearly impossible to keep my eyes on his face instead of his cock, because through all of this, he's still not covering himself up first thing in the morning. Some things never change. "I thought you were still sleeping. Your door is closed."

I stroke Mittens's cheek, keeping my eyes on Jaxon as I murmur, "Did you hear that, buddy? Daddy called me Mommy. You'll never get rid of me now. I have a child to look after."

Red heat rushes up Jaxon's neck, pooling in his cheeks. Turning around, I hide my smile as I shift Mittens to one arm, fill two bowls with equal portions of Trix and Lucky Charms, and top them off with milk.

"We always knew I was your real mama, huh, buddy? We let Daddy take his time coming around to certain concepts, that's all." Mittens bops his forehead against mine. "Yes, we do."

I place him at his mat, dumping his breakfast in his bowl while Jaxon fills his water dish and avoids my gaze. We lean over at the same time, nearly bumping heads when we set the dishes down.

I flash him a charming grin. "Hi."

Another adorable flush of his cheeks, and his gaze dips to my mouth, throat bobbing. His eyes flick back to mine, widening, and he snaps upright. I follow suit, much slower, sliding one cereal bowl over to him and taking the other for myself, leaning against the counter as I shovel it into my mouth.

He looks at the cereal in his hands. "Thank you."

"Your cock looks great today. No scratch marks. Mittens is taking it easy on you, huh?"

Jaxon chokes on his cereal, and it's about as close to a laugh as I've heard from him since Nashville, so I'll take it.

"Are you excited for your first game back tomorrow? Google says it's your first time being in the final round of the playoffs." I polish off my cereal, tipping the milk back as I watch him try to figure out how long I'm going to keep talking to him like nothing's wrong. The answer is forever, or until he shuts me up with a kiss, whichever comes first. But fuck me, I'm cracking this man wide open before he steps on the ice tomorrow.

The boys managed to win three consecutive games against Nashville, taking the third round, becoming the Western Conference champs, while Jaxon watched from above in a suite with the GM. Tomorrow, they begin the final round of the playoffs, and I'll be damned if I'm letting Jaxon step on that ice for his first game back without giving him an *I'm proud of you* kiss first.

"Gran said she's got the whole neighborhood coming over to watch you play. She's not sure she has enough space in the living room."

He halts, his hand and spoon frozen in midair as his shocked gaze slowly rises to mine. "You talked to Gran? Without me?"

"Every night. She calls after she gets off the phone with you to make sure you really are doing okay, because she suspects you're lying to her. We do the crossword together, and she gives me my daily Jaxon fix by entertaining me with stories from when you were a kid, like that time you got your head stuck between the spindles on the staircase."

"I was five," he mutters.

"Eight. She promises she has a picture." Tugging the candy bowl on the counter toward me—the one that was mysteriously refilled yesterday and set next to the brand-new bouquet of pink tulips that also mysteriously appeared yesterday—I pop the tip of a Sour Key in my mouth. "She's going to show me when we go out there to visit this summer. Says she's got a whole whack of pictures I'll wanna see."

Jaxon's mouth opens. His mouth closes. Opens again. Closes. Opens. "I . . . I . . ." There it goes, closing once more. He shakes his head, shoving his bowl in the dishwasher. "I have to get dressed for my team meeting," he calls over his shoulder, speed walking down the hall, shutting his door behind him.

I look at Mittens as he licks his paw at my feet. "One thing about me, Mitts? I'm gonna smother you with love until you have no choice but to accept that it exists, and that it's real." Mittens meows his agreement, tossing himself down on his back, belly up as he rolls around. I join him on the floor, rubbing his belly like the good cat mom I was born to be. "That's exactly what we're gonna do, buddy. We're gonna peel back those layers on our favorite onion boy one by one, and we're gonna love every one of them, aren't we? Yes, we are, marshmallow. Yes, we are!"

There are those footsteps again. They slow, stopping a few feet away, and I look up when a throat clears.

Jaxon looms above us, looking rightfully confused and a little uneasy, dressed in a pair of dark blue shorts and a gray T-shirt that hugs his broad shoulders and trim waist in a mouth-watering kind of way, *Vipers Hockey* on both of them. He takes in me and his cat, sprawled out on the kitchen floor, then sinks his fingers in his light brown waves before tucking them beneath his backward baseball cap, another sight that has me resisting the urge to bite my knuckles.

"Um . . . what are you doing?"

"Snuggling with my son."

Oh my God. Is that a—oh my God, *it is.* The corner of his lip is twitching. He's trying not to *smile.*

Hold on to your tits, Lennon. Don't react, don't react, don't react.

Jaxon wipes his hand over his mouth, taking that tiny quirk with it. "Um, so, I'm gonna head out for the team meeting."

"Okay. I'll be here."

His eyes search mine, looking for any hint of duplicity. I wonder how much it hurts, constantly wondering when someone is going to leave. It guts me every time he looks at me like this, questions the truth behind three words as simple as *I'll be here* or *I'm not leaving;* I can't even imagine how much it *kills* him.

He opens his mouth to say something, but a knock on the door cuts him off. He frowns, heading to the front hall, I assume, since I can't see him from my spot on the floor.

The door opens, and two seconds later it slams closed.

"Who—" Another knock cuts me off as Jaxon opens the door again.

"Has no one ever slammed a door in your face before?" Jaxon drawls, the words slow and arrogant, but the anger laced through them is unmistakable. "I find it hard to believe I'm your first, but just in case it wasn't clear, you're not welcome here."

I shoot up to sitting, clutching Mittens to my chest as I wait to hear our guest's response.

"Where's Lennon?"

My heart stops, falling to a pit in my stomach at the voice I haven't heard in over three months, one I'd gladly never hear again.

"None of your fucking business," Jaxon spits out.

"Do you speak for her?"

Jaxon barks out a laugh, and I scramble to my knees, then my feet, because he can't get in a fight today. He needs to protect his head, and he needs to play tomorrow. The person standing in the doorway isn't worthy of taking any of that from him.

Arrogant blue eyes come to mine, and a pigheaded, shit-eating smirk pulls in a set of dimples in his fair, freckled cheeks.

"Hi, angel," my ex-fiancé murmurs.

Jaxon crosses his arms over his broad chest. "Honey, this piece of shit is at the wrong apartment. I'm gonna see him out real quick."

"I'm not at the wrong apartment." Ryne's gaze moves down me. Before it can come back up, Jaxon steps between us.

"You must be. Because I know you didn't just call her angel."

Ryne's eyes flick to Jaxon, lighting with challenge as he tilts his head. "Have you had fun playing house with my wife?"

Jaxon laughs. Dark and low, a threatening sound that sends a shiver of excitement scattering down my spine. "You wanna get this one, honey? Don't wanna step on your toes, but I'm happy to handle this."

"Nope, I got it." I cross my arms over my chest as Jaxon steps aside, making space for me. He pulls an apple from the basket on the kitchen island, leaning against the wall as he chews it. "What are you doing here, Ryne?"

"I'm taking you home, Lenny," the man says like it's the simplest thing in the world, as simple as his thoughts, or the way he wielded the pencil dick hanging between his legs. "It's been nearly six months. Don't you think this little temper tantrum has been going on long enough?"

"Definitely." I nod. "Go on."

"I've let you have your fun, fuck around with this . . . this . . ."

"His name is Jaxon."

"I know his name. How do you think I found his apartment? Plenty of scorned women online who love to talk about having spent the night here with him." Ryne grimaces. "He's been taking advantage of you, angel. You were hurt and confused, lost, and he took advantage of that."

Jaxon buries his guffaw behind the aggressive crunch of his apple.

"You abandoned your family. Ran away and left them heartbroken over your selfish decision. You abandoned *me*."

"Is that all?"

He nods, leveling me with a look that's surely meant to be some sort of mix of endearing and empathetic. Instead, it's remarkably reminiscent of Ben Stiller's Blue Steel look in *Zoolander*. Come to think of it, he's just as short. "It's time to come home, Lenny. Let's put this behind us and move on. Do you have your ring?"

"I sold it." Twelve hours later, Second Chance Home received an anonymous donation of twenty-five thousand dollars.

"You—" He clenches his jaw. "Okay. That's okay. Just use your imagination for me, then, all right, angel?"

"Huh?"

He pulls a black velvet box from his back pocket—the same box my engagement ring sat in the night he proposed—and sinks to one knee. He opens the empty box and flashes me his famous grin. "Lennon, will you—"

"*No!* Are you for fucking real, Ryne? Get up!" I scrub my hands over my face as Ryne scrambles to his feet and Jaxon chokes on his apple behind me. "Jesus Christ, what are you thinking?"

"I love you. I've wasted too many years to let you throw this all away over a little blow job."

"Wow, well, when you put it like *that.*"

His eyes light, and he starts sinking back to his knee.

"*Get up!*" I shout, and teensy footsteps thunder across the floor. Before I can stop him, Mittens hisses, launching himself at Ryne's thigh. His penis is simply too small to use for batting practice.

"*Ow!*" Ryne howls, clutching his thigh, and Jaxon's choking on his apple again as Mittens continues to spit hisses at the man I nearly married. "Fuck! What is that, some sort of demon cat?"

"Yes." I scoop up my sweet angel kitten, press a *good boy* against his ear, and then pass him back to Jaxon. "All right, let's start from the beginning. Where were we?" I click my tongue against the roof of my mouth as I recount everything Ryne's said in the last two minutes. "Ah, right. You asked if I agreed that this little temper tantrum has been going on long enough. Quite frankly, I do. It's been nearly six months, Ryne, as you pointed out. You simply need to get over it and stop acting like an entitled brat. I know your grandmother told you the world revolves around you, but it doesn't."

His jaw hangs, and I'm really beginning to worry about all the choking Jaxon's doing back there. Which brings me to point number two.

"I was hurt, confused, and lost when I came to Vancouver; you're right about that. But Jaxon didn't take advantage of me. In fact, if anyone used anyone at first, it was me. I wanted to forget you, and I wanted to know what it felt like to feel good for once in my life. Jaxon was the perfect man for the job. But I never could've suspected that he'd also help heal the hurt. Clear the confusion. That he'd help me find myself. I was hurt, confused, and lost when I met Jaxon. And now I'm none of those things."

Jaxon's coughing dies, and he grows quiet behind me.

"Abandonment is a big, serious word, Ryne. I don't like it. Because you're right, it is selfish. And yes, I was being selfish when I left. But I didn't abandon anyone. I left, after talking with my family, because staying wasn't a choice that served me. I was selfish, because for once in my life I had to be in order to give myself the love I deserved. Because I deserved better than what you gave me. I deserved loyalty and communication. I deserved support for my dreams and someone who showed up for me when they promised they would. I deserved love, Ryne, and I deserved *better*."

My fists shake at my sides, my chest heaving and pulling taut as I glare at the speechless man before me. The one who clearly expected me to roll over for him, because I'd done it so many times before. I failed myself for so many years, put myself last. Leaving Ryne was the first time I put myself first. It was the first time I told myself what I wanted mattered, and believed it. It was the first time I showed up for myself, but it wasn't the last. Because I've spent the last five and a half months showing up for myself every damn day, and I'm going to spend the rest of my life doing it too.

Because I fucking *deserve* it.

A sudden, familiar warmth touches my back, and my shoulders fall away from my ears. My fists loosen, fingers uncurling. My chest falls, and a heavy breath leaves my lungs.

"You don't get to show up here after all the ways you failed her and act like you deserve any place in her life," Jaxon tells him, the quiet words firm and final. "You had one job in your relationship, and it was to love her. You failed. You failed to respect her, to listen to her, to root for her. You failed to be her friend, and you failed to be her partner. Day after day, you fucking failed her. And you don't get to show up here now and pretend like you deserve even the consideration of a second chance."

Another step, and Jaxon is beside me, unshakable as he defends my worth the way I wish he'd defend his own. The way I'll always defend it for him. Because that's what a partner does, isn't it? Reminds you you're worth it on the days you feel like you aren't.

"Get out," Jaxon says. "You're not welcome here."

Ryne's eyes bounce frantically between Jaxon and me. "Lenny Bean, are you—"

"Ah-ah." Jaxon holds up a hand. "She said everything she wanted to say to you. You're talking to me now." He steps in front of me, and I bite back my triumphant smile at the way Ryne shrinks, eyes wide as he backs himself into the hallway. "I'm trying really hard not to fight anymore. Lennon doesn't like it, and I don't want to scare her. I think she'd forgive me, though, if yours was the next face my fist met."

Oh, fuck. My coochie's awake.

"I have no patience for people like you," he continues, still stalking toward him. "People who think they're free to do whatever they want, and that the people they hurt along the way are just casualties. People who think there are no consequences for their actions. You hurt her. Long before you stuck your pencil dick somewhere else. You took away her passions, her voice. You deprived her of all the little things that would have made her feel special. Jesus, how hard is it to get her some pink fucking tulips once in a while to let her know you see her, that you appreciate her?" Jaxon shakes his head. "She deserves someone who does things just to make her smile. She deserves better, and you had the chance to give it to her. You chose not to."

He grips the edge of the door, filling the open space, and Mittens bursts through his legs and out into the hall, hissing and wielding his claws like weapons. Ryne tumbles backward, and Jaxon chuckles as Mittens makes his way back inside.

"Good boy," he murmurs, and right before he slams the door in Ryne's face, he tells him, "Goodbye." With his back to me, he hangs his head. "You okay, honey?"

"Mhmm. Yup." Super turned on, but I'll keep that to myself. I touch his wrist, bringing his eyes to mine. "Thank you."

"Nah, that was all you, tidbit. You know your worth, and you fed it to him."

"I thought I knew my worth, but you cemented it."

His gaze falls, and he rubs the back of his neck. "You give me too much credit."

"I give you exactly as much credit as you deserve, Jaxon." Wringing my hands, I take a deep breath and step toward him. "I—"

—frown when a knock on the door cuts me off for the third time in the last ten minutes.

Jaxon's face twists with surprise, then anger. "I can't believe that motherfucking piece of sh—oh. Garrett. What are you, uh . . . what are you doing here?"

"Thought we could ride together to the arena." Garrett flashes an easy, soft smile, pressing a drink into Jaxon's hand. "Chocolate Java Mint Frappuccino. Your favorite summer drink." He winks at me, handing me something beautiful and pink while Jaxon short-circuits over the drink in his hand. "Pink Drink with oat milk for our nut-free queen."

"My angel," I murmur, wrapping Garrett in a hug. "Wasn't that thoughtful of Garrett, Jaxon?"

"Yeah, that was . . . thanks. Thank you." He swallows, looking between us. "Uh, you coulda texted first."

Garrett nods. "Coulda. Did, actually. Three times. Called too. Twice. Your phone broken, or you just ignoring me?"

Jaxon's cheeks burn bright red.

I grin, clutching my drink to my chest. "Just a couple of besties, doing bestie things." I shoo them out the door. "Well, you two better get going. Coach will wonder where you are."

"Or Carter," Garrett grumbles. "He panics when anyone's late for anything." His phone pings, and he sighs at the screen. "There he is now. *Meeting's in ten, are you okay?* Followed by three question marks."

Jaxon pulls out his phone. The corner of his mouth hooks. "I got five."

"We better get going." Garrett salutes me. "Catch up tomorrow morning, Len?"

I salute him back. "Have fun."

Jaxon pauses, glancing at me as Garrett heads for the elevator. "You sure you're okay?"

"Positive."

He watches me for a moment before nodding, turning to follow Garrett.

"Hey, Jaxon?" I reach out, catching his hand. "I'll be here."

He looks down at the connection, the way my fingers twine through his. And before he walks away, he squeezes.

I wait for the elevator to close before I head back inside, locking the door behind me. Mittens follows along as I take my Pink Drink out to the balcony, pressing his face to the glass panel so he can watch the cars below.

"What should we do today, Mitts? Wanna go for a walk? Maybe get an ice cream cone?" I sip my drink as the breeze dances through my curls. "We could go down by the water, see if you can catch any fish."

He meows like he likes the sound of that.

"Okay, it's settled. We'll get an ice cream and walk down to the water." My phone rings and I fish it out of my shorts, my brows jumping at the name on the screen. "Hello?" I answer cautiously.

"Hey, Lennon," my landlord greets me happily. "Got some good news for you. Your apartment is finally ready."

My heart plummets to my stomach.

"You can move back in today."

30

ENOUGH

Jaxon

IT'S A FIVE-MINUTE DRIVE TO the arena, and I panic for all of it.

I worry that Ryne will come back while I'm gone.

That Lennon will come to some grand realization, the one I keep waiting for her to come to, and she'll stop waiting for me to get my shit together.

And I worry about what Garrett's going to say in the safety of his car.

But when we pull into his parking space at Rogers Arena, he still hasn't said a word.

"Um, did you . . ." I shift in my seat ". . . wanna say something?"

"Nope."

"Oh. Okay. Cool."

He waits for me to get out, then falls in step beside me as we head for the doors. Then he stops.

"You know what? Actually, yeah, I do wanna say something. You can want some space. You're entitled to it. But you're one of my best friends, and I consider you my family. Not only does it hurt when you ignore my calls and messages, but it makes me worry."

I want to deny it, argue that the only person who's ever worried about me is my gran. But I see it. Etched between his eyes, the same ones that bounce between mine, beg me to hear what he's saying. In the tension stacked in his shoulders, the hands curled into fists at his sides. So instead of arguing, I stay quiet.

"Need some space? Cool. Take ten seconds to text me back and let me know you're safe and you'll contact me when you're ready. I know you're going through it right now, Jaxon, and I know you think you have to do it alone. But you don't. So if you don't wanna talk, that's okay. I'll sit beside you in silence so you know you're not alone. That's what family does."

I open my mouth, but I don't know what to say. I want to tell him everything. How terrified I am that one day, when I go, they'll have no choice but to leave me in the past and move on, no matter how slow they do it. How desperately I want this to work out exactly the opposite of every time before this. Not just with Lennon, but with all of them.

And I don't know how to put that into words without laying all of me on the line.

The truth is . . . I'm afraid to be vulnerable. I'm afraid to tell them how much they mean to me. How much I love them. Because I do. These guys have a special, once-in-a-lifetime way about them, the way they accept each other so wholly and without question, show up for each other day in and day out. It's rare to find that, and I can't accept that somehow, after all these years, *I've* found it. Surely, I can't be lucky enough to keep it.

So "I'm sorry" is what I tell him. "I didn't mean to make you worry. I'll text you next time."

"Thank you." He pulls his phone out while we walk through the halls, heading to the conference room. "Carter's gonna be ten times worse than me, by the way. He's been acting like he's getting dumped all week." He sighs, typing a message out before tucking his phone away. "He really doesn't handle rejection well."

"What do you mean?"

Another sigh. "You'll see."

I can't imagine what he's done that I'll—*oh*. I stop in the doorway of the conference room, where Carter is dressed from head to toe in black. A black hoodie, hood up over his black baseball cap. Black sweatpants, even though we're now in June, and it's seventy-two degrees outside. "Is he going to a funeral or something?" I whisper to Garrett.

"Or something. He said he's in mourning, and he's wearing all black, like the shadow over his aching heart." Garrett points at me. "That's an exact quote."

Carter's eyes coast the room, and when they land on me, he leaps to his feet. "Jaxon! *Jaxon!*" He waves aggressively, as if I could possibly miss him, then shoves Adam out of his seat and straight to his ass, pointing at the now-empty chair. "I saved you a seat. Here. Right here." He pats my back when I cautiously make my way over, then shoves me down into the chair. "Next to me."

"What's with the hood?"

"Oh, this?" He rips it off, spins his hat so it's on backward. "Just vibing. You know how it is." He claps his hands, thumbing at the tables running along the back wall. "Want me to make you a plate? I'll make you a plate." He disappears before I can tell him I'm not hungry, and Adam's just finally dragging himself to his feet, plopping down in the chair beside me.

He frowns, crossing his arms over his chest. "He could've just asked me to move." His gaze slides to me, softening. He squeezes my shoulder. "Love you, buddy."

An arm comes around me from behind, putting me in some sort of headlock. Emmett presses a loud kiss to my head. "Love you."

Garrett plops into the seat to my right. "You already know I love you."

"*Garrett!*" Carter shrieks from where he's loading up two plates with food. "Out! Get out! *I'm* sitting beside Jaxon!"

"Jesus fucking Christ," he mutters as he shifts into another seat. "Coulda sworn Olivia only gave birth to one baby."

I snicker, then fold my lips together when I realize it. They're good. Fuck, they're *so* good at making me forget. At making everything feel normal. At making everything feel light again. It's effortless, too, like all they had to do was walk into the room and turn on the light.

Our GM pops his head into the room, and it quiets. "Hey, guys," Axel says.

Carter stops on his way back to his seat, and I swear he puffs his chest out. "Axel." He flicks his head up. "Hey."

He's trying to be intimidating, but the smirk Axel wears says intimidated is the last thing he feels. They've been doing this little dance for a while now, since Jennie's studio opening when Axel asked Carter's mom to dance, and then to have dinner with him.

"Apologies, but we're running a bit late. Hang in here if you want, go for a walk, whatever. Be back in a half hour."

The five of us stay seated while the rest of the team disperses, grabbing snacks on their way out the door. Axel salutes us before he turns to leave.

"Oh, hey," Carter calls after him. "My mom told me to tell you she can't make your date tonight. She's busy, and also, she doesn't wanna."

"Oh, hey," Axel calls back. "Your mom told me to tell you she can't make it to your place for breakfast tomorrow morning. She's busy, and also, she's *my* breakfast."

Carter gasps. "How *dare* you!" He shoves the plates into my hands and dashes to the doorway, poking his head out. "*Holly Beckett is an angel!*"

"Holly Beckett is *my* angel!" Axel yells back.

"Unbelievable," Carter mutters, sinking down beside me as Adam, Emmett, and Garrett head to the snack table. He tears one of the plates from my hands. "These were both supposed to be for you, but now I'm worked up." He shoves a sprinkle doughnut in his mouth. "I wa' gonna make 'nana pancakes fo' him fo' bweakfast tomowwow, 'cause he wikes dem." He swallows, licking his fingers. "He can forget it now."

"I always wanted to be bilingual," Emmett murmurs. "Never dreamed the second language I'd learn would be Carter with his mouth full."

Adam sighs. "We're all fluent in it."

"Jennie knows it better than anyone, though," Garrett says. "Every once in a while, I'm like, *what the fuck did you just say?* And Jennie will just repeat Carter's entire sentence like it was in perfect English, never misses a beat. *A lifetime of practice*, she always says when I ask her how."

"Ollie's getting pretty good at it," Carter says.

"She has no choice," Emmett reminds him. "She wants to spend the rest of her life with you. Cara's constantly reminding her that's the path she chose."

"Rosie thinks it's cute when we talk with our mouths full." Adam shrugs. "She says it's adorable that we all have this sort of secret language, and that we spend so much time together, we have no choice but to become like each other."

"I'm terrified of losing Lennon and everything I love in my life," I blurt out, and *holy fucking fuck*, it feels so damn good.

The room goes silent, and I stare down at the plate in my shaking hands, my knuckles white from how tight my grip is on the flimsy cardboard.

"Oh my God," Carter breathes out, shaky and barely audible over the thud of my pulse. "It's happening," he whispers. "Britney's Bitches . . . *assemble*."

Somewhere I'm conscious of the soft shuffle of feet as the guys ditch their plates, make their way back over to us. Chairs shift, turning to face me, and my friends surround me as they take a seat, waiting for me, for whatever scraps I'm willing to give them. For the first time since Bryce died, I want to give them everything. I want to trust someone with all my pieces, even the ones no one's ever loved. I want someone to help me carry them, because I'm too damn tired to carry them on my own anymore.

So I swallow the tightness in my throat that feels a lot like fear, close my eyes, and jump.

"I've been trying . . . I've been trying so damn hard to be better, to be what people want. It's never been enough. It's never been right. *I've* never been right, not for anyone. And I'm just waiting for Lennon to realize that. To realize there's someone better. Someone who follows instructions, doesn't put his ass on the line every single time he steps on the ice because he can't figure out how to stop using his fists." I drop my face to my hands, running my fingers through my hair, tugging on the strands. "I forgot her name. I forgot her fucking *name*, because I couldn't help it, couldn't ignore a few words meant to get me worked up. And I tried. I swear to God, I really tried. I saw the look on her face the week before, saw the fear. And I didn't want to be responsible for that again." My chest rises sharply, my breath rattling against my rib cage. When I release it, my body sags with relief, eager to give up the fight. "I failed her. I'm gonna fail her over and over. And every time, I'm gonna wonder if this is it. If this is when she realizes I'm not worth it. If this is when she walks away, same as everyone else."

Emotion clogs my throat, building behind my eyes. I lace my fingers together, resting my elbows on my thighs, chin on my hands, and I try to breathe through it. It's sharp and painful, the tightness in my chest, stretching across my shoulders, churning in my stomach. It runs through my body, right down to my toes, and my feet move of their own accord, bouncing quickly. I close my eyes to the feeling, the urge to flee that always wins, and a single tear drips down my cheek.

"When I lost Bryce, the only solace I found was in thinking that life couldn't get any worse. That I would never know another loss that would hurt me the way his did. And then his parents left. And when I withdrew into myself because I felt like I couldn't breathe anymore, all my friends left, because I wasn't the same person they'd known. And when I fought too much in LA, in Carolina, in Nashville, when the only thing I was good at became the risk teams weren't willing to take anymore, when I got traded, I lost my friends, my family, all over again. They moved on, forgot about me, and I could never figure out what about me made it so easy for them to do it."

Another tears slips out, followed by another, then one more. I swipe them away, but then Carter lays his hand on my back and something inside me breaks. Or maybe it was always broken, gripped tightly in my fists, bound by fear, fear of being judged. And by speaking it out loud, the fear slowly dissipates. It runs over my hands, gently prying my fingers loose. It sifts through the cracks like sand, spilling at my feet, finally free after all these years.

"It's not just Lennon I'm afraid of losing," I admit on a fractured whisper. "I never wanted to make Vancouver my home. I wanted to treat it the way I'd been treated all these years. I wanted to remember, for once, that no matter how much I'd grow to love it, no matter how many friends I made, how easy it was to convince myself I'd found a place here, that this wasn't my home. That it never could be. Because one day, I'll get traded. I won't be worth it anymore, and I'll have to get on a plane and leave all of this. Leave a family I try to convince myself every day doesn't actually love me the way they seem to. Because I know what loss feels like, the kind where people become so intertwined with your life you can't imagine it without them. And I am so fucking *tired* of getting my hopes up and putting myself through it, over and over again." I pull in a deep breath, and my shoulders shake as I let it go. "It was supposed to be easier to push you all away before you could leave me."

One moment, I'm sitting here, Carter's hand on my back as I crack myself wide open, spill everything I've been holding on to for way too many years.

And then I'm on my feet, wrapped up in the middle of four men who wind their arms around me, holding me tight while I let it go.

Except it feels a lot like they're hugging a twelve-year-old boy who lost his best friend, and somewhere along the way, himself.

For the first time in my life, I don't have to hold myself up.

And nothing has ever wanted to make me fall to my knees more.

"You're forcing it on yourself," Emmett tells me as we break away, taking our seats again. "You're so scared about the possibility of Lennon leaving, about not being enough of a reason for her to stay, that you're forcing the loss on both of you. You think you're gonna fuck up. You think you'll be traded, you'll make her upset, you'll argue, and you think that she's just going to up and leave because you're not worth the fight. But have you ever stopped to ask her if *she* thinks you're worth the fight?"

"Have you ever stopped to ask if *we* think you're worth it?" Garrett looks me over, his gaze swimming with my pain. "Because for the last year and half we've been looking at a teammate and friend we call family, someone we can't imagine our lives without, and you've had one foot out the door the entire time, waiting for things to end."

"We're all scared of things," Carter murmurs. "It's what you do with that fear that matters. You can spend your life pushing away the people who want to love you because you're afraid one day you'll lose them. Or you can cling to it. The love, the happiness, that full feeling that makes you realize how truly empty you were before them. Life is hard enough as it is. There's no reason for any of us to do it alone."

Adam meets my gaze, the emotion he holds there so palpable I feel the way it crawls over me, a hand at my back. "At the end of the day, the only person you need to be enough for is you. But for what it's worth, you've always been enough for us too."

The words crash into me at full speed, splintering apart, millions of tiny slivers that prick my skin, work their way underneath. I've spent so many years focused on other people's opinions, I haven't stopped to consider my own. And now? Now I've spent too many years focused on their words that they've become mine too.

Not outgoing enough. Not gentle enough. Not sensitive enough. Not resilient enough. Not disciplined enough. Not flexible enough. Not fast enough. Not memorable enough.

Not enough. Not enough. Not enough.

When will I be enough?

It's a question I've been asking myself for years, a knife lodged in my chest, twisting itself deeper each time I dare ask. But the pain is nothing compared to the question I find myself asking right now.

Why am I not enough for myself?

"We're not going anywhere, Jaxon," Carter says. "All of us could be traded. We could be spread out across North America, and we are *always* going to come back to each other, because we're family. Me, Garrett, Adam, Emmett. *And you.* You are part of this family. Sure, we didn't have you two years ago. Now we do, and if we lost you, we'd never be complete again."

I hang my head, trying to feel the words. To let them soak in. To believe them.

"I wanted to hate you," Garrett whispers suddenly. "So badly, when you stepped off that plane, I wanted to hate you. And you made it impossible. Didn't even fucking do anything, just showed up day after day, and then I was looking for you." He drops his head, lacing his fingers together. "You were there for me when my dad almost relapsed. When I thought I was losing Jennie."

"You're there for the kids, reading them bedtime stories, carrying them on your back, making them feel safe," Adam says.

"You're there for the girls," Emmett adds. "Day in and day out. Lending them your ears, holding them up when they need it." He smiles. "Doing face masks and eating junk food and just giving them nights that make them so happy, have them forgetting about the hard stuff for a couple of hours."

"You've been there for us every day, Jaxon." Carter looks at his hands, wringing them between his knees. "On the ice, and everywhere else that matters. You're always there." His eyes come to mine. "Can't do it without you."

Emmett cocks his head. "What does Lennon deserve?"

Fuck. What *doesn't* Lennon deserve?

I blow out a heavy breath, rolling my shoulders as I sit up, thinking about the world I'd give her if I could.

"She deserves . . . stars. Fifty million of them instead of ten thousand. She deserves pink tulips, and extra shelves in her shower. A spacious countertop for her hair products, and a big window in the bathroom that gives her the best natural light to do her makeup. She deserves someone who wraps her hair for her on the nights she's too tired to do it herself, and silk sheets on her bed just in case. Homemade instruction manuals to help her learn, a telescope to help her dream, and watching the Northern Lights dance through the sky. She deserves someone who hears her, who sees her. Someone who accepts all of her, without question and eagerly. She deserves love."

Emmett's eyes move over me. "Sounds exactly like the way you've been loving her."

Before I can respond, the door opens, the quiet room suddenly alive with laughter and chatter as everyone files in again, grabs a second round of snacks, finds a seat.

Coach heads to the front of room, whistling to get everyone's attention. "Sorry about the delay, guys. I promise, we'll keep this quick so everyone can head home and get some rest ahead of game one tomorrow. Let's start with the best news, shall we?" He looks up with a grin, gesturing at me. "Riley is officially back on the ice tomorrow, thank fucking fuck." The room erupts with hoots and hollers, and my ears burn as I drop my face, a grin crawling its way up it. "Jaxon, we can't do this without you. We've missed you. Now for the love of God, take care of your head. This team isn't a team without you. We love you, buddy."

It's a funny, powerful thing, the way something can shift your whole perspective. Because this morning I woke up and wondered how much longer I had left with the people I love. And now, as my team gathers around me, twenty-three men that dogpile on top of me right here in the middle of the room, I can't imagine ever being anywhere else.

When Garrett parks in front of my condo an hour later, killing the ignition, he looks at me. "Can I ask you something? You talked about what Lennon deserves, but what do you think you deserve?"

I look out the window, at this beautiful city I've refused to call home. A place that's given me everything I've ever wanted.

"Friends," I answer quietly. "Family. Home. Lennon." I look down, knees bouncing as I whisper the thing I've wanted more than anything my entire life. "Love."

Garrett grins. "Yeah, you do. So go take it."

I'm going to. I swear, I'm going to. I hype myself up the whole elevator ride, telling myself no one can love Lennon better than I can, better than I have been. I tell myself that this time, I've given myself to the right people, the people who are going to appreciate me, always make space for me at their table. I tell myself I deserve it.

And then, as I exit the elevator, I find Lennon in the hallway, grunting and groaning as she lugs boxes of IKEA furniture out of the apartment, lining it against the wall. The same furniture she's been storing here since her own apartment flooded.

"What are you doing?"

She startles, hand on her heaving chest as she spins around. "Oh. Jaxon. You scared me." She bats a handful of curls off her forehead, trying to stuff them back into the clip haphazardly holding the rest of her hair on top of her head. It's useless, and somehow, the entire clip dislodges, beautiful chestnut spirals spilling down around her shoulders.

She gestures at the boxes. "Moving all this stuff out."

My heart kicks itself into overdrive. "Why?"

I know the answer. I know it before she says it. I was expecting this, pushed her to it, and yet when she answers me, my world still skids to a stop, throwing me from the mountain I've just conquered, tossing me carelessly to the ground when I've only just managed to get to my feet.

"My landlord called. My apartment is ready."

31

I GOT YOU, HONEY

Jaxon

"You're moving out?"

The words come out exactly as frantic as I feel. They hurt, every one of them, like Lennon's shoved her fist down my throat, plucked each one out of my chest in excruciatingly slow motion.

"I—"

"Y-y-y—" Christ, I'm stuttering. Losing it, if I even still had it. I shake my head, taking in the sight around me, boxes upon boxes of furniture that were meant to make up her home, her home away from me. "Y-you . . . you can't. No. You can't." I don't know what I'm doing, how I wind up here. Pulling the box from her hand, shoving it back through the door, inside my apartment. I just know she can't leave me. "Please." I grab another off the wall, pushing it inside, then another.

"Jaxon." Lennon watches me, mouth gaping as I take every single box, shove it back where it belongs. She reaches for one, eyes widening as I pull it away. She scoops up the smaller items, kitchen utensils with the tags still on, dish towels and pie plates, and she dumps them all in a box that she clutches to her chest. "Jaxon, what are you—"

"You can't leave!" I blurt out, hands trembling as everything bubbles up to the surface. The fears, the insecurities, all the years I spent self-loathing. My thoughts run rampant, screaming at me

that she's leaving for a reason, just like we knew she would, just like everyone else.

But my heart screams at me to stop. To stop running, stop hiding, and for once in my goddamn life to stay. To fight for the ending I want. To fight for *who* I want. Who I want to be, and who I've always been beneath the fears, the labels, the self-doubts.

To fight for the life I deserve.

So when I open my mouth, I don't know what's going to come out of it. I just know I'm going to stand here and give it my all before I let her walk out of here.

"What do you want me to say, Len? What do you need to hear? Because I'll tell you everything. You want to know why I have every place I've ever lived tattooed on my body except for Vancouver? You want me to tell you how I finally, *finally*, gave up? That when I was traded to my fourth team when I was only twenty-six, I was tired of telling myself this place might be it, the place I finally get to stay, the place I get to truly call home? Because I am. I'm so fucking tired of trying to belong somewhere, of getting my hopes up just to get traded when I fuck up, when they find someone who can do my job better than me, just to be forgotten by the people I called family while I was there. That's why I pushed you away. That's why I pushed everyone away. Because I've never been enough, Lennon, and I didn't want to be here when you figured it out."

Hot tears slide down my face without my permission, and I watch Lennon's heart break in real time. The way her face crumples, the longing in her eyes to hold me, comfort me. The tears that gather in her incredible brown eyes, spilling down her cheeks. That tremble in her chin as she watches me wipe my tears away, her chest heaving in time with mine.

"You want me to beg you to stay? To tell you how badly I wanna be the one who reminds you how much Advil to take, massages your back when you've got your period? The one who makes a detailed instruction manual for your favorite lattes, but makes them for you anyway when I wake up first? The one who puts your favorite flowers on the kitchen counter every week just to see you smile, who does your hair routine when you've had a shitty day and aren't up for it? You want me to tell you how I wanna be the one sitting next to you on the couch while you show off all the pictures you took that day, listen to you talk about your favorite ones, smile at the way you you trip over your words because you're so excited, so damn *in love* with your dream? That I wanna be the one who drives you out to the middle of nowhere at midnight just to fucking *stare* at you while you stare at the stars, because somehow, in this whole huge world, I got lucky enough to find you, not once, but twice? You want me to ask you to stay, Lennon? To tell you I'm in love with you?"

She gasps, more tears running free, cascading down her beautiful face while my heart slams in my chest as I struggle to breathe.

"Here it is, honey. I love you. I am so goddamn, mind-blowingly in love with you, and the thought of losing you is killing me. I don't want you to go. This place only feels like a home when you're here." I whisper my final plea. "Please, honey. Please stay."

Lennon stands there, box still clenched to her heaving chest, full lips parted and trembling.

And she says nothing. Nothing at all.

Makes it impossible to miss the way my heart claws its way out of my chest and shatters at my feet.

"Right. Well." I drop my gaze, burying my hand in my hair as I fail to swallow down the searing pain creeping up my throat. I pull my hands free, taking in the violent shake to them before I quickly curl them into fists, turning away from Lennon before she can see. "I can help you . . . I'll . . . if-if . . ."

"Jaxon."

"Um, yeah, just gimme a minute, and then I can help you with the . . . with the-the . . ."

"*Jaxon.*"

I close my eyes, memorizing the way my whispered name sounds leaving her lips. It takes everything in me to turn around, to look at her again, that fucking box in her hands. "Yeah?"

That box falls to the floor.

"I love you too."

And then she's dashing across the kitchen, crashing into me at full speed. Her arms around my neck, my hands on her ass as I hoist her up to me.

I brush her curls from her soaked face. "What? What did you just say?"

"I love you," she cries, laughing through the tears running rampant down her face, wiping at mine. "I love you for reminding me how much Advil to take, and for massaging my back when I'm on my period. I love you for teaching me how to use the complicated espresso machine, and for making my lattes most of the time anyway. I love you for the tulips, for taking the time to learn how to care for my hair, for sitting next to me on the couch and listening to me ramble on about my pictures. I love you for supporting my dreams, for taking me to watch the stars, for looking at me the way I look at them, and the same way I look at you, like I'm the most incredible thing you've ever seen." She cups my face, sniffling, licking the teardrops from her lips. Her gaze doesn't waver, swimming with honesty, raw and vulnerable. "There is no one alive who could love me better than you do, Jaxon. You love me the way I always dreamed of being loved. The way I deserve to be loved. And I'm going to love you the way you deserve to be loved."

The beam that spreads across her face is so stunning, so devastating, my knees wobble. I look away, shaking my head, because this is, without a doubt, the most overwhelming thing I've ever felt in my life. Is it real? Is it mine?

She touches my chin, guiding my gaze back to hers. "I love you."

Tears gather all over again in my eyes. She brushes them away, whispering, "I love you," against my cheek.

"One more time." I swallow against the tightness in my throat, licking my lips. "One more time. Please."

Soft lips sweep over mine. "I love you, Jaxon."

My mouth collides with hers, fingers sinking into the thick spirals at the nape of her neck, gripping them tight in my fist. My legs move, walking us to the kitchen counter, where I sit her on the edge so I can take her face between my trembling hands as my mouth moves with hers. I pull her head taut, looking down at her as I catch my breath. Except, staring down at her, at the world I hold in the palms of my hands, all I do is lose it.

"Where did you come from? How did you walk into my world out of nowhere and knock it off its axis? I took one look at you and started falling, terrified every damn moment, from the top right down to the bottom. But you were there. You were always there, honey." I press my lips to hers, tasting her tears. "Thank you for falling with me. I don't think I could've survived falling alone."

"I think you can survive anything, Jaxon. You are so much stronger than you realize." The smile she hits me with is soft and gentle, everything Lennon. "But you never have to be strong on your own again. You've got me, and I'm not going anywhere."

"Yeah," I murmur, coaxing her mouth open with mine, sweeping my tongue against hers. "I got you, honey."

"And for the record," she manages on a whimper as I trail wet kisses down her throat. "I was never leaving."

My head snaps up. "What?" I look at all the boxes, and before I can ask her what she was doing with them if she wasn't moving back into her apartment, there's a knock at my door.

"C'mon." Lennon hops off the counter, scooping up a box on the way to the door. Two women with carts greet her, and when they start loading the boxes up, I slowly approach them.

Lennon gathers the final box, the one she dumped all the kitchen stuff into just minutes ago, and tucks it on top of one of the carts. "That's the last box."

"This is incredible," one of the women says. "Thank you so much."

"Are you sure we can't reimburse you some of the cost?" the other asks.

Lennon shakes her head. "Please, just take it. I don't need it."

"What's going on?" I ask quietly as the women disappear into the elevator. "Where are they taking your stuff?"

"To the domestic violence shelter for mothers and children. I was never leaving, Jaxon."

"But you said—"

"My landlord called and said my apartment was ready. I told him I didn't need it anymore."

"You were never leaving," I whisper. "You were always going to . . . to . . ."

"Stay. I was always going to stay. I don't walk away from the people who need me, Jaxon. Even if they're afraid to admit it." Her hand slides along my jaw as she steps into me, and I lean into the warmth. "I don't know when I fell in love with you. It happened slowly, I think, but maybe we planted the seeds that first night. One day I just looked at you, and I knew. It was like my world stopped, and all I could focus on was the way I felt in that moment, like I'd come alive, stepped out of the shadows and into the sunshine, embraced all of me for the first time in my life because I'd found someone who let me be me without ever asking me to change a thing. Someone who saw me and just . . . appreciated me. Exactly as I was. There is nothing in this world that could pull me away from you, Jaxon. You are my best friend, my line, and my home. Why would I ever leave?"

She shrugs then, a saucy smirk crawling up her face. "Now if you'd have let me speak, I would've told you all that. But you were intent on delivering your monologue, and it was so beautiful and heartfelt I couldn't bear to stop you once you started."

A growl rumbles in my chest. I stoop down, wrapping my arms around her knees, tossing her over my shoulder. I clap a hand to her ass as she squeals, bouncing along as I cart her off to the bedroom.

The truth is, she deserved the monologue. Honestly? I think I deserved it too. I've spent too many years questioning my worth, trying so damn hard for people who didn't matter. The only person I should've given that time to was myself. All I wanted was a friend or two in my corner, someone to call family, someone to cheer for me. But I should've been cheering for myself. Lifting myself up. Because through this all, I've been a good friend. I've given everything I've been capable of giving to the people I cared about, time after time. I showed up for them when insecurities whispered in my ear, reminding me how the time before ended, and the time before that.

Lennon deserved my words today.

Carter, Garrett, Adam, and Emmett deserved my words today.

I deserved my words today.

I won't do it perfectly every day, but, fuck, I'm gonna try. Because if these are the people I get to call family? If this is the place I get to call home for this season of my life? I must be doing something right.

I lay Lennon down on the bed, and a lump beneath the blankets springs to life, scattering out and onto the pillows. Mittens looks around for a moment, blinking the sleepy, dazed look from his eyes, his white and orange fur disheveled like he's been hibernating in a cave for the last three months. When he spies us, he meows, tossing himself onto his back, wriggling around with his belly out.

"Mitts, I love you, but I'm about to make Mommy scream for Daddy when she comes all over my cock, and I don't think you should be in here for that."

He climbs to his feet, and I think he's gonna listen to me for once in his life. Then he plops himself down on Lennon's chest and nuzzles the fuck out of her neck.

"Nooo," I whine. "Those are *my* boobs to lie on and *my* neck to nuzzle."

He whips his head around, hissing at me before he goes right back to nuzzling Lennon, and I swear to God the little shit pauses to glance back at me, gloating.

Lennon snickers, cuddling him to her chest as she stands. "I know, buddy. We had a beautiful Mommy-son day today, and now Daddy's ruining everything for you. It's not fair. How about we do a fashion show tomorrow morning, huh? We'll get up early and put on your best outfits, take lots of pictures, and then post them on your Instagram so everyone can see how handsome you are?"

With his paws on her chest, he pushes up, bopping his forehead off hers, and I watch as the two of them disappear into her room. I don't have the heart to tell them I'm keeping Lennon in bed until the moment we need to leave for the arena, and also, I don't wanna risk my balls. Sweaty jocks and cat-attacked cocks don't mix well.

Lennon returns a moment later, closing the door softly behind her. "Think he's down for the night," she whispers, coming to stand between my legs. "Being a cat mom is so challenging. You have no idea."

Laughing, I pull her into me, pressing my lips to her torso as she threads her fingers through my hair. My fingers dance up her sides, inching her shirt up as they go. It disappears somewhere behind her, and she moans as I grip her hips, flattening my tongue over one nipple, then the other. I suck them into my mouth, tease them with the gentle nip of my teeth, the roll of my tongue, and she keeps me there, head thrown back, fistfuls of my hair in her hands. Hooking my thumbs into her shorts, I wiggle the tight denim over the wide flair of her hips, let them fall to the floor at her feet, her pretty pink toenails. My palms glide up her thighs, squeezing her ass as my mouth slides across her perfect, copper skin.

Her hands leave my hair, grabbing the hem of my shirt, pulling it over my head. She guides me to my feet, where she trails the tip of her finger over my chest, down my torso, lighting me on fire with her touch. She works my shorts and boxers off, smiling as my cock springs free, poking her belly, saying hello. With her palm on my chest, she pushes me down to the bed and climbs on top of me, straddling my lap, and my brain goes haywire.

"I love you," I blurt, and when her gaze comes to mine, I cup her face, bringing her closer. "I love you, Lennon. And I've wanted love for a long time. But I didn't know it would be like this. I didn't know it would be infinitely better than the very best things my imagination conjured up. Being with you feels like the first time I looked through your telescope. It feels like seeing fifty million stars when I'd only ever been able to see ten thousand. It feels like an impossible rainbow of lights dancing through a black night. Like a storm that's been living for hundreds of years, and meteors falling from the sky. Love feels like looking at you and not understanding how something as beautiful as everything you are exists, but just accepting that it does, because a world without you means a world without light."

I turn her over, spreading her out below me as I settle myself between her thighs, press my lips to hers. My cock rubs against her center, warm and soaked, inviting me home. Her hips lift, our palms sliding together, fingers twining as I hold her hands on either side of her head as my mouth moves against hers.

Kissing Lennon is like that first sip of coffee on a cold winter morning. She's everything warm and rich, this cozy feeling that sinks into your bones, settles all your racing thoughts. She wakes me up, slow and steady, chases away the fog, makes me feel ready to take on the toughest parts of my day.

But I think that's always been Lennon. She stepped into my life, and every erratic thought quieted. She chased away the confusion, one day at a time, until slowly, a whole new world came into view. I stepped outside of my comfort zone, pushed back against the fears. I didn't do it every day, and sometimes the days I tried were the same days I failed, but I showed up. I tried again.

And isn't that what progress is? Isn't that the best we can ask of ourselves?

"I'm going to show up for you," I promise her on a whisper, swallowing her gasp as I sink inside her. "I'm going to show up for you every day. And I'm going to do my best to show up for myself too."

"And on the days you struggle to show up for yourself?" The pad of her thumb skates across my lower lip, her eyes following its path. She looks up at me, and I memorize the sight, the devotion that shines so bright in her gaze, the gentle smile she wears just for me, the deep flush staining her copper cheeks as she meets me, one slow, deep thrust after another. "I'll show up for you extra on those days."

She captures my mouth with hers, kissing me fiercely, and I give her all of me in return. I bury myself inside her, give it all up, and she takes it without question. I chase her orgasm with my own, exploding inside her as she clings to me, and when I bury an *I love you* in her neck, she gives it right back, pressing the words to my forehead, sweeping them across my knuckles, painting them over my palm.

"You're worth it, Jaxon," she whispers. "You've always been worth it."

32

DRESSED FOR REVENGE
(SPOILER ALERT: I'M NAKED)

Lennon

I'M NOT SURE I'LL EVER get used to this.

It's a sight most of the world will never be blessed to see.

So, naturally, the only logical thing for me to do is videotape it and post it to Instagram. It would be selfish of me to keep it all to myself, and one thing about me? I'm extremely charitable. A modern-day saint of the people, if you will.

I creep a little farther into the living room, aiming my phone at the floor. It's where Jaxon lies, sprawled out in the evening sun streaming through the windows, holding Mittens above him as he serenades him.

"Silly kitty, chunky kitty, I kiss your tiny nossse." He brings the cat to his chest, pressing a loud smooch to his pink nose before lifting him into the air again. "Fluffy kitty, handsome kitty, I love your extra toesss."

Mittens meows, pawing softly at Jaxon's face. When Jaxon sets him down on his stomach, Mittens crawls up it, booping his head off Jaxon's jaw, his nose, his cheek, his forehead.

"Ohhh, I know, buddy. Daddy loves you. Yes, Daddy loves his handsome, chunky marshmallow." He rolls onto his stomach, chin propped in his hands, feet kicking behind him, and the poor guy has no idea the camera is rolling. "You're my bestest friend," he says, taking Mittens's face between his hands, showering him in kisses. "Yes, you are. Well, Mommy too. Just three extremely pretty best friends, living their very best lives. Mommy's the prettiest, though. We're so lucky to have her, aren't we? So lucky."

My heart warms, and I end the video. I consider cropping the last bit off before I upload it to Instagram—Mittens's page and the Vipers' page, oops—but I want everyone to know Jaxon's living his best life ahead of game seven in three days, the Stanley Cup Final. Also, it's extremely fun to set Carter off, and not being included in a video that lists Jaxon's pretty best friends is going to do exactly that.

So I also send him a quick text telling him to check the app. Oops again.

I step into the room, and Jaxon glances over his shoulder. The grin that explodes across his face when he sees me is hands down the most stunning sight I've ever laid eyes on, and I've had the pleasure of watching the Northern Lights dance through the west coast skyline. I snap a picture, because the Jaxon Smiling folder on my phone has quickly become my favorite place to waste the day away.

"C'mere," he murmurs, flipping onto his back, crooking his finger at me. He pulls his phone out of his pocket when it pings, frowning at the screen. "Why did Carter just text me 'how dare you not name me as one of your pretty best friends' in all caps?"

"I'm sure I have no idea." I lower myself to his lap, my mouth to his. "What were you two doing in here?"

Mittens shoves himself between us, crawling on top of Jaxon's chest.

"Just reminiscing. We used to be a couple of bachelors. People called us the world's most handsome dad-and-son duo."

"No, they didn't."

"Iconic, they said. Alluring. Said they'd never seen anything like it, probably wouldn't see it again in their lifetimes." He tilts his head, shrugging. "Mittens and I were just saying we wouldn't change a thing, because it led us to you."

"Life was so tough for you as a hot, successful, single dad."

"You don't know what it's like out there, Len. Vultures everywhere, trying to get a piece of us." He scrapes his palms up my thighs. "We're lucky to have made it out alive." He sniffles. "I could really use a blow job right now."

"Oh, fuck off." I laugh, swatting his shoulder as I climb off him, scooping Mittens up. "Mitts, your daddy is unbelievable."

Jaxon claps a hand to my ass, hooks a finger through the belt loop on the back of my denim shorts, and tugs me back against his chest as he stands. His mouth dips to my bare shoulder, dragging wet kisses up my neck, pausing at my ear. "Unbelievably lucky. Now go get some shoes on. We're going out."

"But I just got home," I whine. "I thought we were gonna watch a movie."

"This is better than a movie."

"Little in life is better than *She's the Man*."

He groans, tossing his head back as he follows me to the door. "For once in our lives, can we watch *anything* other than *She's the Man*?"

"Name a better romcom and we'll talk, Jaxon." I stuff my feet into my Crocs, staring him down as he does the same. "You can't, can you?"

He rolls his eyes, taking the cat from my arms, kissing his head before setting him down on the giant dog bed in the living room. As we ride the elevator down to the parking garage, he humors me while I list all the reasons Amanda Bynes and Channing Tatum deserved an Oscar nomination.

"Should I have brought my telescope?" I ask as we race across the bridge, heading toward North Vancouver.

"Nope."

"Okay. Are we going to Carter and Ollie's? Adam and Rosie's? Gar—"

"Nope."

"Are we—"

"Oh my *God*, you're so *annoying*."

I grin at him, the setting sun casting him in an amber glow. "Annoying's always been your type."

"*You're* my type," he mutters. "Just you. Now be patient. We'll be there soon."

I pin my arms over my chest. "I'll be patient, but I won't be quiet."

"Yeah, you're never quiet."

"You love that about me."

He smiles to himself. "I do. Don't know what I'd do if your voice wasn't in my ear all damn day." He sighs, tapping his finger on the steering wheel. After a moment, he tells me, "I'm feeling weird about the game. I thought I'd be nothing but excited, but instead I feel kind of sad."

I squeeze his forearm, sad for him. Vancouver and Pittsburgh have traded wins and losses back and forth for the entirety of the final round over the last two and a half weeks, sitting at three games apiece now. They play game seven of the Stanley Cup Finals in three days, this Saturday. It's Jaxon's first time in the finals, and I want this to be everything it should be. "What's on your mind?"

"Gran's not gonna be there. She should be." He swallows, his grief palpable. "She's the only one who's stood by my side since day one. She sacrificed so much so I could chase my dream, and I . . . I want her there."

"I'm sorry, Jaxon. I know how badly she wants to be there. It means so much to both of you." Gran's slowed down a lot this year. She says all the time she spent chasing after Jaxon is finally catching up to her, and she's not comfortable flying out alone.

"I've been thinking a lot about Bryce too," he admits quietly.

"He'll be watching," I tell him firmly. "I know he will."

Jaxon smiles. "Yeah, he will. I feel him, I think." He worries his bottom lip between his teeth. "I've been thinking about his parents too. I'm not mad at them, you know? I never have been. Just . . . heartbroken. But I think about how impossible everything felt when Bryce died. How I thought I couldn't possibly live the rest of my life without him. I didn't play hockey for a year, thought I'd never touch a stick again. It reminded me of him, and I didn't want to be reminded of what I'd lost." His throat bobs as he keeps his eyes on the road. "He was my best friend, but he was their son. Their only baby, their world. They were barely seventeen when they had him. And I can't . . . I can't imagine what it was like for them. I don't want to, but I've found myself doing it a lot lately. I don't think they walked away from me because they didn't love me. I think they walked away from me because they looked at me and all they saw was their son, the life he'd never get. I spent so many years running from that loss, and I think they did the same." He sniffs. "I guess I wish I could just tell them . . . tell them that I understand. That I forgive them. That I still love them, and I always will." He swipes at the single tear the moment it falls, and like always, it triggers mine. "I bought two tickets for them. Got too nervous to reach out." He lifts a shoulder. "Who knows? Maybe they'll watch, and maybe somewhere, they're proud of me."

"They're proud of you, baby. How could they not be?"

"Thank you, honey." He smiles at me, eyes moving over my tears. "Now I gotta take those tears away. Hmm . . . Should we have an adoption party for Mittens?"

I choke out a laugh, drying my face. "An adoption party?"

"You know, something where you stand in front of a judge and promise to be his mommy for the rest of time." At the look on my face, he frowns. "Judge too much? We can skip the judge. Just our friends and family. You can say a few words where you promise to love him and me forever, and we'll do the same."

"That sounds a lot like a wedding, Jaxon."

"A wedding? Psssh. No, not a wedding. Don't be . . . you're so . . . *a wedding*. Ha." He tugs on the collar of his shirt, smiling. "Mitts would look dapper as fuck in his tux, though, prancing down the aisle with rings tied to his collar, huh?"

"*So* dapper. Wonder what he'd ruin that day."

"The vows, probably, when he decides to attack my nuts in the middle of them."

I snort a laugh, and Jaxon chuckles, threading his fingers through mine, bringing my hand to his mouth. The kiss he sweeps across my knuckles is sure and steady, but I swear I hear the wild thrum of his heart as it races, the way it always does when he's trying to figure out how to broach a certain topic.

"Is that something you want one day?" he asks cautiously. "A wedding? Marriage? Or did what happened with Ryne change your mind?"

I skim my teeth across my lower lip, imagining the wedding that was supposed to be. So many people I didn't know, people that weren't important to me. The image changes before my eyes, a picture of what a perfect wedding would look like. Except the only thing at the end of the aisle is Jaxon, waiting for me with a brilliant smile.

"Yes," I tell him. "I'd like a wedding one day. A marriage with my best friend."

"Cool. Cool, cool, cool." He nods, clicking a beat out on his tongue, knuckles blanching with his tight grip on the steering wheel. "Hey, Len?"

"Mmm?"

"You're my best friend."

My heart smiles, a beam so bright it warms me from the inside out.

We pause at a stop sign, and I lean over the console, taking his face in my hands, pressing a kiss to his mouth. "And you're mine."

Two minutes later, we're weaving through a quiet, familiar neighborhood. We pass Emmett and Cara's street, then Garrett and Jennie's. Carter and Olivia's, then Adam and Rosie's. When we turn into a small court, pull up a long, gated driveway, park in front of a stunning two-story modern colonial home, my pulse races.

"What are we doing?" I ask, Jaxon towing me from the car. "Where are we?" I spin around on the cobblestone driveway, taking everything in. The gorgeous garden, the oversized front porch, the mixture of stone, dark siding, and wooden beams that make this house incredible. And God, the mountains. What a spectacular, breathtaking backdrop.

Jaxon takes my hand, leading me up the front steps.

"Who lives here?"

He just smiles, punching in a code on the keypad. When it beeps, he opens the door, hand on my back as he guides me inside.

I take in the grand entryway, all the exposed brick, dark wood, the floor-to-ceiling windows. "It's empty. Nobody lives here? Is it for sale?"

He kicks off his shoes, and I follow his lead, stumbling after him when he heads into the first room off to the right, a cozy little den with a bench seat at the window. "Nice little spot to curl up with a mafia romance."

I blink at him, then dash after him when he heads across the hall, opening the glass pocket doors, stepping inside a spectacular room with built-in bookshelves.

"Tons of space for all those mafia romances."

"And the *why choose* ones," I whisper in wonder.

"And the sapphic ones. The, uh, alien ones, and, uh"—he rubs his neck—"I'm pretty sure I saw one with tentacles or something."

"Yeah, that's a great one." I spin around, nearly crumbling in front of the stone fireplace. "So this is a library?"

"A library. An office." He shrugs. "For a photographer who likes to read or something, I dunno."

I cock my head, but before I can question him, he claps his hands. "Let's go upstairs."

Upstairs is more of the same, one stunning bedroom after another. Oversized bathrooms, linen closets galore. The last room at the end of the hall is the primary bedroom, with cathedral ceilings and another stone fireplace, French doors that lead out to a spacious balcony, the mountains right there, right in the backyard, so close you can taste them.

My heart patters as I take in the en suite bathroom, the soaker tub, the extra-wide glass shower. The double vanity with more counter space than a girl could ever hope for. I join Jaxon back in the bedroom, where the nerves are rolling off him in waves.

"Four bedrooms? Wow. Roomy."

He pulls his hat off, raking his fingers through his hair. "I guess some people like kids and shit."

"Kids and shit," I murmur. "Do you? Like kids and shit?"

He shrugs, knocking on the door frame. "What is this? Wood?"

"Jaxon."

He grabs the top of it, pulling on it with both hands, knotted muscles in his gorgeous, tattooed arms flexing. "Seems sturdy enough."

"*Jaxon Eugene Riley.* Look at me right now."

His head hangs, shoulders slumping. He spins around, huffing, looking up at me with ginormous puppy dog eyes.

"Do you want kids, Jaxon?"

"With you?"

I nod. "Hypothetically speaking."

Color floods his cheeks, turning them the sweetest shade of ruby red. He wrings his hands, gaze bouncing around the room, before it finally lands back on me. "Yes."

I smile, walking by him. "Okay."

"Uh . . . okay?" He chases after me, catching me on the staircase. "You didn't . . . um, hey, you didn't say if you wanted kids."

"With you?"

He nods.

"Hypothetically speaking?"

He shakes his head, the tension he holds pulling his brows together, dragging the corners of his mouth down. "Real."

I grin. "Yes."

Relief slides through him, and he punches a fist through the air. A fist that he quickly stops, looks at with wide eyes, and hides behind his back. "Nice," he whispers. "That's nice."

Snickering, I bounce down the stairs and through the hall, mouth dropping when I come to the open-concept kitchen and living room. "Holy shit."

"Yeah, yeah, it's amazing, but come look at this." He grips my hand, tugging me through the kitchen, down a small hallway. He pauses at a glass door, glancing back at me with giddy anticipation. Then he opens the door and steps aside. "After you, honey."

My heart free falls from my chest, spilling to a puddle at my feet. Something thick settles in my throat as I step inside the dark, round room, something I can't swallow down. I don't know how I get there, but I find myself in the middle of the room, slowly twirling around, taking it all in.

Windows. Every inch of this space is enclosed by windows. From the floor all the way to the . . . the . . . the . . .

"Jaxon," I gasp, and my heart restarts, pounding a frantic, unrelenting beat against my rib cage as I look up. Up at the glass ceiling. At the last bits of orange light that disappear. At the navy sky. At the stars. All the fucking stars, dancing right here above us. Tears pool in my eyes, blurring my vision. "It's . . . it's . . ."

"An observatory," he whispers, chest against my back as he winds his arms around me. "So you can watch the stars every single night."

I blink, and my tears spill down my cheeks. "What did you do?"

"Nothing. Well, nothing I can't take back." He lifts a shoulder. "Just a little deposit to hold it, in case you like it."

"You want to live here? With me?"

"I'd live anywhere with you, Lennon, so if this isn't it, that's okay. If you want something different, we can keep looking. If you aren't ready and you wanna stay put in the condo a while longer, that's cool too. It doesn't matter to me where we call home, just as long as it's me and you." He moves in for a kiss, stopping at the last second. "And Mitts, obviously. He'll want his own bedroom for all his shenanigans. And he'll need a big closet for all his outfits. I thought about getting him a cat brother or sister, but he feels like an only cat to me."

"He wasn't made to share the spotlight."

Jaxon indulges me with a kiss that severs every connection in my brain, until my limbs turn to limp noodles, and he's got me pressed against a window, his cock hard and rocking against me. "Do you like it?" he asks, and the softness in his voice brings me back to earth.

I sling my arms around his neck. "I can't imagine anything more perfect."

"So, does that mean . . . ?"

"Yes."

He blinks at me beneath the moonlight. Opens his mouth.

Closes it. "I wanna ask you if you're sure," he whispers, "but I'm not going to give you the chance to change your mind."

"I'm not ever changing my mind about you, Jaxon."

"Thank God, because I had this made for you." He pulls out what I think is a bracelet, a diamond-studded letter J hanging from the delicate gold chain, next to a heart, an L on the other side, but then he sinks to his knees and fastens it around my ankle. He hums his approval, palms gliding up my thighs, and then he unbuttons my shorts, slowly tugs them down my legs, my panties following quickly. When he pushes me against the glass, he grins up at me, devilish and playful. "You know what they say. One woman's anklet is the right man's necklace."

In one fell swoop, he hooks my legs around his neck and buries his face between them. He flattens his tongue against my pussy, drags it up, moaning about how good I taste, how wet I always am, and then he sucks my clit into his mouth.

It takes me two minutes to come on his tongue. Two embarrassing minutes before I'm shattering around him. And he doesn't stop, doesn't let up as I ride out my orgasm on his face. He drags his thumb through the soaking mess between my legs, pushes it into my ass, and makes me come a second time while he's feasting on me. This time, I last a whopping thirty-six seconds. I know, because he makes me count each agonizing one.

Chest heaving, I yank off my shirt as he strips, slow and arrogant, and I'm desperate to wipe that smug smirk from his face. "Jaxon," I whine, rubbing my thighs together, chasing the friction I need. "Hurry up."

He tsks, tilting his head as he fists his cock, pumps it slowly. "So impatient today. You need to be taught a lesson."

Oh, God, yes. I drop to my knees before he can ask, mouth opening as he stalks toward me.

He pushes my curls back, strokes my cheekbone. "Look at you, honey. So desperate for my cock." The pad of his thumb runs along my lower lip. "Think you can take it?"

I nod eagerly. "Mhmm."

He chuckles. "Of course you can. Ask nicely, honey."

"Please, Jaxon. Can I have your cock?"

"So polite. That's not the way I'm gonna fuck your mouth, though."

"Prove it."

A grin explodes across his face, and he sinks inside me in a single thrust, hitting the back of my throat. "Jesus," he groans, gripping my face. He pulls out slowly, pushes back in. Over and over, faster and deeper each time as my throat relaxes. "Such a good fucking girl," he pants. "Fuck, this mouth is heaven."

He pulls out of me without warning, tugging me to my feet. My back hits the glass, and my eyes roll to the stars above me as Jaxon hikes my leg around his hip and plunges inside me. He grips my chin with a shaky hand, forcing my gaze back to his, hazel eyes hooked on me as he pistons inside me, one powerful, breath-stealing thrust after another.

"I fucking love you. Christ, I love you. Scared of how fucking much I love you, Len." His eyes close for just a moment, the shake of his head so small I almost miss it. And then his mouth is on mine, prying me open, his tongue sweeping inside. I claw at his shoulders, yank at his hair, pull him closer as he fucks me, because I want him everywhere. I want to taste his pleasure, swallow his moans. I want to feel the way his tongue moves when he cries out my name, and I want everyone to know he does it just for me.

"Up for a little revenge?" he asks, the words hoarse and stag- gered. I follow his gaze to the floor, where my phone is spilling out of the pocket of my shorts. When I look back at him, he cocks a brow. "Yes or no, honey. Your decision."

Adrenaline courses through me, pushing me toward the edge. When I nod, Jaxon scoops my phone up, plunging back inside me without missing a beat. With one hand, he holds me to the window. With the other, he finds MOTHERFUCKING PIECE OF SHIT in my contacts. When it rings, he hits the speaker and sets the phone on the ledge, pounding into me.

"Lenny Bean?" Ryne's frantic voice comes over the speaker. "Angel, are you okay? Did you change your mind?"

"No," Jaxon grunts. "She didn't change her mind. Yes, she's okay. Better than okay."

"What the—"

"Shhh. I'm fucking my girlfriend."

My head rolls over my shoulder, pressure building low in my belly. Jaxon hooks his arms beneath my thighs, jerking them up, spreading me wider, his pelvis slapping against my clit with each thrust.

"Oh, fuck," I whimper, back arching.

"What the fuck?" Ryne bellows. "What's going on?"

"I already told you. What aren't you getting?" He pulls my head taut, dragging his tongue up my throat, pressing his damp forehead to mine as he holds my gaze. "Go on, honey. Spell it out for him. Tell him who's fucking this pussy."

"*You,*" I cry, nails biting into his shoulders. He strums my clit, pulling his name from my lips, over and over, while strings of expletives explode from Ryne's mouth.

"Look at this cunt. Soaked and greedy, taking me so deep, stretching around me. So fucking perfect. You take my cock so good, honey. So fucking good."

"Oh my *God.*" My eyes squeeze shut, legs quivering, threatening to give out when he pulls out of me, spins me around, and bends me over. He sinks back inside me with a single, punishing thrust that has me screaming his name, and when he pushes his thumb inside me, the edges of my vision go blurry.

"Hang on for me, honey."

"I can't." My head wags side to side as I struggle to hold on. "Oh my God, I can't handle it."

"You can," he promises, "but this piece of shit never gets to hear you come again." He slaps his hand over my phone, finger hovering above the *end call* button. "Hey, Ryne? On your honeymoon, I fucked the ring right off your fiancée. Fucked her the way she deserved to be fucked. Best night of my life at the time, but it just keeps getting better. I'm gonna fuck her the way she deserves to be fucked for the rest of my life. I'm gonna love her that way too." He ends the call, wrapping his hand around my throat, burying his face in my neck as my spine shakes, my walls squeezing him tight.

"I thought the best revenge was a happy life," I manage.

"Sure is, honey. Second best is being fucked the way you deserve to be fucked for the rest of your life. Third best is making sure your pencil-dick ex knows it." He flips me over, captures my mouth with his, and drives himself inside me, deeper than he's ever been. I don't know if the stars I see when I shatter around his cock are the ones in the sky or the ones he put there. All I know is my name leaving his lips as he explodes inside me is the most beautiful sound I've ever heard. And the most beautiful sight? Watching him sink back to his knees, gather the cum leaking from my pussy with two fingers, pushing it back inside, all while those hazel eyes sparkle with mischief. They flick to me, and he grins, the tip of his tongue touching the corner of his mouth. "Just practicing."

He presses his tongue against my pussy, drags it through my slit, grabs the back of my neck, and kisses me. The taste of us swirled together on his tongue melts my brain, and my eyes roll back as I cling to him, his sweat-soaked body pressed tight to mine.

He disappears—naked, and with only his hand covering his cock—out the front door, returning two minutes later with blankets and pillows, and we spend the next hour lying together beneath the stars.

"Did we just buy a house?" I whisper against his chest.

"I think legally it's already ours. I came on it; it's mine."

"Oh, wow. I must have missed that one in the rule book."

"It's in there. Look it up."

Laughing, I press my lips to the spot over his heart. "I love you. I can't wait to make this our home and paint everything pink and decorate for every holiday and hook my audiobooks up to the speakers and watch Mittens terrorize you and poor Magic Mike first thing every morning." I heave a dramatic, happy sigh. "Doesn't that sound like a beautiful life?"

"Life's been beautiful since you walked into it, Lennon. Doesn't matter what it looks like, because through it all, I'm only gonna be looking at you."

I sit up so I can get a good look at him. His eyes flick to mine, rolling.

"Yeah, I know. Who knew I could be so thoughtful?"

"I did."

"It's been said I'm sweeter than sugar."

"I doubt anyone's ever said that to you, even Gran."

"This one time, she said my attitude was worse than sour milk." He frowns. "It was three weeks ago."

I bark out a laugh, and he tugs me back down beside him. Curling into his side, I lay my cheek over his heart, watching the stars twinkle above us as he twirls my curls around his fingers.

"Honey?" The single word is as soft as the featherlight brush of his fingertips as he trails them up and down my arm. "You once told me to look for Bryce in the stars. That I'd find him there, lighting even the darkest nights. But I didn't know I'd find so much more there."

His gaze comes to mine, all the love and gratitude he holds there unwavering. "Do you know what I feel when I look at the stars? I feel love. I feel at peace. I feel at home, honey. That's what I found in the stars. I found my home."

33

THE BEFORE, AND THE AFTER

Lennon

THIS MORNING, I WOKE UP and thought the boys would act like adults.

I thought they'd be wearing their game faces all day. That they'd put the shenanigans aside for one day and focus on the task ahead of them: the final fight for the Stanley Cup.

I thought wrong.

"*Move,* Garrett!"

"Do you have *any* rhythm at all?"

"It's fucking embarrassing!"

"He's doing his best, but his best isn't good enough!"

"Can you get out of my space? I can't shake my ass when you're crowding me like this!"

I sigh, putting my phone down as a fight ensues between the boys in the hallway. "Can we get along for one minute? *One* single minute. That's all I ask. I'm trying to take a nice video, and it's like nobody practiced—"

"I did!" Jaxon shouts. "I practiced!"

Carter shoves his finger in Garrett's face. "We all know who didn't practice!"

Garrett throws his hands in the air. "I practiced! I practiced so hard! Jennie cried, I was practicing so hard!"

Emmett rolls his eyes. "We all know the real reason Jennie cried."

Adam crosses his arms over his chest. "Because Garrett's such a horrible dancer it brings tears to her eyes."

Garrett gasps, hand pressed to his heart. "How *dare* you. How dare *all* of you. You know what?" He fixes the button on his suit jacket. "I don't need this." He makes to storm off, but doubles back right after he passes me. "I, um, really wanna do the video, 'cause watching them makes Jennie fucking elated, so can you guys say something nice about me and then we can go again?"

Jaxon gestures at him, searching for words. "Uh . . . your ass looks extra bubbly today in those pants?"

He sniffs. "I've been doing extra squats."

Carter juts his hip. "No one pops a hip like you, but I'm a real close second."

Emmett sighs, scrubbing the back of his neck. "You never give up, and that's admirable, given how horrible you are."

Adam runs his fingers through his curls. "You, uh . . . you look really nice in your suit. Very handsome, buddy."

Garrett points his nose toward the ceiling. "Thank you. I know." He claps his hands, dashing back to his spot in line. "All right, let's go. And everybody back up, please. Give my booty space to work its magic."

They give him space, all right. And Garrett's booty? It works some type of magic. Not sure it's the type of magic he hoped for as they sing and dance along to "Firework" by Katy Perry, but as I leave Jaxon with a good-luck kiss on the lips and the rest of the boys with one on their cheeks, I know it's the type of magic that's going to get this video over a million views on the Vipers' Instagram. After all, we now have the biggest social media fan base of all the NHL teams.

I make my way out into the family waiting area, where everyone is buzzing, alive with excitement for the Stanley Cup Final. I'm only a little jealous of the custom denim jackets the girls are decked out in, their titles—or future titles—stitched and bedazzled along the back, their favorite numbers below them, embroidered patches unique to their relationships with their men scattered throughout. Take Olivia, for example. She wears *MRS. BECKETT* in rhinestone letters, *87* stitched below. Her patches consist of a tiara, a slice of pumpkin pie, a stack of Oreos, *world's hottest teacher*, and *MILF*. And she's rocking it.

There's only, like, the smallest sliver of me that regrets insisting I didn't need one. I mean, I knew I wanted one. The girls knew I wanted one. That's why they asked me no fewer than twenty times if I was sure, and why I had to leap on Cara's back, put her in a headlock to stop her when she said, "I'm just gonna order you one."

Just kidding; that didn't stop her. I mean, she didn't order it, but she did toss me off her back with no effort at all, and then I was running through her house, shrieking at the top of my lungs as she chased after me. Afterward, Olivia congratulated me on fulfilling the rite of passage.

Anyway, I have my good-luck Stanley Cup vest, hand crocheted by Gran herself, with Jaxon's last name and number stitched over my heart. Jaxon's got one, too, except his name and number are on the back, a paw print, camera, and star over his heart. Even Mittens has one, except it says *Daddy* on the back. They arrived the morning of game one, and we've walked into the arena before each game, holding hands in our matching vests.

Not Mittens, unfortunately. Mittens isn't allowed at the arena, so last night we went for milkshakes, brought Mitts on his harness, and everyone wore their vest. We got a lot of attention, and Mittens soaked every moment of it up like the slutty little cat he is.

Ireland, Lily, and Connor are wearing denim jackets, too, their daddy's numbers painted on their cheeks. Holly, Carter and Jennie's mom, is here with Hank, Ireland's pseudo-great-grandpa, and he's quite possibly the cutest old man I've ever seen, his fluffy white hair hidden beneath a ball cap that says *CARTER BECKETT'S #1 FAN*, a picture of the two of them with their arms around each other printed on his T-shirt. Garrett's parents have given up trying to manage his three little sisters, Emmett's brothers have put each other in headlocks no fewer than five times, and Adam's parents are trying their damnedest to wrangle all the kids from Second Chance Home, who are all here on Adam's dime.

But the three people I'm looking for, the same ones I've been waiting for the last two hours, still aren't here.

"Lennon!" One of the security guards waves his arm in the air. "Got some people trying to get in, say they're with you?"

"Yes! Send them in, please!" Gripping my camera in my hand, I start dashing toward the door, only to skid to a stop when my eyes land on the people rushing toward me.

"Lennon! Thank God, angel. I knew you'd let me in." Ryne stops in front of me, gripping his knees as he catches his breath. And the person he's with? His fucking grandmother.

"Oh my fucking God," I mutter. "Have I died? I'm dead, aren't I? Because there's no way you're here right now, standing in front of me."

"Uh, Len." Cara stops beside me, face twisting in disgust as she takes in the same sight I'm seeing. She waggles her finger up and down in Ryne's direction. "Who's this dipshit?"

I sigh, checking my nails. They're painted blue and green for Jaxon. "My ex."

"Your—" She snorts a laugh, folding her lips into her mouth. "Oh, babe. You really dated down, huh? Poor, sweet girl. Well, you have our sixty-nine king now." Her gaze goes back to Ryne, moving down in slow motion, then back up. "I didn't expect you to be so short."

He scoffs. "I'm five-nine."

"Five-seven," I correct.

"Average height."

"Mmm." Cara props her chin on her fist. "Short, but definitely not a king," she murmurs, and she might as well have strapped me to a rocket, because she's just launched me straight into outer space.

"Lennon, please," his grandmother drawls when I manage to get a handle on my cackling. "Don't be rude. It's not very becoming of you. And in a crowd, no less." She smooths her hand over her stiff coif. "Though I suppose theatrics in crowds were always your thing."

The loudest guffaw that's ever guffawed sounds from behind me, all four of my girls echoing my disbelief. I know they've got me, which is why I simply stand back, let them handle this.

"You did *not* just say that, lady."

"Theatrics? I'll show you fucking theatrics."

"You wanna know what's not very *becoming*? Your grandson, coming down the throat of someone who wasn't his fiancée *at his wedding rehearsal.*"

"You wanna know what's *gonna* be-*coming*? Lennon, after this game, with the six-foot-five Stanley Cup champ."

"Mommy." Lily takes Rosie's hand. "Why's this lady being mean to Auntie Len?"

"Because she's old and miserable, sweetheart."

Connor points a teensy, threatening finger at her. "You *old* 'n mis-a-bubow!"

Ireland makes claws with her hands and . . . hisses. Interesting.

"For heaven's sake," Ryne's grandmother mutters, pinching her eyes. "It's a zoo in here. Ryne, angel, let's hurry it up."

"Hurry what up?" I ask, and immediately wish I didn't.

Because the PIECE OF MOTHERFUCKING SHIT pulls out a velvet box and sinks to his knee before me for the third time in his life.

"You cannot be fucking serious."

"Lenny Bean, angel, I love you."

"Did he just call her Lenny Bean?" Jennie whispers.

"I'm gonna be sick," Olivia breathes out.

Ryne reaches for my hand, and Lily smacks it away.

"Don't touch him, Auntie Len! He might have cooties!"

"Will this change your mind?" He flips open the box, revealing a hideous, gaudy ring, and I clamp my hand over my gaping mouth. "I got you a new one, worth twice as much. Since you sold your old one."

"Have you lost your mind? Kids, cover your ears. Was me screaming my boyfriend's name while he was balls deep inside me not clear enough for you?"

"I'm willing to forgive you, Len—" The crack of a fist against his face silences the entire floor.

My jaw unhinges, eyes bugging as I watch him clutch his bleeding nose, his grandmother panicking, crying out for tissues, and something about reconstructive surgery for his no longer perfectly symmetrical face.

Cara's hands fly to her mouth. "Oh my God. Oh my *God*. Oh my God, I hit him! I punched him right in the nose! Did you see that?" She jumps up and down, grabbing me by the shoulders. "Did you see, Len? *I punched him!* Oh my God, that was *exhilarating!*" She spins around, grinning. "Who got that on video? Anyone? Emmett's gonna *lose it*. I can't wait to show him!" Slipping the tip of her thumbnail between her teeth, her eyes glaze over. "He's gonna fuck me so good tonight."

I clutch Cara's hand in my trembling one, letting her pull me back into her. "The answer is no," I tell Ryne. "It was no three days ago, and two weeks before that. It was no when you called me four weeks after our wedding rehearsal to see if I'd had a change of heart, and no when you texted me two weeks before that. It's a big. Fat. Fucking. *No*. If you cannot get that through your head, I'm going to file a restraining order, or waive my boyfriend's new no-fighting rule."

"You're behaving irrationally," his grandmother argues in a hushed voice. "People have urges, Lennon. It's meaningless. What matters is who he comes home to, who he's providing for. If he has to satisfy his urges elsewhere here and there, so be it. We keep our heads held high and move along."

"Who the fuck is this 'we' you're talking about? Because it sure ain't me. And by the way, 'people have urges' is a funny way of saying 'cheating, dishonest, cowardly piece of shit.' If that's the life you've lived, I feel sorry for you. But that's not my life. It never will be. I respect and love myself far too much to settle for anything less than what I deserve, and what I deserve—*who* I deserve—is Jaxon."

I keep my gaze off Ryne, because he truly isn't worth a second glance, not a single moment more of my time or energy. Plus, it looks like Emmett's brothers are about to gently escort him outside, and out of my life.

My gaze coasts the space, and when I find the three people I've been waiting for being ushered inside, I smile.

"Excuse me. Jaxon's guests are here."

Jaxon

I'M TERRIFIED CARTER'S DRAMATIC PERSONA is rubbing off on me.

Because everyone else is at least half-dressed, and instead I'm sitting at my cubby, head in my hands, in nothing but my underwear.

"What if I fuck it up?" I mutter.

"You won't," Garrett says.

"I might."

"It's a team effort," Emmett adds.

"I haven't fought in six games. I'm overdue."

"You're doing great," Adam murmurs.

Groaning, I throw my head back. "Can you just second-guess me for once in your life?"

"Nah."

"Why would we do that?"

"We think you're great, and you've proven your worth and skill tenfold over the last six games, without throwing a single punch."

A gasp rings through the room, and I look up at Carter, staring slack-jawed at his phone.

"Phones!" He snaps his fingers at us. "Check your phones!"

I pull mine out, a notification from our group chat at the top of my screen, covering my background photo of me, Lennon, and Mittens, drinking our milkshakes and watching the sunset.

Olivia: Sooo . . . Len's ex just showed up here with his granny and proposed with a new ring???

"What the—"

"Ho-ly *shit*."

"Didn't you literally call him while you two were christening your new house?"

My fingers fly across the screen, blood pounding angrily in my ears.

> **Me**: Pardon the fuck out of me?

Jennie: He called her Lenny Bean.

Rosie: It was utterly horrifying.

Olivia: Vomit-inducing.

Cara: I PUNCHED HIM IN THE FACE. I DID IT. I NAILED HIM SO GOOD.

Emmett: THAT'S MY FUCKING GIRL!!!

Jennie: Ireland bit him in the leg.

Carter: THAT'S MY FUCKING PRINCESS!!!

Rosie: Connor sternly told him he was a "berry" bad boy, then charged at him, shrieking at the top of his lungs.

Adam: THAT'S MY BOY!!!

Olivia: His granny said we were raising troublemakers.

Cara: So then I charged at her, shrieking at the top of my lungs *hair flip emoji*

Garrett: Are . . . are we the troublemakers?

Emmett: We're the troublemakers, baby!

Carter changed the group chat name
to The Tea Is Hot But Carter Is Scalding.

Carter: i'm sorry, len. it was a good name n
it had a good run. but every1 knows this one
is better. it's not personal. luv u.

Carter: p.s. jaxon wants 2 know how big the
diamond was so he can double it

                              Me: I did not say that.

Carter: oh so u don't care if ur ring is 2nd
string when u propose???

                    Me: Why are we talking about proposals?
                    We've been dating for like 2 seconds.

Garrett: Best 2 seconds of your life.

Lennon: Best 2 seconds of your life.

Garrett: HA! JINX!

Lennon: JINX! Buy me a Coke!

                    Me: Also it's not about the ring size.
                    It's about the love.

Emmett: Sounds like something someone
with a small dick would say.

                    Me: Lennon, honey, how big was the
                    diamond? Asking for a friend.

Carter: (he's the friend)

I slam my phone down, leaping to my feet. "I'm going out there.

I'm finding him." I sink back down to the bench, crossing my arms, knees bouncing. "No, Cara took care of him. Naturally." I leap to my feet again. "I have to make sure Lennon's okay."

Ignoring my name as they call after me, I dash across the dressing room. When I reach the door, all four of them scream my name at the same time.

"*What?*"

Emmett gestures at my lower half. "Dude, put some fucking clothes on."

"Huh?" I look down at myself, my pink boxer briefs with Mittens's heart-shaped face scattered all over them. I have another pair at home with Lennon's face on them. "Oh. Right. Oops."

Thirty seconds later, I'm bursting into the hallway in my socks, shorts hanging haphazardly off my hips, tugging a shirt over my head.

"Jaxon?"

I spin around, bouncing off the wall, and Lennon's giggle makes my heart smile. Her warm hands coast up my sides, gripping the hem of my T-shirt as she slowly frees my head, pulling the soft cotton down.

"What are you doing?" she murmurs.

"I came to find you. To make sure you're okay. Also, I need to know how big the diamond was. Is Ryne still here? Should I punch him? I can punch him. Just once, right in the dick. Are you okay? You're beautiful. I love you." Bracketing her jaw, I bring her mouth to mine. "Wanna find a closet and have a quick good-luck fuck before the game? I'll settle for seven minutes in heaven, just kissing, plus some hand stuff."

She drags her hand down her face. "Can you behave for once in your life?"

"No." I squeeze her ass. "I've always been bad at following rules. Ask Gran."

"It's true," a soft voice says from behind me. A voice I'd know anywhere. "A real pain in my ass, he was."

My heart races as I look down at Lennon, the guilty grin she wears. When she turns me around, bringing me face-to-face with the small old woman pushing her walker toward me, her salt-and-pepper hair tucked beneath a Vipers cap, dressed in a vest that's nearly identical to mine and Lennon's, that heart sputters to a stop.

She grins up at me. "Wouldn't change him for the world, though. My favorite of all my pains, and I have many."

"Gran," I whisper, right before I dash over to her, scoop her into my arms, clutch her tight to my chest. "*Gran.*"

Her weathered hands cup my face, blue eyes shining with tears. "Oh, sweetheart. I've missed you so much."

"How did you get here?" I murmur against her hair. "I thought you couldn't travel alone."

"Your sweet Lennon was going to fly out yesterday morning, pick me up, and fly in with me. That was the original plan."

I glance at her over my shoulder, standing there wearing a bashful smile as she wiggles her fingers at me. "But—she was with me all day, so how did you get here?"

Gran smiles, gently pushing the hair from my forehead. "I flew out with two old friends instead."

"Oh? Who? Is it Dawn and Marie, 'cause they always . . . always . . ." My words get lost in my throat as Gran steps aside, and the two people behind her step forward. My chest heaves, gaze bouncing around them, taking them in. The hands clasped tightly at their stomachs. The jerseys with my number on the arm. The pins on their chests, all with my name, but a different logo for each. One for LA. One for Carolina. One for Nashville, and one for Vancouver. Almost as if they've been watching me this whole time, keeping up with my life from afar.

My heart squeezes as I follow the shock of red hair tumbling down around the woman's shoulders. Those deep brown eyes on the man, red-rimmed and swimming with tears.

It's been nearly sixteen years, but I'd know these faces anywhere.

"Jaxon," the woman whispers, and all the love I've been missing, the grief that's gripped me so tight, falls down my face as tears as Bryce's parents take me in their arms.

"I'm sorry." The broken words crawl up my chest, squeezing out of the viselike grip on my throat that, for the first time in forever, feels like it's slowly easing. "I'm so sorry."

"No, sweetheart." Bryce's mom takes my face in her hands, tears streaming down her face. "You don't have a thing to apologize for."

"We're the ones who need to apologize." His dad swipes at his tears. "We were young and foolish. We were so damn broken. It's not an excuse. We just didn't know how to survive. We looked at you, and all we could see at the time was a life Bryce would never have."

"I was broken too," I whisper. "And every time I looked into the mirror, I saw the same thing you saw. The life Bryce would've done so much better at than me. And the kid who was too slow to save him."

"No, Jaxon. You were there with Bryce in his final moments, and that's the only thing that's brought us peace all these years."

"Lennon reached out to me on Facebook two days ago," his mom tells me. "We didn't know if you'd even want to see us, even though she said you did, but we had to try. It's taken us years to get here, to get to a place where we feel strong enough to move forward, to finally make real progress. Years of therapy, grief counseling, and marriage counseling. Hell, we passed preadoption training ten years ago, but every damn time we think we're ready to grow our family, we get scared all over again. One step forward, two backwards. God, we're *tired*. So damn tired of failing. Failing ourselves. Failing you. Failing Bryce."

"We're sorry, Jaxon," his dad says. "We're sorry we walked away when you needed us most. We're sorry for hurting you. We know it's not enough. That it'll *never* be enough. But sixteen years later, damn it, you deserve to hear the words."

"We love you, sweetheart." With shaky hands, she reaches into her purse, pulling out a Ziploc bag filled with ticket stubs. Ticket stubs dating back nine years. Vancouver. Nashville. Carolina. Fuck, my debut game in LA at eighteen. "We've watched you every step of the way. Been so damn proud of you. You did it. You worked for it. And you deserve it, Jaxon. You deserve everything good in your life."

Suddenly, every racing thought in my head stills. All the insecurities that have spent years attacking my self-worth, bubbling just below the surface where I can keep them contained if I try hard enough, begin to wane. The frantic pounding of my heart slows to a steady, gentle thrum, and everything is quiet.

You deserve everything good in your life.

It's funny, isn't it? A lifetime of people walking away and never looking back left me scrambling for validation, for connection. Left me desperately chasing a version of me I'd never be able to attain. It took nearly sixteen years to realize the reason I'd never been able to be better was because there was nothing wrong with who I was in the first place. I'm still working on it, struggling every day to accept that I truly am deserving of all the good things in my life, a struggle that gets easier every day with my family by my side.

And a handful of carefully selected words, spilled out like the tears cascading down their faces and mine, wipes the slate clean with a single sweep of the hand. Because life is too short to hold grudges, and if I've learned anything, it's that hurt people are desperate enough that they'll do whatever they think they need to do to ease the pain, that we're all just out here doing the best that we can, wherever we are in life.

So when I tell them, "I forgive you," there isn't a piece of me that doesn't feel it. There isn't a bone in my body that doesn't feel the weight of all that heartache shifting from my shoulders, the way my chest expands like I've finally broken the surface of the water, and I'm taking my first full breath in ages.

"Why?"

"Because that's what family does. And you'll always be family to me."

Six months ago, I convinced myself I was alone in a room full of people. I watched my friends with envy as they expanded their families, loved and were loved without condition. I sat there and refused to see that when they expanded their families, they expanded them to include me. That when they loved without condition, that love extended to me too. They accepted me the way families are meant to, and I sat by day after day and convinced myself none of it was real. I waited for it to end, for it to be robbed from me the way it always was, and I wasted so much precious time I'll never be able to get back.

So when I step onto the ice forty-five minutes later and see all the people in the stands, the ones wearing my jerseys, people who love me, who want nothing more than for me to succeed in life, when I look at the team that's stood by my side even when I tried to push them away, I'm overwhelmed by the power that courses through me. The confidence. I feel unstoppable, invincible.

Jesus, what a wild thing it is to be loved.

That must be why when the "Cha Cha Slide" comes on during warm-ups, I'm the first one sliding into position, why nobody rocks the ice better than me for those brief minutes, even though Carter insists it's him.

When we head into the dressing room after warm-ups so they can flood the ice, Lennon follows with her camera. She snaps picture after picture, her phone off to the side and recording while

Coach steps back, letting our captain hype us up the way only Carter knows how to, screaming about a team who never gives up, a team who deserves this. A team he's proud to call family.

We head back through the players' tunnel, and I pull one glove off, hooking my finger through the belt loop on Lennon's skintight leather pants, dragging her into to me.

"Still can't believe Gran didn't put my number on the back of your vest."

She arches one perfect, dark brow. "Jaxon, you asked her to crochet *king* below it. You wanted me to walk around with *RILEY 69 KING* on my back."

"Oh, well, *excuse me* for wanting everyone to know I take my diet very seriously. People are always asking me what I eat; the answer is my girlfriend's delicious cunt."

"You're filthy." With a fistful of my jersey, she tugs my mouth down to hers. "I love it." Her lips touch my ear. "Win tonight, and I'll let you feast on it while I swallow your cock."

A long, loud sigh comes from beside us. I look up at Adam, leaning against the wall, head down. "Needed a minute before the game. Saw you guys having what I thought was a sweet moment, so I thought it was safe to come back here for some quiet. That'll teach me, huh?"

"Walked yourself right into it, bud." I clap him on the back as the team takes the ice. "C'mon. You're gonna rock it, Adam." I pop a kiss on Lennon's cheek before following Adam, pausing in the doorway. "Hey, tidbit!"

She glances at me over her shoulder, a small smile playing on her lips.

"You're not my line, Lennon. It's Vancouver. It's Carter, Garrett, Adam, and Emmett. I stepped off the plane feeling lost, and that wasn't new to me. But the hopelessness was. I managed to hope for the better with every trade, but it got harder each time. When I came to Vancouver, that hope was gone. I had nothing left to give. Nothing left to find. Nothing left to hope for. And those guys out there? They took one look at me and said, nope, that's not gonna work here. They drew the line, and I slowly stepped over it. You're not my line, Lennon. You, honey? You're my after."

With a wink and a grin, I step onto the ice, watching as my girlfriend wipes her tears away before they can fall, her nose scrunching.

"I love you. Now I'm gonna go win us a cup." I gesture at her camera. "Make sure you get my good side."

I give my all on the ice. Put every bit of myself out there. I show up for my team, the same way these guys have always showed up for me. I keep myself in check, keep my fists to myself, peek at the people who matter every time someone tries to pull a penalty from me to knock us down a player.

I play fair, but I don't play nice. This body was made to defend, to push, and I do just that, pinning Pittsburgh's offense against the boards, knocking them off course. I do my job keeping the puck away from Adam as much as I can, and when there's only thirty seconds left in the third period, I'm exhausted, desperate for a break.

The game is tied at one apiece, heading for overtime. As we line up for a puck drop in our end, I take a moment to soak it in. I want to win, but the truth is I've already won. This has been the best year of my life, and it's only June. I have everything I need, right here within my reach. I want the cup, but I don't need it. If I never get to touch it, never get to see my name on it, I'll be okay.

Carter bends, stick across his thighs as he waits for the ref in the center of the circle. "Hey, Jaxon?"

"What's up, buddy?"

"Love you."

I straighten as the players around us chuckle.

Carter's eyes come to me over his shoulder, right along with his smirk. "I'm waiting."

Clearing my throat, I get back into position as the ref holds the puck out. "Love you too."

The puck drops, and all hell breaks loose as Carter battles it out with Pittsburgh's centerman. He pokes the puck between his legs, and Garrett scoops it up on the other side, passing it across to Emmett, who races down the ice. He gets rocked into the boards, a clean hit he shakes off, but the puck is already barreling back into our end, Pittsburgh's left winger charging toward me. I match his every move, skating backward so I can track him. When he moves to dash around me, I lay my body into his, knocking him to his ass.

I take off out of our end, firing the puck off to Garrett when I cross the red line, the boys following him into Pittsburgh's end as he dodges a defenseman and heads behind the net. He pauses there, the puck moving back and forth on the blade of his stick as his eyes bounce around the ice, taking in everyone's position. They come back to me, waiting just inside the blue line, and he smirks. Stepping out from behind the net, he hurls the puck toward me.

I don't think. Don't even let the puck hit my stick first. With three seconds left in the game, I wind up, shift all my weight to my right foot, swing forward, and let that puck fly when it slaps against my stick. Pittsburgh's goalie dives right, his glove coming up to nab the puck out of the air.

But the puck sneaks over his shoulder, hits the back of the net, and drops to the ice.

The buzzer blares. The fans explode. And my teammates pile on top of me.

Lennon is the first one on the ice five minutes later when they roll out the carpets for the photographers, sobbing uncontrollably but acting like she's not, trying to laugh her way through it.

"I didn't even like hockey six months ago," she weeps as I skate toward her. She lifts her camera, snapping a picture of me as I come closer. "It was just a job. And now I'm a-a"—she hiccups, taking another photo—"*a puck bunny!*" I stop in front of her, and she sniffles quietly, staring at me through her camera. "God, you're so fucking handsome."

"Len?"

"Yeah?"

"Put the camera down, honey."

She slowly lowers it, showing me her tear-streaked, soaked face, and when I open my arms, she leaps at me, wrapping her legs around my waist, arms around my neck. "You did it," she cries into my neck. "You got your dream."

I squeeze her to me, Carter, Garrett, Adam, and Emmett hollering as they watch us. My eyes coast the arena, where the girls are sitting with the kids, crying and snapping photos. Where my gran sits behind them, crying with Bryce's parents.

And back to the woman in my arms.

The one who gave me the courage to take my final steps.

My after.

"Yeah," I murmur. "I got my dream."

Epilogue

OOPS

Jaxon

JULY

I have a new favorite ice cream flavor.

"Cookies 'n *Cold Brew*?" Sarah gags, stumbling up the path ahead of me, a scoop of pink bubblegum ice cream hanging on to her waffle cone for dear life. "Who wants coffee-flavored ice cream, Jaxon? That's *gross*."

"People who like coffee, *Sarah*. Plus, what's not to like?" I gesture at my triple-scoop cone. "Coffee ice cream, chunks of cookie, and a gooey chocolate ripple."

Truth be told, the only time I get out for ice cream anymore is with Sarah on our weekly walks. Lennon and I have taken to making ice cream at home to be safe. Every Sunday evening, Mimi sends us a list of ingredients for our grocery shop on Monday. When we get home, she videos in and the three of us make it together. This week, we made roasted banana chocolate chunk, and I swore I saw God at the pearly gates. Lennon was mad at me for a solid three hours, because she said now Mimi knew what I sounded like when I came.

Mimi texted her later that night to apologize for creating such orgasmic recipes, sending Lennon off the deep end all over again. I stood quietly at the kitchen counter, watching her go off while slowly shoveling the best ice cream I'd ever had into my mouth.

"I'm gonna get a tattoo."

I choke on a cookie chunk, tears gathering in my eyes while I try to swallow it down. "You're twelve!"

"Not now, you dingus. When I'm eighteen."

"Oh. Okay. Good. What are you gonna get?"

"I dunno yet. I have some time, but I was thinking . . . maybe a hockey skate? To remember you by."

"Remember me? Where you going?"

She sits on the bench, looking up at me with big brown eyes. I take a seat next to her.

"Where are you going, Sarah?"

"West Virginia."

"West Virginia." I chuckle, licking my cone. "Good one, Sare."

She stares up at me, and my stomach does this funny twist. "I'm being adopted, Jaxon. My new family is from West Virginia."

"Adopted? Sarah . . . that's incredible." I wrap my arms around her, and my cone tumbles to the ground. "Goddammit," I mutter, scooping it up and tossing it in the trash. "Wait. West Virginia? But . . . that's so far. And . . . this is Canada."

"My social worker said it's called intercountry adoption. I'm a little nervous about moving, but mostly I'm excited to have a family. But we won't be able to go for our ice cream walks anymore, and I'm really sad about that."

"Hey." I toss my arm around her shoulders, hugging her to my side. "We can have virtual ice cream dates. And you know what? I'm from West Virginia. It's pretty there. And my gran still lives there, so who knows? Maybe you'll be close, and you can visit with her. She makes the best grilled cheese. And then every time I go home to visit Gran, I can visit you too."

"That would be amazing. Maybe one year, you can come for Christmas. My second parents said I could invite friends to come visit, but I don't really have any friends other than you."

"You're gonna make tons of friends there, Sare, and me and Lennon will come out to visit."

She smiles at me, and we sit in a silence as she finishes her ice cream. "You know what's really cool, Jaxon? They were at your hockey game, too, but I didn't even see them. Or maybe I did, but I didn't know them then."

"Really?"

"Uh-huh. That's how they heard about the home, when we were on the jumbotron. They're a little bit older, but they're really nice. And you know what else? They had a son before. He played hockey, too, like you. Isn't that cool? But he died when he was twelve."

I still, my heart skittering to a stop.

"They did their adoption training ten years ago, but every time they thought they were ready to adopt, they got scared. When they showed us on the jumbotron at your game and talked about the home, they thought it was a sign. They came to the home two days later, and I asked if I could do their hair. They let me do their makeup, and paint their nails, and . . ." Sarah's chin trembles. "I wasn't too messy for them. I spilled my makeup, and they said it was okay, that it could be cleaned up. And then they helped me, and they never even yelled at me to hurry up." She looks up at me, and the tears gathered in her eyes restart my heart. "I wasn't too messy or too slow for them."

Swallowing the lump in my throat, I squeeze her hand. "You deserve a family who loves you for who you are, Sarah. One who loves you every step of the way."

"I think I'd like to have a family like yours," she says quietly. "You and Adam and Carter and Garrett and Emmett? I want a family that loves me the way you guys love each other. And I have a really good feeling about this. Every time they call, I feel really happy, like when you show up to take me for ice cream."

My hands quiver, and I curl my fingers into my palms in an

effort to stop it, my pulse racing. "Did they tell you what their son's name was?"

"Bryce. Isn't that a nice name? He had red hair, like his mom, and big brown eyes. He looked really nice, Jaxon. I bet he would've made a good big brother, and an amazing best friend."

I pull in a deep breath that shudders in my chest, and when I let it go, memories of my best friend dance around us. In this moment, he's right here with us; I'm sure of it.

"Yeah," I murmur. "I bet he would've."

"YES, BABY. THAT'S IT. THAT'S the money shot. Work it for me, handsome boy. Work it for Mommy."

I stand motionless in the patio doorway, watching the scene unfold before me in our backyard.

The scene is Lennon, sprawled out on her stomach in the grass with her camera, AirPods in, and Mittens, spread out on his back in the kiddie lounge chair we bought for him, wearing his mermaid fin and matching triangle bikini top, Lennon's heart-shaped sunglasses tucked over his eyes. An empty beer bottle is strategically placed to his left, a half-eaten cupcake to his right, and Goldfish crackers are spread out around him.

He stretches, belly out as he rolls left to right, and I scrub a hand over my face as Lennon clicks away on her camera.

"You're a star. A natural. Yes, lemme see that belly. Gimme fierce kitty. The people want it." He rolls onto his belly, front paws stretched out, ass in the air. "*Yes*, Mittens, there it is! You are such a good boy, aren't you? Yes, you are! You're Mommy's best boy!"

I march over to them, disgusted by the sight. "Are you kidding me right now?" I gesture at Mittens when Lennon startles, rolling over to look at me. "He needs a hat, *Lennon*. It's a summer photo-shoot, the sun is shining, and he's in a bikini! He's fair-furred! Make it make sense!"

She grins up at me, wide and saucy. "I know you're saying something, 'cause I can see your mouth moving, but—" She points to her earbuds before pulling them out, and her phone auto-connects to the sound system in the covered porch.

"—his massive hands cupping my breasts, rolling my nipples between his thick green digits. His bottom cock sinks into my pussy, and his top cock works its way into my ass, inch by delicious, aching inch."

I tilt my head, leveling her with an unimpressed look. "Really? He has two cocks? And I'm sorry, did she say green digits?"

"He's a dragon shifter," she says simply.

"'I'm going to fill both your holes with my seed, over and over, until it's spilling out of you and you're swollen with my child.'"

My brows lift, and I point at Lennon. "Now there's an idea."

She rolls her eyes, ending the audiobook and peeling Mittens's outfit off him. "You wish, fuckboy. I require at least a year of fucking first, and a ring on my finger." She holds up a hand. "To clarify, because I'm secretly afraid Ryne has supersonic hearing and is about to come running, I want a ring from *you.*"

My chest puffs, and I prop my fists on my hips, rocking back on my heels. "So you're saying you wanna marry me."

"You already know I want to get married."

"But you've never specifically said 'I want to marry you, Jaxon.' For all I know you could be talking about anyone."

Lennon takes Mittens's face between her hands, rubbing the tip of her nose against his. "Daddy knows Mommy wants to marry him, but he just wants to hear me say the words so he can walk around for the next five to ten weeks reminding me and everyone else that I said it." Her playful gaze lifts to mine. "I want to marry you, Jaxon."

I snicker. "Mitts, did you hear that? Mommy wants to marry me."

Lennon's eyes narrow as she strokes Mittens's forehead. "Hey, wanna know something cool and weird that happened today?"

"I love cool and weird."

"Oh, then you're gonna love this." She sets Mittens on the grass and climbs to her feet, swiping through her phone before she hands it to me, showing me an email. From *National Geographic*. "They received my photo of the Milky Way at twilight over Porteau Cove, and while they don't usually accept unsolicited submissions, they're happy I sent it. Apparently, it would be perfect for an issue next spring."

I scan the email, the request to see more of her work, and the amount they've offered her to license the photo. "Holy fuck."

"Right? For a picture I took just for fun."

"That's amazing, honey. Congratulations." I pass her phone back, kissing her forehead. "That's so cool."

"Yeah, but I haven't told you the weird part yet."

"Oh?" I fold my lips into my mouth in an effort to stop from outing myself.

"The weird part is I never submitted a photo to them."

"Oh. Oh, wow. Yeah, that is weird. Hm." My head bobs, and I squint at nothing. "Well, maybe they saw it on your, uh . . . Instagram."

She pins her arms across her chest, hip jutting, brow arched.

"*Oh*. Ohhh, wait. I think it's coming back to me. Yeah, now I remember." I grip my head and close my eyes, like I have to force the memory. I give her a gritty grin. "I, uh . . . submitted it to them."

"Jaxon Eugene Riley!"

I spin away from her when she lunges for me, and I dash inside, racing for the staircase. "I have to take a shower! Don't be mad at me!"

"Why did you do that?" she shouts at me from the bottom of the staircase.

"Because your work is beautiful and you deserve to be in

magazines and I want you to quit working with the team!" I slam my mouth shut, pausing at the top of the stairs. My gaze falls to Lennon, staring up at me with wide eyes.

"You don't want to work with me anymore?" she whispers.

"What? No. No, no, no, no." *Fuck.* I jog back down the stairs, taking her face in my hands, brushing my thumb over her sharp cheekbone. "Len, I'd die a happy man spending every day with you. None of the guys get to spend as much time with their wives as I do, and it'll crush me when we lose that time. But your dream isn't hockey. It's stars. Sunsets and meteor showers. Northern Lights and mountains when the sun touches them just right." I look at the giant canvas hanging in the hall, one of the many shots Lennon got of Mittens lounging in the Stanley Cup. "You also do magical cat photoshoots, and I think that might be something worth exploring," I add on a whisper, and she chokes out a laugh. "You're a phenomenal photographer, honey. I just want you to choose something that makes you happy."

"What if staying on another season is what makes me happy right now?"

"Then stay on another season. I'm going to support you no matter what you choose, but I'm always going to push you to chase your dreams too."

She turns toward my palm, pressing her lips there. "Thank you, Jaxon."

I hold out my hand. "Wanna shower with me? The limo's not coming for two hours."

She slips her hand into mine, and we walk up the stairs together, past the paint cans in the hall, the boxes in the spare rooms. We moved in three weeks ago, and our only priority was setting up our bedroom; that's where we've spent most of our time since the hockey season came to an end. Lennon went shopping with the girls one day to help Jennie pick out her wedding dress, and I set up her observatory while she was out. She was so excited when she got home, we didn't leave the room till morning. Slept on the couch, right there beneath the stars.

Our quick shower turns into thirty minutes of loving on her beneath the spray of the water. When we're done, we lie together on the bed while I tell her about Sarah's adoption, how somehow in this whole huge world, Bryce's parents found her, and she found them.

With the tip of her finger, she traces my newest tattoo while she listens. It's her favorite thing to do when we're lying here, following the shape of the mountains on my chest, brushing her fingers over the Northern Lights, pressing her lips to every star painted over my heart. There are exactly thirteen, one each for me, Lennon, the guys and girls, and the kids, with plenty of space to add more down the road. And right there at the top, is Sirius, the brightest star in the sky, watching over us.

"We both found our families," I tell her at the end, and when she presses her lips to mine and curls into my side, everything is right with the world.

An hour later, once we've dropped Mittens off at Garrett's parents' place for the weekend, we grab our bags and head out onto the front porch to wait for our friends.

"What are you thinkin' about over there, tidbit?"

"Sometimes I wish I could go back in time, to when we were little. I'd find you, and I'd hug you." She strokes my cheek, smiling through the pain living in her eyes. "I would have loved you back then, you know. Would've done everything in my power to make sure you knew how incredible you were."

I take her hand, brushing a kiss across her knuckles as the limo pulls up our driveway. "I know you would've."

She grabs her purse, and I grab our suitcase, heading for the steps.

"Hey." I catch her elbow, turning her back to me. "I love you, honey. And loving you, being loved by you . . . it's worth every fucking heartache. I'd do it all over again if it meant I got you in the end."

All that pain dissipates, her eyes softening. "You've got me. In this lifetime and the next."

"In every lifetime, honey."

"Let's fucking *go*, lovebirds!" Emmett shouts from the sunroof, hat on backward, sunglasses on, shirt buttoned haphazardly. "Vegas, baby!"

"Oh my God," Lennon murmurs as I open the door for her, and Carter, Adam, and Emmett all topple sideways out of it, piling on top of one another.

Rosie sticks her head out, hand over her little baby belly. "Yeah, they're drunk already. Don't ask how. We live five minutes down the road."

Garrett raises his hand. "I'm not drunk, but I'm so fucking psyched. I've never been to Vegas just for fun."

"Can we go again next summer?" Olivia grumbles, pointing at the belly peeking out of her shorts, bigger than Rosie's even though she's due a month later. "You know, when I can drink?"

Carter scrambles to his feet, gripping my arm. "I'm sorry!"

"Well, you can be sorry at home with your five-month-old twins and your two-year-old daughter next summer while the rest of us go to Vegas."

"I can do it," he argues, climbing back into the limo after Adam and Emmett wiggle their way through. "I'm Superdad, remember? I'll be totally fine. It's you guys I'm worried about. You'll have no fun without me there. Just be sad, missing me the whole time." He grins at Cara as he takes a seat beside her. "Hi, Care," he coos, wrapping his arms around her.

Cara rolls her eyes, popping a new bottle of champagne as I climb in behind Lennon. "I need to catch up."

Jennie snaps her fingers in Carter's face. "I need you to sober

BECKA MACK

up. We're hitting the karaoke bar tonight, and I can't have you embarrassing me on stage."

"Yes, *Mom*." He claps a hand across his mouth and giggles. Yes, giggles. "Oh my God! Look how cute!"

I follow his gaze to Adam and Emmett, passed out, their heads resting against Olivia's and Rosie's shoulders.

Cara shoves a glass of champagne in my hands as the limo pulls out of the driveway, and I tell them the most exciting news they'll hear today.

"Oh, hey, by the way, guys, no big deal, but Lennon said she wants to marry me."

IN MY DREAM, I'M NOT hungover when I wake up.

In my dream, the sun doesn't blaze a hole straight to hell through my eyeballs when I wake up.

In my dream, Lennon's mouth is on my cock when I wake up.

In real life, I'm so hungover I can't move without feeling like my brain is slamming against my skull.

In real life, I open my eyes and scream a throaty, barely there scream as the sun streams in through the windows and tries to tear out my corneas.

In real life, Lennon's mouth is not on my cock, but in my ear, saying my name over and over.

"Jaxon?"

"Mmm."

"Are you awake?"

"No."

"Can you wake up for me?"

Yawning, I roll over, trying and failing to pry my eyelids open. "I can do anything for you, honey."

"What's that?"

I sigh, dragging a hand down my abdomen, cupping my boner.

Rock hard, but then I always am for Lennon in the morning. "Magic Mike, sayin' good mornin', honey. Now, come on." I reach out, capturing what feels like her wrist, dragging her toward me. She's warm, the same way she always is, and I just wanna cling to her. "Come sit on him."

"No, not that. *That.*" She touches my finger, and my eyes flip open at the weird, unfamiliar feeling.

On my hand—*on my left fucking hand*—is a gold fucking wedding band.

I shoot up in bed, grabbing Lennon's left hand and pulling it to my nose.

It's unnecessary. The diamond on that engagement ring is so big, it's impossible to miss.

Just like the gold wedding band beneath it.

"Jaxon," Lennon whispers, intoxicating eyes bouncing between mine. She's quiet, breathless, but there's an air of excitement in her voice, one that matches the frantic pounding in my chest. "Did we . . . ?"

Thousands of memories rush through my mind. Blurry, drunk memories, laughter and tears and me on one knee. Lennon asking if I was sure, then falling into my arms when all I said was *please.* Fucking *Elvis*, a little white chapel, and my friends screaming in our ears. Adam saying *I told you so*, Garrett collecting too much money, Carter asking the attendant if we could get shirts with the picture of us kissing on it, Emmett and Cara lost in each other on one of the pews, Olivia, Jennie, and Rosie weeping, Gran, too, watching over FaceTime.

Lennon brings a trembling hand to her mouth. "Jaxon, we—"

Our bedroom door bangs open, and Carter strolls through it.

"Hey, newly—" He skids to a stop, covering his eyes as he screeches. *"Cover up!"*

I look to Lennon, but she's got the sheet pulled up to her chest.

Her eyes shine with amusement, and she aims a pointed look at . . .

Magic Mike. Damn it.

"Oh. Oops." I toss a pillow over my dick. "Maybe knock before you burst in here!"

"You know I don't think before I act!" He lowers his hand shield and pulls something blue out from behind his back. "Figured you'd want this, though, now that it's official." He grins at Lennon. "The girls had it made for you when they got theirs, even though you told them not to."

He tosses it onto her lap, winks at us, and shuts the door behind him when he disappears. "I told you all, I give it six months! Six months, and they'll be married, engaged at the least!" I can't be sure, but I'm almost positive he's cackling. "That'll be the last time you all bet against me."

Lennon holds up the denim jacket, bedazzled to shit, just like the ones the girls wore to the Stanley Cup Final. There's an embroidered camera stitched on one arm, a honey pot on the other, stars scattered throughout it, and an orange and white cat.

"We got married last night," she whispers, and I'm already shoving her arms through the jacket, pulling it on her. "Jaxon?"

I scramble off the bed, yanking on her hips until she's on her hands and knees, her ass in the air and *my* last name staring up at me.

"Did you hear what I said?"

I grip her hair—we forgot to wrap it, which is just as well; looks like my hands were buried in it all night—and turn her head, capturing her mouth with mine. She opens for me on a sigh, our tongues sliding together, and I dip two fingers into her soaked pussy. She's always fucking wet and ready for me.

"I heard you," I murmur against her lips. When I back away, lining the head of my cock up with her slit, her eyes come to mine over her shoulder, dazed, hooded, so damn in love. "You said we got married last night."

I slam my hips forward, sinking inside her, grinning as she tears the sheets right off the bed, screaming my name, a spectacular, incredible sound that the rest of the hotel guests surely hear.

"Oops."

Acknowledgments

To LISSA AND MAYA. I am beyond grateful for your time, effort, and invaluable feedback while writing *Fall with Me*. Thank you for pointing out areas where I lacked knowledge and understanding, for encouraging different thinking and wording so that I could build a better world with stronger characters, and for having constructive conversations with me as I learned. I appreciate you.

To Erin, Hannah, and Ki. I love you, I love you, I love you. You know I'm big on PDA.

To Megan, because without you, I'd probably still be lying in bed, scrolling through Instagram, telling myself I'll get to writing this book tomorrow. You deserve the world. I can't wait for you to find it.

To Meredith, for making my life infinitely easier. So happy and lucky to have you here.

To Lulu, Hannah, and Hannah (omg I have so many Hannah's in my life), for listening to my hour-long ~~podcasts~~ voice notes and not getting sick of me. I'm grateful to have you in my little corner of the world.

To Anthea, because you are incredible and make this journey so fun and a lot less scary.

To Pete and Stuti, for seeing my worth and pushing for it when my backbone fails me.

To Sierra and Hayley, and everyone at Zando, for a wonderful new partnership and an exciting journey.

To Miss Bizzarro. Your encouragement will never be forgotten.

To my family. You are everything to me, and I love you endlessly.

To my readers, for falling in love with my characters over and over again, for screaming about my books, for supporting me in whatever way you're able to. Where would I be without you?

And to my older brother, always, for giving me this gift when you left this earth. I miss you.

The Fall with Me Playlist

1. "Mr. Nice Guy" – Suriel Hess
2. "Slingshot" – Zach Seabaugh, Chance Peña
3. "Everything Falls for You" – Seaforth
4. "Fallin' All in You" – Shawn Mendes
5. "Wildfire" – Cautious Clay
6. "Think I'm Gonna Love You" – Michal Leah, Caleb Hearn
7. "Bigger Than The Whole Sky" – Taylor Swift
8. "I Wanna Remember" – NEEDTOBREATHE feat. Carrie Underwood
9. "Feel Like This" – Ingrid Andress
10. "Scared To Start" – Michael Marcagi
11. "hate to be lame" – Lizzy McAlpine feat. FINNEAS
12. "How Do You Dress for the Rain?" – Sam MacPherson
13. "Start" – Sam MacPherson
14. "More of You" – JP Saxe
15. "You Are In Love" – Taylor Swift
16. "If It Weren't For You" – FINMAR
17. "The View Between Villages" – Noah Kahan
18. "i am not who i was" – Chance Peña
19. "See The Light" – Stephen Sanchez
20. "Fall Into Me" – Forest Blakk
21. "I Got You, Honey" – Ocie Elliot

About the Author

BECKA MACK IS A SELF-PROCLAIMED sarcasm queen, professional (and neurodivergent) procrastinator, and super fan of dragging you through hell on the way to a happily ever after. In another life, she was also a kindergarten teacher.

She enjoys writing contemporary romance with lovable and flawed characters, loads of humor (sometimes of the immature variety), and enough angst and heartache to yank on your heartstrings, because she secretly thrives on the tears of her readers.

Becka lives in Ontario, Canada, with her husband, kiddos, and four-legged babies.